Goodnight Eleanor

✤❧❀❧✤

November 5, 2005

Dear Gerri

Mary Margaret Bayer

Oh, to breathe the breath of the past in the quiet pages ahead....

Margie Bayer

Note for Librarians: a cataloguing record for this book that includes Dewey Decimal Classification and US Library of Congress numbers is available from the Library and Archives of Canada. The complete cataloguing record can be obtained from their online database at:
www.collectionscanada.ca/amicus/index-e.html
ISBN 1-4120-4726-9
Printed in Victoria, BC, Canada

TRAFFORD

Offices in Canada, USA, Ireland, UK and Spain
This book was published *on-demand* in cooperation with Trafford Publishing. On-demand publishing is a unique process and service of making a book available for retail sale to the public taking advantage of on-demand manufacturing and Internet marketing. On-demand publishing includes promotions, retail sales, manufacturing, order fulfilment, accounting and collecting royalties on behalf of the author.
Book sales for North America and international:
Trafford Publishing, 6E–2333 Government St.,
Victoria, BC v8t 4p4 CANADA
phone 250 383 6864 (toll-free 1 888 232 4444)
fax 250 383 6804; email to orders@trafford.com
Book sales in Europe:
Trafford Publishing (uk) Ltd., Enterprise House, Wistaston Road Business Centre, Wistaston Road, Crewe, Cheshire cw2 7rp UNITED KINGDOM
phone 01270 251 396 (local rate 0845 230 9601)
facsimile 01270 254 983; orders.uk@trafford.com
Order online at:
www.trafford.com/robots/04-2534.html

10 9 8 7 6 5 4 3

Preface

It may seem strange to be writing a book about a city that I spent only nine short years living in. My parents, having seven energetic children and a father with North Dakota roots that was pulling him back to the country, transplanted the family to a farm in Hobart near Maple Valley in 1969. When our family drove to downtown Seattle to take in Ivar's Fish & Chip Bar and the Ye Old Curiosity Shop, I was in awe of anything that seemed nostalgic to me. At an impressionable age, the charming old brick buildings, dark alleys, light poles and shops fascinated me. And while the salty air filled my senses and a strong breeze pressed against me as I stood on the piers over Elliot Bay, a thirst for what took place years ago only grew stronger. As our station wagon meandered throughout the city, turning corner after corner, my attention did not rest on the pedestrians as they hustled to and fro in the 1970's.

Rather, my thoughts and senses were engaged elsewhere, many decades earlier to be precise. Although my roots as a Seattleite are etched only on the surface, I am proud to say, that on my mother's side roots go much deeper.

As a child, my great grandmother, Anna Margaret Nist spent her first night in Seattle on the tide-flats of Elliot Bay. As newcomers, the owner of the shanty did not share a little detail which occurred nightly. While the family slept, the tide did not as it came into the cabin and soaked everyone.

Her father, Jacob Nist, wanted all six of his sons to have good and steady employment, thus he started the Seattle Box Company.

My great-grandfather, John Reisinger arrived in Seattle the day of the Great Fire, June 6, 1889. He had made his way from Austria to America after his father's sudden disappearance.

Coming from a large family, John ventured to America to start a new life for himself and to send money back to his mother. And that he did until World War I when the contents of packages from America were emptied and letters from Austria were opened.

John and Anna Reisinger were married on August 2, 1900 at Sacred Heart Church in Seattle, Washington. They raised five children; Richard, Marie, Catherine (author's grandmother), John and

Geraldine. For some years they owned a grocery store which is now the site of the present REI store. Chief Seattle's daughter, Princess Angeline often came into their store wearing everything she owned. She and other Indians would trade woven baskets for goods. The family lived above the store and had fond memories of seeing fire works from the Seattle Times roof top on the 4th of July. My great grandfather delivered goods to homes in a wagon pulled by a horse named Prince. With the birth and success of the Pike Place Market which was hard on many grocers nearby, they eventually sold their store. John Reisinger was a self-taught electrician, and Anna, while raising her growing brood, helped support the family by selling cleaning supplies to the well-to-do on Queen Anne Hill. And when the family dog Brownie had puppies, my great grandmother boarded a trolley for the now popular market at Pike Street to sell them.

Prior to researching the Suffrage Movement for this book, I never understood nor fully appreciated what women went through and endured for the right to vote.

Growing up, I had endless questions for my grandmother, Catherine Reisinger Eddy about her Mama and Papa. Some were answered, some were not. Although Catherine had tuberculosis for a while and recovered, Richard also had it for sometime but did not get over it. Sadly he passed away on June 8, 1924. He had just turned 22.

The following story is a story of sorts, filled with history and fiction, memories passed down and memories made up. I have tried to capture the flavor of an era that I truly believe I should have been born into. Since I was not, writing about it was the closest I could get without having lived it.

A final note: The characters and events are fictitious; any similarities to actual people or events are purely coincidental.

Contents

On June 7, 1889, the day after the Great Fire, property damage was in the millions. A good portion of downtown businesses were leveled from wharf to pier, from University Street all the way south to the tide flats. There was no loss of lives compared to the London Fire or the Chicago Fire. The sleazy wooden buildings in the lower end of town were gone. The rats and fleas had been incinerated. Out of the estimated one million rats which perished with the city, only one sat out of harms way.

Seattle was still a young city after having shaken the ashes from her skirts twenty years earlier...

On top of the gradual slopes which push away from Lake Washington, homes yearning to be mansions line the dirt streets in naked rows. Young trees next to pavement sidewalks are no taller than the new electric lamps at each street corner. Homes perched on knolls above the street look down on their neighbors and the tops of chimneys almost equal in height with the new telephone-electrical poles. Like many others, the home of Col. Blethen, publisher of the Seattle Times, and neighbor across the street, the Duffy's, rose to the occasion.

A few blocks away, a father and two sons have gathered for supper which is being served by Mrs. Lucyna Nidhug, a middle-age Scandinavian woman. For nearly two years she has endured low wages while her employers surround themselves with the finest comforts, clothe themselves in the finest garments, and smoke the best imported cigars in the billiard room behind the parlor.

For two years she has forced her ears to ignore the Miller's gloat of superiority over others; God, weak men, women, and immigrants were thought little of in the Miller's poverty stricken intellectual minds. Laboring without pay raises or gratitude, she supports her husband and his drinking; for her money is his, for she is allowed no claim to her own earnings, few as they are.

To-night she is very tired, as she has the right to be. She carries china plates and bowls to the lace covered table. The Miller men do not care if the candles resting in the silver candelabra are without flame, or if their housekeeper's arms are void of strength after the day's washing. The bowl of vegetables slips from her tired fingers and crash to the kitchen floor. She hears "Stupid woman. Worthless immigrant!" muttered loudly from the walrus mustached Mr. Stuart

Miller, Sr. His clumsy housekeeper has reminded him to cut her low wages even lower.

As she gathers her skirt and lowers her exhausted body down for a moment before cleaning up the vegetables, there is a roar of laughter from the dining room. The elder Miller speaks as if he were reciting verses from a Bible but laces his voice with mockery. He was agreeing with a native-born politician named Thomas Watson who recently was quoted when asked of his opinion of immigrants, "The scum of creation has been dumped on us. The most dangerous and corrupting hordes of the Old World has invaded us. The vice and crime which they have planted in our midst are sickening and terrifying. They represent the worst failures in the struggle for existence."

The kitchen door suddenly and quite violently swings open and supper momentarily ceases as the men look up at their angry housekeeper.

Mr. Miller Sr. asks his oldest son, Stuart Jr., "What the hell is wrong with her?" while he continues chewing.

She towers over Mr. Miller Sr., hissing through partially clenched teeth, "My name is Lucyna Nidhug! For two years not one of you ungratefuls has addressed me by my proper name!"

"Names, names… Who gives a damn what your name is…" Mr. Miller Sr. spouted, "You should be thankful no one hasn't choked on the dumb thing—"

"Especially one that sticks to the back of a person's throat!" Stuart Jr. added.

"Now—get on with the rest of dinner," Mr. Miller Sr. grumbled quickly without looking up at the bothersome woman.

She stood there breathing heavily, shooting daggers at the repulsive father, then at Stuart Jr., the honey-tongued son who walks in his father's shadow— the servant-son. And then at Todd, the university student, a cold hearted young man, though not quite as ill-bred as the others, but just as repulsive because he is one of them.

"As God is my witness," seethed Mrs. Nidhug, "I have never permitted myself to stoop so low as to hate any man! If I stay in this house a moment more I will succumb to the disease of bigotry which suffocates the air in this house. I release myself as your housekeeper!"

Turning towards the front door she holds her head up in pride but a deep voice barks at her.

"Return to the table at once! You cannot quit! You cannot afford to quit. Have you forgotten that in that wooden shack of yours is another worthless immigrant….your husband who is forever drunk? Is he taking advantage of 'this land of opportunity' by drinking it all? You traveled so far to find out that your sort are not wanted or welcome in America."

Mr. Miller Sr. laughs a deep, humiliating laugh, and then shoves a heaping fork full of food into his mouth. "Now get back in that damn kitchen and don't forget your place in this house again! Thomas Watson was right. The scum of creation has been dumped on us."

Another round of humiliation breaks from the table as all three Miller's roar with laughter.

Mrs. Nidhug spins around. Her face is red, her eyes brimming with tears, and her body shakes from anger and exhaustion. The lace table cloth is quickly in her grasp and before everything settles on the Oriental rug, the emotionally haggard woman is out the door. Although her feet tries to escape, she makes it no further than the porch walk when a pair of strong hands clenches onto her shoulder and the back of her waist shirt. Her shrieks fill the late summer evening as she is spun around to see the fist of Stuart Jr. suspended in the air. Neighbors resting from the warm day stare in shock from their porches while one of the Miller boys had a grip on the poor woman. His fist was still in the air as he came to realize that he was being watched.

"Get it over with you coward!" she hissed, expecting to feel his painful knuckles any moment.

But the voice of his father yells at Stuart Jr. from the door, and Stuart hesitates a moment or two as he takes in the pleasure of watching the pitiful woman shrink from him in fear. Such serge of empowerment puts a smile on his face. He hears his father yell at him once more, and regretfully, he releases the older woman and pushes her against the black iron fence.

"I feel sorry for you people!" she says unsympathetically, after putting herself on the other side of the gate. "Sooner or later," she proclaimed, pointing to the sky with a stiff finger, "God Almighty will deal with unkind people like you. I will be waiting and watching for His hand to sweep over this house."

"And what will he do?" the young man asked sarcastically with a loud laugh.

"That is up to Him!"

"Oh, why don't you go home and get drunk with that lazy worthless husband of yours."

As she hastily walked away with neighbors shaking their heads, the woman said under her breath, "I shall be praying hard. Very hard!"

August 29, 1909

The dragon flies and hornets are abundant this year. I do not know if there is any significance in their numbers concerning the weather for this coming winter.

Eleanor leaned back in the chair as she waited for the ink to dry on the page of her journal. Eleanor sighed in the pleasure of her own company in the quiet bedroom that she shared with her two younger sisters, Alice and Marie. At the moment they were in the company of their Papa and Mama below on the porch along with her two brothers, Richard and John. From the open windows of the dormer which pushed out from the roof, she could hear the muffled voices of her beloved family drift up to her.

Eleanor took up her fountain pen once again.

Mama is sitting in her cushioned rocker working on some delicate crochet piece that she hopes to give to each daughter on our wedding day.

Papa is digesting every column of the Seattle Star in silence. After, and not during a page, he'll adjust his thin round spectacles higher on his nose.

Marie no doubt will be sitting close to Mama working on a simple needle and yarn project. For some reason, Marie was born a nervous child which the rest of us hasn't a clue as to why, but we try take it all in stride. It isn't her fault that this ill-fate has been issued to her in this life.

Alice is the reader of the family. Mama is constantly asking Marie and I what time Alice blows out the light at night. I can truthfully say that I do not know for I am asleep before her. Mama is worried that Alice's eyes will tire and that she will need glasses like Papa. I doubt a pair of spectacles will discourage Alice from reading! She will be sitting next to Papa waiting impatiently for him to finish each section. Mama gently scolds her for tapping her feet as she waits for him. Sometimes I wish Papa was a faster reader, but I think he does exceptionally well since having learned the English language on his own after arriving in America when he was 19 years old. That must have been dreadfully difficult to leave one's family behind in Austria. What Papa needs to do is give Alice the paper first, and after finishing each section, then give it to Papa. That would save a lot of toe-tapping. But Papa is the head of this house-hold and to even suggest such an idea would be out of the question.

John could be doing one of two things. He and his older brother may be on the front steps having a chat of sorts while innocently gazing at porches which grace our dirt street. Depending on the hour of the day, a young lady may post herself on her front porch as we do, or retreat to her backyard if the setting sun is too bright in her eyes. If there are no young ladies sipping a cool drink on front porches, John may be checking his bee hive in the side yard. (Most likely he will be enjoying Richard's company.) He is quite proud of his little hive and enjoys selling the honey. Although he is not in High School yet, (a week away) he has plans to buy an automobile before any of us.

And then there is my dear Richard. He is Mama's first born. He is and always will be my favorite sibling. That is not to say that I do not care less for the other three, but my heart does not hold a special place for them, as it does for dear Richard. Alice, Marie and John are younger. I was born directly after Richard, and after a brief rest, the others were added to the family.

The words to describe Richard and I would be few, if it were possible to explain us at all. I'm afraid if I attempted to do so, description would diminish what is and always has been between us.

A nice breeze has blown across the desk and I can feel autumn in it. Soon it will be winter and the cold rains will come. Although Mama does not speak of it in front of us, I'm sure her thoughts, like mine have turned to dear Richard's fragile health.

I best join the others downstairs. Mama does not like it when her family is apart for too long.

Eleanor

September 2, 1909

It has been a long, busy day as my cracked, purplish fingers can't deny. (I do not understand how apple juice can turn skin purple though.) For a good part of the day, Alice, Marie and I peeled, cut and cooked the wind-fallen apples from the side yard.

Half the apples were black and wormy inside and had to be discarded. What a waste! The rest we cooked down and made sauce. For all our work, I thought there would be more pint jars on the kitchen table.

I fear the remaining apples which still require another month are already riddled with those bothersome creatures. We shall not be enjoying very much warm sauce over toast this winter I'm afraid.

Goodnight,
Eleanor

P.S.

Richard cut the last roses of summer (with Mama's permission of course). One vase was put on the kitchen table, one in the living room, and one on our desk next to me. Thank you, Richard dear.

I found an appropriate little poem in this month's issue of "The People's Home Journal. It is titled: *A SONG OF SEPTEMBER*

The blades are brown and withered, the tops are dried and ripe,
There's music in the fiddle, there's comfort in the pipe;
Persimmon's in the hollow and the cider's in the shade!
The great corn-captains totter, the ears are in the husk,
The whippoorwill is calling down the wood road in the dusk;
Swing down the fields of fodder, pile high the fodder stack,
The coon is in the willow and the possum's in the sack,
The goldenrod, a glory of yellow plumes, makes bright
The fields that catch its living ray of golden autumn light;
The coveys in the orchard whirr up at every tread,
The sumach's fires have faded and the sweet gum's turning red.
Swing low, ye fodder binders, the black crow sails on high;
When tops and blades are gathered then the harvest we'll lay by;
The sweet September weather sifts its glory o'er the hill,
Oh, ring around the rosy by the old sweet-cider mill!

September 3, 1909
Sunday

I have been at this desk, quietly sitting with my journal open for a long, long time. All I can do is look out our window and take notice of the change beginning in certain trees. My eyes have not wondered far from them. I can count on the cool nights of autumn to bring change. A change in the weather is always welcome and comforting. After a long rain; the sun appears. After a hot summer; cool breezes flow. After gray and rainy winter days, beautiful white flakes fall from heaven above. Changes such as those I greet with open arms…. but this afternoon….. my life has suddenly been changed in a blink.

I'm afraid that if I describe our visitor and his reason for paying our family a visit, I will harbor unchristian thoughts. Help me Lord to reiterate the facts and not the turmoil in my heart.

Papa and Mama have always felt that it is not a child's place to share in certain concerns of the household. Although Papa and Mama work very hard to provide for the family, financial worries can be seen on their faces. Although we are not allowed to speak of such things in front of them, at night while tucked snugly in our beds, we quietly discuss what our parents will not. To-day, our unexpected visitor changed all that.

He, Stuart Miller, Jr. drove down the hill and parked his impressive automobile in front of our house. The mile walk could have been easily managed and enjoyed, but I understand now that he "needed" his automobile and not his feet to travel quickly away from us. As soon as Papa saw who it was he folded the Sunday newspaper on his lap, and Mama put down her crochet needles. They nodded their heads to Mr. Miller, which was more than gracious on their part, considering who was standing before us. I know that Richard and John would have loved to have asked, "Where is your father? Oh, yes, that's right, he sends you to do all his dirty work."

I almost felt sorry for Mr. Miller, so out of place, so overly groomed for the occasion of having to carry out a job for his father. Any compassion ceased when he explained to us and to any listening neighbor that my dear Papa has been late on the house payments. Poor Papa stood up and told the young man that he did not care to discuss it in front of his children. Mr. Miller's laugh was insulting as he told Papa to sit down and that he did not care what Papa wanted. Papa did not sit down, nor did Richard and John after that. We were told that the Miller's are without a housekeeper and wanted one of us girls to work for them. Our employment at the Miller household would make up for the difference of what our Papa cannot come up with.

To end his horrible speech, his eyes carefully surveyed Marie, Alice, and I. Stuart let his eyes roam over me as he told Papa and Mama that it didn't matter who was chosen. That would be up to us. I did not care for the way he looked at me, nor did my brothers for they made their way down the steps and towards Mr. Miller.

Over the noise of his motorcar, he said that he expects one of us a week from tomorrow.

Before any of us removed ourselves from the porch, my family knew, as I did, even before Mr. Stuart Miller Jr. make his way for his automobile, that the future of one person had already been determined.

I, Eleanor, must give myself over without resistance.

I will be submissive.

I will pray for the ability to recover from this day's turn of events, and for the strength to adjust easily.

I must work hard in the face of adversity, and not let any action on my part tarnish my family's good name.

Goodnight, Eleanor

September 4, 1909
Monday

I have never dreaded a Monday morning in my life. While waiting for the trolley to take me downtown to the Insurance Company, the morning cloaked me in cold and dampness. Autumn is here. I'm sorry to say that I was poor company to the others who waited with me. If only they knew my troubles. If only I could have told them. I hope I gave no one reason to suspect that there was something wrong. But after Friday, I shall not be riding on the wonderful trolleys that share the streets with horse drawn carriages and automobiles. The noise and wonderful confusion, the fever and madness of daily life in the business district has been my life for the past three years.

The Miller's do not care that my fine clothes which I made will have to be put away. Nor do they care that I graduated with honors in school. It was important to me to be the fastest typist, the best bookkeeper, the quickest stenographer. My handwriting won many awards in high school. (Mama was very pleased with such an accomplishment.)

I can still see the look on poor Mr. Whiting's face when I finally had to tell him the bad news. He knew right away that something was terribly wrong when I entered his office. My dear sweet white-haired employer crumbled in his chair as the shock of my words took hold of him. There really hadn't been an easy way to make it less painful for the aging man. I truly intended to be brief and save the tears until I returned home, but that was not the wish of Mr. Whiting. Pounding his fist on his desk, he demanded to know who was stealing me away from him. Was it another insurance firm? Was it a bank? It hurt me so to see this otherwise kind and gentle man agitate himself, and I feared that if I did not tell him the whole story he might have had an attack right then and there.

I found myself crying and Mr. Whiting said to me, "You have every right to cry my dear. I know what kind of man Mr. Stuart Miller is— and his sons. He is a bitter man who loathes the rest of mankind. He sold his code of values a long time ago. His lifeblood is keeping the lower class always in his dept. They cower at the mention of his name. Mr. Miller has made his living off of those poor souls. One day, he will stand trail for all his wrongful deeds which has devoured his soul. Pray, oh, do pray, dear citizens of Seattle, that God is surely our true vindicator!"

On the trolley home, I wondered if Mr. Whiting had forgotten that I was still in his office as he spoke to the window, his hands behind his back. I don't think he would have spoken so freely if he hadn't been so upset.

I wonder when I shall be able to return to Mr. Whiting and my friends.

I wish Papa would have informed us of just how badly our financial difficulties were, so extra income somehow could have been brought in. Now I will be under the unpleasant thumb of the Miller's.

Dear Lord, please send more guardian angels to protect me on Monday.

Thank You, Eleanor

September 9, 1909
Saturday

Dinner consisted of Mama's good Beef-Barley soup, thick slices of bread with my raspberry jam, and apple pie that Alice made. (She is getting better with her crust.)

The clock in the living room chimed a half-hour past one in the afternoon. I truly believe that a house would not seem as cozy if it were without a Westminster clock.

After Marie and I washed and dried the dishes, and put them away, Alice swept the kitchen floor and then ran a mop over it.

Our bedroom is a little on the chilly side to-day so I have brought my journal to the kitchen table. The stove is warm and keeps me company. Under gray skies crows can be heard ka-kaing in the corn patch searching for any left-over ears. They will be lucky if they find one, for we canned quiet a few quart jars three weeks ago. I look forward in anticipation in making Corn Chowder soup this winter with biscuits or cornbread.

The lingering aroma from dinner smells good, as does the coffee which I'm enjoying.

There is something special about autumn. There is almost a humming of excitement, anticipation, new energy in the air. A new season is taking hold.

My thoughts keep returning to the top of the dresser in our bedroom. There sits a lovely card signed by Mr. Whiting and my fellow colleges. A book of poems from Mr. Whiting, and personal note from Mr. Whiting. On the other end of our dresser is a letter from the Miller's. It was addressed to Papa and Mama, and in the note they gave us their house number and a key to their house. That was all. I suppose someone shall greet me Monday morning and give me the particulars of how their household is to be managed. What meals they do or do not care for. I can only imagine that the Miller's residence can not differ terribly from our household. Cooking and cleaning, is still, cooking and cleaning.

Good-day
Eleanor

September 11, 1909
Monday

My ink pen, if it could, would put something down about to-day. It does not understand that I'm not sure where to start.

After arriving back home after the hour of nine, everyone was anxious and curious as to what the Miller's house was like. I gave them a description of the parlor and of the dining room since those were the first rooms I saw upon entering the quiet house.

"There was a predominately rose patterned floral carpet in shades of rose and green on a beige background. There are chairs and a parlor table with an embroidered cloth and a lamp placed on it. A rocker sat in front of the double window which was curtained with expensive lace in a flower and scroll pattern. In a corner was a beautiful Roman couch. Against the left wall as you leave the parlor is a combination desk glass enclosed bookcase. A dark and lonely large brick fireplace which was filled too high with ashes faced opposite the windows. There were potted palm trees near the light, and scattered large photographs of three men hung from expensive wallpaper. Behind the parlor is a billiard room for the men.

Opposite the parlor is the spacious dining room which an imported maroon wool carpet covers the entire floor. I cannot even begin to describe the patterns throughout it, nor guess at the cost. The table is of dark, thick, heavy wood, and the carving designs on the upper legs and feet are nothing short from breathtaking. Another piece is the matching buffet with brown marble, lots of drawers, a mirror as tall as I, and enough carving work to employ a man for several years.

I did not know if Papa and Mama would allow me to describe the father's bedroom, but I think they too were curious. Mr. Miller's room was the largest of the four on the second floor.

Aside from a large bed, and high ceiling, there was a sitting room furnished with a commode, armoire, dresser, chest, table, chair, and more imported lace curtains at the window. Dark maroon wallpaper in a fleur-d-lis design covered the whole room. The walnut commode which had a towel bar and double doors was located near the bed. A white china pitcher and bowl on top had a blue design of baby birds sitting on top of a scroll. Wild roses, butterflies and berry vines covered the rest of the pitcher. To my dislike there were four rats at the bottom of the scroll. Mama says that was the style during the

1870's through 1880's, a period of realism using nature's designs in dress and household furnishings. (I can do without the rats!)

The top of the large walnut dresser was covered with a lace scarf on which a jewel chest tray, and sterling silver dresser-set sat. The dresser-set was engraved with scrolls, flowers, and a monogram. It included a hand mirror, hairbrush, comb, and clothes brush. A large walnut armoire which matched the rest of the furniture had a place for hanging clothes and more drawers for storage. The last piece was a linen press with shelves and two doors holding linens, bedding, quilts, pillow shams, and other household dry goods.

I was glad that everyone seemed satisfied with what I told them. Mama said that I looked very tired and that maybe I should take my bath and go to bed early. I'm glad Papa and Mama did not ask who met me at the door and all the particulars of the day. Had they known what was in store for their daughter, the Miller's would have received a tongue lashing from Papa. This is a record of how my first day unfolded.

After catching the electric street car at the bottom of the hill, we were pulled to the top by a wonderful device of counterweights that are under the street. For this I am thankful! When the line ended, my walk up the scenic hill began. Arriving at the black iron gate, I stood for a moment to catch my breath and to unpin the key which was kept safe inside my coat. Opening the beautiful etched glass door, I stood inside a very quiet house. Not a soul greeted me. I stood there listening for any signs of life. I spoke out loud to inquire if anyone was home. I think I almost heard an echo as I stood there realizing that I was on my own. My first thought was to look around for a note explaining my duties and what I should expect on my first day. There was no such note on the table in the hallway, or in the dining room, or on the fireplace mantle. My curiosity led me into the kitchen in hopes of finding instructions on the table, but there was none.

After removing my sweater and sitting in a rocker near the large and terribly ornate stove which is larger than ours, I was thinking how kindly Mr. Whiting had received me on my first day and how he made me feel at ease. I wonder how he is doing to-day. I wonder if he knows how much I miss my former job.

Although it was not my wish to give myself an orientation tour of a strange house, I did not have any other choice. Wouldn't Papa and Mama simply be horrified if they knew! I can just see Alice along side me, if not dragging me from room to room, poking her curious nose into everything. I'm sure she would have been amused, but I was not. What was I supposed to do? I was upset due to the lack of instruction. What time would the men be home for supper? What type of meals did they like? What grocery and meat market did the Miller family have an account with, and what day or days of the week did they deliver? When food and household items are needed, will they be purchased on credit? Am I to wash and iron their shirts, or, does a Chinese laundry service frequent this street?

I stood in that big kitchen with my hands on my hips and almost stomped my foot. But as I stood there, my thoughts turned to Mama and a calmness came over me. I know that back home, she must have been praying for me at the same time I was thinking of her. If she had been there, being the sensible woman she is, how would she have conducted herself given such circumstances?

A good part of the day was spent getting acquainted with the wood and coal range in the kitchen and removing the ashes which I deposited in a corner of the backyard. The icebox does not have a water tray underneath like ours. Rather, a drain pipe follows the floor and pokes through the wall to the outdoors. And what the last housekeeper had fixed for the Miller's was still in the icebox. Goodness!

The house was in terrible disorder and it would take more than a day to put it to right. I have a feeling that men in general, especially the Miller men haven't a clue of how long it does take.

As the day progressed, my worries increased about the supper situation. If there had been a block of ice above the food it would not have mattered. Everything was spoiled and had to be thrown out. I doubt if the door had been opened since the last housekeeper was there. Tomorrow I must look for the card and place it in the dining-room window. Stuart had no idea where it was.

As dusk settled in, the first footsteps to enter were those of Todd. He did say "Hello," after he gave me a nose in the air glance. I in turned asked him if he knew when his father and brother might be returning home. Todd shrugged his shoulders and walked away, climbing the stairs away from me.

"Mr. Miller," says I, "the proper response is, "I'm sorry Miss Eleanor, but I do not know."

Todd stopped, turned, and gave me a look as though someone actually had the audacity to address him.

A belittling voice replied, "No, I do not."

"Thank You," I replied, watching him ascend the stairs and disappear around a corner.

Although I let out a sigh of temporary relief, my poor nerves had been agitating my stomach throughout the day. By the time Todd came home I was feeling almost ill. So I paced in front of the fireplace and chastised myself for not baking at least a few loaves of bread as I had thought about doing earlier in the day. But then, how ridiculous a sight sliced bread and water would have been! I wanted to be back at home—away from those awful, nasty men!

Within twenty minutes I heard the front door open. I summoned every bit of courage I had and met Mr. Miller Sr. and Stuart Jr. in the hallway. Mr. Miller Sr. sniffed the air and asked why he did not smell supper. Stuart Jr. asked why the table was not set. At this point I was shaking inside but miraculously managed to say, "Good-evening. My name is Miss Eleanor... As to your question of dinner Mr. Miller, you are correct. You do not smell supper.... because.... there is no supper to fix."

I wish my family could have seen the stunned look on their faces which turned from stricken dumb to boiling anger. The poor dears! I pray that I recover from the profanities that bursted out of Mr. Miller's mouth. Suddenly, my emotions snapped and I fell into a fit of tears when Mr. Miller called me a stupid and incompetent female. He stomped up the stairs yelling at the top of his lungs that I was fired and that my Papa just lost his house. Hearing this made me cry even more.

A blurred figure, one forgotten Stuart Miller, stepped forward and caught his father's attention with a sharp, though respectable, "Sir!—" In the brief moment in which the large man ceased to move, Stuart asked for leniency without a sympathetic note in his voice. "Perhaps, under the circumstances, we could make allowances for the girl." Stuart paused, and to my surprise, Mr. Miller only growled. Stuart cleared his throat. "Let us not make any decisions while we are troubled by the discomfort of hunger. Surely, another house will not benefit us, if we discard the pleasing prospect which comes with it, before, another chance is given."

My eyes rose to where Mr. Miller Sr. stood on the handsome stairwell, and his eyes, nasty, mean and full of evil, bore down on me.

"She is your concern!" he barked.

Mr. Miller Sr. slammed his bedroom door, and turning to me, Stuart made a gesture towards the parlor and watched me with unashamed intensity as I took a seat. I asked if I may have a note-pad and a writing utensil. Stuart went to his father's desk and found them.

I was told not to waste his time as he was starving and would now have to go back down the hill. A door slammed and the pounding of descending feet was soon followed by the brief figure of Mr. Miller Sr. The front door slammed. Stuart swore openly for now he would have to walk to the street car without his father and their nice motor car. Stuart told me to be quick about my business.

Satisfied with my questions, I flipped the tablet closed, and to my astonishment, Stuart Miller took leave of the parlor and the house—though, not quietly.

I wanted to cry again. Instead, I retrieved my sweater from the hall and went home.

Goodnight,
Eleanor

September 22, 1909
Friday

I saw my first Bewick's Wren this morning. His long, black beak nervously stabbed at the ground under the hydrangea bush next to our front porch steps. I've never seen a bird flick his little tail up and down so. Although I've never heard him, Mama tells me that the Wren sings as though its lungs are bottomless.

Papa and Richard got a few more residential odd jobs to-day.

The sunlight was glorious this morning and a swirling breeze was touched with a bit of coolness. Our street must be home to several families of Chickadee's for they bade me 'farewell' with their sweet 'chick-a-dee-dee-dee.'

Marie has come in to lie down on her bed. I wish our beds were new and were without noisy springs. Every time Marie makes the slightest movement the bed squeaks. I do not speak out loud of such annoyances, for dear Marie has a way of unintentionally construing what has been said to other members of the family.

Funny that Marie should ask how things are at the Miller's. I was just thinking that two weeks have come and gone already. She is complaining how tired her frail body is after a week of school. She worries what she will do after graduation in two years time. I'm afraid to confess that her life may never extend further than our house. Poor, Marie. She constantly reminds me to be thankful for a bright mind and strong body. Without those abilities, I could

15

not complete all the baking, cooking, cleaning, scrubbing, clothes washing, clothes mending, and trips to the ash pile each day. I will admit that at the end of the week I am very, very tired. But we still have our beloved house which the Miller's are never going to get their hands on.

Goodnight,
Eleanor

September 24, 1909
Sunday

It was difficult getting out of bed this morning. Alice and Marie robbed their beds of top covers to wrap around themselves and stood at the window exclaiming that all the house roofs were white with frost. I should have pried myself out of bed last night and opened the green trunk at the end of Marie's bed. Extra blankets and quilts stored there would have given me a pleasant sleep. Instead I shivered. Stubborn people deserve to suffer.

Alice bounced on my bed to wake me but I covered my head and told her to occupy herself elsewhere. She laughed and said that she would join Marie in the warm kitchen, and if I wasn't downstairs in five minutes she would send Richard up. Under the covers I rubbed my hands together and closed my eyes and thought of the long day which waited for me tomorrow. I dreadfully miss being with other people. I felt independent, looked forward to each day. I was treated with respect. Not once, in two weeks has the Miller's paid compliment to any of my meals. Papa, Richard and John are forever thanking us women.

I must have been in deep thought for Richard made it up the stairs without my notice.

"I understand there is a sleepy young lady in here somewhere," Richard teased from the doorway.

"There is and she wishes not to be bothered."

"Do I hear voices from under the covers?"

The springs creaked and the mattress sank as Richard lowered his body on my bed.

"Richard, do you think Papa and Mama might not take notice if one of us is not in the pew this morning?"

"Are you speaking to the blankets or to your brother, my dear sister?"

I uncovered my head to see the smiling freshly shaven face of Richard already dressed for church.

"How do you manage not cut yourself with that horrible instrument?" I asked while allowing my fingers to follow different paths across his face.

"A steady hand and some luck," he grinned. "I'm supposed to drag you downstairs you know."

I let out a deep sigh and looked at my dear brother. He placed a hand on either side of my hidden body and looked down at me. "El, are the Miller's working you too hard?"

My lips couldn't give him the answer he wanted, but his warm brown eyes knew the answer. "I'll be all right." I tried to reassure him. "Really, I will be."

Richard sat up and took a handful of my hair into his hands.

"Are you and Papa securing more steady jobs?" I inquired.

Richard nodded and brought my hair to his face and breathed in. "We've been picking up a lot of odd jobs here and there."

"That's good."

Richard nodded again and swirled my long hair on top of my head.

"Come on El. It's nice and warm in the kitchen."

"Is the coffee done?"

"Just waiting for you. I'll pour you a cup so you'll stay awake in church."

"Doubtful."

"I'll fill your cup twice."

Richard slowly rose from the squeaky bed and made his way to the door.

"Can I sit next to you so I can rest my head on your shoulder and sleep?"

My brother eyed me tenderly as he stood on the threshold of our room, his hands pressing on the door frame, his body leaning forward. His attention was riveted on me. Silence passed between us. A knowing. An understanding. I slowly lifted my head off the pillow and sat up.

Richard removed his hands from the door frame, and for a moment of magnetic rapture, enchanted grounds were tread upon. But, oh! How the mind is not ignorant to the slightest movement of flesh…my heart was pierced even before his foot moved away.

I did sit by Richard and he kept an eye on me as the Latin

words wanted to lull me to sleep. What would I do without my dear Richard?

Eleanor

September 25, 1909
Monday

Another beautiful morning, but no Wren's. Haven't seen him in a week. Maybe he's taken up residence in a neighbor's yard. There are still plenty of Chickadee's and House Sparrow's to greet me on my long walk to the Miller's house. Although I do love and appreciate the cheerful sun as it reflects against homes and of trees with autumn hues, if I did not wear my hat I would go quite blind.

This is the beginning of the third week at the Miller's and during this time I have received interesting looks from the Miller's neighbors. I can understand their stares, their slight nods, their looks of pity. I can read their faces. I can almost read their silted mouths. They wonder what circumstances has brought such a fine young lady to that house for employment. Not to belittle domestics, but I do not look like a peasant girl from Ireland or the Old Country. I should be in an office wearing my nice clothes, greeting customers whose eyes discreetly follow me about the office as I prepare their paper work. I do not know if Papa and Mama would consider such glances improper, for they are a far cry from the look that Stuart Miller gave me at the end of his visit three weeks ago.

I almost forgot. I received a nice letter from dear Mr. Whiting asking if I would consider working on Saturday's. Since my departure, the organization of the office has quickly eroded. Mr. Whiting described his new secretary as being close to an imbecile as they come. His wife convinced him to hire a niece, and against his better judgment did so anyway. According to my dear former employer, his niece can not handle pressure nor can she find her way out of a box. Poor thing! I'm not sure who I feel most sorry for; Mr. Whiting or the young lady. The offer sounds good. It would mean more money for Papa and Mama, and a little for myself. It would mean putting a whole disastrous week to right in one day. The thought of using my God given talent with numbers brings a smile to my face. Mr. Whiting has said many times that my mind is as sharp as a needle and that my mere presence illuminates joy in what otherwise would be a gloomy office. Isn't he sweet? I remember once during lunch break, one of my girlfriends whispered to me that I have fallen under notice of many clients, and that she has heard men ask Mr. Whiting of my 'availability' status. We had a good chuckle over that one. I shall have to give Mr. Whiting an answer soon. Very soon.

Goodnight, Eleanor

September 26, 1909
Tuesday

This morning Papa rode with me part way up the hill. Word is spreading from neighbor to neighbor that Papa can just about fix anything. He is very smart and cleaver. Funny how people do not want to figure things out for themselves like Papa has.

It was strange sitting next to him. I cannot recall the last time I had Papa all to myself. Since we did not have far to travel our conversation lightly touched the subject of the changing season. I will have to ask Mama if Papa has always been so quiet. I wonder what he was like as a child. While growing up in Austria. While he was courting Mama.

The electric trolley car came to a stop, and forming a slight smile with his thin lips Papa whispered, "Be a good girl."

"Have a good day, Papa."

As the trolley moved forward, I waved a small wave and noticed how my Papa's smaller than average build was looking even slighter. Were tired shoulders that bore the worries of his family to blame? I do not like to see my Papa so solemn.

While kneading bread dough first thing this morning, I thought I heard footsteps and coughing from an upper room. I did not think the coughing belonged to Mr. Miller Sr. for it was not deep as if he were trying to rattle his intestines. My curiosity was ceased for the cough belonged to Todd. He came into the kitchen and sat down at the table. No greeting came from him as he squinted off the beautiful morning light. He watched me fold, push and turn the white pile.

"So that's how you girls do it," Todd said in a very hoarse voice.

I turned to him and smiled. "Yes, Mr. Miller. This is how we 'girls' do it."

He let out a sigh declaring dry conversation.

"Have you enjoyed my bread?"

"It's all right."

"Just, all right? I'm surprised how a whole loaf can disappear at one meal with only crumbs remaining as evidence of my 'all right' baking."

Todd was silent for a few moments. His chest rattled and he mumbled, "Whatever."

Putting the dough in a greased bowl I covered it with a cloth to keep it warm while it rose. I began cleaning up my mess when Todd coughed and crinkled his face in pain.

"How long have you been ill?" I asked.

He sat staring at me as if wasting time were a form of amusement.

"Mr. Miller," says I, "you remind me of Pharaoh."

"Who?"

"Pharaoh and Moses. Heard of them?"

Todd shook his head.

"I think you would have liked Pharaoh. He was afraid the Israelites would out number the Egyptians, join his enemies, fight against him and leave the country. So he tried oppressing the Israelites by forcing them into hard labor and used them ruthlessly."I slightly turned away from the work board and made eye contact with Todd.

"God had a plan and sent Moses to soften Pharaoh's heart. Moses had one request, and that was for Pharaoh to let the Israelites go. But Pharaoh was such a stubborn man that even after God turned the Nile into blood, sent plagues of frogs, gnats, flies, killing all Egyptian livestock, and sent festering boils on man and beast. There were more plagues. Hail, locusts, darkness which could be felt for three days. Still, Pharaoh was stubborn and didn't listen to Moses."

I washed my hands and waited.

"Well….what happened?"

"Every firstborn Egyptian died. Men, women, child, and beast."

The kitchen was silent.

"Did this Pharaoh have a child?" Todd finally inquired without trying to sound interested.

"Yes. Yes he did," I gently replied.

I asked Todd if he had ever read the Bible. Todd said that his father does not believe in the Bible.

"I would be interested in knowing what 'you' believe in. Not your father, but you, Todd Miller."

The kitchen was very, very quiet. The eyes of Todd Miller fell from my face and they just….they were just lost within his own thoughts.

Then I told him to stand up.

"Why?"

"Like I say, you and Pharaoh have much in common. He was a very stubborn man. Very stubborn. If he would have cooperated, his army would not have been swallowed up by the Red Sea."

Todd slowly pushed his chair away from the table and stood up.

I went to him and placed my fingers under his jaw and felt for swelling and lumps.

"Sore?"

Todd nodded his head and looked down at me.

He coughed a few times and I put my head against his chest and told him to breath deep. I looked at him with concern. "I'm going to have you gargle every half-hour with a warm water-salt solution. That should help your sore throat. While you are upstairs gargling, I will be making a mustard plaster. I want you to lie down on your bed and wait for me."

"What does the mustard do?"

"It breaks up the congestion in your chest. Now go."

I think Todd was more nervous than I at the thought of exposing his chest as I laid the smelly mixture on him. I can not count the times Mama and I have made that dreadful concoction.

While Todd suffered quietly, I sat with him, softly singing and humming while catching up on some mending.

As another day was over, I made my way to the foyer where I could hear the voices of Mr. Miller Sr. and Stuart Jr. drifting from the billiard room. As I was putting on my heavy sweater, Todd slowly made his way down the staircase. He looked as though he wanted to thank me, but didn't know how. He put his hands in his pockets, stopping close to the last stair which allowed him to look down on me. My ears and my heart were waiting for just a little bit of thanks. But none came. Instead, he asked me what my name was. I made my back straight and lifted my chin. I told him that if he did not know my name by now, it was not my obligation to tell him. I opened the door but hesitated.

Todd hadn't moved from the stairs when I turned around and sternly asked, "Certain things do not matter to this family...do they?"

With that I went home.

Goodnight,
Eleanor

September 29, 1909
Friday

The skies were quite gray this morning which darkened all rooms of our house. I spent a short time observing the assortment of birds from the kitchen window while sipping my coffee. Maybe our fine feathered friends feel safer in our established neighborhood, for I do not see as many on top the hill. It gave me great pleasure to see the Steller Jay in his beautiful blue coat. And although he did not stay for long, the Downey Woodpecker nervously searched for food in the bark of the apple tree. The Robin whom I have not seen for some weeks flocked to our yard and flew from one tree to another. I wonder if the change in the weather has stirred excitement in the birds. Or, do they know that tomorrow is the last day of September? What do they know that we do not?

The week has been a busy one, for to-day I made enough bread (hopefully) to last till Monday morning, and also made a pan of sticky buns. I do not know what the Miller's do for meals on the week-end. Perhaps they dine out. Perhaps I should not care what the Miller's do in my absence.

Since Tuesday I do not think Todd has been out of the house. After having spoken such words with him, he stays in his room and sleeps for hours at a time. I suspect all the studying and staying up late eventually does take a toll on one's health. His coughing sounds better—thanks to the mustard plaster. On Wednesday I made a pot of chicken soup which Todd allowed me to bring to him. He watches me as I bring him meals and when I take the dishes away. That young man puzzles me. While quietly putting away his shirts in the armoire this afternoon, I thought he was asleep so I tip-toed about his room. My back was turned to him when he spoke to me.

"What color is your hair?"

Taken by surprise, I turned to him and replied, "Pardon me?"

Todd was resting his arms behind his head. "Your hair. What color is it?"

"My hair? Oh, I suppose you could call it dark brown, though Richard says it reminds him of shiny melted chocolate."

His eyes and silence rested upon me. Was such a habit acquired from other students at the University, I wonder? Do they pine their hours away, resolving beforehand, as a standing order, that such behavior should be dispensed to all mankind?

"Is that all, Mr. Miller?" I asked. More silence. I turned to leave and was almost out of his room with the tray when he spoke bluntly.

"Is my father paying you to take care of me?"

I stood in the doorway long enough to digest his question when Todd asked me a second time. Putting the tray down, I went to him and sat on the end of his bed. (If for no other reason, my feet and legs needed the rest.)

"Let me ask you a question. Would it bother you if he were?"

Todd shrugged his shoulders.

Our eyes studied each other.

"Well, is he?" Todd asked again in a rather snobbish tone of voice.

I could not help but grin at that strange young man.

"No," I replied kindly. "People are not paid for acts of kindness."

"Why not?" Todd asked with indignation as he crossed his arms.

"Why not?" I cried in profound dismay. "Mr. Miller, people, decent people, do things out of the goodness of their hearts, usually without even thinking twice about it. It is something people just do."

Todd's face was firm as was his lips.

"Can you imagine what would have happened if our Lord would have expected payment for healing the sick, giving sight to the blind, cleansing people of leprosy, bringing dead people to life as if they had only been asleep. He removed demons from people. He did all those things not expecting payment or thanks."

Todd Miller's eyes did not leave mine as my little speech did not fall short of his attention; regardless of his lack of belief in the Bible.

I removed myself from his bed, smoothed my skirt and apron and took the tray from his room. I heard him move in his bed.

"Do not bother me for the rest of the day," Todd so ordered, mumbling into his pillow.

As I sit at our kitchen table looking at the black windows, my heart almost feels sorry for Todd Miller. I think his heart has been cold for so many years that it either doesn't know how to thaw out, or, if it is, the thawing is too painful. I shall have to pray for him.

Goodnight,
Eleanor

October 3, 1909
Sunday

The weather has been a mixed bag since last night. The wonderful pitter-patter of rain drops on the roof above our bedroom brought me comfort while I laid in bed, not wanting to sleep just yet. Marie always has disliked the 'noise' that rain brings. Once in a while I must ask her to hush herself so I can enjoy it. She complains that she is unable to sleep. I wish we could tuck her away in a little corner downstairs on such nights. There is something wonderful about the sound of rain on roof tops. Not on the neighbors roofs, not on the Miller's, but only on ours. It reminds me of large angel wings wrapping themselves around our humble home; they do not want to let go for there is love and warmth within our walls.

Expecting rain on the way to church, I was very surprised to see the sun dominate the morning sky which was still cloaked in clouds, though not with dark ones. Our next door neighbor lady has a cute saying which Mama repeated, and most of the time, proves to be true. It goes:

"If there's enough blue in the sky to make a sailor a pair of pants, it should be a good day."

Fellow streetcar riders who couldn't help but overhear, smiled at Mama.

"I've never heard that saying," someone offered, "but it certainly is cute." And that began a cheerful little conversation that continued to Mama's delight, after the lady rider removed herself from the streetcar as she blended in with the rest of the flock going into Sacred Heart Church.

But Mama's cheerfulness quickly came to an end upon entering the church. To-day is a sad day for our neighborhood. A twelve year old boy who lived around the block from us passed away last night. He had been fighting influenza, but like so many others, he could not escape the contagious disease. Out of respect, the pew which the family regularly occupies was left empty. Two large white bows hung from the ends of the wooden seats. Mama was very upset for she is sympathetic for the grieving mother of the deceased. All through Mass she dabbed her eyes and sniffled. I don't even want to think about who is going to be next on our street, the next street over, and all the other streets which make up the landscape of Seattle.

At night, Alice and I speak in whispers, asking each other if we have read this or that article concerning the unseen hand of death that sweeps over the nation. There are long columns in the obituary portion of the paper. It is ironic, don't you think, that mankind can build the automobile, harness electricity, build glorious universities, and brag that civilization is moving forward. Is it progress when death cannot be stopped? Who can stop influenza and tuberculosis? The wealth of high society cannot buy off this evil, for their bored children die alongside everyone else.

The house has been quiet on purpose since we came home from church….on account of Mama. Alice, Marie and I made baked chicken, baking powder biscuits, mashed potatoes with pan gravy, and cold slaw salad. Papa brought a tray up to Mama but she did not care for it.

This morning she promised to play her mandolin for us after church. John was to play his harmonica, Alice would play the piano, and Marie and I would sing. It feels as if a stranger is in our home to-night. Our dear house is never this quiet. I do not like it.

Richard and John have come into our room and quietly shut the door behind them. John says that Mama is crying. All five of us children are sitting down. Alice says that she does not know what to do in a quiet house. Everyone else agreed. Marie said that I am lucky for I have my journal to keep me company.

I made the suggestion of finishing off the apple-cobbler that we had for dessert, so everyone has left the bedroom except me.

May tomorrow be a better day for Mama. She will probably keep Marie or Alice home to help with the washing. I wish I could help Mama. Tomorrow will be week four at the Miller's. I forgot to pray for Todd this morning after seeing the white ribbons. I will say a prayer for him now.

Goodnight,
Eleanor

October 4, 1909
Monday

I received a lovely embossed wedding invitation from my good friend Miss Minnie Douglas. The three of us, Miss Douglas, Miss McAfee, and I were close friends during school. I have not seen her in a while and did not know she was even engaged. Inside the envelope was a separate note saying that she expects Miss Ernestine McAfee and I to be her attendants. The wedding will be Saturday,

November 6th. I found the lack of details puzzling since she did not make mention how they made their first acquaintance, and, what is the occupation of the groom-to-be.

Miss Minnie Douglas has been the "chatter-box" between the three of us, as she always has managed to speak about herself. If she had not had an ounce of loveableness and charm about her, I dare say Miss Ernestine or I would be friends with her. For a young society girl living on Millionaire Row, to befriend the likes of Miss Ernestine or myself, we could only reason that she chose two daughters born of immigrants for enlightenment and entertainment. We must have supplied her upper-crust society mother with numerous headaches and fits by mere mention of our names—which one cannot tear apart from at birth. Not that we would ever dare to do so in order to squelch man's prejudice. Where Miss Minnie delights in such free independence as not conforming to her station in life as a Millionaire Row daughter, Mrs. Douglas puts the blame entirely on her husband and his scores of past mistresses. Although he or she could not disclaim the notion that perhaps in some not yet explained scientific way, that Mr. Douglas' vices have round-a-boutly unsettled the cart, for Mrs. Douglas has never had a relation on her family side that showed an independent streak—until little Miss Minnie was born.

Very soon I shall witness the union of Mr. and Mrs. Howard Wallingford.

> Goodnight, Minnie Douglas-
> I wish you all the happiness
> in the world.
> Eleanor

October 5, 1909
Tuesday

I look forward seeing the welcoming lights in our windows as I approach our home in the black of night. My heart is warm and glad when I pull myself up the front steps, but to-night my tired feet could not walk any faster. I went straight to my bed to lie down.

I am almost too tired to write to-night. I think it was the extra cleaning, clothes and bedding washing after Todd's sickness. He is fine. And no, he never thanked me. I suppose I should just realize that it will never happen and leave it at that.

Alice was so dear to-night. After seeing me dead like on my bed, she drew me a nice bath and set out my nightgown and put my dirty apron in the soaking tub. I heard her humming the tune of "Happy Birthday" while I soaked. I asked her why she was singing it.

"Oh, poor, poor Eleanor. The Miller's have made you so exhausted that you have forgotten what tomorrow is."

My hand flew to my mouth as I apologized to my dear sister who would be turning eighteen in a matter of hours.

Mama warmed dinner for me but to her quiet dismay I only picked at it. While Alice kept company with me at the table, Mama looked at me with concern. I could not hide my tiredness.

Marie came into the kitchen and started complaining that she has to do everything now. Mama told her to hush and to go to her room, and that she did not want to see her until morning.

Alice almost didn't want to mention it, but tomorrow at the Alaska-Yukon-Pacific Exposition is "Apple Day," and a no charge day. Richard said that he would accompany us on the trolley. Mama and Papa wished to stay home, for their one and only visit proved too strenuous for them. Alice knows that I do not arrive home until late and would feel bad if I did not go with them. I told her that she was too sweet, but I wouldn't mind if they went without me. Perhaps I could go just before the Exposition closes on the 16th.

According to the article in the newspaper which she showed me, "Apple Day," October 6, will see the Washington apple in all its glory. Visitors to the Exposition will know that it is apple day even before the carloads of apples are distributed, for every avenue and walk of the grounds, to say nothing of the buildings, will be decorated with the luscious fruit. Directly in front of the Cascades will be erected a pyramid of apples 32 feet square at the base. Every county in the state that raises a pippin has offered barrels of apples and these will be given away to fair visitors.

Before I went upstairs, I asked Alice's forgiveness that I did not get her a present for her special day, perhaps as soon as I can earn extra money. She said, that every day those wicked men do not get our house is like a present to her. Bless her heart. I hope everyone has a good time tomorrow. The weather should be pleasant.

Goodnight, Eleanor

October 9, 1909
Saturday

It is Saturday already. I heard the rain early, early this morning. It is very dark and wet beyond our cozy walls.

In last Sunday's paper there was an advertisement for electric irons. How wonderful! I can only imagine the time it will save! No more nine pound sad irons that have to be heated on the range. Perhaps ironing will not be an all day job. Electricity has only been available in homes within the city for a few years, so electric irons may help a few women in Seattle. On Monday I would like to ask Mr. Miller about purchasing a clothes wringer so I will not have to do so by hand. I do not understand why they have so few modern conveniences which would help enormously with the tiring job of washing and ironing. It cannot be to the lack of finances. As tight as money is in our family, we all worked together and purchased a hand-cranked clothes wringer when they came on the market.

I wonder just how much the job of cleaning clothes have changed since Mama was a girl. I wonder what will be available five or ten years from now. It seems that great strides are taking place to improve and ease woman's household duties.

After I began working at the Miller's I asked Mama if I could borrow her little book on washing and cleaning hints for women. It really should be titled, "A Week of Woeful Work for Women Without Rest." I want to take the time and write down the important and useful information which my Mama and I use at this time in our lives. Although the writing will be time consuming, I want to have it down on paper so someday, when I am very old, I can look back and see how progress has changed. Perhaps my daughters, grand-daughters, (and eventually, great-granddaughters) might find such facts interesting by then.

Just a personal note: The day-to-day schedule was meant for the house or farm wife who could start soaking clothes on Sunday and begin on Monday, as our family does. At the Miller's I begin soaking on Monday and start washing on Tuesday.

Good-day
Eleanor

MONDAY

An oval shaped copper container called a boiler is brought into the kitchen. It holds about twenty gallons of water. Place over two stove lids. While the water is heating, prepare the starch for sizing and set aside to cool. Heavily soiled items that had been put to soak in warm soapy water the night before are removed from the tub and put into a dishpan or pail until it is time to wash them. Soiled handkerchiefs are soaked in salt water separately.

The laundry is sorted ready for the tub and the boiler. White clothes are first and separated; lightly soiled whites for the tub; cotton sheets, tea towels, etc. for the boiler. Next are the colored ones: light colors first, medium colors, and finally the dark clothes. These are washed in this sequence because of the natural dyes used in the fabrics which fade. Men's outdoor pants and overalls follow, and last, the colored socks.

Two galvanized tubs are placed on the kitchen chairs and filled with water. The first tub about half full of cold water. Hot water is added from the boiler to a medium washing temperature used for washing the light-weight, delicate, and least soiled items. White goods put into the washtub for scrubbing are sheets, towels, men's white handkerchiefs and other stained or heavily soiled pieces. Put these in the boiler to boil and soap is added for extra cleansing. Dry clothes are never put into the boiler as the hot water set stains. When ready the hot sudsy clothes are lifted from the boiler by using a round stick about thirty inches long. The laundry in the boiler is removed and goes to the washtub and then through the rinse.

The wash is rubbed on a washboard using home-made soap. Soap is applied to soiled portions, then the clothing is rubbed on the board, returned to the water, swished around to remove excess soap, then wrung out and placed in the rinse water contained in the second tub.

Rinse: take out of the water, let it drip momentarily, then with both hands holding the garment or cloth twist in opposite directions in a wringing motion. Or use a clothes wringer which clamps to the side of a tub. The clothes are put between the two rollers and the handle turns to guide them through and press out excess water. Guide the clothing with one hand and turn the handle with the other.

Battling dingy laundry

Tea towels, hand towels, and other items used on a daily basis.

Rinsing is done in cold water so soap suds do not completely dissolve. The residue is still in the material and eventually creates a dingy look. Boiling the white goods. Three or four balls of compressed powdered bluing are tied in a piece of white cloth and added to the last rinse water, swished around until the right shade of blue is achieved and then remove. If the bluing is left too long the white clothes have an undesirable bluish cast.

Heavy soiled clothes

Lye soap is used to loosen heavy soil in men's work clothes while they soak. Soiled colored clothes that can not be boiled are put in the washtub to soak in warm sudsy water to loosen dirt/heavy soil. While these are soaking the white clothes are rinsed and blued. Do not forget to stoke the fire—keeping the water hot and supper cooking!

The second tub should be at least half full of cold water for rinsing the clothes. This tub needs to be changed at least once or twice, using fresh water. The cold water for rinsing out the soap becomes "scummy" and leaves a residue in the colored clothes which dims the brightness of the color and will stiffen the cloth. Vinegar sometimes is added to the water to cut the "scum."

Starching

Starching prevents soil from being imbedded into the garment so when it is washed soil and starch are removed at the same time. Also cotton or linen materials wrinkle easily even after ironing. Water is added to dilute the cooked starch, the strength depending on the amount of water added. Deciding on the strength of starch is by trail and error. Heavy starch is used for such wash goods as men's shirt fronts, collars, cuffs, women's aprons, curtains, pillow slips, pillow shams, lunch cloths. White clothes are done first; colored next, in the light to dark sequence. They are dipped in the starch water which has been prepared earlier, wrung out, and hung on the clothesline to dry. As the starch is used the strength becomes thinner and materials needing a lighter starch are done last. When the wash is all done, dip a pail of water for mopping the floor. The wet clothes are carried to the backyard in a wicker basket and are pinned on the line with a common pin made of soft wood.

Recipe for Starch
3 T. dry fine starch
1 quart boiling water
Pinch of salt

Piece of clean tallow (or butter) the size of a cranberry.

HINTS:
To keep colors from running in washing black prints, put a teaspoon of black pepper in the first water. Salt also sets black.

Alum sets green.

To take spots from wash goods rub with yolk of egg before washing.

To make linen white, boil one teaspoon of turpentine with clothes.

Spots on towels: A little ammonia in enough water to soak articles, two hours before washing. One cup for overnight soaking. Save the water and use it on the house plants.

TUESDAY
Ironing
In hot or cold weather the cook stove is always in use. On Tuesday clothes from Monday's wash is ironed. Ironing boards are made of wood. On Tuesday morning, irons are placed on the stove and anything that needs ironing is sprinkled with water to moisten and then rolled up tightly to dampen throughout. The sprinkled clothes are wrapped with a towel and placed in a wicker basket ready for ironing. The daily chore of keeping the stove top clean is done differently on ironing day. The surface is polished by using a brick wrapped in a clean old cloth, rag, or blanket piece. This keeps the stove clean for the irons. Sometimes irons heated on the stove have black soot or grease on them. Each time an iron is removed from the stove it is rubbed on an old cloth or brown paper to clean it. The cloth is kept at the end of the ironing board near the iron trivet. Beeswax and salt rubbed on the iron also helps to keep it clean. If the iron is too hot it can scorch the material, then the wash goods have to be treated and returned to the washing. Testing the heat of the iron is done by moistening the end of your finger and quickly touching the surface of the iron. It is ready if it sizzles. If in doubt, it is tested on the old cloth kept nearby. A sad iron weighs about 9 pounds.

When pressing is needed, a clean white cloth, of 12' by 18' size, is dipped in cold water, wrung out and placed on the garment or seam to be pressed. A heavy tailor's iron is applied to the pressing cloth causing steam which smoothes the wrinkles and sets the seams.

The iron dries the pressing cloth and presses the garment. This iron weighs between 13 to 15 pounds.

To clean hat bands:
Magnesium chalk is used to clean men's and women's hat bands. Dust as much of the powder as can be absorbed into the band to clean way the grease. Brush remainder away and allow to air.

WEDNESDAY
Mending
While the midweek batch of bread is rising, work on the mending. To do work by hand requires knowing several basic stitches: the overstitch, the running stitch, the backstitch, and the buttonhole stitch. (These skills were handed down from Mama to me.) Sewing buttons is a constant chore, and also mending button holes. Buttonholes are reinforced if they are torn, frayed, or stretched too large to hold the button. A simple running stitch is made all around the opening and a buttonhole stitch is done over this. Needles, thread, scissors, and thimble are used in the sewing basket which is always kept close to a comfortable chair. A button box or jar is also kept handy near the mending so the lady or ladies of the house can sort out the right size button to replace the one lost.

When the bread it ready to bake, set aside the mending and put the bread in the oven. Always keep an eye on the fire to make sure it has enough wood, then return to your mending.

I pray that someday, the task of washing clothes will become easier for women. Amen and Vote for Women!

Good-day again,
Eleanor

October 10, 1909
Sunday

Alice was excused from church this morning on account of her feeling "poorly." Her "curse" began last night and Mama says that God should forgive women if we do not attend once in a great while. Before I left I gave Alice a hot water bottle, set her into a comfortable chair by the fireplace, gave her a few aspirin pills and a Good Housekeeping magazine. John cannot understand what all the fuss is about. He wouldn't. All men wouldn't. It has been said, that females are privileged to have bodies enabling one to bear children. Are we to feel privileged when our bodies writhe in pain one week a month while wearing enough cloth "there" to accommodate a small pillow? Are we to feel privileged while wearing these beastly corsets which make breathing so difficult? The days of such suffering in whale bone or steel may soon be over. Doctors have been telling women for decades to discard their corsets. I cannot tell you how uncomfortable they are. But to discard it would immediately mean a wider skirt is needed for the skirts are made to fit after the corset has been tightened around the body. I will feel privileged after I remove it and throw it away! Privilege indeed! I wonder if Mama and Alice feel as I do. While I was employed at the Insurance Company I felt privileged to work at a place where men took me seriously. Mr. Whiting would not have it any other way. His kind, I'm afraid are very rare.

Alice is begging me to go to the Alaska-Yukon-Pacific Exposition next Saturday which ends after 138 days. I have sent word to Mr. Whiting that I will be at his office next Saturday. If I do not go the Exposition I will surely regret it for the most successful Fair ever held in any country is close to being over. On that day everything will be wide open, and the wildest scenes of carnival will reign supreme. (So the Sunday paper says of the last day of A.Y.P.E.) Grotesque costumes, car loads of confetti, millions of tin horns and cow-bells, steam whistles and sky-rockets will be the order of the day and night. Everybody will know everybody else; bands will play "There'll be a Hot Time: and "We won't go Home till Morning."

Exhausted or not, Alice and I will attend in the evening. I cannot forget to ask Richard if he will still be escorting us. I wish we had an automobile, but what a luxury. I have heard that a prosperous family buying a $3,000 touring motor car will probably spend another $3,000 a year to run it.

Another annoyance about the female myth: women cannot possibly learn to drive the automobile. If we want to vote, I suppose we need to show men that more than a handful of us dainty creatures can handle such a machine.

Goodnight,
Eleanor

October 11, 1909
Monday

I am upset but I am not surprised that Mr. Miller Sr. turned my request down flat after I asked for a washing machine device. I am quite convinced now that all the other domestics employed on top this grand hill have it easier than I. I see China-men coming and going every day on this street. Can you imagine, having someone else do your laundry? How nice and how costly!

I found Mr. Miller Sr. resting in the parlor after dinner, reading the evening paper and smoking his smelly cigar. I was hoping that he would be in a half-agreeable mood right after my good dinner of pot roast, stuffing, corn, cranberry sauce, spice cake and coffee. To boil our little conversation down to what it amounted to, it went like this. Mr. Miller does not care how long it takes me or anyone else in the future to do the laundry. Nor does he care if it takes all day to iron their clothes.

I composed myself and replied, "Tuesday is washday so you will have a pot of soup and bread. If there is clothing on Wednesday which is dry, you men might have any left over soup or beans. And on Thursday, depending on how much mending there is to do, you may receive a larger meal."

Mr. Miller, not caring what I had to say had already begun reading the newspaper while puffing away on his cigar. I doubt if he heard one word of what I had said. Come tomorrow he will be wondering what a bowl of soup and a slice of bread is all about. The Miller's may not care if I am doing the work of two or three people, but I do. And I will hold out until I receive a clothes-wringer!

Alice just told me that there is a new publication managed by suffragettes, called "The American Suffragette." The magazine will be issued monthly and will be on sale at news stands for 5 cents. The subscription price is fifty cents a year. She is wondering if I would like to subscribe since she does not have a job.

I think Alice with all her time and energy should be the one in the family to lead us further towards votes for women. She obtained a "Votes for Women," pennant of the suffrage movement from a young woman down the street who has been practicing speeches on top a wooden box in her backyard. According to this young lady, a "Votes for Women," pennant floats below the A.Y.P. banner at the upper-most peak of Mount Rainier. A Dr. Cora Smith Eaton who placed it there while climbing with the Mountaineers, knows that no political or equality plea was ever carried to greater heights on the American continent.

Richard had some interesting news about President Taft tonight. After his "opening day" visit at the Exposition, he likes the Northwest immensely and says he is coming back next spring. President Taft likes to travel and the people of the Northwest will be glad to welcome him many times during his term. It has even been proposed that the national government be removed to the West during the heated summer months, as Washington, D.C. is too torrid. The people of Puget Sound believe this is the ideal location if a change is made. I do not know of many Puget Sound people who like the idea of more politicians in the Northwest. We do not need another Washington, D.C.

I best get ready for bed. Tomorrow is my big wash day and I need my rest. I look forward to serving the Miller's soup and bread. If it's good enough for our family on washday, it will be good enough for them, too.

Goodnight, Eleanor

October 12, 1909
Tuesday

The pressed linen was laid on the dining room table. The candles were lit in the shiny candelabra. The bread smelled wonderful and its lovely warm aroma drifted throughout the house. The good plates and the bowls and the silverware waited patiently for the Miller men. On the back burner a pot of beef barley soup waited. I waited.

Downstairs on the clothes lines which runs the width of the Miller's house hangs the wash which I labored over to-day. The heating system sits in the middle of the basement and the wash lines run all around it. Since to-day started and ended as a wet, gray and drizzly day, I had no choice other to be in the gloomy basement. I do not care for it down there for too many shadows pry on my imagination.

While I hung up the many pieces of articles, I felt very relieved that in the kitchen, slowly simmering, was dinner. My day had already been made easier.

I waited for the Miller men to gather around the table. When they were all seated, I carried out a plate of bread with a little smile on my face, and upon my return I brought forth dinner in a large soup server. One by one I filled their bowls and placed the soup in the middle of the table. The look on the men's faces was beyond priceless. I turned to leave and started for the kitchen door when Mr. Miller Sr. roared at me.

"What in God's name is this?!"

"This is dinner, Sir. Have you forgotten what to-day is?" I asked very sweetly.

"Damn it! I know what day to-day is. It's Tuesday!"

"Yes, it is. For a moment I thought you had forgotten about our little conversation we had last night."

Oh, the glorious silence! The father glared at me. The sons stared at the father. I smiled at all three and said ever so sweetly, "Enjoy your dinner!"

Oh, how I wished to have heard their conversation, but I was busy washing the dishes and humming my favorite songs.

The only thing which could have made my day complete, is if I had not been stricken with the "curse" after I came home. I must be losing weight for I did not notice as much rounding in my stomach this time. I read somewhere that a women should drink apple vinegar in her water during meals which is supposed to "lighten the flow." One of these days I should actually try the suggestion to see if it is beneficial.

Goodnight, Eleanor

October 13, 1909
Wednesday

I was reading an old issue of Good Literature from June of 1900 and found a poem entitled *"A WOMAN'S WORK."* I understand how that poor woman feels—Is this how our life is to be for generations to come?

> *When breakfast things are cleared away*
> *The same old problem's rising,*
> *For she again sits down to think*
> *Of something appetizing.*
> *The dinner she must soon prepare,*
> *Or give the cook directions,*
> *And great is the relief she feels*
> *When she has made selections.*

When dinner things are cleared away
The problem that is upper
Is just the same with one word changed—
"What can I get for supper?"
She wants to give them something new,
And long is meditation,
Till choice is made, and then begins
The work of preparation.

When supper things are cleared away
Again her mind is worried,
For then she thinks of breakfast time
When meals are often hurried.
She ponders o'er it long until
The question is decided,
Then bustles 'round till she makes sure
That everything's provided.

That "woman's work is never done"
Has often been disputed,
But that she's worried is a fact,
And cannot be refuted.
The worry over what to eat
Is greatest of these questions,
And glad she'd be if some one else
Would make the meal suggestions.
E—

October 14, 1909
Thursday

Yesterday was not a pleasant day for me. The "curse" so fitting the name, has brought horrible pains to the back of my legs, and since yesterday was ironing day I spent a great deal of time standing. I know that it was not right to complain to myself the way I did, but all I wanted was to go home and lay down with the wonderful hot water bottle on my stomach and have half a dozen wrapped in towels to put under my legs. Horrible thoughts go through a woman's head when she is in pain, especially when she knows that she cannot do much about it.

37

I am thankful that the Miller men did not eat all the soup on Tuesday, for that is what they had last night. I forget who started to say something about soup again, but as you can imagine, I was in no mood to hear their nonsense concerning left-overs. As dim-witted as men are in the matters of "female things," even they took note of my sour tone of voice and kept their opinions to themselves. It did not bother me in the least to look Mr. Miller Sr. straight in the eye and remind him that it was "ironing" day.

Unfortunately, ironing day did not end yesterday. Unlike drying clothes on the line in the sunshine, they do not dry as quickly downstairs. Oh! And to make my day worse, after supper last night, Stuart wished to speak to me in the parlor. He asked me if I iron his father's bed sheets. I told him I do not. He smiled a peculiar smile and told me that from now on he wants 'his' bed sheets ironed. Not only the pillowcases, but the sheets, too. Can you imagine! And then, he informs me that his white shirts are not white enough. He demands that they are to be whiter. Since men do know anything about bluing balls, I had to explain to him that if I left them in the bluing solution longer than usual, they will have a bluish look to them. I tried to explain that only so much can be done to whiten whites and that I was doing the best I could. Stuart Miller came close of accusing me of not making him look as good as or better than his father. Interesting, isn't he?

I don't think Richard is the only one coming down with a sore throat. For the past few nights Mama has put a wet handkerchief under a wool sock and wrapped it around his neck. That along with gargling salt water should do the trick. I suppose I best do the same.

This evening after a simple meal of meat loaf, boiled potatoes, cut green beans and pan rolls (no dessert), I cleaned the kitchen as quickly as I could and quietly left the Miller's house. After having been deposited at the bottom of the hill by the street car, in my hurry to reach home I tripped on the uneven sidewalk where the grass meets the pavement. I do wish I had a lantern to see by. But I am home and in bed with a hot water bottle. My saintly sister, Alice, is taking care of me. What would I do without her?

I cannot imagine what it would have been like living with all brothers as Mama did being the only girl with six older brothers. Who would take care of you? Who could she talk to if she did not care discussing personal matters with her mother? As a young woman, how would she and her mother discreetly wash and hang their monthly cloth to dry, in a household of seven men?

I am very thankful for dear Alice for she is cleaning my skirt. I had to apologize for almost running her off the stairway as I was in such a sad and miserable state of emotional turmoil as the "curse" is known to bring on (not to mention the other happenings of the week.)

Speaking of emotions, Alice started laughing and said that she just had to tell me something amusing. The young lady down the street who gave Alice the "Vote for Woman" banner came to our house after school to-day. She, being Frances Harper, is in Alice's class, and the two are just now becoming good friends.

Getting back to the 'emotional' issue, Miss Harper gave Alice a copy of past quotes from men and women concerning the suffrage movement. A Reverend Father Walsh, of Troy, New York, spoke at a "Mass Meeting" organized by the Anti-Women's Suffrage Association in 1896.

"A woman's brain evolves emotion rather than intellect; and whilst this feature fits her admirably as a creature burdened with the preservation and happiness of the human species, it painfully disqualifies her for the sterner duties to be performed by the intellectual faculties. The best wife and mother and sister would make the worst legislator, judge and police.

The excessive development of the emotional in her nervous system, ingrafts on the female organization, a neurotic or hysterical condition, which is the source of much of the female charm when it is kept within due restraints. In...moments of excitement...woman, therefore, carries this power of irregular, illogical and incongruous action; and no one can foretell when the explosion will come."

Alice and I busted out laughing, and unfortunately for poor Marie, she happened to come into the bedroom just as we broke out in a fit of laughter. Marie, of course, thought we were being rude to her and quickly retreated downstairs.

I asked Alice where Mama was during Miss Harper's visit.

"Well," says Alice very coy like, "Mama was sitting in her chair very quiet like, tending to her crochet work, her eyes down, her hands working faster and faster as Frances read that piece of...... nonsense."

"Did Mama say anything?"

"No—I'm sure she wanted to though! She did tell Miss Harper

that she was welcome any time, especially if she had "news" to share.

While reading the newspaper as sleep was gradually overtaking me, lying under wonderful layers of blankets, I came upon a letter that Elizabeth Cady Stanton dictated to someone on her death bed on October 25, 1902. It was addressed to Theodore Roosevelt. In closing, she reminds the President of the United States, that Abraham Lincoln immortalized himself by the emancipation of four million Southern slaves. He likewise, who was already celebrated for so many honorable deeds and worthy utterances, should immortalize himself by bringing about the complete emancipation of thirty-six million women. Twenty four hours later, Elizabeth Cady Stanton was dead. She would have been 87 on November 12th. She left behind a very sad and lonely old friend, Susan B. Anthony. It will be four years this coming March 13th, that another pioneer for "woman's rights" has passed on.

I remember, just hours after her death, how the newspapers across the nation said so many unkind things about her. A North Carolina paper, the Charlotte News, went as far to say, "—that although she was fervidly sincere, she was guided by an evil star. And when the angel of death called for her she was forced to look back over a life strewn with little but failure. She never realized the fact that the great majority of American women cared not for suffrage. Had she realized this she would have spent her energies in a more profitable and worthy cause.

No, the good women of our country do not want suffrage. They care nothing for "rights" and "franchises." They are happy and content to reign in the happy kingdom of the home. They esteem more highly the work of rearing the children aright and making the home cozy and attractive than they do for the matter of the "ways and means" of getting Bill Jones elected as coroner. They have a work, a calling apart and by far more sacred than that of making good laws and steering the Ship of State.

Our good women have ever been happy in their God-given work, and that they may be content and happy in it forever is our earnest wish."

Remind me to never visit the state of North Carolina!

Eleanor—

October 15, 1909
Friday

The night air is chilly as it should be for the middle of October.

I paid Richard a visit as soon as I came home. Mama ordered him to stay in bed all day. Being the ripe age of 22 should give him license to do what one likes, but Mama and I agree, especially with Richard, that little things can quickly grow into big and serious illnesses. Poor Richard spent a boring day flipping through John's five and ten cent magazines. Heroes such as Fred Fearnot, Nick Carter, and Bowery Billy spring from every page (as John puts it), saving some helpless girl from an oncoming train, or rushing in front of a team of mad horses, catching the woman in his arms and staggering out of harm's way. I should write George Patten and make the ludicrous suggestion of publishing just "one" issue where the female saves the male. Wouldn't that cause a stir!

My hopes of going to the Exposition may be over, for Richard should not be around all those people if he is feeling poorly already. Mama hopes that I will stay home after my day with dear Mr. Whiting. I know I should, for my sore throat isn't getting better with being so tired day after day. Though, for five straight weeks I have not experienced the kind of enjoyment others my age are having. It would be nice to spend just a few hours, within the throes of the crushing crowd of thousands, just to remind myself that there still are people on this earth, other than the Miller's.

A few weeks ago, the daily paper said that Exposition officials have been given to understand that they need not look for any let up in the tourist traffic during the present month and that it, will extend right up to the close of the Exposition. Representatives of the Northern Pacific and Great Northern railroads declare that their Eastern advices are to the effect that the rush to the Coast is still on and that their roads are carrying as many passengers as it is possible to supply service for. I wonder how many of these tourists will want to make the Northwest a permanent home after taking a brief glance at our land and its resources.

Speaking of the railroad, wonderful news is on the way! The first move in a war declared upon all northwestern railroads by James J. Hill's lines, will result in reducing the time for carrying the mails between Chicago and Seattle, ten hours. A proposition to this effect has been made to the post-office department. The new mail train is to leave Chicago daily at 1:50 a.m. and the schedule calls for its arrival

41

in Seattle at noon of the third day. All sections of the Northwest will benefit from this new arrangement. Just a year ago all western roads entered an agreement to lengthen schedules to the Pacific Coast. See what happens when only men have a say so in such matters?

Dear Richard will not have to worry about not escorting us to the Exposition tomorrow night. Alice has gone downstairs with bubbles under her feet after giving me a pocketful of news. Apparently her friend, Miss Frances Harper has an older brother who can drive us in their father's motorcar. Funny I can't recall his name. I have never seen my sister's eyes sparkle so.

The young man sells automobile parts at Broadway Automobile Co., on Broadway and Madison Street. Alice was warned by Miss Frances Harper that we will be getting an ear full of the types of auto's they sell there. She, not I, is impressed with the fact that they have the Packard "30", Pierce Great Arrow, Winston, Cadillac, Wood's Electric, Knox Waterless, and Trucks. Was it Barry, or Bertram? Oh! Bertie! Bertie Harper. If this Bertie Harper says one remark concerning women and our inability to handle such a machine, I will find other means to get us home.

Before coming home to-night, Miss Harper was encouraging Mama, Alice, and I to attend one of Emma Smith DeVoe's meetings, for she is leading our state's campaign.

Before the Northwest Territory became a state, women had twice won the vote, and then twice lost it in the territory's Supreme Court. Something has to happen soon. Only three states have equal suffrage. Wyoming was first in 1890, then Colorado in 1893, and finally, Idaho in 1896. It has been a long drought. Will the women of Washington State have the right to vote in 1910?

I think I will retire even before Alice or Marie. I am very exhausted and feeling poorly myself.

Goodnight,
Eleanor

Nate

The young man sat near the bust of James J. Hill, the "Empire Builder." He thought it was an appropriate and timely tribute to a really great man while he was yet "in the flesh," instead of the customary habit of paying post-mortem tributes. Nate witnessed the unveiling months ago, for he was one of the 2,100 men who made the Alaska-Yukon-Pacific Exposition possible. Crossing his strong arms across his chest, his rough hands snagged his wool coat. The evening was a little chilly as his breath hung in the air.

To-night he might let his feet wonder over the grounds again, perhaps covering some of the seven miles of lighted walkway for the last time. Or, he could stay seated on the curving steps leading up to the Manufacturers Building. Nate leaned his head back and felt dwarfish by the magnificent columns behind him. It was going to be difficult leaving the Exposition. He had made many friends; those who worked with him were decent men; men trying to make an honest living.

Nate leaned against one of the columns, out of the way of the crowds. He enjoyed watching people come and go, exclaiming wonderful praises on this building or that building. He almost felt shameful, that among all the hardworking men who put up the Fair, he really did not have to have been there, at least not for the sake of pay. Prior to coming to Seattle, Nate paid the Yukon a visit. He was not expecting to find much gold since the big rush was pretty much over. But it was there. And he found it. The Yukon had been good to him. Very good. He had managed to slip out of Alaska quietly without being robbed or killed.

But to-night, Nate's thoughts ran in many directions. Although he pondered about his new wealth which could take him anywhere or could buy him anything, he wondered about his life. There wasn't too much that Nate hadn't done or tried. There was the back breaking work of laying down railroad. He worked the wilderness, raping the forest for the sake of building new homes. He worked at shingle mills but left on account of the dangerous work which left men without fingers, hands, or limbs. Nate pressed his eyes shut. He was still trying to forget. For a while he was needed as a stump farmer, blowing up what remained deeply rooted in the soil, refusing to let go of what always had been to make way for homes, vegetable fields, and dairy pastures. Hard work he never shied away from.

It had been a long time since he left Seattle. He was thirteen then. Now, fourteen years later, Seattle looked very, very different. There were jobs for everyone who wanted one in the Pacific North-west now. The idea of settling down kind of interested Nate. If the Seattle area did not keep his attention, there was always Oregon. A million dollar cement plant near Portland would be breaking ground in December. The plant was expected to cover twelve acres which could keep his hands busy for a year. Nate leaned back on the column and drew his eyebrows together and sighed. He didn't know. He just didn't know.

At least he wasn't in any rush to leave the boarding house that he and his single brown trunk was renting out. Winter was not too far off, and Seattle's mild climate would be a welcome relief compared to the mid-west or the east-coast.

Nate was getting stiff and a little cold on the cement steps. He looked down on the cheering crowd as they glanced up at the sky-rockets which lit up the smoky-black sky. The air was filled with noises of tin horns, cowbells, steam whistles and more sky-rockets. Not far away bands played but he could not tell what pieces they played. The grounds were covered in confetti and he was glad he was not on the clean-up committee.

The hour of the evening felt late, and according to his pocket watch it was half-past nine. As Nate was putting his time piece back in its pocket, he noticed a small gathering was forming some distance ahead of him. He was a little curious for the voice of a female rose above the crowd and above all the noise. It was more than natural curiosity which propelled him forward as he separated the crowd with his arms and body.

"Someone help me—please! My sister has fainted!" a young miss was frantically pleading.

Nate pushed aside the gawking observers and knelt down beside the handsome young woman whose face was very pale, and whose eyes were closed while her head was cradled against her sister's bosom.

"What happened?" Nate asked.

"She just fainted! It's my fault making her walk so much to-night, especially after not feeling well and being so tired. I'm sorry Eleanor. I'm so sorry!"

"Let's get her off the ground," Nate suggested as he had already begun to scoop up the limp body of one 'Eleanor.' After getting a good grip on her through yards of material, he let her head gently fall back on his shoulder.

"Is she going to be all right?" the worried sister asked.

Nate looked down at the young woman who rested in his arms.

"I don't know, Miss."

It was true. He didn't know. But what he did know was that she was lovely and that her name was Eleanor, and she was in his strong arms.

His thoughts were interrupted by a male voice.

"What's going on?"

"Oh, Bertie! Eleanor has fainted! I think we should get her home right away!"

"Of course, Alice."

It suddenly dawned on the young man named Bertie, that someone was holding the fainted sister. His eyes rose up to the unknown face of Nate and they narrowed slightly at the stranger.

"I thank you for coming to our aide, but I can take her now."

Bertie held out his arms, but to his dismay they stayed empty.

"Miss Alice, is it? Where is your motorcar?" Nate inquired.

"We came in the Harper's motorcar. Bertie's father owns the Broadway Automobile Company," Alice quickly replied, nodding to Bertie with a little smile. Such an impressive fact should have made Mr. Harper beam with pride but failed to do so.

In its place, a wrinkled forehead unpleasantly emerged, for how could this irksome stranger brazenly insinuate that a woman might own, let alone try to operate such an expensive machine, even if it was on the borrow from his father.

Nate fairly ignored the irate shorter fellow.

"Then please, Mr. Harper, show me the way."

The young man named Bertie Harper did not move and he glared at the man who was holding Eleanor close to himself.

"I do not wish to sound ungrateful, but if you will be so kind as to place the young lady in 'my' arms, you may go about your affairs which we are keeping you from."

Nate smiled at the young man who breathed and harbored jealousy toward him. Knowing fully well that he may be infringing on another man's claim, should have caused shame in Nate for such conduct was unbecoming of a gentleman. But this rare opportunity of stirring and assisting Mr. Harper's vexation was too good to pass up.

"I have nowhere to go, but to deliver this young lady to your motorcar, Mr. Harper. She is quite safe, for I have no intention of running off with her."

Eleanor was starting to moan and Nate took a few steps forward on purpose to force Bertie in the direction of his motorcar.

"This way," he growled, walking quickly through the crowd, followed by Nate and Eleanor, and her sister who was almost trotting behind them.

As the foursome cut across the grounds to the parking area, Alice thought it was her duty to explain her sister's situation to the stranger.

"You see….she had the perfect job at the Insurance Company, but they made her quit. Though she has agreed to work Saturday's for Mr. Whiting because the office is in total shambles. Since Eleanor is the oldest of us girls, it was up to her to work for those beastly men. They are working her to death, as you can very well see! Eleanor has not had a rest in five weeks and was so looking forward to the last day here. After she left Mr. Whiting's office she bought a new hat from her good friend Miss Ernestine McAfee. Oh!— Her hat! Her new hat is gone! In all the excitement I did not notice!"

"Sorry—neither did I," Nate added.

"Eleanor will be sick about it!" Alice wailed. "She traded dozens of jars of her best raspberry jam for that beautiful hat. Now who knows how long it will take to save up for another just like it."

"Here we are," Bertie proudly announced as he reached a touring car. Alice gathered her skirts and lifted herself up on the running board and sat down while Bertie brought the automobile to life. He was too busy with the machine to notice that the stranger had carefully placed Eleanor next to her sister.

"Take care of her…" Nate whispered to Alice before he stepped down from the running board.

"Thank you, Mr—?"

Bertie Harper threw the motorcar into reverse, turned the steering wheel sharply, and without looking back, dashed forward as he drove off into the night. Alice looked back at him and waved a small wave until she probably couldn't see him anymore.

There was nothing for Nate to do, except go back to his lonely room at the boarding house and go to bed. Except sleep was not on his mind. At that moment, Nate would have traded a good portion of his newly acquired wealth if someone could lead him to the young lady named Eleanor.

October 17, 1909
Sunday

Have you ever been in such a mental state in which your pen has been suspended of duty, for the hand awaits the mind, and the pen awaits the hand.

I am supposed to be resting in bed while everyone is at church, but how can I rest after last night? I best start from the beginning.

First, I spent ten hours at the Insurance Company which is in such a state of cruel disorder, that I found myself growing angry with Mr. Whiting's niece for having unraveled my organized office. (I must remind myself that it is no longer 'my' office.) I am there only to put things to right. Mr. Whiting handed me an envelope containing wages in cash before I left for the day. He thanked me over and over and said how much everyone misses me.

I felt happy and wanted to treat myself to a new hat. My dear school chum, Miss Ernestine (and her father) owns McAfee's Millinery Shop not too far away from the Insurance Company. She makes very beautiful hats indeed. I am tremendously proud of her for starting her own business in this world which is dominated by men.

I am sick about losing my new hat! Brand new! I finally bought something pretty for myself and then it falls off my head sometime during my fainting spell. Surely, someone at the Exposition must have seen it come off. I cannot barter anymore raspberry jam as payment for another. The family needs the rest of it.

I should explain the reason for my fainting spell. Quite simply I was beyond exhausted. I have not been feeling well lately, and I had not ate much yesterday. By the time Alice and Bertie dragged me all over the Exposition I was finding myself holding onto things for support. I did not want to say how poorly I felt for I could see how Alice was enjoying herself. I just never expected to collapse like I did.

This morning the sky was pink. Now it's a solid overcast of gray. Sometime to-day I expect rain.

I am finding myself procrastinating, for I seem to be at a loss of what to say about a man who carried me for quite some distance in his 'capable' arms across the Fair grounds last night. I have no idea what he looks like, other than the detailed description of what Alice has told me, which is: He was a few inches taller than Richard, she guessed, and when Bertie Harper stood next to him, Bertie looked 'insignificant' in comparison. Alice went on to say that this young man was nice looking, but not overly handsome, but not in the least plain. He was very easy going and decisively a person who takes matters into his own hands. Alice was glad that Bertie did not try to carry me for he may have taken a few steps before I would have slipped out of his arms. She especially took note of his eyes and the tone of his voice. She said it was one of those things that even a woman cannot explain properly, but his voice was so extraordinarily pleasing that she could have listened to him talk for hours. And if he had not used his voice, his warm and kindly eyes would have 'spoken' for him. Every time she thinks of how easily the stranger picked me up as if I were nothing, and how he held me close to him, and the way he took possession of me..... Alice had let out a deep sigh for it made her tingle in a way she's never felt before. She almost got his name, but Bertie was so put out that she almost lost her hat as well.

The drizzle has turned to a light rain, and I am tired. I think I'll crawl back into bed for I am still in my nightgown. I will try to rest and close my eyes, and maybe if I drift off to sleep, the good Lord will bless me with a lovely dream.

All for now,
Eleanor

Eleanor

Eleanor had managed to sleep a good portion of Sunday away, even through Richard's coughing spells in the room next to hers. Mama made sure that the noise in the house was kept low.

She was glad that the rain had ceased for the moment as she walked up the hill Monday morning. She would be glad to get the range going at the Miller's and warm herself. To-day she would need to start soaking clothes for tomorrow's wash day, bake bread, strip the beds, and do other household chores.

After entering the dark house, she turned on the lights and took note of the dark hole in the fireplace in the parlor. To-day would be a perfect day to start a cozy fire in the parlor. Not much heat came forth from the large pile of bricks, but it did give the room a sense that someone was home.

Eleanor went through the Monday morning routine of emptying the ashes out of the range and got her shoes dirty trodding out to the ash pile in the backyard. She went downstairs and brought up kindling and scooped coal into the bucket which she kept next to the stove. Assured that the fire could manage itself, the oval boiler was brought upstairs and filled with water. Eleanor sighed as she carried the wicker basket to the bottom of the staircase leading up to the men's bedrooms and to the bathroom. Her shoulders wanted to slump, which was not a good thing, for it was too early in the day to be weary of her chores.

"Oh, Lord, I think I need your help to-day," she groaned out loud.

Her right hand gathered a handful of skirt and the handle to the wicker basket while her left hand pulled her up the stairs and into the bedroom of Mr. Miller Sr. She opened the door to Stuart's room, carrying the basket filled with linen, shirts, and soiled handkerchiefs. Stripping his bed naked of its sheets reminded Eleanor that he wanted them ironed. It did not bother her to sigh heavily at the thought of more ironing.

Oh, how she wished to be at home with her Mama, to be back in her squeaky bed resting. She would not be able to do so until the sky grew black again. Not for many, many hours. Eleanor wanted to cry but it would not do her any good if she did. Nonetheless, she felt close to it. She told herself that she 'had' to be strong, but the voice inside her was weak and very small. She would, somehow, muddle through to-day.

Taking up the basket which was heavy by now, she crossed the hall to Todd's room, and opening the door, she pushed it a little too hard with her foot and it slammed against the wall. Directly after the bang which the door produced, the unclothed upper part of a man's body shot up from the bed. The basket that Eleanor was holding flew out of her hands and onto the floor with a thud. Her shrieking voice filled the house as she took flight from the room and down the staircase.

Her screams and footsteps then were silent.

He sat upright, propping himself up with his hands. It took him a moment or two to gather his wits. Finally, his disbelieving lips were able to murmur her name— "Eleanor?"

Nate threw the covers off his warm flesh and swung his feet onto the chilly floor. His folded pants and shirt were snatched from the end of the bed and were quickly put on. His socks and shoes were located as well. Stepping over the pile of wash, Nate cautiously put his head out the door and all was silent, for the moment. Part of him remained back in his brother's room, his heart pounding, for it was in total denial of who was downstairs. The other part of him made his way down the steps, across the foyer, softly announcing her name in the silent house. Surely, the young lady who appeared at the bedroom door was not a creation of his brain. She had to be in the house, somewhere, and probably very frightened. His knuckles gently rapped on the kitchen door.

"Miss, may I come in— please?"

He listened for a moment but there was no answer. He gradually let himself in the kitchen. She was standing next to the range, a frightened thing she was, holding a coal shovel tightly in her grasp.

"Stop right there, Mister! Don't even think about coming a foot closer or I'll…I'll…I'll throw one of these burners at you!"

"There's no doubt in my mind that you would do just that!" Nate could not help but laugh, which seemed to make the young lady shake with fright even more.

"I mean it!" she warned, raising the coal shovel higher. "So help me!" her voice was quivering, "if you try anything…I'll…I'll throw hot coals at you!"

The kitchen was filled with his laughter, and pulling out a chair at the table, Nate tried to compose himself.

"Your sister never told me you were this feisty!"

"My sister?"

"Yes, you know…the one named Alice. Had a pleasant chat with her. Quite a charming young lady indeed."

"May I ask when and where you may have had this pleasant chat with my sister?" Eleanor asked warily with sarcasm in her voice.

"Well, that young man named Bertie, and your sister, Alice, walked with me as I carried you to Mr. Harper's motorcar while you were in a state of unconsciousness. It was rather cruel of me to rouse Mr. Harper's temper, though it was amusing watching him suffer as I do believe he may have feelings for you."

Nate's eyes were drawn to her soft brown eyes as they grew wide and watched her lips slowly part.

"I suppose," Nate continued, "it's not Bertie's fault that he lacks the physical stature to carry a delicate young woman as yourself a good distance. I believe Mr. Harper did not care to see you within the folds of my arms which were reluctant to release you, for I thought I would never see you again…"

Eleanor slowly lowered her weapon as she starred at the young man at the table. The color from her face was starting to drain and she began to say, "Oh, my…" but she scarcely had finished.

Nate was there, and once more he held her lifeless form in his arms.

Even before she opened her eyes, Eleanor heard the crackling of the fire. She glanced at the lace curtains which belonged in the parlor, and turning her head toward the fireplace, she saw that the stranger's eyes were totally absorbed on her. And across his face was a look of enchantment. Eleanor wished that her corset would disappear for breathing was difficult. At that moment Eleanor understood what Alice meant by that 'tingling feeling.'

"Is it our destiny that we are to keep meeting this way?" Nate asked with a wonderful warm smile on his face.

She slowly sat herself up from the Roman couch, and while smoothing her hair Eleanor thought it necessary to say, "I'm sorry for that.…I don't know what came over me."

"Perhaps I should explain my reason for being here. I owe you at least that."

Eleanor nodded her head. "Please. My sister never did learn your name."

"No, she did not. Mr. Harper was quite in a hurry to get you home." He paused for a moment. "My name is Mr. Miller. Mr. Nate Miller."

51

He watched the expression on her lovely face change to slight disappointment to confusion.

"Would you like me to explain?" Nate offered.

Eleanor sighed. "Please. And if you do not object, I should like to remain seated."

Nate roamed in front of the nice fire, placing his hands in his pockets. He could not tell her everything, but to pick at pieces of the truth would hopefully satisfy her and at the same time ease his conscious of any misleadings. He politely cleared his throat.

"I had taken up a room at a boardinghouse downtown while taking in the Exposition. After returning from supper Sunday night, I found new occupants in my room and that my trunk was waiting for me downstairs at the reception desk. Apparently I was ousted on account of other means of affluence."

"My, how awful!" Eleanor exclaimed. "Can they really do that?"

"Oh, I'm sure many folks got the boot. With all those thousands of tourists who came to the Exposition for the last night, I shouldn't have been surprised. So, I decided to look up my—"

He had to pause. He looked at Eleanor who was waiting for him to finish. Nate could not use the word 'family' to describe his ties with the men who lived in the big house on the hill.

"—my relations."

"I see…" murmured Eleanor.

"I was told to sleep in Todd's room for he was not expected home. I am quite sorry for that. I assumed someone left you a note…. perhaps? No?"

Eleanor let out a little laugh and couldn't hide the smile that was growing. "Perhaps? No. No, indeed! You see, Mr. Miller, to-day marks the sixth week since I have been here. During that time, not one of your 'relations' has addressed me by my name. Your lips Mr. Miller spoke my name and we have just met. I thank you for that. So, you see, in notifying me that a 'guest' was in the house would have been an unthinkable gesture on their part."

Nate smiled for her honesty.

"Mr. Miller," she began, "I hope that you do not hold my candor against me. You share their last name. Please tell me if I have offended you."

Nate shook his head and looked at the young woman. If only he could be as honest with her. "True, I was born a 'Miller,' but I…" he sighed. "I do not share their philosophy on how life should be conducted. May I leave it at that?"

"Thank you, Mr. Miller."

"Please, call me Nate."

"And you may call me, Eleanor."

"Pleased to make your acquaintance, again. Now, if you'll excuse me, I have some errands to fulfill."

"And I must tend to my chores."

She crossed the room but stopped at the doorway.

"Will you be dining with the rest of the family to-night?"

"What time is supper served?"

"Anywhere from six-thirty to seven."

"I will be here."

Nate went back to his younger brother's room and freshened up. Downtown, there was a certain Miss Ernestine McAfee whom he had to find.

October 18, 1909
Monday

Supper was interesting to-night. There were four men sitting at one table and no one spoke a word while I served. Nate would look up from the table and glance at Mr. Miller Sr., Stuart, and then at Todd. The touching of silverware against the china and the sound of food being chewed was almost more than I could bear. A typical meal would be filled with conversation concerning each man's day. Nate kept smiling at me as if nothing out of the ordinary was taking place. Finally, the Miller men did look up when Nate thanked me for the wonderful supper. And yes, he called me "Miss Eleanor." I gathered by their disapproving glare at their 'guest' that to pay compliment was forbidden, an error in which the heartless, soulless Miller's never make. To do so would be an imperfection of their on going quest for male superiority. A momentary omission of missed opportunity to demoralize the weaker sex. I truly hope that Mr. Nate Miller intends to stay for a while. His presence is like a breeze of clean air in this stale house.

As I was putting on my sweater in the foyer, Nate came out from the parlor and asked if I would like to wait by the fire until my family came for me. He was not amused when I explained that I walk part way home. I was invited to wait in the parlor while he brought the motorcar to life. All the way down the hill I sat in silence next to Mr. Nate Miller.

I could see Alice at the front window separating the curtains as we neared the house. I thanked Nate as he helped me out of the motorcar and escorted me to the front steps.

"It was a pleasure, Miss Eleanor. A lady should not be out in the dark, alone."

He looked down at me with a warm smile and curious twinkling eyes. I did not feel 'alone.'

My feet reluctantly made their way up the steps when I heard my name.

"Eleanor....."

I turned to him. "Yes?"

There was a pause in the night air.

"Goodnight."

In return, I smiled politely and nodded before turning toward the steps.

An anxious Alice waited for me as I closed the door behind me. Her mouth was in shock.

"I know," I said calmly, smiling shyly. "It's him."

"Oh, do tell all! Hurry!" Alice grabbed my hand and dragged me half way up the stairs when she suddenly stopped. "Golly! I almost forgot!" Her face lit up and I was being pulled upward again. "Hurry! I've been dying all evening. My curiosity cannot stand it a minute more!"

"Alice, whatever are you bumbling about?" I laughed while trying my best as to not trip on my skirt.

We rushed into our bedroom, and on my bed were two packages wrapped in brown paper. I slowly sat myself down and took note of the fine print of a certain friend of mine.

"Oh, my…." I breathed.

"Eleanor, open them!"

As the brown wrapper fell away from the first, a lovely hat box with yellow and cream strips beckoned me to lift the lid, and as I did so, my hand flew to my bosom.

"Your hat!" gasped Alice as she carefully took it out of its box. "Who? You don't think….oh, my!"

"I think you ought to open the second one," says I.

"There's a note for you," said Alice as the fallen wrapper revealed. "Shall I read it?"

"Please."

"Dearest Eleanor, an unusually kind and genteel young man visited my business to-day. He did not provide me with his name, but he said that you and he formally met to-day. He explained that it was your misfortune to lose a recently purchased hat, and that he wished to give you another just like it. The young man asked me how well I knew you. I replied that we have been close friends for some years. "Good," says he, "I will leave it up to your good taste to select Miss Eleanor another hat which perhaps, she has been in admiration of."

My dear Eleanor, next time you are in town, I will not forgive you if you do not stop by for a 'chat.'

Fondly,
Miss Ernestine McAfee

Alice very carefully took out the straw hat with the popular Cheyenne front roll. She placed it on me and I moved to the dresser mirror. The brim was rolled high on the left side at the front, and extending almost entirely around the crown was a wreath of pretty white blossoms. A drape of baby blue taffeta ribbon was twisted among the flowers and around the crown.

Miss Ernestine McAfee did well in her choosing. I cannot visit her just yet, for I know that she will want details about a man who is still but a stranger to me.

Goodnight,
and thank you,
Mr. Nate Miller

October 20, 1909
Wednesday

The Miller's house was quiet this morning. I listened for movement above me, but there was none. As much as I adore its Westminster chime, the grandfather clock in the hallway took me by surprise by its announcement that it was half-past seven. My hands tried to calm a pounding heart under thy bosom.

I peered into the parlor and saw the dark fireplace which reminded me that more ashes needed to be disposed of. Removing my sweater and hat I hung them on the tall golden oak hall rack. After putting on my apron, I went downstairs to empty the ashes from the coal furnace. To my horror, after I picked up the coal hod, I saw an ugly beast at the bottom of it. It and its long tail scurried away as I screamed and bolted for the stairs. I thought for a moment that I would be sick. My heart can not take much more of unpleasant, unwelcome 'things.' I leaned back against the cool brick wall and tried to calm myself. The thought of the horrible beast running up inside my skirts made me gather them against my shaking legs. I don't know how long I stood there in the dim basement, but whether I wanted to or not, the ashes in the furnace had to be taken out, and more coals had to be put in.

After cleaning the ashes from the range, I suffered another trip downstairs for more coal. The rows of hanging wash casting shadows in the poor light did not help my nerves. I will have to ask Nate if he could set some traps or leave poison for the rat.

While I cleaned the top of the range and prepared the sad irons, as much as I detested the lowly animal, I was resolved to face whatever there was waiting for me. Through my fear, which I doubt, will never be conquered upon seeing a rat, I made myself go down there in meek bravery.

Last night's heavy rain moved aside for the time being and the morning sun was allowed in the kitchen while I ironed Stuart's bed sheets. Suddenly, a hard bounce hit the window; a sound all too familiar to my ears. I rushed to the window and looked down, but did not see a thing. But I understood what the noise had been and set the irons off to the side of the hot stove. My feet quickly made their way to the front door, down the steps, and around the house. It was there, under the kitchen window that I found the poor little thing.

I carefully scooped up a Golden-crowned Sparrow. How strange that the little thing should be in the sparse neighborhood on the hill. I have heard it in the thicket and brush piles as it promenades from bush to bush singing, "Oh, dear me! Oh, dear me!"

It lay calmly in the palm of my hand, waiting for death to come. Its little feathery body panting and its tiny black-brown eyes were open just momentarily before they half closed. His little delicate feet drew closer to his warm body and its beak was open. I wonder if the poor little thing wanted to tell me something. Did he know that I felt sorrow for him? The panting of his body slowed and his eyes closed. Death must have been near.

Did he follow me up the hill, unintentionally, as I sang my own songs, not knowing that he was leaving behind a safe sanctuary?

Why does it have to be, that the ugly, devious rat lives, and the innocent bird must die?

I do not understand life.

I do not understand it at all.

Eleanor

56

October 21, 1909
Thursday

Nate was the first Miller to open the door this evening. He looked physically ragged as he climbed the stairway and held onto the polished thick banister. Having freshened up and wearing a change of clothes, Nate came in the kitchen and inquired what the delicious smell was. I informed him that they were to have stew and bread. Nate filled his lungs with the aroma of dinner and complained that it was making his mouth water. I thanked him for the kind compliment.

Everything was done for the day and there was a good 45 minutes to an hour before the front door would open again. I waited in the kitchen for a while, but the silence was dreadful. I did not know if Nate wanted to be by himself. I was not enjoying my own company with the knowledge of him in the house, so I hesitantly ventured towards the parlor and found Nate in a chair close to the fire. His face was still and thoughtful for my soft though present foot steps had not distracted his mind, yet.

"Have you come to keep me company?" he asked before turning his head toward the foyer.

The rustling of my yards must have caught his keen hearing.

"If— that is your wish."

"It is," Nate smiled, though wearily.

"I expect the others should be home shortly…" My words trailed off. I was aware that Nate was casting his attention upon me. There was silence. "Dinner is warming on the stove, and everything else is done for the day, and I….."

"Eleanor, please," he breathed ever so patiently, "you do not have to explain yourself to me, or to anyone else. Come sit with me and enjoy the fire."

"If —you truly do not mind?"

"I would appreciate your company," Nate replied with a smiled, though a tired sigh followed.

"Very well," I replied, nodding my head. "I'll be right back with some mending."

I settled into a comfortable chair and started working on some button holes. I couldn't help notice how tired Nate looked as he leaned his head back and gazed at the fire. Sitting quietly for a while I questioned whether or not I should converse with him, for he appeared to be enjoying the quietness of the evening. A comfortable period of time lapsed while he rested his eye lids and stretched his legs out in front of the warm hearth. There was little left to wonder if Nate was not residing in light slumber, for his head was turned toward me, and across his handsome face, light from the fire played with his features; making them all the more agreeable to my female notion of the perfect picturesque man.

"Would I be bothering you if I inquired how your day went?" Nate suddenly asked.

"Ouch!"

I put my finger in my mouth. "That's a fine way to make a girl poke her finger with a needle!" I scolded.

"I'm terribly sorry. Should I take a look at it?"

"Thank you for your concern Mr. Miller, but I will not let you fuss over such a trivial injury."

I could not help but let out a little laugh.

"What?" Nate lightly inquired.

"I've been sitting here wondering if I would be disturbing you if I were to ask you the same," I confessed.

"You were, were you?"

"Yes, I was."

"Eleanor, you could never disturb me," Nate replied reassuringly.

I returned his kind remark with a smile, and perhaps without being aware of the obvious, our attentions towards the other felt very natural. But then, why does my heart race when he whispers my name? It is nice to have someone to talk to in that big house. I look forward to evenings now, even if it means seeing Mr. Nate Miller for just a short time.

Since he had inquired, I spoke of the poor bird that hit the window, and I confessed that I buried it in their backyard. I then mentioned that a nasty intruder with whiskers and a long tail was hiding in the basement. Nate was more than happy to do something about it as soon as he could purchase some items. I almost forgot to thank him for the hats.

Upon asking him how his day had gone, Nate sat up and turned toward me. He had spent most of the day walking around the wharves that sat on pilings overlooking Puget Sound. Nate has secured a job of unloading sacks of lime and other imported cargo off sailing ships.

I wanted to ask if he would be staying with his 'relations,' or take up a room closer to the waterfront. I did not ask for that would be prying into his affairs. As much as my curiosity would have to suffer, time eventually will relieve my mind in hopes that Mr. Nate Miller will not remove himself and his trunk from the premises.

After another quiet dinner, Nate kindly drove me home.

E—

October 22, 1909
Friday

To-night Papa asked me to join him next to the brick hearth which was so warm and inviting. On autumn and winter evenings, we can usually find Papa and Mama in front of the fire. Papa quietly asked how things were going at the Miller's, and about Mr. Nate Miller. I dare not say that I work for atheist's, for I do not think Papa and Mama would want me there if they knew. From what I have gathered from Todd, I'm sure the three are. I wonder if Nate walks with the Lord or not.

Papa says that Richard is planning on attending night school to learn about telephones. Apparently, Richard has been interested in telephone construction for sometime now and wants to learn more about those big wooden boxes. With the rise in popularity, as more and more people are placing telephones in their homes, Richard thinks this would be an opportune time to educate himself on transmitters, receivers, switch hooks, generators, lightning arresters, wet and dry batteries, and ringers.

It seems as if I haven't spoken to my brother in a long time. At least not the way we used to. I dearly miss our long conversations.

The rain has not let up much since last night. I'm thankful that it postponed itself until Nate drove me home. I am wondering if he feels obligated to bring me home from now on. That concern has been on my mind. I simply cannot wait in the parlor or the hallway and pretend that family is coming to fetch me. I do not want Mr. Nate Miller to be burdened with me.

John has started playing the harmonica in his and Richard's room. He is getting very good at it, but I'm afraid the pounding of rain on the roof is threatening to mute his practicing.

Last night, while resting under our warm covers, Alice and I waited for Marie's heavy breathing to become apparent which meant she was fast asleep. I listened to the wonderful sound of the rain storm in the dark, and could picture fallen leaves adhering to the cold, wet ground. Even though they might, even when the wind blew just right, they were at the mercy of the pelting rain which did not allow them to rise above the earth.

Alice asked me in a whisper, hesitantly, if beauty was a bad thing. I could only reply that God created beauty in nature, and therefore it could not possibly be bad. "Why do you wonder?" I asked.

"Miss Frances Harper was told, that beauty serves only to find husbands.....and it is in general, a young lady's face which determines their fortunes. The consequence of this," Alice went on to say, "is that they are often prudish before marriage, and dull and tiresome afterwards."

I did not know what to say for neither of us are uninteresting creatures.

The room was quiet for the moment, but I had a feeling that my sister's head was still swimming with provoking thoughts, and that I would be her provisional ear for her curiosity.

And I was correct.

"Eleanor?" Alice quietly asked again.

"Yes?"

"Promise you won't be upset or startled if I repeat something?"

"Depends. Would Mama approve of it?"

Alice gave a little grunt of disappointment in the dark.

"It's just an interesting quote from a Ralcy Bell. Frances read it to me the other day."

"Well, all right...."

Alice's spirits instantly rose along with her voice which was now above a whisper.

"According to 'Ralcy Bell,' "The average man too long has looked upon the female of his kind principally through the little pig-eye slit, which sees only sex...."

"Alice!" I spoke her name far above a whisper too, which caused Marie to stir in her sleep. She would have woken for sure if it hadn't been for the rain which continually assaulted the roof. Quickly continuing on, Alice ignored my verbal reprisal.

"His eyes are no better than buttonholes burned in a blanket—they are just about as perceptive. His cunning little primitive eye is no improvement on the brute's; his optical evolution ceased in a fringe of lashes. When he sees sex, he thinks he sees all there is to a woman."

Silence.

"How's that!" huffed my sister.

More silence followed.

"Alice....."

"Yes, Eleanor?"

"I'm not sure that I approve of the material that you are memorizing from Miss Harper, but I do envy your God-given ability to do so."

"Goodnight, Eleanor."

"Goodnight, Alice."

I was grateful that our room was black, for I did not want my sister to see my own curiosity stirring upon my naive face.

E—

The Miller Men

Nate Miller drove Eleanor home while there was a quick break in the weather. Although the black October sky could have changed its mind at any moment, he drove a bit slower, for he was in no hurry to get his father's housekeeper back home.

He was very quiet for Eleanor's sister had spoken words at the Exposition. "…..you see, she had the perfect job at the Insurance Company, but 'they' made her quit. She has agreed to work Saturday's for Mr. Whiting because the office is in total shambles. It is up to Eleanor to work for 'those beastly men.' 'They' are working her to death. She has not rested and was looking forward to the Exposition…."

At the time Alice's words meant nothing to him. Little did he know that Eleanor worked for his father and brothers, otherwise known as 'those beastly' men. He found Alice's description of his family interesting. True, he had not seen any of them, or spoke to them in fourteen years, but there was an unsettled feeling in his gut that he did not like.

He knew his father. He had speculations of his father's 'preoccupation's' which were none of his business as a youth. But Nate's mother, his dear mother whom he was so close to began developing illnesses. She would get better for a while, but never completely. What illness that was corrupting her still youthful body was never mentioned. Within two years his beloved mother was gone.

The procession of horse drawn black carriages on that warm July day still haunted him. Nate remembered the numbness of his body as he sat alone for hours that day; not feeling, not thinking, not existing. He did not want to feel. He did not want to live. He wanted his mother.

A pair of women dressed in black taffeta were chatting around a corner of the house, sure that they could talk freely of their deceased friend and of her 'beastly husband' who killed her, because he, like hundreds of other men were 'sexual drunkards,' addicted to the 'social evils' of Seattle's brothels.

No one understood why he left home so young.

Nate could not stay in the same house with his emotionally detached father.

His two sons did not weep the way the middle son did. They

missed her at first, for nature would not let even them be nonobservant to her lack of presence. In time, his brothers grew angry at her for abandoning them.

Convinced that he knew the truth, Nate added more distance between he and his father.

At the age of thirteen, the distance had been decided.

Part way up the hill, Nate Miller pulled off to the side of the road. He put his hands to his face and cried.

Tomorrow he would visit his mother.

Upon returning to the big house, as he followed the foyer which led him to the massive stairway, he heard a deep clearing of a man's throat. Nate stopped and took a few steps back toward the parlor. His father was raising his body out of a chair, and briefly eyeing him, nodded his head for Nate to come inside. Nate stood on the threshold, placing his hands in his trouser pockets. His father threw his cigar into the fire, and reaching for another on top the mantle, asked Nate if he cared for one without looking at him.

"No, thank you," he replied.

His father lit the cigar and went through the drawn out process of puffing on the smelly thing. Tilting his head back, his features rolled and twitched across his face. A hand rested on the mantel while the other was occupied with the cigar.

Without looking at Nate, he delivered a heavy tone of voice, sparing all effort of dispensing a hint of fatherly concern. "Haven't seen you in a while."

With his hands kept deep in pockets, Nate let his eyes drift over the carpet, then to his father's shiny black feet made of colt skin, with partially seen black buttons running up the sides.

"No, Sir," His reply was somewhat cool and bitter. Nate's usual voice was swallowed up by his dislike for his father.

Nate took note of the gray checked wool Cassimere suit his father wore as the older man stood stiffly on the brick hearth. He thought of his black oil string pants, his heavy oil double slicker coat, and the squam oil hat that kept him dry on the Elliot bay docks. What different worlds the two worked in.

Mr. Miller Sr. coughed and drained his throat, spitting into the fire. The foul sound made Nate ill as his father spat again.

"I assume that you have not done as well as the rest of us." His statement was not a question, but more of a guessed fact.

"Sir?"

His father finally turned his face to his son and ran scoffing eyes over his simple garments. The young man who kept his distance from him was a commoner, unrefined, unpolished, almost countrified. The thought of a suit on the able-bodied structure almost made the father laugh. The young man stood stock-still at the doorway as does a stranger in a foreign house.

"Have you made your fortune?"

The young man looked down briefly before answering him.

"I believe that I have done well…."

The father's mocking laughter filled the parlor. "A trunk and the clothes on your back? Fortune indeed!"

The young man drew his shoulders back and hardened his jaw, casting a raw, piercing look at the older man.

"My, my, my… Is my success a thorn in your flesh?"

His father had not changed at all. His rancid, demoralizing personality hit Nate like the stench of a dead carcass.

"If it pleases you, my trunk and I will be gone by morning…."

Nate turned to leave but his father spoke in a raised voice, "Your brothers should spend some time with you….I don't know if they even want to, but I will give them the chance."

"……if I were to stay, but if I am not welcome here I will find other accommodations, and my brothers may visit me if they wish."

His father turned back to the mantel and looked in the rectangle mirror.

"The spare room is never used anyway. It is up to you." The cigar was thrown into the fire and his father walked towards the billiard room, sweeping the heavy maroon curtains aside.

Nate stood there starring at the same fireplace that he and Eleanor had sat in front of. To-night the flames appeared as yellow ice.

There was a movement across the room, and standing just outside the billiard room, a passage of warning and hostility made its course from Stuart to Nate. The older brother kept his eyes on Nate, and taking a long drink from his glass Stuart dropped the curtain behind him, separating himself from the stranger that shared his last name.

Upstairs, in the spare bedroom, Nate sat on his trunk. He did not know how he could possibly stay in his father's house. But leaving would mean that he could not delight in the simple pleasures that Eleanor offered. A smile here, a nod there. No other woman, except for his dear mother, entertained his immediate thoughts as Eleanor did.

Little did his father's housekeeper realize just how much she was in Nate's thoughts. Knowing the truth would turn her fair cheeks scarlet and her soft brown eyes downcast. Amid the inner reasoning and claims that shroud its self within a victim of noble yearning toward the fairer sex, a dreadful thought suddenly arose. Did the young Miss have a beau? If so, he did not accompany her at the Exposition, and so far, Nate had not heard from her lips of a suitor. Though an unspoken suitor did not guarantee of one not existing, it was near improper if not in poor taste to inquire for his benefit and his alone. Nate knew that his dear mother would have never approved of him being so forward in asking a young woman, so he would stay at his father's house until a proper opportunity presented itself. Nate prayed with all his heart that favor would blow his way, for he could not bear to lose Eleanor.

October 24, 1909
Sunday

The sun was very bright this morning. I should have greeted it with enthusiasm— like I used to. I was not ready for it—did it not understand how uncheerful it made me? Did it not understand how used up, worn out my being is? I am starting to loath anything which takes my precious sleep from me.

Upon opening my eyes, the gas light was glowing in my room as it was black outside. I heard the squeaking of bedsprings, and just as I was going to ask Alice to please hush herself, I heard a cough, and turning my head, I saw the wonderful face of Richard who was gently trying a new waking suggestion on me.

"Hello, sleepy head."

"Hello, yourself."

"Did it work?"

"Did what work?"

"The noisy springs. I was thinking of taking the covers from you again, but that usually results in me getting in trouble. Thought I'd try something new."

"Bless you, now go away."

"Want to know how long you've been napping?"

"No."

"Three hours."

Richard got up from Alice's bed and told me to scoot over as he sat on the edge of my bed. He looked down at me with his brown eyes—but they weren't just looking at me, they were trying to look into me.

I sighed too deep a sigh. I raised my eyebrows and tried to smile a little.

"Ele…..I've never seen you so tired before. I'm worried about you."

I took his hand and squeezed it. Oh, how good his warm skin felt when he placed his hand against my cheek. Just then something crumbled inside me. I felt it welling up and bit my lip, but a tear quickly rolled down the side of my head and hit the pillow before I had a chance to dab it away.

"Oh, Richard……" I sobbed.

I partially rose from the bed and fell into the comforting arms of my brother. He gently rocked me like a child, his hands held me through my thick hair that fell against my back.

"I'm sorry….I hope you are not ashamed of me."

"No," Richard whispered, "you are just very, very tired." He was quiet for a moment. "Do you want me to speak to Papa about the Miller's?" he half whispered.

I took my head off his shoulder and brought one of his hands up to my cheek. I smiled at my dear brother. "I know you would, but I won't let you."

"And why not?"

"Because if I were taking Saturday's off I could rest and not be so bad off."

"Are you going to?"

"No."

Richard coughed a little and asked. "Why not?"

"Because, Mr. Whiting is paying me $3.12 an hour each Saturday compared to the Miller's 15 cents an hour."

Richard eyed me. "Am I to understand, that Mr. Whiting is giving you the same amount of wages for one day of work that you used to get for five days work?"

"Yes!—And it was all Mr. Whiting's doing. Not mine. He would not let me argue with him on the subject. That—we should be thankful for!"

"But it's not worth it when your sister is losing weight and falls asleep on her brother's shoulder every Sunday…….not to mention her snoring."

I smiled at Richard. "Don't you like my snoring?" I teased.

"Almost as much as I adore hearing you read," my brother hinted with a warm smile. "May I?" he asked, rising from the bed to retrieve my book from the dresser.

"I do not think there is one poem in this book that hasn't been read at least twice or thrice," I happily sighed as I opened it up. "All right, Richard dear, what would you care to hear to-night?"

Richard closed his eyes and thought a moment. "How 'bout…let's see…um…page 288…bottom."

He opened his eyes and I turned to the page of his request.

"A Denial"
by Elizabeth Barrett Browning

We have met late—it is too late to meet,
of friend, not more than friend!
Death's forecome shroud is tangled round my feet,
And if I step or stir, I touch the end.
In this last jeopardy
Can I approach thee,—I, who cannot move?
How shall I answer thy request for love?
Look in my face and see.

"I might have loved thee in some former days.
Oh, then, my spirits had leapt
As now they sink, at hearing thy love-praise!
Before these faded cheeks were overwept,
Had this been asked of me,
To love thee with my whole strong heart and head,—
I should have said still…yes, but smiled and said,
"Look in my face and see!'

"But now…God sees me, God, who took my heart
And drowned it in life's surge.
In all your wide warm earth I have no part—
A light song overcomes me like a dirge.
Could love's great harmony
The saints keep step to when their bonds are loose,
Not weight me down? Am I a wife to choose?
Look in my face and see—

"While I behold, as plain as one who dreams,
Some woman of full worth,

67

Whose voice, as cadenced as a silver stream's,
Shall prove the fountain-soul which sends it forth,
 One younger, more thought-free
And fair and gay, than I, thou must forget,
With brighter eyes than these...which are not wet—
Look in my face and see!

"So farewell thou, whom I have known too late
 To let thee come so near.
Be counted happy while men call thee great,
And one beloved woman feels thee dear!—
 Not I!—that cannot be,
I am lost, I am changed,—I must go farther where
The change shall take me worse, and no one dare
 Look in my face and see."

The room fell silent. Very silent. Then Richard swallowed and looked at me.

"So farewell thou, whom I have known..., And one beloved woman feels thee dear—Not I!—that cannot be, I am lost, I am changed,—I must go farther where the change shall take me worse, and no one dare look in my face and see..."

I brought myself over to Richard and took his hands in mine, but suddenly, he began to cry and his hands left mine as they covered his face.

"Richard, Richard," I pleaded softly as I moved myself before him. "Please forgive me!"

I had not seen my brother cry since we were children, and the sight of my beloved caused pain in my heart and I wept, too. He leaned his head against my stomach and put his arms about me. The voice of the unknown spoke. The voice of fear spoke. Our words were too powerful and painful; our hearts felt regret from having read the poem. Out of the tender silence, we did not need to speak. I could only hold his head and stroke his soft brown hair.

He whispered my name in a strange way, and unwrapping his arms from about me, took hold of my arms and pulled me down. Richard started coughing even the more. His distress bore into me and his wet eyes followed mine as I knelt down before him. Oh, the sadness, the bitterness, and affliction I saw! My dearest Richard then took my hands into his and crushed them against his lips and pressed his eyes shut.

"Oh, Ele!" he cried.

His pain which I shared was almost unbearable; the depth of his misery tormented my heart close to physical aching.

"Richard, please tell me what is troubling you so!"

He kissed my hand and whispered, "Mama..." I watched him swallow hard followed by a long cough. "Mama...was talking about...if...the time should ever come...if my health...should...get the better of me...of where to send me..."

His voice trailed off and he kept his eyes fixed on mine which were suddenly filled with new fear. A grim heaviness gnawed at the inner cavity of my existence.

"No...that will never come about. No...no," I stammered, shaking my head. "No..." my voice wanted to be strong and to deny all and everything. "No..."

Richard held my head still in his hands as he spoke words that even I could not give comfort to.

"While you were napping, I overheard Mama speaking to Papa. They do not know that I know." He paused. "Nor must they."

Through the floorboards we heard Alice beginning to play the piano. One would know the fingers of Marie, Alice or myself. The sweet, gentle sound floated up to us, and folding my legs under myself I rested my head on Richard's knee. He stroked my head and whispered that my hair still looks like shiny melted chocolate in the dim light. And in the pervading spirit of fear, I prayed at the feet of my brother, but most of all, I silently and earnestly prayed that we would be forgotten.

E—

October 25, 1909
Monday

Week 7 at the Miller's.

A delightful surprise was waiting for Nate and I upon arriving at my house. Three carved and lit pumpkins sat on the front porch. Nate just had to get out of the motorcar to get a better look. The center pumpkin was tall and skinny; an expression of ghastly shock on its face. The two which flanked him were fat; their devious eyes glancing inward showing growling teeth.

Nate asked who might have been so creative. I informed him that John is the artistic one in the family. Nate told me to tell John that he did a marvelous job. There are only a handful of homes that are displaying jack-o-lanterns so far. Maybe as Halloween draws nearer we'll see more.

During the summer, an older gentleman sings out, "Potato man! Potato man!" as his wagon slowly makes its way up our street every few weeks. Mama waves to him but does not buy. The potato man passes through our neighborhood until late October, when he sells pumpkins for Halloween, and then we will not see him until late spring.

I have been working on Minnie Douglas' wedding present. It isn't fancy (as far as wedding gifts go), but I hope she likes it. It has been a while since I have crocheted edging onto pillow cases. I am trying an exquisite overlapping fan design that hopefully Minnie will cherish as a heirloom.

This Saturday Minnie's mother is hosting a luncheon for her only daughter. (Minnie has a younger brother.) I am anxious to see what Mrs. Douglas has prepared—it should be nothing short of spectacular—even for a luncheon.

Thoughts of secrecy around this wedding have stirred my imagination when I think of the short notice which I have been given. I don't know, maybe this is how things are done. Maybe this is how the Douglas' do things. Whatever their reason, I am glad that Minnie has secured a husband, because as long as I have known her, that seemed to be the main ambition in her life.

I cannot help but compare the roads which my two best friends have set for themselves. Miss Ernestine McAfee no doubt will want a husband 'someday,' as we all do, but for the moment she is an independent bird, doing what she has always said she would do—to be a business woman. For a short while I treasured my independence. Ernestine still has hers.

Both Ernestine and I are daughters of immigrants, and we have taken every opportunity to better ourselves in the country of our birthplace. We are of the lower-middle class, but I believe with Miss Ernestine's success of fulfilling the on going idolization of material things for working and non-working girls, she will rise quickly to middle-class.

Miss Ernestine can always tell when a young lady steps through her door, whether or not she is truly 'independent' and needs to 'make a living', verses the individual who needn't work, but does so briefly so she may say that she was a 'working girl' before snaring a husband.

One day while visiting Miss Ernestine, in the company of only her and I, she explained.

"The first young lady opens the door, hesitating as her figure stands under the tinkling of the door bell. Her mouth is in awe, eyes relishing every plume, feather and flower. She clenches her little purse against her chest. It is she, whom I treat as if she were royalty. For if her purchase is the only one she makes from me, I hope my treatment towards her is never forgotten. But the second young lady, the one who is merely passing time, opens the door wide—to pause on the threshold for the public and I to take notice of. Her walk is calculated and stiff—perhaps too much starch in her skirts is to blame. Her eyes are dreary as they do not pause over a single item, or me, for she has stood before me many times, finally waving a delicate hand at one of my creations. It is placed on her queenly head and I escort her to a mirror where I begin my duty of 'sale by flattery.' For a brief time, that unmarried woman has the freedom to express her love of self, her desire to possess things.

For both women, having come from different social and financial classes, she prides herself— for her independence has led to the love of luxury—she is triumphant."

Perhaps that is why I went back to work on Saturdays for Mr. Whiting. It is my one day in which I feel triumphant as an individual, as a woman. It does not bother me that most of my wages go to help our family. It is the fact that I am in a position of considerable importance. I am efficient, discreet, and have been referred to as Mother Superior as I kept order in that office. I know everything and remember everything. According to Mr. Whiting, no man could do their job nearly so well (or cheaply) as I.

Marie and Alice are preparing to retire for the night, so I best close.

Very soon, whoever is available to do so will be making wonderful caramel apples, popcorn balls, taffy, and cookies for Halloween. I suppose by the time I arrive home, everything will be done, but I will look forward to the sweet, tantalizing smells which will fill our home for hours.

Goodnight, and sweet
dreams, Eleanor

October 26, 1909
Tuesday

A thick blanket of fog covered the world this morning. A 'first' this autumn.

Mama made pancakes and bacon before everyone went their separate ways. This morning I wore my long coat and even put on my fascinator which kept my ears warm.

This evening Mama and I waited up for Richard. Last night after coming home from school he had an awful headache. Again to-night, he had another bad headache. Poor Richard. He looks so tired after a few hours of studying. I'm glad that Richard is pursuing an interest of his, though for how long before Mama needs to intervene for his sake.

The living room was cozy to-night. I moved a chair close to the fireplace so I could read the daily paper which I have not done in a while. Papa was at one end of the couch with his head back against the cushions, his eyes were closed and he was softly snoring. Mama was at the other end doing some button hole mending.

At the Miller's to-night, I had to suffer through another quiet meal. Actually, I should say that it was Nate who suffered since it was not I who had to sit with the other men. Maybe I should start humming softly while I serve supper tomorrow night.

I wonder how many more days Nate will stay there. His trunk is still at the end of his bed and the armoire is empty.

Around half-past ten this morning the fog disappeared and the sun came out, but now it is black again—a color which I see too much these days.

Nate drove me home again. I was trying to slip out to-night without notice, but even when I do not think I'm being watched, it seems as if he is keeping an eye on me. He asked if I had a ride home, and as much as I wanted to bend the truth, I couldn't. I feel awful, for I can see how tired he is. I do not want Nate to worry about me.

> Goodnight,
> Eleanor

October 29, 1909
Friday

Only two more days until Halloween and every house within

eye sight has a lit pumpkin on their front porch. To-night Richard came home in time to take a walk with the family. It has been a long time since we have all been on a walk around our neighborhood. We stayed out perhaps fifteen minutes. Every house beckoning us further down the street; further into the night. The chilly, damp air has a way of nestling under one's clothing, trying as we might to wrap our arms about ourselves, many breaths quickly disappearing as words do in passing.

Richard tried to hand pieces of taffy around to everyone, but our giggles gave us away. Mama thought it was pretty funny that Richard was trying to be sneaky.

Making our way round the neighborhood, there were other families doing the same as we. Papa and Mama of course took a moment to say "hello" to each. We happened to come upon Bertie and Frances Harper only long enough for Alice and Frances to send giggles into the night air. I noticed Miss Harper was looking at Richard with interest as does a young lady who is cooing over a hat which she has been admiring—but cannot purchase—yet. I did not scold my jealous feelings toward Miss Harper for she was treading on sacred grounds between brother and sister. She may gladly have John who is equally charming and good looking, and although he may be a few years younger than she, that should not be a deterrent on her female mind.

It wasn't until we were back in our cozy little home, drinking warm apple cider with fresh banana bread and oatmeal cookies, when Marie asked me if I took notice of Mr. Bertie Harper taking notice of me. Everyone apparently did and thought that I should have acknowledged him. I'm sorry, but I would not hand over even Marie to Bertie Harper.

The skies were laden with dark clouds early this evening and a few hours before night fell, a pinkish brown hue filled the sky between earth and the dark clouds. It was very unusual and unsettling to see a tint of brown mix with pink.

Tomorrow I can only work a half day for Mr. Whiting since Miss Minnie's luncheon is at one in the afternoon. I'm sure she will want to show us her beautiful wedding dress and veil, and while we sip on fine bubbles Minnie will explain in great detail what is expected from her attendants. And after we have rehearsed our parts mentally, her mother will remind Minnie what flavor the cake will be and its towering height, how many bottles of champagne will flow, what type of flowers have been plucked and imported to be added in the draping ivy vines.

I shall be envious while in the atmosphere of wealth, a grievous failure on my part, but it will quickly depart from my heart once I put some distance between the Douglas' and myself.

I have never wished for our family to have 'extra means' like the Douglas family. From my estimation, their family is no happier than ours. Perhaps Mr. and Mrs. Douglas have grown refined and stuffy over time. Are persons of wealth entitled to change their natural behavior which God imprinted upon them? I don't know. Miss Minnie has always been my friend. Even though she denies changing throughout the years, Miss Ernestine and I were always waiting for that day when our friend would take up friendship with girls from important, affluent families. We held our breath during the summer prior to becoming 'freshman.' Mrs. Douglas wanted her daughter to attend Holy Names Academy, but Miss Minnie did not want to be separated from her friends. There ensued a lengthy battle between daughter and mother over the summer, and after a two week 'illness' which prevented Minnie from eating or rising, her mother gave in. Minnie quickly recovered.

I truly am looking forward to tomorrow.

> Goodnight,
> Eleanor

October 30, 1909
Saturday

What an interesting day it has been. How do I begin to describe a day that should have been memorable but ended in tragic bewilderment?

After putting in a short day with Mr. Whiting, I waited for Miss Ernestine so we could ride the street car together to Miss Minnie's house. To-day started out so lovely— not a drop of rain in sight— the sun shone for the occasion— the autumn foliage gracing the streets with orange, yellow and brown damp leaves. As the street car went up the hillside away from Lake Union toward Queen Anne Hill, Ernestine and I sat close to each other, holding hands while our mouths were in awe of the lovely homes. Little did we know of the sad amusement that would unfold soon under the Douglas' roof.

I expected to see Minnie rushing out the door to greet us, but instead a shy frail girl answered the door and silently took our coats. We were told to wait while she placed our outer-ware out of sight, and upon her return she asked us to follow her into the parlor. There were three girls who we did not know. They were not like Ernestine and I in anyway shape or form. In their lovely dresses they looked superior; their mannerisms made us feel inadequate; the tilt of their delicate chins were measured; their practiced voices were not wasted on us 'common girls.'

Ernestine and I made the effort of introducing ourselves to the three upper-class girls. At least we knew our manners where introductions are concerned! Their response was a simple nod. For a few minutes we let our eyes roam the exquisite parlor, but one can only do so far so long. The three sat with the stiffest backs, casting glances under their lashes and delicately speaking to each other in subdued throat clearances. I would have liked to assisted them by a sound smack of my hand upon their backs. Their behavior was rude yet entertaining—if there was any other way of describing these girls of the upper-crust in Seattle.

We heard the rustling of skirts and stood up, only to be greeted by a fidgety and nervous Mrs. Douglas who was saving her good graciousness and smiles for later—perhaps after everyone had taken leave of her house.

"I am sorry ladies, but Minnie can not come down directly..... she is suffering from too many butterflies of the stomach which is causing her to not feel her usual self."

We all mumbled some polite offering for poor Miss Minnie.

"While we wait for my daughter to come down, perhaps in-between bouts, let us retire to the dining room and begin refresh-ments," Mrs. Douglas announced.

I'm not sure who felt more awkward at the time, Mrs. Douglas or the five of us following the stiff figure around a corner where a table was laden with hors d'oeuvres, a bottle nestled in ice, and fine cut glasses waiting to be filled. Sprays of lovely flowers took center stage on the lace covered table and in the corners of the room. It was all very elegant, considering how things were going, until Mrs. Douglas turned to Ernestine and I. We were 'instructed' to open the bottle and pour, then, we were to ask Minnie's friends what they cared for on their plates.

Mrs. Douglas gathered her skirts and was gone. Ernestine and I looked at each other, our blank expressions lingered only long enough to digest Mrs. Douglas' meaning. Ernestine looked at me in a way that only a friend could do, or understand. She promptly opened the bubbles and I holding our glasses in the air, toasted the absent Miss Minnie and took healthy sips.

"Miss...." One of the three girls finally spoke. "Are you not going to pour for us?"

"Miss...." replied Ernestine in a similar mocking tone of voice, "Have your dear legs suddenly become unproductive in the course of walking from the parlor to here?"

Oh, my! If Ernestine doesn't have a wonderful way with words just at the right time! You would have thought that little delicate thing without manners had been slapped with leather gloves all of a sudden.

Another one of the three addressed me next. "Miss....did you not hear Mrs. Douglas? It was her wish that you two....girls.... act as hostesses for us."

I glanced at Ernestine and then turned to the girl and gave her a most sympathetic look.

"I am most dreadfully sorry, but I did not bring my apron......"

I kept my glance steady on her.

"You mean we must serve ourselves?"

Ernestine took another sip. "Eleanor dear, do you think they have a clue?"

"Tragically, Ernestine, I think not."

"Perhaps their Papa's should buy them some manners instead of squandering their wealth on party dresses."

As quick as a 'jack-in-the-box' the young ladies vacated their chairs and huffed, "Well— I have never been so insulted in my life!"

"Then please, do tell us, how does it feel?"

Due to their lack of an answer, Ernestine and I were suddenly alone in the dining room. There were voices down the hall and Ernestine poured more bubbles as the front door was shut. She put the glass to her lips, and by the time Mrs. Douglas stood in the dining room doorway, Ernestine had it devoured. I thought Ernestine's little performance was superb, and the only thing keeping me from laughing was the cross look on Mrs. Douglas' face. Actually, 'cross' isn't quiet the appropriate word.

"Girls..." the word fermented on her tongue and her dark eyes flashed between Ernestine and me. "What—did you two do to cause Miss Minnie's friends to leave so....abruptly?!"

Oh, that Ernestine! She placed an innocent hand upon her chest and says to Minnie's seething mother, "Mrs. Douglas, Miss Eleanor and I are as shocked as you appear to be. Those lovely young ladies departed with such speed as if a swarm of bees were after them. What a shame too.....Miss Eleanor and I were having such a wonderful time....and then, without any notice....off they flew!"

"I see," says Mrs. Douglas.

Her steely suspicious eyes swung over to me. "Miss Eleanor....."

"Yes, Ma'am?"

"What can you tell me?"

"It's true. Miss Ernestine and I were having a fine time, despite the absence of the guest of honor. Yes, well.....the last thing I remember is....we were paying compliment to the detail of their dresses.....and then to our utter bewilderment, they were gone." I looked at Minnie's mother as I clasped my hands together between my bosom.

"Mrs. Douglas, were we improper for doing so?" I asked innocently.

Mrs. Douglas could only accuse us with her penetrating eyes.

"No, of course not." She cleared her throat and stood next to the doorway. "I think it would be wise if you two girls went home as well....."

"Mother....." It was Miss Minnie's stern voice.

Mrs. Douglas rushed to her daughter and pulled her into the hallway where a low hum of whispering could not be deciphered. Finally Minnie came into the dining room wearing a gown of satiny ivory material and lace that flowed when she came to us. Her long light brown hair was braided down her back and a matching satin ribbon bow was knotted at the end. I'm afraid to say that Miss Minnie did not look her vibrant self as her face was tired and pale. She hugged us both, and then her eyes paused at the table and a hand went to her stomach. Poor Minnie! She asked us if we wouldn't mind going to the parlor instead.

Our dear friend was so sorry that she ruined the party for everyone, saying that it wasn't 'supposed to be this way'. She hoped that the neighbor girls weren't too much for us. It was her mother's idea to invite them, not hers. She told us briefly what our roles would be as 'maids of honor.' Minnie says that we are equal friends to her and she did not want to stick to tradition by having only one 'maid of honor.'

As Minnie spoke she was holding her stomach again and she was not looking at all well. She managed to give us the horrible news that her new home will be in Portland, Oregon before she vomited.

In a flurry, Mrs. Douglas ran us out of the room; the shy little maid handed us our coats (which we had to put on outside) and there we stood, feeling awkward and ill ourselves. Poor Minnie though!

What a day! Mama would like me to set the table for supper so I best put my writing things up stairs and hurry back down.

> What an interesting after-
> noon.
> I hope Miss Minnie feels
> better soon.
>
> Eleanor

October 31, 1909
Sunday

We arrived home from church—thankfully not marred by black bows this week, but death was at our doorstep for a beautiful fine feathered friend. Actually it was the first time I have seen its kind—almost hawk like. By now I have forgotten who noticed it first. I found the heavy brown paper that my hats were wrapped in and placed the deceased on it. I carried the poor thing up to the back stoop and found what type of bird it was in my North American Bird book.

Being brown above and streaked below with rusty tones, it was a 'she', verses a male which has a pale gray back with wing tips of black. She is a Northern Harrier, or a Marsh Hawk and when fully grown measures 16 to 24 inches. The deceased was a youth—only about twelve inches in length. Her eyes are yellow and scornful, her yellow waxy legs are ridged, but the toes remained curled and sharp. During a hunt they fly close to the ground and take small animals by surprise. Seldom do they pursue their prey in the air or watch quietly from an exposed perch, as do other birds of prey. Their hearing is keener than other hawks; I wish she would have paid more attention to where she was going.....

John dug a hole for me in the backyard for the poor, poor thing. I cannot recall a season in which so many birds have ended their lives by hitting windows. It is starting to disturb me. I found it difficult to speak of her in the past tense. I know she is gone for her body was cold and her heartbeat was not felt in my hand. Perhaps if her eyes had been closed when we found her; when she laid on the cement stoop for description reference; when I gently rolled her in the brown paper; when the brown dirt covered the brown paper which covered the brown bird...... Her eyes are still open, even in death.

I almost forgot that to-night is Halloween night. Dear Richard had better not have eaten all the taffy meant for the little kids. I think I will join the others downstairs. Our room is chilly.

Happy Halloween!
Eleanor

November 6, 1909
Saturday

The wedding occurred at the home of her parents on Saturday afternoon, November 6th. Miss Minnie Douglas exchanged vows with Mr. Howard Wallingford. It was a very quiet wedding, only the near relatives and intimate friends of the couple being present. After the ceremony, a wedding luncheon was served and at 4 o'clock Mr. and Mrs. Wallingford started for their new home in Portland, Oregon.

They had planned to slip away, but the bride had told it very confidentially—to a few girls in her club, and the result was that at least twenty-five people were at the station to wish them fare-well. Among the surprised were the newly-weds, the mother of the daughter, Miss Ernestine and I.

At present, I am trying to picture Minnie, I mean Mrs. Howard Wallingford, on the Oregon bound evening train. I wonder if she is longing to be back in her father's house which she knows so well, or is she anxious to set up house, thinking right this minute of her position as the 'Lady of the House.' There is no doubt in my mind that Minnie has already thought out simple little details, from what type of font should she care to have on her calling cards, and to whom lives on such and such a block from her handsome home. (Although it might be fun to imagine planning such flamboyance around one's day, I would not care—truly—to want the responsibility of keeping up a pompous life-style.) However, I cannot see the new Mrs. Wallingford in any other role, for she has told me that the estate which Mr. Wallingford has chose is beyond stunning. He told the bride-to-be that she should not be alarmed if she finds herself lost within her new home.

I do not think Minnie fully realized the implications of the matrimonial yoke that had been placed upon her as she laughed and made pleasantries that echoed in the King Street Station. Even Miss Ernestine and I could not help notice that our dear friend, who was to be whisked away at any moment, showed no emotional indication of parental discontinuation or detachment. She flitted about as if she were amusing the members of the social clubs that she previously belonged to. Perhaps her insecurity or denial of the situation took claim; her mind withdrawing, regressing to the simplicity of childhood.Minnie's loveliness and charm complimented her evening attire so that any despondency that the new bride might have felt was not evident to the party who begged for tidbits of any size concerning her new mansion in Portland. This party consisted of the social club—young ladies who relish in their own joy of airs and self gratification. Did we not fall under Mrs. Wallingford's notice, you may wonder? I'm afraid that while our wedded friend experienced no immediate suffering in the role as Queen Bee, Miss Ernestine and I bore the cross of inconsiderate neglect, though not without concealed grievance.

Her new husband chatted the entire time with Minnie's father in one of the tall wooden benches while the rest of us eagerly waited in sad anticipation for a voice to ring out, "All aboard! Now Boarding for Portland.....Boarding now...All aboard!"

Although it is not my place to offer comment on my good friend and her husband, I feel compelled to do so concerning my knowledge of Mr. Wallingford. I do not wish to be critical of her choice of a life-long companion, but Mr. Wallingford is not a compatible mate for the energetic, free-flowing and independent Minnie.

After all farewells were given, and the train departed from sight, we, Miss Ernestine and I boarded a trolley at South Jackson Street and headed back home in the dark. I could tell that Miss Ernestine was busting at the seam for a chance to talk. Quickly surveying the sparse population of passengers, she sat close to me regardlessly and whispered, "What did Mr. Wallingford mean when he said, 'Mrs. Wallingford and I expect a kind reply very shortly, Miss Eleanor?'"

I shall have to repeat just what I told her because the following incident has left both of us speechless.

Before Miss Minnie floated down the grand staircase as a harpist played a beautiful wedding melody, and while Mrs. Douglas cried, Mr. Howard Wallingford suddenly presented himself behind me and whispered in my ear, "So you're the cause of our wedding date delay. You must be Miss Eleanor."

I turned around and was forced to step back. "I beg your pardon?"

"We were to have been married Thursday, as is proper, giving the newly wed couple ample time to settle in their new home. But Minnie said that we must wait for a Saturday so a 'Miss Eleanor' could be present. My well-nigh wife seems to be accustomed to getting her own way....Such unconformity has breathed its last breath for a certain vir...a young flower."

I did not know what to say after having been addressed so crudely by Miss Minnie's fiancé. What was I to say and do, other than to mouth, "Yes, I am Miss Eleanor...."

"Of course you are, and quite the picture Minnie painted of you.....verbally. I can see now that she did not do you the justice that you deserve...."

Mr. Wallingford lowered his chin and raised his eyebrow. He changed the tone of his voice and the look in his eyes as if I were a delectable peach to be had. I glanced down at the floor wishing that someone would come to my aid.

He went on. "She was so thoughtful in describing her best friend to me. 'Miss Eleanor has a profusion of beautiful, shiny, dark hair. A lovely, sweet, innocent face. Soft, gentle, brown eyes that melts a man's heart, and a figure that stirs a man's appetite."

My ears could not understand why this man was speaking as if he thought he possessed such liberties to do so. If such words had been spoken by a lover, they would have been gladly accepted and deemed appropriate. I was too shocked and my tongue was rendered useless.

Miss Ernestine kept patting and holding my hand, for I think she was also speechless.

Thankfully someone took me by the elbow and motioned to where Miss Ernestine and I were to stand, which was opposite Miss Minnie's brother and a gentleman friend of Mr. Wallingford. Throughout the short ceremony, I paid little attention to the words of the minister which were locking my friend into matrimony—Oh! How I wished to have spoken up....but what would I have said? Who would have believed me? And so I stood next to Minnie, who unknowingly stood beside a man who was drenched in the cologne of pre-marital infidelity.

As the trolley car clicked over the tracks, Miss Ernestine held my hand and said, "You poor, poor thing!"

"No," said I. "Poor, poor Minnie."

Together we echoed, "Poor, poor Mrs. Wallingford."

For a few moments we were silent. Thinking that was the whole story, Ernestine moved a few inches away and let my hand go. I turned to her and lowered my head as well as my voice. "Ernestine..." I whispered.

She lowered her head also and looked at me from under her lashes. Ever so quickly she bumped herself against me and took up my hand once more. "There's more?"

"I'm afraid I haven't told you the worst of it."

"The rotten scoundrel!" she hissed somewhat louder than expected.

"Shhh....."

"Sorry!"

"Ernestine, promise me a hundred, a thousand times, not even on your death bed, never to let this pass your lips!"

"Promise, promise, promise!!" Ernestine quickly crossed her heart with flying fingers.

"All right..." I glanced around at the passengers who seemed to take no interest in our little chat. "Did you notice how I tried to stay beside you during the luncheon?"

"Yes, and you did the entire time...."

"Until...."

Miss Ernestine searched her memory. "Until I needed to use the ladies room...."

I took a deep breath and told my dear friend the awful truth of what happened during her absence. "Directly after you left, Mr. Wallingford found me in a position in which he thought he could speak freely since we were not with the mass of guests around the buffet table.

"Miss Eleanor," he inquired, "my curiosity is begging to know why you could not have been available on Thursday, and what sort of employment have you that you could not remove yourself for even a day?"

I informed the insufferable man that I keep house for a family on Queen Anne Hill, and then a smile of satisfaction intermingled with his facial features.

"How convenient. A nice little package. A housekeeper for both of us. A friend for my wife, a live-in mistress for myself...."

Mr. Wallingford's covetousness sparkled in his eyes in a most distasteful way and I tried to remove myself for I was feeling ill and terrible warm and my skin was prickly. But with each attempt to remove myself from his clutches, I was unsuccessful.

"Mr. Wallingford," I began.

"Call me, Howard."

"I do not believe I will."

"You must."

"Mr. Wallingford, your behavior is very....inappropriate. I beg you to take up conversation—elsewhere."

"That Miss Eleanor, is all the more reason why you need to come to Portland. Mrs. Wallingford will be so busy engaging in all the social clubs that I will be left home alone. My dear Miss Eleanor, please do not looked so stunned. Surely every good woman in Seattle knows what her husband does to pass time while she partakes in the dry societies of old women."

"Mr. Wallingford….." I began.

"I will pay you handsomely and you shall have whatever you wish, including a spacious maid chamber that you can furnish to your liking. Whatever you desire, you shall have. All I ask in return is your affection."

"And what about Mrs. Wallingford?" I asked in a cool tone of voice.

"She may engage in an affair if she so chooses. And, if she is of the curious nature, she may join us as well."

At that moment I felt dreadfully ill! I glanced across the room and saw Minnie in conversation with her relatives. She looked beautiful, stunning, radiant. Poor Minnie.

"Why," I wanted to know, "did a degenerate such as you, decide to choose my friend so you could saddle her with a miserable life."

"Ah, such harsh words. Please be more kind, Miss Eleanor. For to be a 'degenerate,' one would have to more or less have a slouchy gait, low forehead, chin narrow, jaw widening rapidly until it becomes prominent under the ear, eyes near together, and generally restless, receding forehead and chin, back of the head almost in line with the back of the next, ect. Such a man, seen though of pleasing address, will prove to be cruel, selfish, heartless, liable to fail in business or commit some crime,—if a workman, likely to engage in strikes and frequently out of work. They are degenerates in whom the natural mental qualities are illy developed and who are sadly deficient in that most important of all qualities, self-control. He may make a fairly good appearance for a time, but is not in him to do well. He too, will cause trouble. To a careful observer, the signs of degeneracy are always apparent, and such persons should be shunned for companions and especially avoided when matrimony is the end of the companionship. It is not their fault, but their misfortune, and society must protect itself from the perpetuation of such blemishes of character before it can hope to make real progress and secure a preponderance of noble, capable citizens."

I could have fainted from his smug and blistering speech, and I should have fainted as to attract attention, but by that time I was too numb, too angry, and it was too late to warn Minnie that her marriage which was made in haste, in which she would discover now after marriage, when it is too late to retreat, no matter how much it may be desired, was a fearful price to pay for not seeking my opinion of whom she was keeping company with.

While my thoughts chose to despise Mr. Wallingford, he took the opportunity to reach for my hand—this was done quickly and smoothly as he brought my hand up to his mouth. His kiss adhered his lips to my hand and upon my flesh I felt the disgusting tip of a tongue! He must have anticipated my rejection for his fingers suddenly grew firm as I tried to remove my hand from his grasp.

"Howard, my dear," the voice of Minnie sang out. "Eleanor, Ernestine.....! The photographer is in the parlor. Come everyone, time to sit and pose before we leave for the station."

The members of the bridal party departed for the parlor and thankfully my hand was let go. I heard Minnie call out her husband's name again as we left the buffet room. "Coming, dear!" Howard's voice cheerfully rang out.

"You never did answer my question concerning Minnie," I said in a low voice as we walked side by side down the hallway to the lovely foyer.

"Mrs. Wallingford will, not doubt, as women do, inform someone of her—circumstances."

"I don't understand...."

"Let's just say that your friend procured a husband which is what she wanted, and I, so far as I can tell, have what I want....."

We turned into the parlor and as smooth as butter on a hot August day, Mr. Wallingford showed all the desirable qualities of a new son-in-law and husband.

Miss Ernestine and I sat in complete silence for the duration of the ride home.

Our thoughts and prayers are with Minnie to-night. I don't know how I feel about marriage after to-day. This day, (unfortunately for

Minnie, but perhaps to my advantage), has shed too much light on man's true vices in life. I shall have to pray very hard for my dear friend.

Goodnight,
Eleanor

November 7, 1909
Sunday

I found a nice poem in this month's The People's Home Journal entitled, *"An Autumn Prayer"* by S.W. Gillilan.

*When the dead leaves quiver earthward in the
twilight of the year
Comes the time of love and dreaming, when
the days of days appear;
Purpling distance, mellowing sunshine, trees
aflame with red and gold,
Air brimful of life's elixir—nectar on Olympia
old
Was as water in its weakness when compared
with this, methinks,
And I wish life's chain were endless with sweet
days like this for links.
Music greets my every footstep in the dead
leaves, rustling here-
When the ripe leaves quiver earthward in the twilight of the year.
When the leaves come trembling earthward
in the gloaming of the year,
Then this life's perennial sweetness seems a
thousand times more dear;
Yet the million gorgeous death scenes that em-
blazon every wood,
As the leaves in splendid shrouding quit their
dying brotherhood
To return to earth that gave them in the spring
so tearfully,
Breathe a prayer like an incense through the
very heart of me;
"When life's sap is flowing feebly and my rest*

is drawing near,
May my time for trembling earthward be the
gloaming of the year."

November 8, 1909
Monday

Yesterday our family went to a funeral. The deceased had lived with one of her sons whose house is across the street from ours. Besides raising her own family, the daughter-in-law took care of her husband's mother for many, many years, we understand. She was 94 years old.

I thought for sure that it would rain in the later afternoon, but the day only produced a nasty chill. Alice and I took a very short walk this evening. A comment was made that it felt like snow was in the air.

All the pumpkins are gone from the steps of every home. The streets are darker—lonelier. I suppose I never realized how brief a jack-o'-lantern's life is. We did enjoy their toasted seeds and the pies that Mama made from them. But wouldn't you agree, if you were a pumpkin, how depressing it would be, knowing that as soon as a family chose you, carved you into eyes and smiles, it would only be a matter of time—a fortnight before your flesh turned moldy, your exterior softened, caving in. And if that wasn't bad enough, while lying in the cold, wet, bare vegetable patch, crows pick at you in the daylight; rats and raccoons chew on you in the dark.

I almost forgot! Speaking of raccoons, a few days ago one met death under the cement birdbath bowl. He must have smelled the water in the bowl, and standing up tall, probably thought he could climb up there. Except the top was not secured onto the base and it toppled right down on him, the edge landing in the middle of his body. The poor thing. John offered to bury it next to the Marsh Hawk. I wonder what else is next.

Week nine at the Miller's.

Rain, rain, rain. Every time I looked outside to-day it was raining. I was glad to keep the coal furnace going, and no, the rat has not been caught as of yet. I kept the fireplace in the parlor cozy, and during my lunch break I settled into a chair close to the warmth and relaxed. Last Thursday was a horrible day. The 'curse' started and my legs hurt so bad that I found myself close to tears. There is so much to do on Thursday's that there isn't much time to sit down. I wish that a woman's back, stomach and legs did not have to suffer so. Although the other half of the 'curse' is a nuisance, I wish we could have the choice of that or the pain. Not both.

It has been twenty-two days since I officially met Mr. Nate Miller. I was wondering while the rain kept falling and falling, how poor Nate was managing down on the piers. While kneading the bread dough I looked at the gray wet day outside and thought of Nate. While upstairs in the men's bedrooms, stripping linen, putting clean linen back on, I thought of Nate. Working outside on such a miserable day as to-day, I couldn't help imagine how drenched and chilled to the bone he must have been. I wondered if he wanted to be in front of the fireplace, reading the evening paper, enjoying a cup of coffee. He usually comes into the kitchen and says 'hello,' tells me that dinner smells marvelous, somehow convinces me to let him sample dinner, and then asks if he may have a cup of coffee, if, it isn't too much trouble.

This morning while cleaning Nate's room, I felt a strange yearning to be near him. The time that I am with him is very brief, when he visits me in the kitchen after he comes home. Then there is supper, but he is with the rest of the Miller men. Then there is the drive home, but that does not take long. I found myself sitting on Nate's bed, running my hand over his bedspread, glancing at his trunk at the end of the bed, wondering with horrible curiosity what might be in there. On the dressing table there was a picture of a handsome woman with her small child, and my eyes and body were drawn to it. She was sitting down, and the child of perhaps two years of age, was standing on the same chair next to her. She was very lovely, gentle and kind looking. The child's hair was in ringlets, touching his shoulders, and the mother and the son leaned against each other, their heads touching. I could not stop myself to see if there were names on the back of the photograph which was held in a swinging wooden frame. The inscription read, "Mother and Nathaniel, two years old, 1884."

I have been wondering ever since, what became of her. No one ever speaks of her. Other than the one in Nate's room, there is no other picture of her elsewhere in the house. Strange, but it is not my business to ask. Maybe someday Nate will confine in me what I am dying to know.

I almost forgot to mention what happened after supper.

Mr. Miller Sr., Stuart, and Todd 'finally' have been carrying on conversations at the table like they used to. The tension is broken.

Once in a while someone will ask Nate what is happening on the waterfront.

To-night, Nate was the last one to finish supper, and while I was in the kitchen with soap-suds up to my elbows, he brings his plate, glass, and utensils in. Then he says to me that I may want to blow out the candles. I looked at him in a funny way, grabbed a towel to catch drips from my hands and went to the dining room, only to find that the candles had already been extinguished.

Upon my return, standing at the sink was Nate with soap-suds up his arms.

"Mr. Miller," says I, trying to scold him, "that was dishonest of you to trick me."

I was not very convincing by the smile on my face.

"I would like to think of it as being 'clever.'"

"But….I can't let you do my work!"

"You aren't. Grab a towel and start drying."

"But….what if….you can't…"

Nate stopped scrubbing for a moment.

"Miss Eleanor, if you insist on using your lovely voice, please teach me one of the songs that I often hear you sing."

It was very awkward, but oh, so pleasant to have Nate join me in the kitchen. I was on pins and needles most of the time, expecting the other three Miller's to come into the kitchen and start raising their voices. Nothing of the sort took place.

Mama wondered why I was home earlier than usual. I told her that I had 'help' in the kitchen. You should have seen her face. Mama said that that young man 'cannot' be a Miller.

When a day ends like it did to-night, I shall be thankful for Nate's help and company, even if it was for only one night. Thank you Lord for small favors.

> And thank you, Mr. Nate
> Miller

November 10, 1909
Wednesday

During the early evening as the day was drawing its curtains close, I stood on the Miller's front steps and spent a few minutes in adoration of the setting sun. It sat on the dark horizon, surrounding itself in a chilly, pink hue, stretching and thinning across the south-western sky. My breath went farther than the end of my arm which I quickly brought back to my body. I only wanted to see how far the cold air would take my warm breath......My knitted wool shoulder wrap that Mama made me years ago felt nice, but my neck and face longed for the warmth of the kitchen so I went back inside.

Once inside, I could smell my ham-shank soup and pan rolls. Oh, how delicious the aroma was! I started soaking the white beans yesterday, and this morning I chopped carrots, celery, and onions, adding them to the ham-shank and white beans. The kitchen smelled wonderful while I ironed and did more wash.

Since the cold weather is here to stay, the four Miller men are wearing their wool and fleece lined undershirts and drawers. More wash to do. Nate wears wool flannel and jersey shirts to work. More wash to do. And then there are his heavy overalls. But knowing that they belong to Nate doesn't bother me as much. Silly, isn't it? Ironing Stuart's sheets, and scrubbing the removable fine linen collars and cuffs is very time consuming. Those items must be impeccably clean. The majority of the cuffs and collars are worn by Stuart. That man may change both four to five times a day. I'm beginning to wonder if he has a 'cleanliness image' that he feels he must maintain.

I should be wearing my union suit soon, though by the time I would get to the Miller's house and start moving around all day, I would be overheated. A simple matter, it could be, if females were not bothered with so many layers to complete an outfit. To take a union suit off, I would have to remove a skirt, waist shirt, an under-skirt or petticoat, a corset, the corset cover which goes under the corset, unsnap the hose supporters and remove my heavy ribbed wool hosiery.

And then there is man who goes his merry way in comfort. It is not fair!

There is usually a few hours of 'mending time' in the evening on 'soup' nights, and to-night I sat in front of the fireplace in the parlor securing buttons on garments. The table was set, the rolls were done, the soup was warming on the back of the stove, and I was exhausted from a full day's work. Oh, how I am coming to enjoy the time in front of the Miller's fireplace after everything is done. I found myself relaxing and getting sleepy. I thought I could close my eyes for a moment, just a brief moment while my needle and thread sat in my lap.

I awoke, but not on my own. A hand was touching my face.....I remember saying Richard's name out loud for I had forgotten where

I was. I slowly left my slumber and opened my eyes to discover Nate standing in front of me. I was terribly embarrassed for having slept on the job, but his smile and reassurance that we were probably the only one's in the house brought some comfort to me. As Nate stood by the fire to warm himself, I casually stole glances at him as he stood there in his dirty flannel shirt and dirty overalls. I should have been ashamed for I know it is not proper for young ladies to stare at young men, but my eyes were watching his face; his tired and dirty face. Nate was watching the fire and I was watching him. Was that so wrong, I wonder?

I gathered my sewing, and put it in the basket for tomorrow, and standing up, my hair loosened and tumbled down my back. The light in the parlor in the evening is not good, and Nate came to my aide to search for the comb. He found it and handed it to me, after he looked at it briefly. I cannot describe the way he looked at me as I twisted my hair and put the comb back in place. He seemed to gather some sort of tender pleasure from watching me put up my hair. Like Alice said, his eyes do speak for him.

I shall not forget the touch of his hand on my face, nor the tender way he looks at me.

Goodnight,
Eleanor

November 12, 1909
Friday

It has been quite chilly this week. As Thanksgiving Day comes closer, it seems as if autumn is behind us, and winter is right around the corner. When I do step outside, the cold air bites at my nose and cheeks. I do miss the autumn when the elements were gentler on the skin.

This morning while Papa was getting the paper from the porch, he happened to observe an interesting event from a nearby maple tree. He hurried back inside to announce that there was a special sound taking place outside. Papa, Mama, Alice, Richard and I put on our sweaters and stood on the sidewalk looking at our neighbor's tree. There had been a heavy frost during the night, and in rapid procession the weighted brown leaves quickly flitted through the air and hit the ground with a 'thud.' I have never heard leaves hit the ground so heavily before. The tree had already been half stripped by wind and rain, but in a matter of a very short time the tree became bare, depicting dark, cold, naked limbs.

I did not drink any coffee this morning—I noticed I had a sore throat even before I was fully awake. I'm not sure if I'm coming down with a cold, or I could have snored for a long time during the night. Either way, the thought of coffee going down my raw throat was not an appealing thought, so I gargled with warm salt water instead. By this afternoon I was coughing and my eyes were watering, my head hurt, and I wanted to go home.

Mama says that I should stay in bed tomorrow and not work for Mr. Whiting. The thought of resting sounds awfully nice. I wonder if Mr. Whiting would understand if I did not show up. I will call the office and leave a message with whomever may be there, if I decide not to go in the morning.

Being the end of the week, I made a nice dinner of Fricasseed Chicken, Scalloped Oysters, peas, gravy, bread stuffing, and Election cake with lemon glaze. (I found out that this was a favorite meal for President Abraham Lincoln and his wife, Mary Todd Lincoln.) I did not feel like cooking a big meal for the Miller's....I did so because I thought Nate would appreciate my efforts. Maybe it's my way of thanking him for helping me in the kitchen every night, and for driving me home every night. I do appreciate the drive home and enjoy his brief company in the automobile, but I do not understand why he is helping me in the kitchen, especially when he could be doing something else. Maybe I should not question his motives.....though......as he stands so near, I cannot help but notice the hair on his arms when he rolls up his sleeves, the muscles which runs up his arms......perhaps Nate should not stand so close to me......

While setting the table to-night, I remembered a song that Mama used to sing. It is called, *"I Love You In Spite Of All."*

Down by a shady brook......By a swift running stream......Sat a maid and her lover,
Both happy as a dream.....All nature seemed at rest.....As the birds sang their lay.....
He told her that he loved her......Called her his Queen of May.....
Neither in their trysting,
Saw a maiden fall.....A girl who also loved him, Loved him the best of all......

"And who do you love most of all?"

I had not heard the front door open. Nate stood in the hallway smiling at me from across the dining room. I started coughing and instantly turned red. His timing could not have been worse. I did not know what to say so I vanished from the dining room with my beating heart. I was hoping that Nate would settle himself in the parlor before the rest of the Miller's came home, but that was not his plan. He came into the kitchen after removing his outer-ware, and his unsettling gaze fell on me. My cheeks nor my heart had not recovered and he was about to make matters worse.

"Yes?" I asked, my voice weak and in total emotional shambles.

"I have a proposition for you, Miss Eleanor."

"You do?"

"I have this box here....." Nate brought it around from its hiding place behind his back. "If you will sing to me, I will give it to you......"

I laughed and said, "What kind of proposition is that?"

"A terrible one, I'm afraid."

"What if I refuse?"

Nate looked at me with his dark eyes.....I wish he wouldn't do so.....I'm glad he does.

"May I at least sit down?" says I.

Nate swept a hand toward the table and offering me a chair, he joined me at the table.

"Just remember that I have a sore and failing voice to-night......"

"Thou procrastinates too much. Sing."

> *"She wondered from her home,.....*
> *This maiden all forlorn,.....*
> *In her heart kept the secret,*
> *Of a love left unborn,....."*

I started to cough and said that I would have to say it instead of sing it. Nate was leaning on the table, holding his jaws in the cup of his hands. I wish his mere presence would not send my heart beating at the speed of a hummingbird's tiny wings. Does he not know that his glances are waking the woman in me? I slept, but my heart is waking. He is knocking on my garden's door. Does he wish to browse among the lilies, taste the fruits and gather the spices? Is his hand touching the latch-opening? Does he wish to taste the honeycomb and drink my wine which flows in the garden fountain from a stream in heaven? Awake, north wind, and come, south wind! Blow on my garden,that its fragrance may spread, and let him come into the garden and taste the fruit. But please, turn your eyes from me; they overwhelm me.

"Have you changed your mind?" Nate whispered.
I shook my head and slowly whispered the rest of the song.

"She came upon these lovers,
Unconscious of her woe,.....
And heard him say, "I love you,"
Just as she turned to go,.....
She would keep her secret,
Which no time could pall,.....
Her heart was almost breaking,
She loved in spite of all.....
Long, weary days have passed,.....
To the sweet little maid,.....
Who has had many suitors,
But to all she says nay,.....
No one else will she wed,.....
She knows her heart is gone.....
To one who will never love her,
He weds tomorrow morn.....
Seated in the arbor,
His words she now recalls,
yet in her heart she loves him,
Loves him in spite of all.....
I love you best of all.....
Better than all this world.....
Those were the words were spoken,
Those were the words she heard.....
With your dear arms about me,
I care not what befalls.....
Surely, dear, you will not doubt me,
I love you best of all....."

I do not know of any words at this moment to help me...... Perhaps I do, perhaps I want to say, but am afraid to. I understand the tenderness in Richard's eyes when he smiles at me. He is my brother—the one whom I love and always will love. But Nate's eyes were intense and I could almost feel his left arm under my head and his right arm embracing me.

I had to look down at my lap and stare at stains from the day's work.

Something touched my hand—I let my eyes rise from my lap to see his warm hand covering mine. Nate slowly turned my hand over and placed the box in the palm of it.

"Open it," he softly told me.

I slowly opened the box, and inside were two side and one back combs for my hair. They were black tortoise floral design in gold, set with brilliant rhinestones.

I did not know what to say. I think I finally apologized, saying that I couldn't possibly accept them. Nate said that I must.

"Why?" I foolishly had to ask.

Nate smiled and he made my flesh weak once more.

"I want to make a certain 'maiden' happy, wishing she were beside a shady brook, the birds singing to her and her….."

"Supper!" I quickly jumped up, nervously straightening my apron strings. "I must finish preparing supper….." I busied myself at the stove and was glad that my back was facing Nate. I heard him rise from the chair and cross the kitchen floor, and as he left the kitchen he started humming the song—and then he was gone.

His torment continued during the evening. During supper while I served everyone Nate quietly hummed parts of the song. While washing the dishes, he quietly hummed, and on the way home he quietly sang the words to the song.

I do not understand Mr. Miller's torment. He must know how unsettling an evening it was for me. The price to pay I suppose for a handsome set of hair combs……

Goodnight, Eleanor

November 13, 1909
Saturday

I awoke around eight this morning and do not feel any better. I personally spoke to dear Mr. Whiting and told him that if he really needed me, I would come in. Although I would be sorely missed, his instructions were, "stay home and rest." So here I am, in bed, curled up in my warm little cocoon, only coming out long enough to gargle the warm-salt water that Mama brings to me. It sounds as if she may be coming down with something, too. Poor Mama. I haven't seen a lot of the family, except on Sunday's.

After I came home last night, Mama and Marie were downstairs occupying themselves with mending. I nodded to Alice to meet me upstairs, and casually we made our way to our room. I started from the beginning, repeating every word that I could remember from the evening. Alice sat on her bed, unbelieving my good fortune.

"You lucky girl!"

"Was I wrong to take such a gift.....if it was? Was it?"

Alice could only shrug her shoulders and give me a sketchy look.

"Was it improper?"

"Which part?" she asked almost too enthusiastically.

"Well.....Oh, Alice!" I started to pace the room in agitation. "Everything!"

"An example would be.....?"

"Him standing too close to me at the sink....."

I almost laughed from the astonishment which froze Alice's face. "What is *he* doing in the kitchen?"

"Washing dishes..." I replied ever so composed like.

"Oh, my......!"

"I know. I know!"

"Eleanor.....what are you doing while he is doing your work?"

"You may wipe that look off your face right now young lady," I teased.

"I can't," Alice giggled. "This is too good to be true!"

"Yes, yes it is. Well, every night after supper, Nate rolls up his sleeves and washes the dishes. While we hum or sing songs I dry the dishes. I wonder what his arms feel like. I put the dishes away. I wonder how hard his muscles are. He hands me pots and pans. I stare at his strong, rough hands as he rinses a handful of silverware......"

"You best sit down for the color in your face is starting to depart."

I sat beside Alice on her bed, staring at the print on the wall-paper.

"Eleanor.....?"

"Yes, Alice?"

"King Solomon once wrote, 'Do not arouse or awaken love until it so desires....' I think Mr. Nate Miller desires to arouse your heart, my dear."

"Oh, my......"

"Oh, yes!"

I think my heart needs its rest. I shall close my eyes and try to rest with it.

E—

November 14, 1909
Sunday

The family has left for church and the ride there will be quite chilly I'm afraid. The temperature was 24 when Papa looked at the thermometer outside the kitchen window. Mama said that my coughing might be 'somewhat' distracting in church so she thought it best if I stayed home. I have been reading my bible by the cozy fire-place in a comfortable chair with my slipper covered feet on another chair. The floors have been quite cold this month, and it seems that I cannot stay warm if I remove myself from the kitchen.

I wonder if Mr. Nate Miller goes to church. Does he believe in God, or is he just like the rest of the Miller men? I truly hope he believes......he is so different from the others; kind, gentle, giving, sweet in disposition. I think it would be wrong for my heart to have feelings for a man who does not believe in God. If I found out to-day that my heart had to give up Mr. Nate Miller, by tomorrow, it would be filled with grief. I wonder if I should ask Mama if it is improper to ask a man what his religious preference is. I best open my bible again and calm my mind.

Alice mentioned a verse from King Solomon's Song of Songs. I found it. 8:4 Daughters of Jerusalem, I charge you; Do not arouse or awaken love until it so desires.

1:2-4 Let him kiss me with the kisses of his mouth— for your love is more delightful than wine. Pleasing is the fragrance of your perfumes; your name is like perfume poured out. No wonder the maidens love you! Take me away with you—let us hurry!

The king has brought me into his chambers.

Do not arouse or awaken love until it so desires.

2:14—16 Show me your face, let me hear your voice; for your voice is sweet, and your face is lovely. My lover is mine and I am his; he browses among the lilies.

Do not arouse or awaken love until it so desires.

4:9—12 You have stolen my heart, my sister, my bride; you have stolen my heart with one glance of your eyes, with one jewel of your necklace. How delightful is your love, my sister, my bride!

How much more pleasing is your love than wine, and the fragrance of your perfume than any spice! Your lips drop sweetness as the honeycomb, my bride; milk and honey are under your tongue. The fragrance of your garments is like that of Lebanon. You are a garden locked up, my sister, my bride; you are a spring enclosed, a sealed fountain.

Do not arouse or awaken love until it so desires.

I do not think I should have opened the bible to the Song of Songs....at least not on a Sunday.

Why do I feel as if I have stumbled upon indecent reading material? It is in the bible....is it not? I have read Song of Songs before and the verses were nothing more than sweet, pleasant words. Must I admit it to myself? Must I whisper the words out loud? My heart is laughing at me for it is fluttering and swelling at this moment.

Oh, goodness! Oh, my! Perhaps I should have gone to church after all!

E—

November 15, 1909
Monday

To-day is week ten at the Miller's.

It was 27 this morning and thick frost dressed the grass in white.

I am still suffering from a cough which has settled in my chest. For the past few nights Mama has put a mustard plaster on me. My chest is very tender and red. I dread the fiery sensation—I can only imagine a hole is being burned through me. But if the horrible, smelly concoction improves my health, so be it.

A little Winter Wren peeked out from a bush beside the Miller's house as I climbed the front steps. I hurried to find bread crumbs for him and scattered them on the white, crunchy ground.

This morning while gathering garments and wash throughout the household, I came upon an interesting object in Nate's room. At this moment I am beyond embarrassed for I know now where it is kept on a man's body,— although I do not know exactly what its primary use would be. I found our Sears, Roebuck & Co. catalogue after I came home and brought it up to our room. It took me a while to find it. On the same page with elastic stockings, abdominal belts, and shoulder braces, are suspensories. I have never seen one in this house, but there it was on page 804. It is a Genuine O.P.C. Suspensory. The little advertisement is as follows: The best suspensory made. This is the one to buy. This Genuine O.P.C. Suspensory should be worn by every healthy normal man. The vital organs need a suspensory to sustain the nervous vitality, energy and force and prevent strain. Ect., ect.

I am unsure if I should ask Alice if she knows about such things. I don't want to sound naive, but I may have to take that chance. Alice, although younger than I, seems to know more about certain things than I. There's no doubt that she obtains her information from one 'Miss Frances Harper.'

This evening after Nate came home, his behavior was peculiar after he went up to his room to change out of his work clothes. He came through the kitchen, quickly said 'hello,' but did not stop for his usual sampling of dinner. He went downstairs, and then came back into the kitchen. I asked him if there was something wrong. "No," he replied. I asked him if he was looking for something. "No," he replied a second time. In no more than a handful of words, Nate mentioned that he checked the rat trap, and that dinner smelled good, and although he tried to be discreet with his questioning eyes, I saw him glance at the tubs which contained soaking garments. Perhaps one of his favorite shirts were soaking that I picked up off the floor. I do think he may have been a little cross with me because, I found myself alone in the kitchen after supper. I contemplated whether or not I should have said something. I did not.

Speaking of garments, I think I shall have to find my union suit. This cold weather is awfully persistent, and there is nothing worse than drafts going up one's skirts. Burr!!

Goodnight, Eleanor

November 16, 1909
Tuesday

Upon returning home to-night, I found a letter from Mrs. Howard Wallingford waiting for me on our dresser. It was thick and held four pages. Ever since her November 6th wedding I've been anxiously waiting word from her.

My dear, dear friend is with child and she joyfully speaks of the "quickening." It was briefly explained to her by the family physician as thus: "As soon as the uterus has become too large to remain in the pelvis, it rises into the abdomen, sometimes suddenly, causing faintness and sickness. After this the movements of the child, pressing directly upon the sensitive walls of the abdomen, are felt."

Minnie also boasts of the arrest of her monthly discharge which was one of the first circumstances which leads a lady to think herself pregnant. She is grateful that morning-sickness has finally left her.

Her once care-free life-style is now but a cherished memory, for the days and weeks are hemmed in by Howard, her husband, Howard's mother, the family physician, and Minnie's personal nurse. She is constantly being watched and doted over.

"The physician," says Minnie, "will not allow me to call him 'Doctor' as if there is a difference between a doctor in Seattle and a physician in Portland. I must address him as "Sir." I do not care for him as I should, for his self-glorification is evident as he speaks down at me with his fancy medical terminology.

My dear Eleanor, if you should still have memories of me as a young woman who gave herself airs or had a high opinion of herself, I can truthfully say that I do not come close to the breed of people in Portland.

It did not take me long to understand that "Mother" holds a form of reverence over my husband and the household staff as well, and as the daughter-in-law, I am the mistress of the house—whatever that should signify. Her authority is carried with a high hand as she swaggers her handsome figure into this house whenever she pleases. The Wallingford's are arrogant, purse-proud, stately, self-admiring people who enjoy turning heads in the latest fashions. Oh, Eleanor! If you could see the peacock pageantry!

On the days when the physician comes to the house, which is once a week, Howard's mother is also here. 'Sir' and 'Mother' speak to each other as if I were an animal being looked at and treated. 'Mother,' as I must call her, asked the physician to explain my morning sickness to me. (As if I did not understand what nausea and vomiting feels like!)"Morning-sickness occurs on first rising, probably from the uterine vessels being then more congested, and hence the disorder termed morning-sickness. In consequence of its intimate nervous connection with all parts of the body, the stomach often acts sympathetically in comparatively trifling derangements. Cerebral excitement, nervous irritation affections of the bowels, kidneys, liver, diet, dress, exercise, sexual indulgence, etc., are all capable of exciting abnormal action in the stomach resembling that which attends pregnancy."

From the moment I set foot on Oregon territory, everything that my mother never told me has been explained by Howard's mother. She is crudely blunt; a woman of substantial force, having all one's wits about her and all the discrimination which wealth entitles an individual to. I cannot escape from Mother. It has taken some time to get acquainted also with my personal nurse. I must admit that she does keep me company since I rarely see Howard in the evenings. I have recovered from the notion of another woman my age caring for me and pampering me. During the first week in our new home, Mother and my physician paid me a visit and repeated the following to me.

"Now Minnie, I want you to listen very carefully to what is going to be explained to you. Your physician and I spoke of the power of ante-natal impressions before we came up to see you. You must listen very carefully, for this is how children are born either bright or stupid."

My physician bowed his head to my mother-in-law. "Thank you, Mrs. Wallingford."

"There no longer remains any doubt that children may be born strong or weak, beautiful or ugly, talented or imbecile, good or bad, according to the will and wisdom of their parents. What would not a parent give to have his child mentally bright and physically handsome? Before the birth of the child, much may be done by the mother for its future character and development. During the first four or five months of pregnancy, while nature is laying its foundation and framework, you should be faithfully practicing a system of exercise to contribute to the strength and hardiness of your child's constitution. Later, in the sixth and seventh months, when the brain is being formed and matured, you may stamp it with the very quality of your own tastes and pursuits. Surround yourself with beautiful and cheerful objects, communing much with the best books and the most gifted minds, hearing the most eloquent speakers and living in the worlds of literature and art, you may give birth to a genius who will astonish the world and delight your own heart; or, reversing all this and giving your attention to the mean and the sordid, the effect will be seen in the lower and more incapable mental qualities of her offspring."

My new mother-in-law retrieved a lace handkerchief from the folds of her healthy bosom and patted her brow saying to me, "Minnie! Are you listening? Take heed my dear! Growing in your womb is my future grandson....a Wallingford!"

"Now, now, my dear Mrs. Wallingford, take care not to excite yourself," the physician replied in an attempt to soothe my mother-in-law. "Upon examining your daughter-in-law, conception has borne fruit and she appears quiet healthy. But may I add, as to what the new mother sows in this season, so will she reap in the harvest-time of maternity. The temper and character of her child will depend very greatly upon her own, especially during the last months of her pregnancy. Patient, serene, content, gentle, pure, unselfish, cheerful and happy, the sunny being that will be born of her will brighten and gladden all her life; while, if fretful, turbulent, discontented and unhappy during this period—and much more if she be positively vicious—she need not be surprised if she gave birth to a public and private pest, that will break her own heart and be a curse to society. Nothing is now more certainly known, or better understood, among those who have given attention to this matter, than this potential effect of the moods of the mother upon the character of her child. If then she would like to see her children strong and healthy, graceful and beautiful, quick, sprightly, intelligent and gifted, cheerful, obedient and happy, virtuous and respected, the ornaments of society and the lights and jewels of her own heart and home, she must give heed to those immediate laws of ante-natal influences."

Mother and the physician left a few minutes ago. I was questioned and examined again and again.

"Now Minnie," Mother began, turning her handsome features toward me. "Has my son been asking you to unlock the door between your rooms at night?"

"No, Mother," I dutifully replied.

"Good," she nodded her head daintily.

"Are your breasts sore?" she asked as if her question was natural in conversation between a mother and daughter-in-law. My own mother would turn scarlet red if sudden-death had not taken her first, if the word 'breast' was mentioned in her life-time. I turned to the physician and he raised his eyebrows as well. My dear Eleanor, I'm sure you are horribly shocked by all this, as was I upon conceiving a Wallingford child. But apparently, this is how a mother-to-be is cared for in the upper-crust of society where wealth disentitles a daughter-in-law to herself .

"Mrs. Wallingford," the physician asked, "are your breasts tender?"

I nodded my head and dutifully unlacing my gown, presented large swollen breasts that he examined and so stated that they are of proper size and shape, and at present are not deficient, for after confinement, nipples can hardy be said to exist.

"Are you washing the nipples several times daily with weak brandy and water?"

"Yes."

"Is your nurse putting warm, moist cotton cloth over your breasts?"

"Yes."

"Are you still elongating the nipple in preparation for nursing?" he asked.

"Yes."

Dearest Eleanor, I sincerely hope you never have to do this, but I am told it will be for the good of my child directly after delivery when he is allowed to nurse. A very simple and efficient measure to elongate the nipple, I am told, is to tie a piece of woolen thread or yarn two or three times around its base, after having pulled it gently out with the fingers. It should be tied sufficiently tight to keep the nipple prominent, but not enough to interrupt the circulation. The woolen threads may be worn several weeks without inconvenience. Of course a man would not know whether this was inconvenient or not.

"Now Minnie, is your nurse still bathing you several times daily by adding twenty drops of the tincture of arnica in the bath water?"

"Yes, Mother."

"Now Minnie, it is very important to let Miss Young carry out her duties. She is a highly sought-after nurse among 'my' circle of friends. I am pleased to hear her report that ladies with fine, sensitive skin should have tender breasts, since the filling of the breasts stretches delicate skin. Miss Young immediately knew that you came from good breeding upon examining you. I have given Miss Young all authority to care for you according to her own unrestrained discretion. She is being paid well, so do what is required of you. Do not make a fuss while she gives you sponge baths. Do not appear uncomfortable while she gives you vaginal injections of warm infusions of chamomile flowers. When she comes to rub rose oil on your breasts, let her untie your gown. Smile while the flow of your milk is checked. Miss Young reports that there are no imperfections in your milk, and that you will be able to furnish the infant with sufficient, rich milk. You see, Minnie, great care must be taken to protect my future grandson.

Wealth can buy many, many things. Wealth can also buy the

best nurses and physicians who impart vast amounts of counsel and advice. Newly married women are too delicate and modest and often let many afflictions run too long, or for those who cannot incur the expense of calling a physician..."

My mother-in-law sighed, breathing deeply which made the handsome long pearl strand about her neck move as her bosom held up the weight of wealth. "But us Wallingford's do not have to worry about that."

Mother nodded to the physician, and putting his hand under the covers, he examined the mouth of my womb. I best finish this letter for I am expecting Miss Young's soft knocking on my door at any moment. I shall let her 'fuss' over me so she can tell 'Mother' what a good daughter-in-law I am.

Dearest Eleanor, I miss being in Seattle. I miss talking to you. I sometimes wish I was still a little girl. Please write soon, my dearest friend.

> Bunches of hugs and kisses
> Minnie

November 27, 1909
Saturday

Thanksgiving was wonderful. Two of Mama's brothers came out on the train to spend the holiday with us. Uncle Joseph Nist (or Brother Sylverous) is from Pittsburgh, Pennsylvania. Uncle John Nist (or Brother Raymond) is from Buffalo, New York. They are of the Redemptorists Order.

Although Uncle Joe and Uncle John write frequently, it has been many, many years since we have seen them. They send photographs so Mama doesn't forget what her older brother's looks like. I know she wishes that they had stayed in Seattle which would have kept them at Sacred Heart Church, but they did not object at the thought of living so far east when they joined the Order while in their early twenties.

I will have to ask Mama if I may keep a photograph of them between my writings.

I wish we had room for my uncles to stay with us, but it is only proper, I suppose that they stay with their fellow Brother's at Sacred Heart Church. Uncle Joe and Uncle John will visit their other four brothers while they are in Seattle. Uncle's Joe and John often ask in their letters how their nephews and nieces are. I wonder how often my other uncles send letters to New York or Pennsylvania. I believe there was some family disturbance as to who's home would furnish the turkey feast for our out-of-state guests. Our home was chosen (I strongly believe) because Mama is the only female sibling in their family, and because she invites many of the Redemptorists Brothers to our house for coffee, cookies, and pleasantries.

Their stay will end on Wednesday. Mama wants Papa to bring her to the train station so she can properly say 'farewell.' She is already making cookies which will be sent along with sandwiches that they can eat on the long route home. I can tell that Mama is very close to those two brothers. Since Thanksgiving, our Mama has been quieter in speech though her body has been very fidgety. Papa has been spending a great deal of time in the basement, keeping out of the way.

Poor Mama. Wednesday will be difficult for her. I'm sure she has been wondering when will be the next time her brother's will come out this way.

Goodnight,
Eleanor

November 28, 1909
Sunday

It must have been Richard's coughing that woke me up earlier than usual. Through the thin walls I can hear my dear brother pound on his chest, his body falling back in bed, his head hitting the pillow, only to rise again when the massive feather tickles the cavity of his lungs. The rest of his body is still so young. He does not want to let this illness cause worry in the minds of his family.

As I listened to Richard, I remember that Uncle Joseph and Uncle John were concerned with their nephew's state of health. They had asked Mama if he was experiencing a slight rise of temperature in the evening, exhaustion after slight physical or mental effort, digestive disturbances, headaches, rapid, difficult or labored breathing.

As I laid in bed I noticed a different light coming through the window, making the morning appear as if snow had fallen during the night. Richard coughed again and I sat up. The world around our home was not covered in snow but merely a layer of white fog. How deceiving nature can be. For what it was worth, a few thrilling moments of joy ran through my body at the thought of beautiful, clean, white crunchy snow....Richard is coughing a lot this morning.

Having put on my slippers and morning robe, I closed our door and stood in the semi-dark hallway. My hand did not want to turn on the gas light. To do so would have given my eyes ample reason to look at the knob on my brother's door. It would have given me no reason to hesitate in the dark hallway. A chill from the wood floors could be felt through my crocheted slippers. The morning air was cold, as can be expected for being almost December. The thermometer outside the kitchen window has been reading '30 degrees' after the waking hour.

My knuckles gently tapped on their door and I slowly opened it without waiting for a reply. Their room was as chilly as the hallway, just as chilly as ours. I sat myself down on my brother's bed and put my hand on his forehead. His skin felt normal. Richard looked tired and I asked him how he felt. He had a headache which he blamed on the coughing, and mentioned that he woke several times during the night covered in sweat.

In the other bed, John mumbled something about not being able to sleep because of all the coughing going on. I politely told John to 'hush.' He turned away from us and buried his head in his pillow.

I took Richard's hand and kissed it.

I heard footsteps in the hallway and Richard's eyes looked beyond me and he said good morning to Papa.

"Gut morgen kindlich." Papa still enjoys calling us children—even at our age.

I turned and smiled at him. "Good morning, Papa."

He asked Richard how he was.

"Tired," was the reply.

"Ihr stay in bed this morgen," he pointed to the bed.

"Yes, Papa."

Papa left the room and went down the stairs—each step he took his shoes echoed back to us. Richard and I listened to the door which led to the basement open. It cannot be closed completely on account of a snug frame. Soon Papa would have the coal furnace cleaned out and fired up, and then the house would be filled with warmth.

This morning Mama told us that Uncle John and Uncle Joseph would be having dinner with us again, and asked Papa if he would kill two ducks after church. Along with the ducks, Mama plans on serving mashed potatoes, baked squash, boiled beets, biscuits, cold slaw, baked plum pudding, lemon pie and coffee.

We are back from church and I have checked on Richard. He is sleeping. I best change out of my good clothes and prepare myself for a day in the kitchen.

Eleanor

December 3, 1909
Friday

End of week 12 at the Miller's. Three long months have gone by.

To-day is my 21st birthday. It feels like any other day. Nothing special to speak of.

The air was quite chilly and damp with the temperature hanging on at 30 degrees. A thin fog encircled the neighborhood which soon gave way to a bright, yet still chilly morning.

At breakfast, Mama asked me what kind of birthday cake I wished for. I insisted that she did not have to go to the trouble of making a special dessert. "Nonsense," Mama said, just as I knew she would. "I always make the dessert of my child's choice for his or her birthday." I chose one of my favorites— Irish Apple Pie. It is very simple to make (part of the reason why I chose it). You simply cut apples into slices, lay them neatly in a baking dish, season them with brown sugar, add any spice, such as pounded cloves and cinnamon, or grated lemon peel. Add a little water and cover with puff paste and bake for an hour. (It was difficult to see my slice of pie under a mound of whipping cream. My stomach is very happy at this moment).

After supper we all retired to the living room where I received my birthday gifts. I was seated before the warm fire and held my presents in my lap as I waited for Papa to open his pipe stand and settle down on his end of the couch. Papa made me a nice little box lined with felt that I can keep hair combs, hat pins, and the like in. From Mama, a pair of crocheted sofa or chair arm doilies in the shape of butterflies. I was very touched. I went over to Papa and Mama and gave them a kiss on the cheek. And from Marie, she made me a lovely card with birds drawn in the middle, surrounded by leaves and scrolls. Inside she wrote, "Roses are red, Violets are Blue, Eleanor is Twenty-One, and I love you!" Alice baked several batches of my favorite cookies. I passed around the plate stacked with Sugar cookies rolled in sugar and cinnamon, Thumbprints, Fried Knots sprinkled with XXX sugar, and probably my favorite, Krumkake. I almost hate to bite the delicate scrollwork that is embossed on the thin cookie. John played a new song on his harmonica for me.

During my unceremonious birthday party, dear Richard was trying to still his cough. He did not speak much, but elected to force a smile, which seemed to be an effort on his part. With each cough his face would wince in slight pain. Mama quietly asked Richard if he was having another headache. My brother did not answer directly, but his loving, warm eyes met mine, and I could see his concern for himself. He is a bright young man whose health is on the decline. My brother raised his eyebrows slightly and said too calmly while keeping his face towards mine, "Yes, Mama. I'm 'fraid so."

Mama buried her eyebrows and looked at Richard. "I shall be making another appointment with Dr. Henry on Monday. Please make yourself available."

"Yes, Mama."

The room was quiet and I cleared my voice and started to thank everyone.

"Don't you want my present, Ele?" Richard asked.

"Oh....." I whispered in surprise. "You didn't have to." I certainly had not expected him to buy me anything, especially the way he has been feeling lately.

"I was not going to let a silly little cough get in the way of finding my sister a present for her twenty-first birthday," he stated sternly without much of a smile. "Here..." Richard rose from his chair and handed it to me, kissing me on the cheek. "Happy Birthday!"

Under the wrappings was a small book of poems. Opening the book, Richard had written a few lines of congratulations, and turning to a random page there was a Louise Chandler Moulton; years of birth and death: 1835—1908. Alice asked me to read a few lines from the little book.

From: To-night

Bend low, O dusky Night,
And give my spirit rest,
Hold me to your deep breast,
And put old cares to flight.
Give back the lost delight
That once my soul possest,
When Love was loveliest.

Mary Margaret Bayer

From: The Secret of Arcady

I hied me off to Arcady—
The month it was the month of May,
And all along the pleasant way,
The morning birds were mad with glee,
And all the flowers sprang up to see
As I went on to Arcady.

I turned the page and read the title of another poem by the same author called, "When I wander away with Death," but my lips held themselves still as my eyes brushed quickly over despairing and feared words.

This Life is a fleeting breath,
And whither and how shall I go,
When I wander away with Death
By a path that I do not know?

I rose and wrapped my arms around my brother, clinging to him.

"Goodness Ele…..does this mean you like my present?"

I trembled and clung to my brother's body tighter. He coughed and my body shook with his. I hated the illness that would not let him rest. It was as if the illness were the landlord over his body; his spirit and will were tenants. I started to sob…..

"Ele……what's the matter?" he whispered.

"Eleanor…..?" Mama was speaking with a troubled voice for it was suddenly high."What's the matter dear?"

"Here, here!" Richard pulled me away from him and looked down on me. "There's nothing wrong, Mama. Who say's a girl can't cry? Right, Sis?"

I forced myself to stop crying and made myself smile for everyone's benefit.

I managed to thank my family for a wonderful birthday, then Richard handed me a Krumkake which I carried to my room and just had the last bite.

Will Richard turn brittle like my cookie? Will his cough take root in his lungs, in an establishment where germs are mysterious and veiled, until viewed with a x-ray machine?

I fear for my dear brother.

I fear this coming week will dispense us with a report that will be intrusive on our lives, even though the informant was asked to bring to light the news of my brother's health.

Dear God, please take care of Richard.

E-

December 6, 1909
Monday

Week 13 at the Miller's.

It proved to be a very chilly morning at 28 degrees. I put on everything possible to keep myself warm for my walk to the Miller's house. As always, I am thankful upon my arrival. The house is chilly during the first few hours. I have a certain routine, as a person would after having done such chores over and over again for the past three months. Nate still cleans the ashes from the fireplace in the parlor, from the range stove in the kitchen, and from the coal heating system in the basement. I am forever grateful for his assistance.

The first order of the day is to start the fire in the range stove, then feed the heating system its breakfast of coal, and after those two are going properly, I start a nice fire in the parlor.

I have learned to entertain myself during the day with humming and singing. At times, I even find myself carrying on little conversations—harmless—I'm sure. One would imagine that filling the hours between 8 a.m. and 8 p.m. would be quiet difficult. That is what I thought three months ago. I seem to benefit from a daily schedule of baking and cooking for four men with large appetites. There does not seem to be an expense budget as far as ordering meat and poultry. On Monday's a driver from the meat market knocks on the door and hands me the items I requested the previous Friday. To-day I gave him a list of the items that I will need for his Wednesday visit.

I wish I could have given him a cup of coffee for I could see his breath escape into the frosty air shortly after 10 a.m. The young man wore a thick sweater and a cap on his head and gloves on his hands. He is a very quiet fellow, walking in a quick mechanical manner. His eyes follow each sidewalk, each walkway to each house. I have never seen a smile upon his face; it is not a face of sadness but of seriousness; as if he is worried of the crime of forgetfulness.

The ringing of the doorbell interrupted my bread making, but I suspected it was my meat and poultry waiting for me on the other side of the door. I greeted the delivery man 'Good morning,' as I always do, and he nodded to me and said, 'Morn'n Ma'am.' Taking my paper-wrapped bundles, I handed him my list for Wednesday. As he turned to leave, I wished him a 'Good-day,' and he removed his cap. He was halfway down the walk when I found myself calling to him.

"Sir?"

"Yes, Ma'am?"

His mouth was straight and tight, his eyes worried like.

"I was wondering...."

"Av' I forgot' somethen' Ma'am?"

I was dreadfully sorry that I caused him worry as I did not mean to do. I smiled and said, "No," he had not. I have been quite pleased with the deliveries during the past three months. But I needed to apologize for never having asked what his name was.

He poked a finger against his chest, raised his eyebrows, and says, "Me, Ma'am?"

"Yes! I care to know what your name is."

"You do?"

"I do," I replied with a slight nod of my head.

I will always remember that man's face as it softened, knowing that someone cared enough to ask him what his name was.

"Thank you, Ma'am. The name is Otto."

He tipped his hat and then scurried away to the house next to the Miller's.

After I returned to the kitchen, I silently promised Otto that I would bake him a batch of cookies, having them ready on Wednesday.

To-night for supper I prepared dressed duck, onion soup, browned potatoes, stewed carrots, cranberry sauce, boiled rice dumplings with custard sauce, pastry sandwiches, fruit, bread, and coffee.

While attending the upstair rooms to-day, the weather warmed slightly and I opened every window in every bedroom. It has long been believed that proper ventilation is essential to one's health. Mama heard some years ago that closed windows at night keeps foul air in the room, which poisons the blood and brings on disease which often results in death. This poisoning of the blood is only prevented by pure airs which enters the lungs, becomes charged with waste particles, then thrown out, and which are poisoning if taken back again. Mama says that a grown person corrupts one gallon of pure air every minute, or twenty-five barrels full in a single night, in breathing alone.

During the warmth of summer I welcome a fully open window, but to-night, as always, Marie checks to see if our window is open a crack. Marie and I go through a silly routine every night. Right before bed time she opens the window an inch. As soon as she dozes off, I give the window the 'little finger' test. Dear Marie is constantly telling Mama that I close the window at night, which of course, is a falsehood since she does not explain that it is not fully closed. Although I agree with Mama on the importance of ventilation, I do not intend on dying from freezing before I die from foul air!!

Goodnight,
Eleanor

December 8, 1909
Wednesday

Far across the wide dirt street are dark roof tops. Chimney smoke from one brick stack floats across to another roof top. The lowest portions of the heavens are streaked with pink; the pink that only God is allowed to use—for us to enjoy. It is a few minutes before the hour of 4 in the afternoon, and I am writing in the Miller's parlor, in front of the pleasant fire. Dusk has set in already. I do not think there is any harm in resting after I have been on my feet all day. I will not be expecting the front door to open till 6 this evening.

The morning woke reluctantly to a cold heavy fog. Our thermometer read 28 degrees, although, any living soul having ventured out in such weather would have quickly agreed that staying indoors near a fire would have been a wiser choice.

My thoughts and concerns this morning were with dear Richard. The doctor could not see him Monday due to a full schedule.

I foolishly tried juggling baking cookies for Otto and scrubbing bedding on the wash board intermittently. I burned one full sheet of cookies which I threw out for my little feathered friends. At ten o'clock Otto delivered a few bundles containing pork and beef. I in turn presented him with a plate of warm cookies. I should try to keep in mind how cheerful he tried to look after being taken aback by my gesture. I think he may have smiled longer if his numb face would have allowed it. My heart goes out to him!

I tried to concentrate on my duties to-day, but my brother would not leave me be. Every shirt I scrubbed was Richard's. Every long hour has been filled with scrubbing white laundry, wringing out as many drops of water as humanly possible, and then hanging the sheets and shirts, underclothes and handkerchiefs on the lines in the basement.

The white's being finished, I proceeded to scrub, rinse, wring, and finally carry the heavy basket of dark garments to the basement. I pinned shoulders, waists, and feet onto the line. A strange prickly sensation crept over me. I wanted Richard to be with me, and it was there, in the strange shadows that I cried. My mouth tasted the salty tears before I stole a wet towel from its wooden pins. I sat on the dusty wood steps and buried my face and sobbed. At that moment I knew Richard was speaking to me.

The neighborhood beyond the Miller's is gradually disappearing in the darkness of early evening. I'm not sure if I care for darkness to-day. It is intimidating, not being able to see what the eye has seen only less than an hour before. If the lights were to fail at this very moment, (please forgive the ink smear—the chime in the hallway announced half-past four.) I would be afraid to leave my chair, for the protective flames that I huddle near would be my only source of light.

Before to-day, I viewed darkness as a thing that could not be avoided. I did not fear it, but was not entirely comfortable with its coming. At this moment especially, it does not bring comfort to my fidgety imagination which just saw black ribbons; those horrible black ribbons hanging on church pews.

I pray that the remaining night goes swiftly here. I dearly need to be beside my brother.

It is a quarter to five, say the chimes. I must tend to the last details before the men return home.

I am coming dear brother. I will be with you soon.

Love, Eleanor

December 9, 1909
Thursday

The pen which I hold is ignorant of the mental and physical torment that tears away at my being. I have exhausted myself from crying, though salty streaks continue to run down my stinging face.

If the front door should open and a pair of eyes find me before the fire, sitting, not moving, numb to my surroundings, numb to their presence......that is how they shall find me.

It is without regret if the fire in the range is not burning, or if the coal bin has not been touched since morning. I have not removed myself from the parlor for hours, not wanting to move from the warm flames, hearing though ignoring the hours which the chimes wish for me to know.

If I could possibly manage to strike my breast so the under-lying heart would cry in protest, I would have done so, repetitively inflicting self injury until weariness would have rendered me incapable of further punishment.

In the depths of sorrow and cracks of pain which to-day cannot escape from, I am filled with distorted courage. Raw, cold, reckless.... callous....the strain of courage that only numbness can conjure to bring me to leave this house, this very moment......I must be with my beloved brother, my dearest Richard, Richard, Richard......I am coming home Richard dear, I will sing to you in whispers and kiss away your tears and envision armies of shining angels fighting in the shadows of mottling lungs, drawing swords along the path of invasion, ceasing all infection.......

E—

$\mathcal{N}$ate

His day was done and Nate was glad of it for he was weary. He boarded a trolley which steadily made its way from the dark salty waters of Elliott Bay, through the business district of Westlake, up hills and steeps grades, and finally to the top of Queen Anne Hill, where Nate removed himself as did others into the cold dark night, quietly dispersing in their own direction as if having been swept off by an unseen wind.

Although his body wanted to be at rest for the night, his destination laid ahead a few blocks still. Nate wrapped his coat collar closer to his skin, crossed his arms tighter, pressing them to his chest. He was not 'there' yet. His tongue almost slipped and used the term 'home,' but he caught himself and was glad, for his father's house was not a home. It was merely a residence to take up lodging while he figured out what to do with his situation. For the moment he paid his father a healthy sum of his weekly wages which his father took without acknowledgment. It was, after all, only purse money compared to what Nate privately kept in a corner at the bottom of his trunk in his room. It was not that he did not trust banks entirely, for that is where his thousands should have been sleeping at the moment. But he did not want to rouse suspicion and raise curious eyes in his direction. That was not his nature. Who would suspect a well-to-do man living out of a well-worn trunk, working long hard hours on the Seattle docks with the Irish, Germans, Swedes, Italians, Russians.....His own father had laughed in his face that night in the parlor. Little did the elder man realize that the son who stood in plain, everyday clothing, the cloth that was worn by the lower, poorer and deprived portion of society.....little did he know. For a moment Nate allowed a thought to enter his mind. He pictured himself sitting in a plush parlor. Comfortable wealth covered every wall; furnishings to be envied. A beautiful piano against a wall, unplayed; other music pieces upon tables, fulfilling their part as ornamental decorations. A cigar between his fingers; dressed in comfortable evening wear; feet raised upon a maroon velvet stool as he idled the evening away over the Seattle Times, the Post Intellencer, or the Seattle Star.

The environment his thoughts conjured up was as cold and unpleasant as the air which seeped through his coat and clothing. Besides, he disliked cigars. Nate wanted nothing of the sort and let the image of such a life style turn to dust which blew away from his memory and down the dirt street. He approached the corner of 6th Avenue West and West Highland Drive and turned his body right onto Highland Drive. His sole ambition was to make it to the big house which usually was well lit from the side walk. Passing one of the new and few electric lamps on the corner, his father's two story residence with its high peaked roof was just five houses down. Nate noticed that the spindly young maple tree trunks were slimmer in circumference than those of the white lamp posts which greeted him on his left. On his right were newer homes of Seattle; tall and elegant, window panes wherever possible. Wrought iron fences and gates which began at the lamp post ended far from view to the east.

In windows of homes which belonged to families who wished avoidance with the Miller family, the cheery color of yellow spilled forth onto obscure lawns, beckoning a man towards his kingdom-like home, welcoming him into the arms of a loving and adoring wife. Nate surveyed each window and was acutely aware of what he did not possess. Eleanor was not his wife; only his father's house-keeper and cook. She was not in the position to greet him at the door with loving arms followed by warm and tender lips. It was his good fortune though, as a single man, to know that she did not dismiss him from the busy kitchen each night as he was testing the waters of understanding. It was he who greeted her; whose hair fell about her pretty face, little pieces escaping the combs which he proudly purchased for her. On too many occasions he had to restrain himself from wanting to brush her dark hair back from her tired face as she stood close to the warm range preparing dinner. If he were to touch her hair, to touch her weary face, to touch her lips which occasion-ally whispers his name; for a woman does not know, and could not know unless by intuition or revelation, how her sweet voice magi-cally transforms a man's name into something grand. This, to any man, especially one who breathes and hopes in prayer that friend-ship, may one day bring life companionship. He saw her face before him, but it was not veiled in white lace.

Eleanor had grown wearier and wearier. Dark circles under her eyes did not show promise of leaving, and the lips which sang of songs so freely when he first met her, moved less and less frequently now. Nate was glad that Eleanor did not refuse his help after supper with washing and drying the dishes. His actions though did not go unnoticed, for it was unheard of for a member of the superior sex to toil in woman's work.

After bringing her home every evening, he spends his time in the parlor, near the fire, catching up on news in the paper while drinking a cup of coffee until he retires to his room. On one of the nights when Stuart was not interested in a game of billiard, he sat in the parlor with his eyes on Nate's back, filling the air with the stench of cigar; overpowering the parlor with his imported cologne; filling his glass with strong drink. It was during his second or third glass that Stuart usually brought himself to the fireplace. His goal was to intimidate his younger brother; his back to the flames, towering over the brother who was still a stranger to him; silently loathing Nate as he drank the whiskey as if it were water. Nate sipped his coffee and turned the pages of the newspaper. Conversations, as from the night before were usually short and to the point.

Stuart knew that his senses were misleading him; though by scheme or ill design he felt compensated for what was not born in him. The effect of Stuart's vice of liquor employed itself as masculine courage while smoothness tingled throughout his body. Was he not the power behind the throne? Did he not carry the king's whip? Or, was he merely the joker, the agent for his father's profitable yet unpopular business dealings? He braced a hand upon the mantel and took another drink.

"Well, if you aren't the little masterpiece."

Nate heard the slurred words but continued reading.

"Just what do you and that little piece of pie do in the kitchen each night?" Stuart inquired.

Nate lifted his eyes and looked at his drunk brother for a brief moment, then lowered them.

"I asked you a question…."

Nate acknowledged Stuart without lifting his eyes, "Her name is Eleanor. Kindly address her by no other name."

A fit of crowing came from the older brother. "My, my, my! Is there a tone of protectiveness in my brother's voice? How has this come about?"

A wearisome sigh came from the provoked young man.

"I do not think that my personal affairs need to concern you." Nate turned a page but before he could stop his brother, Stuart ripped the evening paper from his hands and threw it into the fire. The flames quickly caught the paper and made it swell, consuming it; thus intensifying Stuart's seething aggression towards his tame and subdued brother.

Nate slowly began to rise from his chair, but a pair of hands were placed on his shoulders and pushed him back down, and kept him down.

"I'll tell you what, brother dear," Stuart began, breathing a mixture of whiskey and the remains of dinner onto Nate. His intoxicated voice was on the rise; more than a touch of stirred amusement thrown in. "I'll make you a trade……my little pieces of desert for that one of yours. I'll give you the names of the girls…..so many, but not enough time to enjoy all those little tarts! Imagine, ol' boy, a 500 room brothel, right here in this city."

Nate tried to remove himself from the chair, but his brother's hands were still upon him. If he wanted to, he could in a flash, have his whiskey soaked brother smashed and pinned against a wall. But at the moment he was trying to stay calm and let things pass without incident. He did not want to fight his brother who was not himself due to hard drinking. It ultimately would serve no purpose other than to cause injury, which Nate wished to avoid, if possible.

"Perhaps another time," Nate suggested.

Stuart removed his hands from his shoulders. "I see…..well you just let me know when you want to toss off the 'ol suspensory belt!"

Nate could feel his face growing warm and glanced down.

"So, it's a deal…..you just stay in the parlor tomorrow night…… and I'll find out for myself what kind of desert you have."

Nate charged at Stuart, and laying hold of his suit, slammed him against the wall. Nate's eyes bore into Stuart's.

"Don't you even think about harming that young lady," Nate warned.

"Why bro'— I do enjoy watching you squirm," Stuart heckled nervously, then he grinned a hideous grin. "Perhaps, I might come home for 'lunch' sometime. What would you say to 'that'—dear brother?"

Stuart's laughing eyes bore into his brother's as they watched Nate come very close. The two men breathed upon the other, waiting for the other to strike the first blow.

Nate broke the silence, speaking carefully, leaving not a trace of doubt, his meaning would not be squandered on speculation. "If you hurt Miss Eleanor in any way….I'll kill you myself."

Stuart moved his tongue about within his mouth, letting the disgusting air hit the flesh of his brother. Nate let go of the drunk, but not before discarding him with physical force. At that, Stuart removed himself from the parlor saying, "You are such a bore, dear brother."

Nate began to turn toward the house and put a hand at the iron gate. His eyes had been following the walk as he was thinking of Eleanor's welfare within his father's house. But something in his immediate area was amiss and his eyes lifted on their own curious intuition of what was not in its usual order. The cold gate stood between Nate and a dark house. For a moment he stood stock-still, digesting all the dark windows, except one. In a swift fluid motion, moved by panic alone, his body went forward, flinging the gate open, bounding up the stairs to the porch where he opened the door with caution. His heart which would not still itself, was like him, afraid of the unfamiliar darkness and what it could mean for the occupant who worked there. The door was softly shut behind him, and from where he stood in the foyer, the only source of light came from the parlor, soft, though leery. The rest of the house lay in a sea of blackness.

His feet crept just on the boundary of the parlor and his eyes fell on a figure sitting in front of the firelight. She was sitting but not moving. The light moved across her frozen face, her eyes not moving except for an occasional blink.

Nate took in the daunting picture in his heart and was crushed by the confusion of it all. Eleanor began to close a thin book and held it in her lap for a moment, then put her hands on the chair's arms and rose, all the while starring into the fire. Her mouth opened but slightly and the word "Richard," was barely audible from where Nate waited. Numbly the figure turned away from the chair and toward his direction, walking with ghost-like personality. Her eyes were downcast on the floral wool carpet, each foot making its course over roses and ribbons of green. Her lips again mentioned the name "Richard." Her voice was of a person in the depth of slumber, unaware that speech was taking place.

Nate could only wait until she came close, until something in her would hopefully open the door of realization. Her eyes lifted slowly as they made their way from his shoes, up his body and to his face. Ever so gradually the composition of her face and her body crumbled.

As he carried Eleanor to the couch, he allowed his lips to kiss her forehead and cheeks, murmuring, "Oh, my poor, dearest love, what has happened? What has happened?"

He was beside her, stroking her hair, pressing the cold washcloth to her forehead, rubbing her limp hands. Eleanor did not come to as soon as he thought she should have. The lights in the parlor were not bothered for Nate did not know what to expect upon the opening of her eyes, but thought it best to leave the room as it were. And in the dim room, tears ran down the sides of her face and she began to sob. Nate scooped her shoulders up and pressed her to him. She clung to him like a scared and frightened child, letting her tears run from her haggard looking body. He allowed his hand to soothe her back, patting it ever so gently.

After she decided that her body was too exhausted to cry further, she ceased, but continued to lay her head on his shoulder. It was then that she revealed the reason for her grief.

"My brother has tuberculosis." She paused. "He is dying."

Nate Miller cursed himself for not really knowing the young woman whom he cared for and secretly professed his love to. He did not know her or her family. That would change. But at the moment, Nate thought it best if he returned her home to her family. He suggested on the way that she ought to take a few days off. His father and brothers would be fine, he promised.

Eleanor climbed the front steps of her house and closed the door without looking back. He sat in the motorcar, his flesh chilled, his mind worried, his heart overflowing in loving rapture of a young woman. But within the thin walls of the house before him, life for one family would change, and no amount of his money could alter its course. There was nothing for Nate to do except return to his father's house, where upon his arrival he walked the hill bound neighborhoods of Seattle until his face was beyond numb.

December 10, 1909
Friday

Needless to say, my early arrival home yesterday brought about a few questions from Mama. I pleaded ill which was not an entire lie in itself. I was ill. Emotionally drained. Physically exhausted. After checking on Richard, who, by the way was not in bed but in the basement with Papa, I took to my bed and slept till Mama woke us girls up this morning. Alice said that she has never seen a person sleep as soundly as I do.

Upon awakening, I had nearly forgotten what the previous day had done to me. Perhaps it was a badly needed long sleep combined with the dawning of another day.....Perhaps the icicle like air pressing against my head distracted thoughts and feelings from surfacing while the frozen world was coal black outside our bedroom windows. Alice wondered out loud if it were possible to suffer frostbite in one's own home. All cheerfulness was stolen from us girls as we wrapped our blankets about our necks as we listened to Mama's voice calling from the stairwell. "Eleanor! Marie! Alice! John! Everyone get up and dress quickly! Papa's in the basement starting the fire."

I reluctantly gathered my cold garments in front of me. "Why," I bitterly wished to know, "must we take off our warm nightgowns and expose warm sleepy flesh to this!" my teeth chattered, "—and then place frozen clothing back on our protesting bodies? Why?" I cried.

"Hush, Eleanor....you're making it worse!" Marie whined pathetically.

Marie, Alice and I continued to complain of the bitter temperature in our room—we could see our breath, which was not amusing. Our pleading for the warmth of summer was futile as we huddled in misery—victims of winter we were. Even my goose-bumps protested as they pinched my skin. I wish we could have dressed in front of the range, but if Papa, Richard or John would have caught us in our undergarments, I'm not sure who would have been embarrassed the most.

Richard was standing with his back to the stove when I came down the stairs. "Good morning!" he said, glancing up at me while his fingers inserted buttons into their proper holes of his long sleeve shirt. Mama was setting bowls and spoons on the table and had her back to us for a moment or two. I kissed my brother on the cheek, ignoring the roughness of his unshaven skin. His eyes met mine, and they, in their own tender, secret and magical way, told me that he still adores me.

Mama went around the table so she faced her stove, clearing her voice several times. As she did so Richard's eyes slipped from mine and to the floor.

"Eleanor," Mama began, "is the water boiling yet?"

I looked at the pot on one of the six round iron lids and saw that the water was ready. "Would you like me to stir in the cereal?" I asked.

There was a pause before her answer. "No....I can manage. Why don't you gather up your outerwear and put them by the front door."

120

I looked at Mama for a moment as she was placing a bowl of brown sugar and a glass pitcher of milk on the table. Richard was pouring himself a cup of coffee and did not respond to my 'under the eyelash glance.'

"Right now….before breakfast?" I asked hesitantly.

Her request was unusual and therefore I felt the need to inquire why my morning routine was being altered. Mama and Richard passed each other as they traded places in the kitchen. My brother sat down at the table and cautiously eyed Mama and I. Mama found the box of cereal in the cupboard and sprinkled the oats in the rolling hot water. She lifted the top to the salt box which hung to the right of the stove. Sprinkling the salt into the pot she replied, "Make good use of your time, Eleanor."

I half whispered, "Yes, Mama," and glanced at my brother who shrugged his shoulders again. I turned and took leave of the kitchen, feeling somewhat confused over the meaning of her statement. As I placed my coat, gloves and fascinator on the arm of the couch, it dawned on my senses that my poor Mama was just as, if not more emotionally consumed by Richard's health than I. After all, she is his devoted mother. I, am just his loving sister.

I'm at the Miller's now, in the parlor sitting quite near the fireplace which is ablaze in glorious warmth. Richard almost had to push me out of our house and into the cruel air which hit my body with astonishing painful force.

John had whistled a short time ago while reading the thermometer. "It's going down! Down, down to 20!"

Mama reminded everyone to put "everything" on so the elements would not get the better of us. I wish I could tell Mama that "everything" I own was not sufficient from keeping unpleasant thoughts about the weather out of my head while I tried to hurry up the hill as quickly as possible without breaking my walk.

I must close my little book and get on with my usual duties.

I shall fill the hours of the day with serious prayer and keep my hands very busy.

Good-day
Eleanor

December 27, 1909
Monday

Can you believe it? It snowed! A white Christmas! Everything is so beautiful.

It has been a while since I wrote last.

Our tree is nice this year. Short white candles were wired onto the ends of branches, and after we sang Silent Night in German they were blown out. Mama and I made a few more German star ornaments to hang on our tree since the original ones she made for her and Papa's first Christmas were getting a little worn. I gave Nate a box of twelve German stars which I left on his dresser next to the picture of his mother.

Did you know that the Miller's don't even believe in putting up a tree for Christmas? I suppose a family is not obligated to have one in their home, but it seems so empty without green branches dripping with ornaments and the lovely whiff of evergreen scent filling one's senses.

My dear friend Ernestine McAfee gave me a discount on the hats I purchased as gifts for everyone in our family. I know that Mama has not bought herself a new hat in a long time, and since Alice and Marie are in school and have no income to speak of, I was proud to be able to hand large hat boxes to Mama, Alice and Marie, and smaller ones to Papa, Richard, and John.

Mama had us girls write our initials next to drawings of ladies in white lawn waists in the Sears, Roebuck & Co. catalogue. Our gift from Mama was not a surprise as to 'what,' but as to 'which one.' It is hard to imagine a catalogue selling such pretty, dainty, embroidered, lacy long sleeve shirts for 39 cents up to 98 cents each. I wonder if the lovely shirt that I will save for Sunday best was sewn by one of the immigrant workers in the Triangle Shop back east. Alice's friend, Frances Harper, says that hundreds of woman who (are ready to strike) work 12 to 14 hours a day in hot, airless rooms. The poor workers cannot talk to each other, breaks and taking a few sips of warm water is frowned upon, and they are timed while relieving themselves. If they are ill and find the need to get well at home, they probably will find themselves out of a job when they return. Hundreds of suffering workers are treated like prisoners because the owners have the windows shut and doors bolted. Frances says that the girls are only paid 10 cents a shirt. A sign is posted on Saturday that says, "If you don't work on Sunday, don't bother showing up

Monday." I cannot imagine working in those conditions, but men, women and children do every day. Working for the Miller's is not bad at all when I think how my working conditions could be.

Oh, do you know what dear Papa gave the family for Christmas? A Brownie camera! I have seen them advertised in the big wish book but never imagined that Papa would buy one. Yesterday, I wanted to take a picture of Richard. In the morning while he was still in bed I asked him if I might take his photo. He had his pillows propped up and had one arm behind his head. I asked if he could smile just a little, but Richard said that he did not feel like smiling. Richard said that he had been awake for a long time before I came in. He had been lying in bed with many thoughts going through his mind. My brother did not want to lie to me. He wanted the photo to show that he was not happy with the knowledge that a disease was in his lungs. I said that he didn't have to smile if he did not want to. I just wanted a photo of my dear brother. After we send the camera in some day, I will put Richard's photo in my journal.

Goodnight,
Eleanor

December 31, 1909
New Year's Eve
Friday

It is strange to think that this is the last of 1909— that it shall be no more after the hands of the clock pass midnight. Although I feel the need to put my finger into time's way, I can almost feel the soft metal push against my flesh, protesting for what cannot possibly happen. Tomorrow will be January 1, 1910. I wonder what the New Year will hold in store for our family.

Forgive me if do not write much to-night. I am so very tired that I feel ill, almost at the point of nauseousness. It has come upon me quite by surprise, for although I was tired after leaving the Miller's, I can't say I was more tired than any other Friday night. Unless, during this past week which I have been "cursed," I have been left physically drained in a matter of speaking. This is a subject which is not "openly" mentioned in our household. As a contributing wage-earner to this family, I have taken on the responsibility of ordering safety belts and sanitary napkins for us four females. I am looking forward to the day when Alice finds employment so the burden will be lifted from Papa and myself.

Alice says that she would dearly love to work at the new Seattle Public Library between 4th and 5th Avenues, and Spring and Madison Streets. I remember the announcements in the papers saying that steel millionaire Andrew Carnegie was to fund the classical Beaux Arts building. Since its opening on December 19, 1906, I wish I might have more opportunities to visit and browse the thousands of books in its collection. Maybe, during the New Year, Alice and I will have to take a street car and travel some 26 blocks south, just five steep blocks uphill from the piers on Elliott Bay.

I have written too much.

> Good Night and Happy New Year!
> Eleanor

January 2, 1910
Sunday

It was a very cold ride to church this morning as the temperatures lately have been below 20 and the paper reports that Lake Union is freezing over. It won't be thick enough for skating on for a few weeks.

Everyone wore their new hats, except dear Richard. He stayed home again. I miss him dreadfully during church. He has always been beside me and it feels as if part of me is missing. My mental being cannot and does not wish to concentrate on the Latin words that fall from the lips of men, women and children. When dear Richard sat next to me I was happy and content with life. Too often, I'm afraid, we would smile at each other, knowing the other's thoughts, especially when a sermon was beyond dry, and in the worst way, we wished to be back home. It is difficult leaving dear Richard home. He looks well but is not well internally.

Upon returning home I found Richard at the piano, softly pushing keys down without making any musical sense. I squeezed in beside him and told him that after I changed my clothes, I would play for him. Although my fingers have not practiced since autumn, Richard did not seem to mind my rusty attempt at bringing the keys back to life. He rested on the couch, closing his eyes though listening.

Mama took up her crocheting and sat near the fireplace. She

was quiet— her tired fingers working steadily making little doll dresses that she will sell at The Bon Marche'. Mama used to play the piano when she was young, but I have not heard her play for years. Occasionally she will take up her mandolin and entertain us. She waits for us to ask her about her youth when she was in a girl's musical group. Each played a mandolin—I remember the picture of Mama—before she married Papa. She was young and so pretty. I wonder if she would mind if I kept it in this journal for safe keeping. Mama, and Papa for that matter, does not enlighten us with details of their childhood or courting days unless we ask. It is as though such information being in the past, should stay in the past, or is deemed unimportant. I cannot imagine Papa volunteering such information about his life before leaving Vienna. I would love to know how he spent his youth in a country that I have only seen on maps. At times, I feel as if our Papa is a stranger—for he is a quiet, private man. I know he loves us and takes great pride that he is an American, and that his children are growing up in a prosperous country.

I truly wish that Mama could have recorded her life. Oh, how special her words would have been to me. For all the events of one's life which hasn't been told with ink and paper—what a waste!

Tomorrow is Marie's birthday. I think I'll make her a card and add a poem or two.

Good-day Eleanor

January 4, 1910
Tuesday

What an unsettling day this has been! Where do I begin?

I have been quiet upset with Stuart as of late. For the past week I have had to change his bed linen every day. Does he not understand what a burden this is upon me? It is hard to explain without knowing its origin, but every morning when I enter his room there is a strange odor that causes me to open the window immediately. Upon its discovery the first time, I was making up the bed but hesitated at the sight of a large wet stain on the linen. It does not have the odor that urine gives off, but whatever it is, it does have a lingering, foul smell. I cannot ask Mama what it might be, so I'll have to settle not knowing what may take place in a man's chambers, in the privacy of his own room.

Now, let me try to explain the events of this morning: Around 10 or 10:30 there was a banging on the front door which I could plainly hear from the kitchen where I was doing the wash. After inquiring, "Who is it?" the stranger on the other side said that he had Mr. Miller with him and to open the door immediately. It did not occur to me or to my imagination at that moment that poor Nate was the "Mr. Miller" waiting on the porch. For as soon as I swung the door open, a stranger was holding onto the bent over figure of Nate who was in terrible pain.

"Miss! Which way to his room?" asked the stranger who was of decent height and build. I directed him towards the staircase and he eyed it unpleasantly. I thought for a moment the roughish man would spit out a profanity or two—and he probably would have if I hadn't been in the same room. "Miss, I'll be need'n your help, if you don't mind."

By the time we reached the top of the stairs, I learned that his name was Mr. Droker, married, father of three young children, with the family living in the Belltown area. I asked Mr. Droker if he had to take the trolley far to get to his place of employment. He glanced at me for a moment and then turned his eyes on the rich wood that led us up and up, stair by stair which caused dear Nate great agony. His eyes settled on the fine floral print on the walls and he whispered, "The Mrs. will have papered walls someday—I'll see to that….."

I was ashamed to have asked such a question and wished I could have taken it back. It was apparent that Mr. Droker lives above the hill from Pier 66, one of the seventeen wharves which are firmly planted along the shoreline of Elliot Bay. I can only hope that his family does not live within the shacks that are perched on the shore below Belltown. Papa says that poor immigrants and Indians live there in poverty conditions among the rats and fleas. I have never been close enough to see if what Papa says is really so. I'm not doubting his word—it's just….well, if it is so, it is hard to mentally picture one of God's creatures living in anything less than our dear house. Perhaps if I stay on the hill, peering down on the towering masts of ships that huddle against long buildings, my knowledge will stay as is. At present, I know there are yacht clubs, canneries, coal bunkers, barrel factories, furniture mills, grain mills, fishing piers, and oil depots on the docks. It was only five years ago that a crowd of thousands, prospectors and spectators alike swarmed Pier 57 during the Alaskan gold rush, and in 1903 President Theodore Roosevelt sailed into Seattle and disembarked at Pier 56. I wonder how many people just do not know, or know and do not care, turning a blind eye to poverty conditions in our own city. I pray that Mr. Droker who was so good in returning Nate home does not belong to the lower-class citizens.

I have derailed myself from the happenings of the morning......

With Mr. Droker's assistance, we sat Nate on his bed and try as he might to not show his pain, I know he could not help himself. Nate asked his working companion if he would be so good as to step into the hallway for a moment, but not to leave. Nate then asked me to open the top drawer of his dresser where I would find a roll of greenbacks. I was instructed to take out five Lincoln's, give them to Nate, and then invite Mr. Droker back in the room. Having done so, I quietly retreated near the door but did not leave, for my care-taking duties had only begun. Even as dear Nate laid withering in pain, he was very gracious in his manner and speech to Mr. Droker. Mr. Droker wished him a speedy recovery, and when the time felt right, one man put forth an open hand as the other wrapped his two hands around the one. What should have been a simple handshake and farewell almost brought tears to my eyes. It was in quiet revelation that made one man's face move as if his flesh worked independent against his will. At a glance Mr. Droker saw that between flesh, there was at least a fort-night, to a month's wages. I will never forget the look on his face. "I can't....."

"Daniel, no arguing," Nate said firmly. "It will get you no-where."

"You are too kind."

"Same for you, my friend. Thank you for bringing me here."

Mr. Droker smiled and nodded.

"If upon your return to the wharf.....if anyone should give you trouble for not being there," Nate paused and looked his friend square in the eye, "you come back here and see me. Promise?"

Mr. Droker smiled and nodded again, this time slowly backing up while offering Nate one last, "Speedy recovery."

I showed him to the front door where Mr. Droker paused and glanced up the staircase. "Never before have I known such a man. Gunna miss him. Time he gets back anotha' fella will have his spot." Mr. Droker looked down at me. "You take real good care of him." Mr. Droker nodded to me and then I let him out of the house and into the freezing air.

Before I went back upstairs, I made a phone call to our family doctor. I rang for LAkeview 4-5662 and asked for Dr. George Henry. After saying hello, he assumed that Richard needed to be seen. When

I asked him if he could come to the Miller's residence, he quickly apologized in saying that he was indisposed with other matters. I immediately begged that if he could find just a few moments to visit one of my employer's son's who just hurt his back this morning, having slipped on some icy boards at the pier while carrying a heavy sack of lime......suddenly I was interrupted.

"Miss Eleanor, excuse me for asking, but which son are you referring to?"

"Mr. Nate Miller, Sir."

On the other end there was a dead like silence, followed by faint whispering which I could not decipher.

"Dr. Henry.....are you there?"

"Yes, I'm sorry. I'll be there directly."

"Do you need the Miller's house number?" I asked.

"That won't be necessary. Thank you."

I quickly went to Nate's room and informed him that Dr. Henry was on the way. At first I thought he was going to object, but even if he tried to put up a fuss it wouldn't have profited him at all. Within ten minutes after hanging up the telephone I heard knocking on the front door. While making his way up the stairs, Dr. Henry quickly took in his surroundings and half-whispered, "Never thought I'd see the day when I put a foot in this house....."

I must add, at this point, that in all the years since I've known Dr. Henry, which is quite a few since he delivered all five of us, there was something different about him even before he crossed the threshold to Nate's room. I do not know if Nate was attuned to the charge in the air, but for most men, I dare say, are unequipped with intuitive sensors. I cannot say what the uneasiness could be attributed to, for even I could not put my finger on the cause. I carefully watched Dr. Henry examine Nate. There was a twinkle in his eyes that I have never seen before to-day. And the extraordinary attention towards Nate's well being almost baffled Nate himself as he turned his eyes to me several times, giving me a wary grin.

I shouldn't have been too surprised when Dr. Henry told Nate that he pulled some muscles in his back, and should not engage in any strenuous activities for a fort-night— possibly up to a month. A bottle of strong pain pills were placed in my hand along with some verbal instructions that I was to follow—being that I was to be Nate's care-giver. Dr. Henry bade his patient good-day, and said that he would be back sometime tomorrow. Once again, I let another man out of the Miller house and into the frigid air.

Upon re-entering Nate's room, we eyed each other with half-uncertainty, for Nate was still clothed and both of us knew that he could not retire for the day in his work attire. And still worse, both of us knew that Nate alone was in no position to discard most of his clothes.

"I'm dreadfully sorry to put you in this uncomfortable position, Miss Eleanor, but I don't think it can be helped."

"It is kind of you, Mr. Miller, to want to protect my virtues from the sight of your physique, but I'm afraid that the sight of your chest will not shock me. I have two brothers who need an occasional mustard plaster, and then there was your brother...."For some reason I stopped short—perhaps it was the look on Nate's face at the word, 'brother.'

"My brother? Which one?"

"Todd."

"What happened to Todd?"

"A few months ago he had a bad cold in his chest." I paused, remembering exactly how his chest looked like, and remembering how hard I tried to not to care—for I was curious, as any young female would be. Richard has laughed at me many times on account that I am practically see-through, and that I fail miserably at any attempts of bending the truth.

"I see..."

I'm sure by then that Mr. Nate Miller did see, for my face was warm from embarrassment. Very carefully I sat him up in bed and watched him grit his teeth, followed by his legs over the edge of the bed, followed by more attempts to conceal his agony. I stood close to him as I slowly took off his shirts, and finally the top of his union suit was off. I am most thankful for the moments that followed, for Nate was preoccupied with his pain and exhaustion and did not notice the shock upon my face. If God had in mind a physique that was covered with taught hills and valleys; a wide chest void of hair; limbs which house thick, round muscles and— I will die if Alice or Marie comes in our room for my face is aglow once more. In summary, Mr. Nate Miller's upper physique, shall we say— resembles a large wash board.

For a brief moment Nate was able to stand while I threw back the covers so he could place himself back in bed. Again, Nate apologized for being the cause of my discomfort, for we both knew that only nurses and wives were permitted to see as much as I have seen.

While the pain pills quickly took affect, Nate asked if I could

sit with him, next to his bed, softly humming or singing until he
fell asleep. And so I sat, singing and humming to one of God's most
splendid creatures, until gradually, his eyes which had been fixed
upon mine, closed.

My heart is warm, for the word "palpitation" has a new meaning
when I think of Mr. Nate Miller.

Goodnight,
Eleanor

January 7, 1910
Friday

Oh, blessed Friday! My body is worn and tired as I sit at our
kitchen table.

I said to Papa this morning, "Wouldn't it be fun to skate one
afternoon, and then come home to cups of cocoa in front of our cozy
fireplace?" He replied that if the freezing temperatures continue,
Lake Union should be thick enough for skating very soon.

It has been a wonderful week having Nate in the house, and
although my work load has increased, it is a pleasure to care for
him. He is always patient and kind to me, always thanking me for
the meals, and now and then, he asks if I may stay and talk to him.
He wants to know about my family, wants to know more about
Richard's health, what my interests and hobbies are, and perhaps, is
more interested in my employment at the Insurance Company, and
of course, my position at his father's house.

I was happy to indulge him with answers to his questions, but
concerning my position here, such information was not forthcoming
from my lips and I prayed that Nate would not pursue the topic. He
did not. However, there was no mistake that in his gentle, teasing
voice, there was insinuation that the matter was only temporarily
dismissed.

How was I to tell Nate Miller that I must work for his father?
And now, with dear Richard unable to work, it is up to Papa and I
to support the family. I wish Papa would have gone to someone else
for a loan, then perhaps, we would not be at the mercy of Mr. Miller
Sr. But since Mama and Papa had to give up their grocery store
a few years ago in '07, during the depression, they have not fully
recovered from their loss. Papa said it was due to the market at Pike
Street that drew customers away from his and other nearby stores.

The merchants coming to Pike Street sold their wares for less than store costs. What inflicted the most injury to the merchants were the excessive rents which were being charged by the landlords. Under such conditions, it was difficult for people of slender incomes to make a living. Several good friends of the family could not afford to stay and were driven away from the city.

Since gold was discovered in the Klondike and in Nome, Seattle's population has dramatically increased. Why, just this past year, the state of Washington found 50,000 people wishing to make this state their new home. When a state swells with that many newcomers, a crush for housing and retail shops occurs. The property owner of Papa and Mama's store offered this reason for the over-charge: The law of supply and demand regulates prices and because there is a brisk demand for stores and residences, therefore prices should correspond. Isn't that a bunch of malarkey!? I think Papa would like to get back into the grocery business someday if the conditions improve.

So, how was I to tell Nate that on that August day last summer, his brother Stuart told Papa that if one of us girls did not 'keep house' for them, a foreclosure sign might be placed on a window pane in our dear little house so all passerby's would see our shame. It did not make any difference to Stuart Jr. if I had to leave my position at the Insurance Company. They needed a housekeeper and we weren't in any position to argue.

As it is, Nate and his father are not on the best of terms. A person passing by the dinner table would tell me otherwise, as they could see for themselves, that the men folk engage in lively business conversation while drinking their spirits and eating my fine meals. But that is just what men do, regardless of whether they care for each other or not. Men, being of the animal nature, may growl at each other while chewing their bone. They may hiss or scorn one of their own; be looked down upon, be despised and mocked; sneered at with nose in the air; viewed with disfavor and even pulled to pieces. But instinctively, they have a need to gather together for food and drink.

Although Nate tries to conceal their ill relationship, a woman can almost feel the pulse of blood rushing between each man. I do not want to be the blow on the wedge that splits the wood further apart. If Nate were to leave, on account of me telling him the whole truth, what would I have to look forward to each day, each evening? I cannot begin to imagine my loneliness......

Since Nate's back injury he feels terrible that he cannot empty the ash bins as he usually does, or is unable to help in the kitchen with the dishes. But what really has been troubling that man is that he has not been able to drive me home. On Tuesday, before I left for home, I said 'Goodnight' to Nate, and was hoping to slip out of his room before he realized that I would have to make my journey home on foot. Unfortunately, Mr. Miller was one step ahead of me.

"Eleanor," he said, "have you asked Stuart if he would drive you home to-night?"

"No, I have not— and will not," I answered in a firm but kind voice. For the first time since I have known Nate, I had to tell him directly how I felt, and that I would not drive home with a man under the influence of alcohol. Nate apparently hadn't thought of what consequences could have resulted from his brother's heavy drinking and apologized. I tried to assure him that I would be fine which was difficult, for he was truly concerned for my safety—for it was plainly written on his face.

If there is one thing which pains me more than anything else in the world, is to see a man physically incapable of doing what he wishes. It must be cruel for his mind and body to be in the immobile state which it is in. I will be worried tomorrow and the next day while I am not at the Miller's. What if his family does not care or forgets about him? Surely the Miller's are not that hard-hearted.

Before I took leave from the Miller's house, Nate asked if my family had a telephone, and I nodded my head.

"When you arrive home, please call here and leave word that you made it there safely."

"I will."

"Promise?"

I crossed my fingers several times over my heart saying, "Promise."

John just came up from the basement as he fed the coal furnace. He asked me why the worried look on my face. I was thinking of the drunken slurry voice of Stuart when I called the Miller house this evening. I was thinking how he didn't even recognize my voice. I am thinking, and know, that Nate will never get my message from his drunk brother. Oh, how it hurts me knowing that Nate will be beside himself with worry. Dear Lord, please tell him that I'm fine. Please dear Lord. Thank you.

E—

January 8, 1910
Saturday

My mind could not rest last night, especially after the disturbing call to the Miller's. I paced around the house, uneasy, worrying with my arms crossed about my bosom. My stewing attracted the attention of everyone, which I wasn't aware of until Papa told me to sit down least I wear out a hole in the floor. For a brief moment I joined him on the couch while he finished reading the evening paper, half speaking to himself as he read every column.

"Governor M.E. Hay is in favor of a "day-light saloon law," permitting the sale of liquor only during the hours between sunrise and sunset....he strongly opposes state-wide prohibition, but believes the local option law now in force a good one. Walla Walla refused to abolish saloons."

Mama, who was sitting in her chair, uttered a funny little sound. "I do not think Governor Hay understands the importance of going dry. What difference will it be to a man who intends to get intoxicated, whether it be in the morning so his poor wife finds his face in the plate of food which she has prepared for him?" Mama's voice was rising slightly and Papa lowered his paper just enough to see over it. "Will there be a long train of men lined up outside liquor stores, hoping to spend their hard earned money that should be used to support his family? I can see it now! While the poor wife has gathered her babies at the table, which is void of husband and father, the children grow hungry and wail for a loaf of bread. That money that her husband has exchanged for the drink of the devil will have burned his throat long before he reaches home!" Mama finished in a huff. "There! I gave our silly Governor a piece of my mind!"

"Yes, you did Mama," Papa replied as he raised the paper back up.

"Well done Mama," said I.

"Ladies," Papa began, "you might be interested in hearing this. 'In recognition of the important part played by voting women in the solution of the divorce evil, Governor M.E. Hay has appointed the president of the Washington Equal Suffrage Association, Mrs. Emma Smith Devoe, a delegate to the National Divorce Congress, to Meet in Washington D. C., from January 14th to 17th, in response to call issued by President Taft. This Congress is to suggest remedial legislation for action by the Senate and House, and in view of the fact that divorces have decreased 77 per cent in New Zealand since the women were given the ballot some fifteen years ago, and that Wyoming, which has had equal suffrage longest has the lowest percentage of divorces of any state in the Union, the Suffragists represented to the Governor that the appointment of some woman would be exceedingly fitting.'"

I wrapped my sweater closer to my chest and crossed my arms in attempting to stay warm. "Some woman would be fitting?" I repeated.

"Exceedingly....he did say exceedingly," Papa reminded me.

As Papa continued to read the paper for Mama and I, I rose from the couch and stood by the fire, listening and learning of the necessity to improve sanitary conditions in little towns in our state where infectious diseases have prevailed during the past several months. Doctors have been appointed in the work of getting control of the contagious disease situation and looking into sanitary conditions in these towns. It is chiefly the mining towns that need attention and where conditions will be investigated.

"Papa," asked Mama, "what is happening in the W.C.T.U. Column?"

"Oh, let's just see now...." Papa turned several pages and found the Woman's Christian Temperance Union column. "Whether the fair state of Washington will continue to have the unenviable reputation of being, according to population, one of the greatest saloon states of the Union, depends on how the good, clean, temperance men cast their votes at the coming elections. Neither God nor the devil is voting. The legal voters have the matter entirely in their hands and according to their prayers or wishes, will the question be decided, NO; BUT ACCORDING TO THEIR VOTES. Thinkest thou, oh man, that thou canst put the responsibility on God by asking Him to take away the saloon? God has placed the responsibility on the voter and the voter cannot change His decree nor shift the responsibility on another. VOTE THE SALOON OUT OF EXISTENCE. So shalt thou put away the evil from the midst of thee."

"Amen!" Mama declared.

The clock which rests on the mantel rang out the hour of nine o'clock, and in announcing that I was going to turn in early, I kissed Papa and Mama on the cheek and said, "Good-night."

I found Marie and Alice reading my magazine subscriptions of 'Good Literature; The People's Home Journal; and Woman's World.' Alice has been devouring every magazine before I have the opportunity to do so. She is enchanted and wooed by the handsome male characters in the stories, and by all the advertisements enticing her to summon up the courage to ask, "Oh, sister dear, do you not want souvenir post cards, or a zephyr wool Newport scarf, or, Oh! You would like these...six pieces of popular sheet music. And Marie, here's something for you and your pale cheeks....Beecham's Pills."

"My cheeks are not pale! Are they Eleanor?" Marie asked in a huff of a voice.

I sighed and glanced at Marie. "I don't know," my answer sounded too weary and uncaring. "Must I remind the two of you that there isn't a soul alive who doesn't have pale skin in the month of January."

"Well, see...." Alice held up the page that was causing so much commotion. "Isn't she just lovely?" Alice cooed. "All because she has taken those pills, and now 'roses have been brought back.'"

"Brought back from where?" Marie's face was turned in puzzlement.

"Now listen, Marie," Alice firmly advised. "A woman's physical condition shows quickly in her face. Pale cheeks, colorless lips, biliousness, sick headache and lassitude indicate conditions which should be promptly remedied, and prudence should lead her to strengthen the system at those times when Nature needs assistance. Taken as needed will prove an efficient relief and a reliable remedy. They strengthen the nerves, purify the blood, improve the appetite and exert a very necessary tonic action on the entire system. Their use is never attended by any disagreeable effects. They are a mild medicine, but a peculiarly efficacious one. Full directions accompany each box."

"How thoughtful," I mumbled in slight sarcasm.

Alice cleared her throat and tossed me a look while I continued dressing for bed.

"Beecham's Pills are a boon to women. They relieve headache, depression, nervousness, increase the supply of blood, while to pale cheeks they quickly BRING BACK THE ROSES."

I climbed into my nice squeaky bed and pulled the covers up to my neck. "Oh, brother!"

Marie, I could tell was mulling over the advertisement's promising words in her mind, contrary to what she had believed a few minutes beforehand. She rose from her own squeaky bed and peered into the round mirror which sat on the dressing table, and patting her face in the ill lit room by way of gas light, she began to float my name into the air.

"No, no, no! Now leave me be you two! I am very, very tired. If you are wanting 'things' so badly just for the sake of 'want,' I suggest you begin doing piecework like Mama and 'earn' your own purse money."

"But, Eleanor!" Alice protested.

"Alice, just remember who pays for those subscriptions which is causing such temptations. I can just as easily cancel them at any time...."

As I closed my tired eyes and melted my body into the soft mattress, I heard no more from Alice or Marie.

Goodnight,
Eleanor

A Sunday to Remember

In the humble two-story house down the hill, a certain young maiden was as restless as a winter wren. She paced before the fire with her arms crossed in front of her, fingers tapping on her sides which felt the whale bone ribs in her corset. Eleanor stopped in front of the flames and looked down, placing one hand against the mantle for support, the other taking refuge upon her hip.

Her family having fulfilled their Sunday worship obligation a few hours earlier, had put dinner behind them, and with the kitchen in tidy order, everyone was settled in the living room engaged in quiet activities. Her Papa and two brothers gathered on the sofa with their backs facing the cold window, passing sections of the paper to one another. From time to time they would glance at Eleanor, then turn to each other with questioning eyebrows.

Her sisters, Marie and Alice, found that their concentration was not devoted to the writing of letters to their Uncle John and Uncle Joseph back east. In part, their sole ambition was to finish the letters and then in the privacy of their room, continue reading one of Eleanor's magazines. Fortunately, they could read in peace for it was a rare occasion that their Mama intruded in the girls room. Although their Mama did not disapprove of such reading, for she herself found valuable hints for the housewife, she felt that romance stories should wait till Monday. She gently reminded her children, that the Lord's Day should be set aside for memorizing Bible verses, corresponding with distant relatives, keeping thy hands busy with a crochet needle, or practicing the piano. But Alice and Marie's thoughts were interrupted by the figure pacing before them. Their glances of slight frustration and moderate curiosity were tossed about the room, for their older sister had given the family only the necessary details of one ailing Mr. Miller on top the hill. From what they understood, which was a healthy assumption, due to their lack of understanding of the Miller men, Mr. Nate Miller at present was being taken cared for. Or, so they assumed.

From her favorite chair, Mama was holding a pillowcase in one hand and needle and colored thread in the other. Her fingers were scattering handsome embroidered forget-me-nots, bowknots and ribbons onto the linen for either herself or for one of her daughters. This decision was not important at the moment, for her thoughts lay in other matters. The performance of her daughter's behavior did not correspond with what she had been told of the Mr. Miller situation. As the mother of three girls, she did not interfere in their private affairs, but on the other hand, did not pretend to be blind of what went on under her roof. There was a veil of unspoken trust between mother and daughters, and in the absence of dreaded 'talks,' she hoped that her daughters were naturally following paths of Christian purity and wholesome ways when not under her watch.

There was no doubt that Mama took great pride in the fact that her three daughters had matured into lovely young women; kind hearted, good natured, a joy to their parents and to society. To turn out a proper female was the ardent prayers and wishes of every mother, for it was a direct reflection upon herself.

Mama was making a bowknot at the moment, but try as she might to keep her glances few in fear that the family would pick-up that something was stirring, she herself felt that Eleanor was troubled about an unspoken matter.

Perhaps it was time to sit down with her daughter, and calmly go about the unsavory task of dispensing words of caution to Eleanor who was of marriageable age. There was a delicate time in which a mother should educate her offspring of how things "are" with the opposite sex. But to enlighten one's mind too early would either cause alarm in the innocent, naive female mind, or worse yet, send imaginations seeking out to discover and build opinions from their own findings.

Due to the fact that Eleanor never had a young man whom she kept company with, such talks were kept tucked away on the shelf. But what of this young man who resided up the hill from them? The one who brings Eleanor home every evening? What did they know of him? What was his character, and could he be the cause for the worn-out floor? Their knowledge went to the extent of what Alice told them during the last night of the Exposition, and, from what Eleanor thought she should share, which was, "Mr. Nate Miller is unlike the rest of his family. He seems to be genuinely kind and sincere, and even asks how Richard's health is, and in general how everyone else is."

Mama and Papa could not whole-heartedly disapprove of a young man who brings their daughter home every evening. From behind curtains they see Eleanor wait as Mr. Nate Miller comes around to the passenger door, opens it and offers his hand to her. Their eldest daughter did speak truthfully in saying that this "Miller" departed sharply in distinction from the other three. He did not wear suits of expensive cut; rather, simple trousers, flannel shirts and sensible foot wear covered his physique which of course indicated a hard working man. His character, nature, and position in society was a pleasant contradiction to the Miller's name. Eleanor's parents, especially her Mama, noted the subtle yet unmistaken caring glances that Mr. Nate Miller himself probably tried to hide as the charming and lovely Eleanor took to the front porch steps as she bade him goodbye.

Mama could not bear this any more. She laid aside her needlework and rose from her chair and gently spoke to her daughter, "Eleanor dear, would you mind coming with me?"

The young woman was deep in thought and needed to be spoken to again.

"Eleanor, dear…."

"Did you say something Mama?"

"Yes, please follow me."

The remaining persons in the living room followed them with their eyes and tried to pick up bits and pieces of murmuring from the kitchen, but their Mama's voice was low, and with Richard's coughing, their effort was futile.

Mama gestured for her daughter to have a seat at the kitchen table, and sitting herself down, she folded her hands on the table in front of her.

"Is something wrong, Mama?" Eleanor asked.

"I was hoping you would tell me," Mama inquired with a tilt of her head and a raised eyebrow. She looked directly into her daughter's eyes, raised a few forehead wrinkles and smiled a soft smile.

Eleanor sat twisting her hands in front of her and glanced at the table, then at the print on the walls, and then back to the table. "Well, I'm a bit worried to-day."

"About 'what' my dear?" Mama breathed out a slight sigh while she tried to keep a patient smile on her face.

As Eleanor sat quietly for a moment, her usually smooth forehead developed wrinkles while she contemplated her choice of words which would soothe her Mama's immediate curiosity.

"I'm not sure if Nate— I mean, Mr. Miller," Eleanor corrected herself, "— is properly being cared for to-day."

"And what would give you reason to suspect that my dear?" Mama asked in a light tone of voice.

"Well, you and Papa know how the other Miller's are….." Eleanor looked sheepishly at her mother, "their character is not popular with our family or others for that matter. And....with all due respect to you and Papa... in knowing them a little bit more than you and Papa... which a person would assume I should... since I've been there from September till now....and,.... well...., I just have this feeling Mama that Mr. Miller, being bedridden as he is, in all probability hasn't had nourishment since I left him Friday night."

A sigh of relief escaped from her daughter, both physically and in breath.

"Eleanor, do you really think that is so?" Mama asked, looking at her daughter, still questioning.

Eleanor sat up straight and put her hands in her lap. "Without going into great detail right now, yes, I do think so. If I should arrive tomorrow and find Na— I mean, Mr. Miller in fine spirits from the care that 'someone' has offered him, then I will have wasted my time in worry. But what if I should hear the wailing for help and nourishment as I climb the staircase to check on him? And, if I should find that he has been neglected, how I am to feel in knowing that I could have done something? I don't think I could ever forgive myself!"

The two occupants at the table sat in silence until Mama straightened herself, opened her watch that was pinned just above and to the left of her heart. Mama sighed and smiled, "It's a little past noon already. Sitting here isn't hurrying your feet up the hill."

"Oh, thank you, Mama!" Eleanor quickly rose and hugged her Mama.

"I'll fix your patient a plate of what's left over from dinner. Go and tidy yourself up. Go now."

Her daughter turned to leave. "Eleanor...."

"Yes, Mama?"

"Since it is Sunday....perhaps you may want to put on your Sunday best, again." The suggestion hung in the air and her daughter blushed slightly.

"Yes, Mama."

About half way up the hill, what feelings that noble acts tend to produce in one's heart initially, began to wan as Eleanor grew closer to her destination. With every step self doubt began to swell in her mind and several times she slowed her gait while carrying the warm stew and bread. Mama carefully wrapped the plate with waxpaper and covered it with several kitchen towels. Even though Eleanor wasn't so sure of herself as she turned right onto Highland Drive, she knew that it was her good fortune that her Mama had agreed to this Sunday visit. She opened the iron gate with a gloved hand and passed through it, and now that she was at the front door, her heart began to betray her confidence. What if Todd, or Stuart, or Mr. Miller Sr. came to the door? Of course someone had to since Nate was incapable of the task. Eleanor suddenly found herself blushing which warmed her cold cheeks. In her anxiousness to fulfill her errand, she unwisely failed to go over in her mind what she would say upon her arrival. An involuntary shiver ran over her skin which quickened her thoughts. She made a fist and knocked on the door soundly. After three attempts which did not produce one voice from within, Eleanor unpinned her house key from inside her coat.

Once inside, she carefully removed her fascinator from her head and listened for life within the house. Her ears turned towards the parlor which was empty of persons, but voices drifted out from the heavy folds of maroon curtains which separated the parlor from the billiard room. The lovely parlor which usually was free from the stench of cigar and clear in atmosphere from clouds of impurities, gave indication that the occupants in the other room had been smoking for several hours. Eleanor let out a sigh. She could hear deep laughter, the clicking of balls, a moment of silence—concentration she imagined, followed by more laughter. She recognized Mr. Miller Sr.'s rough and over-bearing tone, and by now, Stuart's loud and boisterous voice which evolved from heavy drinking. As she stood in the foyer, disgusting profanities hit her, revealing what went on under the Miller's roof while she was not there. And to drink on a Sunday! This she would definitely have to keep quiet from Mama. The voice of Todd was absent and she guessed that he was staying at the University over the week-end. His presence was becoming less and less frequent in the house.

She hung up her coat and looked at herself in the coat stand mirror. She smoothed her hair and pinched her checks, and picking up the bundle, she hoped that the stew was at least far from frozen. She tip-toed across the foyer and then made her ascension to the second floor. Eleanor paused at the landing and looked down at her light blue lawn waist which had silk embroidery inserted with Armenian lace in the yoke and panel front, and there were pin tucks on the shoulder and front that added fullness which should not have made Eleanor blush, but did. The collar about her neck was also trimmed in lace, and she knew that her overall appearance was more than satisfactory. But just as quick as she had paid compliment to herself, she quickly scolded herself, for Nate was waiting and the stew was probably unacceptable to his palate by now. A little fist wrapped on his door, and without any hesitation she heard his voice, and with discretion she entered the bedroom and took in the situation which in her heart she had foreseen.

The young man stared at his angel of mercy in utmost disbelief, for God had heard his prayers which began all of Friday evening. But to actually see his dear Eleanor on a Sunday, standing in the middle of his room....and she was holding something in her hands. Suddenly his stomach growled from hunger and his heart which suffered from the loneliness of her, tightened. Her saw her eyes well up with tears and immediately she hastened to his bedside.

"Oh, my dearest," she wailed, "what have they done to you!"

Her lovely warm eyes were now filled with sorrow and tears as they quickly searched his scruffy, unkempt face.

Nate himself felt his own throat tighten and his eyes were also moist. Still, he could not believe that Eleanor was there, sitting next to him on the edge of the bed, folding back the towels from what was resting on her lap. She continued sniffling and Nate wanted to hand her a handkerchief but he did not have one about him.

"Now, now. Everything is all right. You must stop crying. You are here...you are here."

Eleanor revealed a plate full of stew and two healthy slices of buttered bread, and then she started to cry once more.

"Oh, it was nice and hot at the beginning of my journey. I wouldn't feel right serving you a cold meal! If I would have walked faster and not held back. If I hadn't paused at the mirror nor listened to the voices coming from the billiard room." She sniffled and shook her pretty head and put the plate on the corner of the night stand. "Oh, Nate, can you ever forgive me?" she pleaded.

He could not take it any longer, for any sensible young man who is in love cannot resist what was before him without kissing his beloved on her soft warm lips. And so it happened out of crushing passion, for he was a healthy man full of wants and desires, and his lips lingered upon hers. Her eyes were closed when she departed from his touch, but they did not wander far. His dear little angel wanted more and bent down to him, kissing him on the mouth with such urgency that Nate ignored his pain and put his arms about her, pulling her against him. To his delight, he felt her fingers run through his hair, touch his face; her lips wildly kissing his forehead and his cheeks before they found his lips again. Her heavy breathing was intoxicating and excited animal instincts to pursue inclinations which were beyond premature in their young relationship.

Nature was displaying itself, and due to his unexpected guest, the suspensory belt was not in use, therefore, natural, healthy physical appetites could have given way to temptations, morally unsuitable for unmarried individuals. Before his hands cupped her tender face, he wondered if she too shared the intimate nervous connection between her brain and her own secret parts. Was this condition immediately apparent to the other, Nate wondered. When, at last, as he forced restraint upon himself, it was carried out with deep, torturous regret as he summoned everything in his power to do what was right and proper.

Having withdrawn from him, she sat up and gazed upon the figure that had brought her happiness in ways she had never felt before. Now that she was separated from his embrace, the flood of realization of having lost control of some virtue turned her lovely face to scarlet. Her eyes were full of shame and looked away from him. Immediately Nate took hold of her hands.

"My dear Eleanor, please do not look away. Let me look into your beautiful eyes before unjustifiable guilt removes what innocent pleasure and the pangs of love have experienced."

"I cannot..." she whispered.

"Please, Eleanor. It was not wrong, and surely, after all these months, it could not be helped. My dearest, please do not lower your opinion of yourself, for God himself instilled such feelings in the human race for marvelous reasons! Sooner or later, neither man nor woman can shun what generation after generations desire."

Her hands were tugging away and she tried to rise from his bed.

"Please, Nate. I think I shall die if you go on," she half-pleaded.

"Then I will catch you! Oh, my dear, sweet Eleanor, has no other man ever told you how his heart suffers because of you?"

She shook her dark head and truly looked as if she might faint, but he was not going to be apologetic for revealing his containment of feelings for her.

"Then I will! Whether it be the laws of nature or the laws of God, it is easy to love an acquaintance that we feel we can trust perfectly; we know it simply because we feel it, and we feel it simply because the other party be really being so in her heart causes the feeling. God Almighty gave us this instinct among human beings. The feeling never comes and never stays unless the other party is really true at heart. You see Eleanor, God has made it a law of our being that all the best things are desirable things—and having come from Him, it cannot be so wrong. Can it?"

She looked down at her lap where her hands were still in the folds of his. Gradually the natural color in her face returned and her body began to relax. Nate could see by the slight expression upon her face that she was mulling his words over in her mind and abstained from interrupting the process. She drew her spine straight and took in a healthy breath which made the pin tucks on her front add fullness which brought him delight.

Eleanor delicately cleared her throat.

"If that is so, Mr. Miller, place the blame on God for your cold stew," she said gingerly, smiling down at him.

"I dare not! It was He who answered my prayers that brought you here."

In the duration of over three-quarters of an hour, the cold stew was ate, and Eleanor and Nate made merry and lively conversation as a new chapter began in their lives. And on her return home, she did not hurry, for Eleanor sang a song called "Dreaming" in the chilly air which was sung unashamed.

Out in the still sum-mers eve-ning In-to my heart comes a feel-ing
of love that's true and un-dy-ing; For you, sweet-heart, I am sigh-ing. Down by the stream, where we wan-der'd Un-der the pale moon-light beam-ing,
There's where I ling-er and dream of you Dar—ling Dream—ing.

(Chorus) Dream—ing, Dream—ing, you sweet-heart I am dream-ing of days, when you loved me best Dream-ing of hours that have gone to rest, Dream-ing Love's own sweet message I'm bring-ing, Years have not changed the old love still re-mains, Dream-ing.

Years have gone by, still I love you Tho' there's an-oth-er who won you out of my life you have drift-ed; Yet in my heart You still ling-er. Dream-ing or wak-ing I see you, I can for-give, not for-get you. In life and death I'll a—wait your re-turn while I'm Dream—ing.

January 19, 1910
Wednesday

It has been fifteen days since Mr. Droker brought Nate home. I have just finished washing Nate's breakfast dishes, and in a few minutes I will get on with my washing duties. Already I miss having him in the house. Miss bringing him meals, miss seeing the smile on his face when I came through his door. I miss our little talks while he was confined to his bed. Then, as his back muscles improved he spent his days in the parlor near the fire. I had quite a difficult time keeping him from carrying the coal bucket—I absolutely forbade him least he injure himself further.

At the moment Nate is taking a street car down to the pier where he was employed. He told me that if his position has been filled while he was away, he will come back home, warm up, then board another street car which will take him to 4th Avenue South and South Jackson Street. The construction of the new Oregon and Washington Station began only this month, and Nate would like to be part of the crew. The terminal will be shared by the Union Pacific Railroad and the Chicago, Milwaukee, St. Paul and Pacific Railroad. The Oregon and Washington Railroad, a subsidiary of the Union Pacific, gives the station its name. The president of the Union Pacific Railroad Co., E.H. Harriman has touted in saying that it will be the "handsomest on Harriman lines."

If Nate secures a position with the construction crew, I will be very proud in knowing that his own hands helped erect such a grand building that thousands and thousands of passengers will pass through. Oh! If he isn't one to keep secrets. A few days ago I found out that Nate has been in Washington for the past few years while he partook in the construction of the Alaska Yukon Pacific Exposition. I best stop writing and get on with the beastly wash.

I waved good-bye to Nate from the dining room window as I watched him make his way down the sidewalk. I packed him two sliced beef sandwiches and a handful of cookies, just incase, that if he were hired on the spot, he would have nourishment to see him through the day. I do not understand why men must go about such work in the dead of winter. Why can't construction wait till early spring when it would seem a more appropriate time for all the workers? Mankind should take notice of when the robin returns. Sometimes, I should wonder if nature is wiser than man....

It is evening and I am at the kitchen table. I have finished my supper and have washed and put away my dishes.

Nate did not return until past dark, when the setting of the sun occurred nearly at five o'clock. He was so grateful for the meal I had provided for him this afternoon. After Nate had tidied himself up, he went into the parlor to rest and warm himself by the fire. Shortly thereafter, I went in to see if I might bring him a cup of coffee, but he was fast asleep.

My evening will not be complete without mentioning that Mr. Miller and I had a roe at the supper table to-night! I have been wondering for a long time when that man would complain again about "soup nights." Although I must tell of the incident, I would rather not waste my valuable paper and ink on the subject of Mr. Miller Sr.

After I served everyone, I scarcely had put a foot back in the kitchen when Mr. Miller bellowed out, "Housemaid! Get back in here!"

I stood calmly in the dining room, knowing fully well what was on his mind.

Mr. Miller scowled at me, barking out his orders. "We shall have no more of this dreadful substance called 'soup!' From now on I demand a regular meal!"

"Very well, just as soon as you supply me with a modern clothes washer, I shall have extra time and energy to cook you a regular meal."

Needless to say, after Mr. Miller Sr. hit his fist on the table which caused silverware to jump and soup to splatter on the white cloth, Stuart and his father fetched their own coats and took leave of the house. I fear that one day soon, the beautiful etched glass in the door will fall victim to Mr. Miller Sr.'s violent temper.

Poor Nate did not know what to think and stood up in my defense when his father began using profanities to describe his ruined evening. Nate stood beside his chair watching me dab the wet table-cloth with a towel while I grumbled under my breath concerning the stain which was sure to prove permanent.

"Are you leaving, too?" I asked with a little sarcasm in my voice.

"No, Ma'am," Nate replied a little above a whisper.

"What?"

"I said, 'No,' …because I wouldn't dream of leaving…"

I gathered the remains of Mr. Miller Sr. and Stuart's dinner and replied, "Well, I want to. Finish your meal." I paused for a breath. "I would like to go home!"

Cautiously he sat down and quietly ate his soup, and not more then five minutes went by when I noticed the kitchen door slowly open but did not turn my head in Nate's direction. He kindly offered to wash his own bowl and utensils, but I told him that it was not his job to do so. I heard a sigh come from him followed by a long silence which I did not acknowledge. Nate carefully cleared his throat and asked. "Miss Eleanor, might I ease your duties by purchasing a washing device for you?"

"Certainly not!" I huffed.

"Why?"

"Because I work for your father. Not for you!"

Nate let out an exasperated sigh. "Miss Eleanor, do you truly believe that my father will…"

"Will what?"

Nate sighed again.

"Please, Eleanor. Let me buy you whatever you need. Whatever you wish for, I will give it to you. You know I will…" Nate took a step closer and was looking straight at me while I slowly rubbed a bowl in the bubbles. "I would do anything for you."

At that moment I should have turned to him and thanked him with all my heart—instead, the moment past and then it was too late.

"I will go and see if they took the motorcar. I may need to walk you to the trolley line."

Long before he closed the kitchen door a heaviness in my stomach was present. I am dearly sorry that I was so stubborn with him. My pride ruined the evening and spoiled our walk together as Nate escorted me as far as the trolley. The biting cold air did not sweeten our bitter mood either. After seeing that I was safely on board, Nate tipped his hat to me without a smile. Even before the conductor rang the bell—before he moved the trolley forward, all I could see from the window was the back of a dark figure making its way up the lonely hill.

E…

January 29, 1910
Saturday

Upon returning home from work to-day, Marie told me that one of Mama's brothers had a close call with death as he has been suffering from gravel in the bladder. His wife called our house this morning and said that he had a 105 fever before the stone passed. For quite a few months my Uncle has been experimenting with home remedies such as boiling garden-beets and drinking its juice several times a day. This remedy is said to possess the power of dissolving stones in the bladder. Then he tried powdered borax and cream of tartar dissolved in water—another medical treatment that is said to cure cases of gravel in a few days. I believe he has even tried drinking the juice of red onions for a week (no thank you). His wife kept insisting that he see a doctor, but Mama's brother is pretty stubborn and refused any help. He insisted that home remedies do work. Mama is quiet upset right now, knowing that death was lurking around the corner. I'm not sure what it was that worked, but poor Mama does not need extra worry along with dealing with Richard's failing health. He is not doing well. I think Richard has an appointment with Dr. Henry soon. More x-rays I presume.

Nate has been working on the new Oregon and Washington Station since Thursday, the 20th. I have felt so badly for him this past week with morning temperatures as low as 24. Several mornings and nights we have had heavy, damp, bone chilling fog. And then, starting sometime during the night, a wind has been howling off and on, blowing and rocking the bare tree branches to and fro. I do love a good wind storm. Looking out the kitchen window I can see that a pair of sea-gulls have come in-land and are riding on the strong wind, letting it take them where ever it may.

According to astronomer Prof. Charles Buckhalter of Chabot Observatory, the Pacific Coast will be favored by the Halley comet on May 18th, between the hours of 4 and 10 o'clock p.m. The Earth, he says, will then pass through the last of the 20,000,000 of miles of the tail attached to the celestial visitor, and we will witness the most magnificent display of fireworks ever seen by civilized nations.

Good news for suffragists. I shall write this down according to how it was in the paper.

"Endorsement of their campaign for the Constitutional amendment in favor of Equal Suffrage by the state federation of labor meeting at Hoquiam on Wednesday last, coupled with receipt of a check for $500 from Mrs. Carrie Chapman Catt, a former resident of this state and the first newspaper woman on the Pacific Coast, put new heart into the Camp of the Washington Equal Suffrage Association. It is expected that Mrs. Catt, who is heavily interested in Seattle real estate, will come out the latter part of this month to look after her investments. She is the international president of the Suffragists."

Can you imagine $500? That would buy a nice house in Seattle.

All for now. I think I'll go upstairs and visit with Richard awhile.

Good-day, Eleanor

January 31, 1910
Monday

Yesterday our family joined hundreds of people on the shore of Lake Union. The crowd was giddy, and we laughed at the skaters who wobbled and fell down, but since our family does not own skates, we cautiously walked while holding each others hands. Although we were so cold, we did not want to leave, for Lake Union may never freeze again in my life time. And yes, when we arrived back home, after Papa got the fire going again, we all drank warm cocoa while thawing out.

The winds have unfortunately died down from this week-end. There is something about a good wind storm that excites me. Perhaps it is the sound it makes as is pushes boughs and branches back and forth; limbs creaking as they are pushed beyond their natural bending point. They groan as if they are in agony.

As I waited for the street car to pick me up Saturday morning, gusts blew at my long skirt and several men who waited with me were decent gentlemen and kept their eyes from gawking at the outline of my legs. I had to hold onto my hat with both hands. I was not going to loose another hat—especially to Mr. Wind!

Last night Alice was reading in bed at an early hour. Marie and I put on our night gowns and slipped in bed about the same time. I asked Alice if she was almost done so we could blow out the lights, but her response was a few low grunts and noises. While Marie rolled over and nodded off, I laid in bed with thoughts of Nate on my mind. Although we have not spoke about our kiss since that Sunday afternoon after it occurred, it has been weighing heavily in my thoughts.

A few times I almost convinced myself that I was in need of visiting the 'confessional box' to hastily remove such sinful thoughts that have blossomed from the result of my weakness. And then, Nate's words comes back to my memory, "God has made it a law of our being that all the best things are desirable things—and having come from Him, it cannot be so wrong." Countless times each day I repeat those words when I remember my moment of weakness, and then I do not feel so impure.

"Eleanor?" Alice whispered to me in a low voice in the dusk room.

"What?" I asked.

"Is Marie asleep?"

"I don't know," I replied, lifting my head up slightly and turned to Marie who had the back of her head facing us. "I can't tell. Why?"

There was silence for a moment or two, and the heavy breathing from Marie filled the night air. "Good," Alice said. "She's asleep."

"What's going on in that busy head of yours?" I jested.

"Well, Eleanor dear, I've been reading an interesting article in the Ladies' Home Journal that...."

"You have read before I've had a chance to," I couldn't help myself for interrupting.

"May I continue?" Alice asked, twisting her mouth at me.

"By all means," I whispered.

"Well, this article is a condensed version of another article written by Alice Preston entitled, "A Girl's Preparation for Marriage."

"Another 'Alice.' Oh, dear!"

"You ought to be thankful for all the 'Alice's' and 'Miss Harper's' that have enlightened you and I. If it were not for strong, independent female neighbors and writers, you and I would still be embracing the notions of Mama's ways. Think of that, sister dear."

Alice has no idea just how much I have been thinking as of late.

"I really think every girl should read this, and then make up her own mind on whether this 'Rebecca' did an improper thing or not," Alice's voice softly sang in the dim light.

Our bedroom was not so dark that I could not see the sparkle in my sister's eyes as she turned and smiled at me. Alice has a way of stirring curiosity into her words; to make the listener thirst for knowledge that she should consider, if, someday she should be blessed with the estate of matrimony.

"Would you be so kind as to read me the article, if you don't mind..."

"'Tis no trouble at all. A chance to teach my older sister some-thing is a chance I shall not pass up!" Her voice was laced with good-natured smugness.

"Oh, do get on with it!" I quietly laughed.

"All right. Here goes," she cleared her voice.

"If I had my way every girl should be taught from her early teens that some day, in the natural course of events, Love must come to her. She should be taught that it is her fate, and a very glorious fate. On top of this she should be taught that all her days are, consciously or unconsciously, a preparation for it. She should be told that no gift, no happening of youth is comparable to this of the coming of Love; because, when Love comes, it brings in its hands the keys to a Paradise which she could nowise else nor without Love's aid enter.

If we are ignorant how are we to learn? First, by wishing to know things as they are, and by being willing to accept them as they are. First of all, to get a little at this matter of ignorance as to the big bodily truths—the sacred physical facts. I do not wish to go over them, nor to go into any discussion of the truths of sex. I want merely to tell you that I believe they should be known as simply and directly as any of the other big, simple facts of life. A gardener toils in his garden, side by side with the infinite powers of life and growth, and we delight in and wonder at this partnership of the human with the divine. A man like Luther Burbank interests a nation. A man like Thomas Edison works night and day with the big forces of Nature, and we stand aside with respect and admiration as he goes past. And yet the poorest, most humble man and woman who become the father and mother of noble and worthy human beings are dealing with a power greater than any of these; are sharers in a mightier work, are laboring with more marvelous forces. You may read of electrical inventions, of scientific experiments, of marvels of discovery, with wonder; men may lift their hats to Burbank and Edison. I confess that I rise up more awed at the sight of a noble-faced woman great with child.

GIRLS SHOULD KNOW THE BIG, SIMPLE TRUTHS OF LIFE

I am not making a plea for the promiscuous reading of sex literature. I know girls who have, with the best intent, no doubt, gone in headlong for the sex question, have pored over volumes only suited to a well-prepared, cool, science-steadied mind—to the mind of a medical student or physician; volumes which, far from being good for these girls, put an undue weight on the subject, making it a matter of morbid thinking.

Too much analytic sex reading and sex thinking is one of the surest ways of breaking down even the strongest nerves, as any physician will tell you. This is why so many of the French novels dealing morbidly with such questions are considered unwholesome.

IGNORANCE CAUSES LOW STANDARDS

Generally it is ignorance that causes all of the low standards, and almost all of the unloveliness. How, then, shall I say earnestly enough the things to be said, and how shall I make you see what girlhood, the glory of it means?

The other day I heard a hot discussion between a young and modern girl and her middle-aged and old-fashioned aunt. The aunt had discovered that "Joan's" friend "Rebecca"—a girl of "Joan's" own age—saw no harm in allowing a boy to hold her hand—in giving him the engagement's privileges. The aunt not only rose and shone with indignation—she fairly glittered with it. The end was that "Joan" went to her room in disgrace, her cheeks flaming with indignation. By-and-by we talked things over.

"See here," I said, "I don't think your aunt was fair. It is true, I think pretty much as she does. I mean I was always taught from the time I was a little thing to look with dismay on this sort of thing that 'Rebecca' seems to think is all right. I suppose I would as soon have let a boy hold my hand as I would myself have picked up a rattlesnake."

"Now," my sister informed me, "I will disagree right there with Alice Preston. How can holding a boy's hand be as horrible as holding a snake? Snakes are …you know…. scary, slimy, yucky and scary! At least a boy's hand is warm and…." Alice stopped suddenly.

"Alice?" I looked at my sister directly. "How would one know if a boy's hand is warm?…"

"Oh, fudge! I should have kept quiet. Well, only once or twice, at the most have I allowed Mr. Harper to hold my hand. He has been so persistent."

"How do you mean?" I asked, my voice urging her to continue.

"Well, at first I did not see any harm in letting him hold my hand while he has helped me down stairs and such. Even Papa helps Mama navigate her way up and down stairways. But they are married…." Alice's words trailed off as she reasoned with her own thoughts. "Mr.

Harper likes driving Frances and I around town, along the shores of Lake Washington, and here and there. I do think he enjoys showing off his father's motorcar."

"And when do you find time to fit all this socializing into your busy little schedule?"

"On Saturday's while you are busy at your little office."

"Oh," I replied flatly. "Why do you say that Mr. Harper is being persistent, if you don't mind me asking?"

"Well, he tends to walk close to me and tries to hold my hand if my hand isn't already in my coat pocket."

"I see. Do you wish Mr. Harper to not hold your hand? Or do you wish for him to do so?"

The room was very quiet. I was careful to not hurry her while Alice thought this question over.

"To tell you the truth Eleanor, I don't know."

"Well, give this some serious thought. If you do allow Mr. Harper to partake in such privileges again, you may be letting him to think that there is a binding relationship building between the two of you. It is unwise to allow privileges to others than the one you have promised to marry; for it raises an unpleasant crop of consequences which you should bear in mind, dear sister."

"Oh, pooh!" she softly wailed. "Why can't a woman just hold a man's hand so she'll know what it feels like? I don't want to marry a man just so I can find out what his skin feels like! That would be ridiculous in my thinking. Don't you ever want to know certain things too, Eleanor?"

I was looking up at the dark ceiling and was quiet. How was I to answer such a frank question? Oh, if my sister only knew what a man does feel like! Once that knowledge has taken hold, there is no going back to being innocent. Alice was waiting for a reply.

"I believe that God Almighty planted 'curiosity' in our minds for a reason. I believe that natural curiosity never does go away. I like to think of a rose bud, hidden within the green wrapper of nature, then gradually opening, and finally bursting forth in color and perfume. Curiosity, can be viewed as a nasty weed, going to seed, spreading over your garden of thoughts. Or, it can be a beautiful flower, when untouched on its stem, will last for days and days, bringing endless joy to the beholder. But when the stem is cut the petals fade and whither away. Would it not have been better for the rose to have been looked upon by the beholder, than to have fallen into the hands of the beholder because she wanted to know what the petals felt like?"

"But Eleanor, life is too complicated, don't you think? Doesn't it ever just drive you mad?"

"Sometimes....yes, sometimes."

Alice expelled a heavy sigh. "Should I blow out the light?"

"Did Miss Preston's story end at the rattlesnake?"

"Oh, dear me no. Let's see...." 'I think I got it into my head very early from Ruskin and other sources that girls are Queens, and I one in particular over my own domain. I always made it a great point never to fail of queenly dignity—that, at least, was easy. So though I have known friendship with lots of men, also (and I say it with royal gratitude) the love of some, not one of them would have presumed to take the slightest liberty than a courtier would with a Queen.

SHE DID NOT KNOW: NO ONE EVER TOLD HER

The trouble is, most older people lay down the law, and never explain why the law was made—that this sort of familiarity that your aunt condemns so hotly acts directly and subtly on the nerves of the body, renders them morbidly sensitive, rouses the emotions and passions which it is physically harmful to have roused and played upon; that it wakens and stimulates feelings and instincts and desires that should not be wakened. A girl is not told that, by allowing these liberties that she thinks so little and harmless, her nerves and forces and powers are almost certain to become diseased, and her strength undermined. Yet these are simple and direct and serious enough facts, Heaven knows!—that every girl has the right to know."

By the time I got this far "Joan" was no longer indignant, only earnest and interested. "I did not know," she said very simply; "no one ever told me."

A GIRL'S STANDARDS AFFECT HER MAN FRIENDS

A girl I know, who holds the most lovely and womanly and reverential relationship to every man she knows, said to me one day, when I spoke to her in admiration of it: "Oh, you see, it is easy to be the finest kind of friend to them if you just keep in mind their mothers! It seems to me I can always see their mothers back of them, following me with anxious eyes, hoping with such pathetic eagerness that only the best may come to these sons of theirs, only the best women, only the best experiences. And that makes me just as noble as I know how to be, and if I were in doubt as to my place in any man's life I should make myself face squarely this one question: 'If you were his mother would you be glad at every point to have a girl act toward him just as you are acting?'" This is I think, a very pattern and outline of girlish power and justice and reverence and loveliness.

THE CROWN AND CITADEL OF LOVE

None of us can quite define what Love is; but this we know—that its crown and citadel is the human body. To keep healthy hours, to think sound thoughts, breathe pure air, to dress with loveliness, to strive to be a type of warm, chaste girlishness—these are all of them a preparation for Love's coming.

I wonder if some of you think I have laid far too much stress on the importance and sanctity of the body. Well, I do not think it is possible for us to do so. Next month I want to tell you how I think we can as girls prepare our minds and spirits the more fully and worthily for the coming of Love."

After a long silence, Alice got out of bed and quickly blew out the lamp. The bedroom was black and I could hear Alice crawling into her bed.

"Goodnight, Eleanor," she whispered to me.

I was surprised that my sister did not take up the subject in length. Her topic for the evening was presented on a shiny platter by Alice Preston, the food for thought will be simmering on many a girl's minds after reading her article. But I for one was never told until it was too late. My memory of Nate smothering me with kisses will not go away. My nerves are sensitive when our eyes meet. My emotions and passions have been roused. Miss Preston has not written a falsehood in saying that it wakens and stimulates feelings and instincts and desires…. Are humans to be blamed for waking such things that God Almighty has implanted in his people? Should the rising sun be scorned for waking creatures on earth?

How can a warm heart become diseased? My brother's lungs are diseased. How can a person compare that kind of disease to what a young woman and a young man feel for each other in their hearts?

I would like to know how old Miss Alice Preston is, and if she has ever been blessed with a male acquaintance like Mr. Nate Miller?

E—

February 1, 1910
Tuesday

At school to-day, John's class had a bit of fun doing a memory game in which you pay forfeits for mistakes and also for laughing. John won and received a nice box of chocolates which he has been sharing with the family to-night. It has been some years since I have tasted nice chocolates. Every student took a turn by solemnly saying, "One old ox opening oysters." Then everyone repeats this in turn. Then he begun again. "One old ox opening oysters; two tired turtles trotting to Trenton." The next repetition is "One old ox opening oysters; two tired turtles trotting to Trenton; three tame tigers taking tea."

The following verses are:

"Four fat friars fishing for frogs."
"Five fairies fighting furious fire-flies."
"Six soldiers shooting snipe."
"Eight elegant engineers eating eggs."
"Nine nimble noblemen nibbling nuts."
"Ten tall tinkers tentatively tolling."
"Eleven earnest emigrants eating early eggplants."
"Twelve terrible talebearers telling truths."

John is trying this game on all of us and we can't stop laughing at each others mistakes. I have not heard a good laugh from anyone in months and it makes my heart light. Have we been too busy, too tired, too ill, too worried to allow ourselves a moment of joy? My family is laughing but the sounds are almost foreign to my senses. I wish I could bottle Richard's voice and his laugh without the constant coughing. I wish he was not filling dozens of rags and handkerchiefs full of phlegm. I feel sorry for Mama who has to wash them, knowing that her son is becoming worse, not better. Mama looks so tired now-a-days, and quite often in the evening she falls asleep in her chair with her needle work resting in her lap. Someone covers her with a lap blanket and for the rest of the evening she is deep in slumber until Papa wakes her for bedtime.

It was reported recently in the paper, that pioneers on the west side of the state are predicting an early spring, and if that is true, the rush of new settlers to this state should begin within the next six weeks. The railroads say that this spring and summer our state will begin to reap the benefit of last year's Seattle Exposition. The Great Northern and Northern Pacific officials who were in Seattle this past week stated that there were all kinds of evidence that the rush this coming year would be the heaviest in the history of the state. The roads are well prepared to handle the crowds; and thousands of dollars are being spent in sending out excellent literature calling attention to every section of Washington. I do not know where newcomers would find housing in the immediate Seattle area. A person does not have to go higher than to the top of Queen Anne Hill to see how populated our bustling city has become. Glorious homes crowd the hills and the sweep of construction blows northward to Everett and southward to Tacoma. Thanks to the Seattle-Everett Interurban Railway Company, freight and passenger cars cut through virgin timberland as new steel rails continue to be laid passed Hall's Lake and finally to the community of Everett. At the present time lumber products are seen coming and going more often than passengers since lumber is valued higher than people.

Goodnight,
Eleanor

February 19, 1910
Saturday

I have decided to stay home to-day for the trolleys are not operating after our second snowfall this winter. It all began Thursday night, starting out as tiny flakes here and there. Every nose in the household was pressed against a cold window as we marveled at the beauty of the flakes which grew larger by the hour. By Friday morning, there was perhaps close to four inches on the ground. I thoroughly enjoyed my walk to the Miller's in the white winter wonderland. The air was nippy and the sky was a solid dark gray which was a promise of more snow to come. And come it did indeed! While making bread I kept glancing out the kitchen window watching the snow come down, down, down. I thought it was just my imagination that the sky was growing dusk even though it was around 10 a.m. The snow was thick across the Seattle sky and it did not let much light into the big house. I felt comfortable while doing my chores, keeping the range warm, keeping the fireplace going in the parlor.

Finally around noon, I could not ignore the playful taunting of the snow any longer, and wrapping my wool shawl about my shoulders I stood on the porch for a while. Snowflakes landed on my long skirt, and fell on my hair and my face in a teasing manner. My lungs were filled with the cold air and part of me wanted to run in the snow as a child would, but getting my clothes wet would not be a wise idea, so I dismissed the thought from my mind and went back inside and stood by the fireplace.

As I warmed by backside, I thought of Nate being out in the cold and felt sorry for the man. I was concerned primarily for his safety—working in such conditions could prove treacherous.

During the course of the afternoon I made several trips to the basement for coal and kept the furnace well fed so that when the men returned they would be comfortable. I prepared a pot of stew and waited for the two loaves of bread to rise. For some reason, I found myself reminiscing when I used to make cinnamon rolls every Saturday for our family, and how much everyone enjoyed them. For all the work that went into making them—they never did last long. I remember how I used to mildly complain at the fact....but now I realize how foolish I must have sounded. Had they not enjoyed my baking so, would I have felt worse? I should have baked a pan of cinnamon rolls this morning since I did not make it to the office.

While the bread was in the oven and the kitchen was filled with its comforting warm aroma, I settled down in the rocking chair and mended a few items. I thought of Mama and how tired she has become since Richard has been growing worse and worse. I wanted to be with her in our little kitchen, sipping hot tea and eating delicate little cookies by the warmth of the range. We would quietly share each other's daily affairs, however trivial or trite they may be. One of Mama's favorite songs, "Mother Machree," came to mind and I began to sing it out loud.

> *There's a spot in me heart which no coleen may own,*
> *There's a depth in me soul never sounded or known;*
> *There's a place in my mem'ry, my life, that you fill,*
> *No other can take it, no one ever will.*
> *Sure, I love the dear silver that shines in your hair,*
> *And the brow that's all furrowed*
> *And wrinkled with care.*
> *I kiss the dear fingers, so toilworn for me,*
> *Oh, God bless you and keep you, Mother Machree!*

"Oh, God bless you and keep you, Mother Machree!" a voice suddenly bursted out.

My nerves jumped and my mending fell to the floor. To my surprise Nate stood in the kitchen holding the door open.

"Nate! Shame on you!" I scolded and shook a finger at the man who looked out of place in my kitchen in the middle of the afternoon. "You, you...." I sputtered. "Don't you know that you could give a person a dreadful fright— startling an innocent soul like that!" My hand was pressed against my chest as I gasped for breath.

"Forgive me. I thought you may have heard me stomping my feet on the porch. Here, allow me..." Nate already was bending down to pick up the shirt that I was tightening buttons on when I realized his jacket was wet.

"Your jacket looks awfully wet for a short walk home."

"I'm afraid it wasn't a short walk," Nate admitted.

"How far?"

"Two or three or four, I suppose."

"Blocks?" I asked.

Nate shook his head and sneezed.

"Bless you!"

"Miles."

"Miles!"

I quickly rose from my chair and was behind him in a moment.

"Goodness! Let's get your coat off..."

"The rails were gradually disappearing this morning and the street car operators warned us that if the storm kept up all day there might not be any evening service."

Nate moved his shoulders back to ease the jacket off, and taking hold of it, it nearly slipped from my fingers. It was heavy and made my hands cold. I quickly glanced around the room and decided to drape it on one of the kitchen chairs and pulled it close to the range.

"I've been watching the snowfall all day but I didn't know it was that bad."

"It's getting pretty thick. Too tricky to work in so they told us to go home."

When I turned back to Nate I caught him shivering. Something inside of me brought me to him and I placed my hands upon his wet shirt.

"Nate, you're drenched to the bone!"

"I suppose I am. What shall we do with me?"

There was something in his voice that made me lift my face to his. He was looking down at me with soft teasing eyes. My heart quickened and I secretly admired his dark eyes, and in doing so, I almost forgot his question.

"I...I think we ought to have you sit by the fire."

"And you?"

"Follow me, please," I softly replied as I avoided his eyes and ignored his question. I instructed Nate to stay put in the parlor until I returned, and hurrying to his room I gathered dry clothes, putting all except a shirt in the bathroom. Returning to the parlor with the flannel shirt, I asked Nate to remove his wet shirt and undershirt.

He took the dry shirt and asked, "Do you wish to leave the room while I change?"

"I thank you, but that won't be necessary, Mr. Miller. I will turn around."

In the hush of the parlor I heard the undoing of shirt buttons as Nate stood close to me. My breathing quickened without my permission. As we stood before the fireplace with the mirror above it, my curious eye turned and looked at it. In the reflection of the mirror, I could see his wet shirt coming off, but what I really saw was Nate watching me as I was watching him in the mirror. I put my hand out and his wet shirt was placed in it. Next he reached for the bottom of his cotton shirt and pulled it over his head, exposing once more, all the glorious hardness of muscle and flesh that God had bestowed upon him. My whole being trembled in delight and in fear.

My inner body no longer reacted as if it were a girl, for I understood then, and I understand now, that to tell my flesh that I cannot participate in the familiarity which is growing in me, is becoming more and more difficult. I understand now why Miss Preston approves of such laws governing the human body. As she put it: The nerves of the body, renders them morbidly sensitive, rouses the emotions and passions which it harmful to have roused and played upon; that it wakens and stimulates feelings and instincts and desires that should not be wakened.

Nate reluctantly took leave of the parlor without word, and drawing himself a warm bath, he did not come downstairs for over an hour. While he read the paper in the parlor, I brought him coffee and lunch, and went about my day as if nothing had happened.

As afternoon turned to early evening, Mr. Miller Sr., nor Stuart came home. Nate guessed that they would be staying at a hotel downtown until the storm passed and that we might as well have an early dinner in front of the fire in the parlor. We spoke of the snow-storm and wondered how long it might last. Nate related the progress of the new train station, and I gave him the latest news of Richard's health. Nate looked concerned when I told him that there has been talk of moving Richard to a tuberculosis Sanitorium where he would receive daily care under the guidance of doctors and nurses.

I called Papa and Mama and informed them that I was fine, and that after supper Mr. Miller would walk me home before evening settled in. As we made our way through the snow, Nate asked me if I could sing "Mother Machree" again. Mr. Miller says that he has never heard a more lovelier voice than mine and wondered if I sang in a church choir. "I do not," I informed him. He says that I should so everyone could enjoy the sweetness of my voice.

It is good to be home and to know that Nate made it home safely. He rang our number after he returned back up the hill, and the only words he spoke were, "Good-night, Miss Eleanor."

I wanted to speak to him, but my family laid curious eyes upon me and their ears were straining. In a matter-of-fact tone I replied, "Yes, thank-you Mr. Miller for walking me home, and in letting me know that you have returned. Good-night."

E—

March 9, 1910
Wednesday

Last Tuesday, on the 1st of the month, one of the worst train disasters in U.S. history occurred near the small town of Wellington, near Stevens Pass. An avalanche roared down the Cascade Mountains taking with it two Great Northern trains and 96 lives.

After a snow delay in the town of Leavenworth, two Great northern trains, the Spokane Local passenger train, a Fast mail train, five or six steam and electric engines, 15 boxcars, passenger cars, and sleepers headed toward Puget Sound on February 23rd. After passing the Cascade Tunnel, heavy snowfall and avalanches made it impossible for the train crews to clear the tracks, and so everyone waited six long days in blizzard and avalanche conditions. On the 26th, telegraph lines went down. On the last day of the month, the weather turned to rain with thunder and lightening. Thunder shook the snow-laden Cascade Mountains alive with avalanches. Then it happened. According to Charles Andrews, a Great Northern employee, sometime after midnight, he was walking towards one of the warm bunkhouses when he heard a rumble. He turned toward the sound and described what he witnessed:

"White Death moving down the mountainside above the trains. Relentlessly it advanced, exploding, roaring, rumbling, grinding, snapping— a crescendo of sound that might have been the crashing of ten thousand freight trains. It descended to the ledge where the side tracks lay, picked up cars and equipment as though they were so many snow-draped toys, and swallowing them up, disappeared like a white, broad monster into the ravine below."

To be buried under snow must have been horrible. To wonder if help would ever come. To escape with injuries but to be alive. I have been thinking of the train disaster all week and am thankful that none of my relations work for the railroad. I thank God that 23 people survived, but for the 96 who were killed, I hope that they were in deep sleep and did not suffer as their last moments on earth came to a close. May they rest in peace with God Almighty.

I do not like death. I despise even looking at the word. Old people, their time on earth has been plentiful. Those individuals I do not weep and lament over so. Their time has come. But for Richard.... he is so young in the eyes of time.

After supper last night, I kept company with him in his room, sitting in the chair next to the door. For some time now, John has been sleeping on the sofa in the living room. He does not care for the arrangement and is growing impatient with the situation. I know he is afraid, just like the rest of us. If, Richard is taken from us, who will John have to talk to? Who will love and adore me? As I read the evening paper to him, the pitter-patter of rain danced on the roof, its feet growing louder and louder. I stopped reading and looked toward the ceiling. Richard's eyes followed mine. It was a lovely, wonderful sound for a moment—the moment passed. Then the rain beat upon the roof unmercifully, the sound filling my brother's room. The noise made me lonely and tense....something it has never managed to do.

"Richard," said I, "can I imagine myself beside you, keeping you company, you comforting me? Would that be all right?"

"Ele, what took you so long to imagine that? Don't you know that every hour that you are away from me, I am constantly thinking of you? I wonder what you are doing, what you are thinking. Wonder if you are thinking of me. Do you Ele? Do you think about me as I'm wasting away here, becoming less and less of a man? Tell me you do, Ele."

Tears were running down my face and my mouth tasted the salt as I wiped them away.

"Dearest, Richard! How can you ask such a thing? How can you doubt what always has been between you and I? No matter how sick you are or will become, my fondness for you will never change. Do not forget that. Do not let your illness let you think otherwise. When you close your eyes to-night —" I starred at my brother lovingly as tears were staining my smiling face.

"When I close my eyes to-night Ele, what will I see?" my brother asked, his own eyes sparkling.

"When you close your eyes to-night, spring will come to you, for she will give you warmth, comfort and love. I give you permission to lay with her, for time is short. I am saying this because we do not know what to-morrow will bring. To-morrow may be too late. Do not fear dear brother, for I have given you permission to indulge your imagination in what is being robbed from you. I say this with a clear conscience and a happy heart."

Richard made himself comfortable and then closed his eyes.

"You lie beneath an apple tree, laden with open pink blossoms. The air is sweet and warm, and the grass beneath you is warm and tender. Above you, baby blue sky is gentle to the gazing eye as soft, billowy clouds float on by. Spring has come to you and wishes to make you happy. She drops her soft pink petals upon your face, upon your sweet mouth. Do you see the daffodils and tulips beside you? Spring is inviting you to drink its nectar as the soft, delicate petals open. What you find deep inside is yours. Gather what you want. Stay as long as you wish. Can you feel the warm breeze that spring has brought to your valley? Are you swaying deep within the flower, holding onto the sweet nectar, drinking in the divine fragrance of the passage of spring? Can you see the rose bud swelling? She is tender to the touch. Are her dark glistening new leaves like velvet? Is spring as soft and warm and tender as the yellow down of a chick? Does spring bring you joy, Richard dear?"

The room was quiet and my dear brother was looking at me with angry, grieving eyes. I did not understand. "What is the matter, Richard?" I painfully wished to know. I stood at the foot of his bed.

"No, Eleanor, it does not," he said sharply. "Spring has not, and never will bring me joy." His voice was rough and was not steady and Richard began to cough up phlegm.

"Please, Richard, do not be upset with me! Please tell me what I have done to upset you. Please, Richard!" I begged.

He looked at me with cruel brown eyes, and the flesh of his face was ridged. Why was he torturing me so?

"Blow out the light Eleanor and leave me be. You need to go now," he said ever so sternly.

He rolled over on his side as I stood holding onto the end of his bed feeling numb.

"Go! Get out of here!" he shouted.

Backing out of the room I began to cry and almost fell over the chair, and in the hallway faces appeared and voices wanted to know what was the matter. I ran to my bed and buried my face in my pillow and cried.

Sometime during the night I had a dream. I found myself walking softly to my brother's room and quietly lay with him. I did not speak. But in gentle whispers he said to me, "I knew you would come back. I knew you wouldn't let me die without knowing what spring would be like."

I gave my brother the taste of spring. In whispers of whispers, he told me that he never imagined that spring was so tender, warm and divine, and that her petals were soft to the touch. The rose bud swelled and sweet nectar flowed, but the seeds did not stay in the valley, for they floated away on billowy clouds.....

E....

April 2, 1910
Saturday

I have returned home early from the Insurance Company. I tried staying away as long as I could, but the dampness and chill from the outdoors weakened me and forced me back home. May God forgive me for telling Papa and Mama that 'there wasn't enough work on my desk to finish out the day. When will be the best time to explain to Papa that I no longer work there? Mr. Whiting, my dear former employer has been replaced by his nephew, Mr. Douglas Whiting. Due to heart problems, the older Mr. Whiting decided to retire. I did not know of this until this morning. I will miss him dearly. If possible, I should like to keep this matter from Richard. He surely does not need another worry.

I should for the sake of clarity, revisit the events leading up to when Mr. Whiting asked me into his office.

The trolley car was cold as usual this morning and very few men spoke as we made our way to downtown. I was one of a handful of females who boarded and was given a seat by a polite gentleman. As we traveled to the business district, sitting on cold wooden benches, I thought of Minnie in her mansion with servants waiting on her, having her own personal nurse taking care of the mother-to-be in ways I don't think I should ever mention to Mama. I will not say if Miss Young's methods are proper or not, for every household is different. I can only imagine how different the 'wealthy' must live. Though, I do get this feeling that dear Minnie is unhappy since her new husband is rarely there. That would make any new bride unhappy to say the least.

As our trolley neared Westlake Avenue, our driver rang his bell and waved to other drivers as we passed a half-dozen cars. My heart quickens and I hold my breath as each car cuts in front of us, and then we cut in front of a black or green one without a scratch. I watch the drivers every Saturday morning and they are not flustered for their timing is perfect.

Like a faithful steed, the trolley stops at the corner of Fourth Avenue and Pike Street, in front of the five story building that has the words, "SEATTLE BUSINESS COLLEGE" affixed to the edge of the roof. A young boy of seven or eight sells the Seattle Star newspaper on our corner. I can hear his voice and the voices of other children who covet each street corner as their own. He is small and lanky, and the bundle of newspapers under his arm seem to dwarf his weedy little figure. As I step off the trolley, his pleading brown eyes are fixed on mine, as they are every Saturday morning. "Paper, Miss? Won't you buy a paper to-day?"

"I'm sorry, not to-day," I tell the poor little thing as I smile at him. In the few seconds that I am allowed to, I quickly observe his outfit which never changes. Upon his straight brown hair an ill fitted cap sits. Over a dingy shirt that once was white, a gray wool sweater with wide black edging covers his cuffs, around his neck, down the front and around the bottom of the sweater. Every Saturday he wears dark knickers and black stockings and his dear little brown shoes are dirty and worn. I wonder if there are holes on the bottom of his soles.

I found myself standing on the street corner observing this little boy whose eager eyes had already left mine and moved onto other passerby's. I could not help but notice his slightly protruding ears that were red from the cold. I'm sure his little hands were just as cold since he did not wear mittens. I started to turn away, but something in my heart was tugging and I turned back to him.

"Excuse me," I said.

"Changed your mind, Miss?" he asked as soon as he saw me turning back to him.

"I'm sorry, but I'm not in need of a paper to-day...."

"Oh," he replied, casting his eyes with crushed hope downward. The dimples at the corners of his mouth slumped and I quickly found my tongue.

"It would please me, if you could tell me your name."

The young boy starred at me for a moment and blinked. "Why do you want to know, Miss? Am I in trouble for something?" He moved away from me a step or two, and his brown eyes were filled with skepticism and uncertainty.

"No, oh, no! I didn't mean to cause you alarm. I am just curious as to what your name is. I see you every Saturday standing on this corner....and, I don't know, just knowing a face without knowing a name is rather sad I think. Don't you agree?"

"I wouldn't know, Miss. Names don't buy newspapers. Faces do."

"I see." I opened my little purse and found twenty cents. "Here.... I want you to have these."

The boy looked at the coins and then at me.

"I want you to buy yourself something to eat. Perhaps a hot bowl of soup and two slices of bread, or ice cream and cake and a glass of milk. Would you like that?"

"Oh, yes!" His little face brightened and the dimples dove into his cold, rosy cheeks. I placed the coins into his hands, but just as I did so, I ceased his joy and slowly watched his moment of happiness crumble. He shook his head and mumbled, "Can't..."

"Why not?"

"If my Mama or Papa found out I spent twenty whole cents on myself, I wouldn't be able to sit for a whole week!" The boy rubbed his backside and contorted his face into convincing suffering.

Oh, how I wished I could have bought him a warm lunch at Frey's New Cafe and watched the poor little thing devour whatever he wished. But I did not want to go against his wishes, for I did not understand his family's situation.

He put his palm out to me, wanting to give the coins back. "Here, you best take them back."

"I'll tell you what. You keep them and give them to your Mother and Father. Tell them that Eleanor gave it to you. OK?"

"Yes, Miss. Thank you, Miss."

"You are very welcome." I smiled and turned to go for I was already late for my job.

"Miss!"

I heard his voice call me and I turned around. He gave me a little smile and said, "My name is Roy."

I smiled and nodded to him, and then turned away from the corner of Fourth and Pike. As I made my way under several awnings, I was careful not to hurry and take extreme steps. I kept my chin at a pleasant height and rounded my shoulders, for my carriage was a display of utmost grace. Although I kept my eyes forward, I was well aware of the male population behind the nine windows which I pass to get to my office. When my curiosity weakens me, I have on a few occasions made eye contact with the male office worker. It is terribly difficult not to be curious, especially when 'watchers' know when I will pass by their offices at a certain time. Mama's 'words to the wise' has been imparted upon us girls hundreds of times; "An ill-bred, uncultivated young woman acknowledges the presence of men while they work. The little seed of suggestion, insinuation, may grow from the curious eye and stirs up feelings in the male animal that you may have falsely advertised."

I know Mama means well, but is casting a quick glance to my right truly viewed as bad taste in character? I flaunt nothing except meekness, gentility, and a pleasant smile.

It would be far easier if God had put horse blinders on the side of our heads, then the hungry appetite of nature would not be encouraged, solicited, seduced, enticed, stimulated or aroused. Since the beginning of time, has not the fairer sex always enticed man, captivating his attention, charming him with her soft ways, whetting his heart for the sole purpose of yearning for her and her alone? Shall I take no notice of the opposite gender? If my eyes were devoted in taking in only the admirable and note-worthy sights of Seattle, I can say that the time doing so would be ill-spent, fruitless, and unbeneficial in curbing a young woman's ripening passion for romance.

Did Mama never keep secret reflections in her young heart? In the strictest of confidence, did her mind ever wish to know if her hazel eyes, dark hair and creamy complexion opened the eyes of a young male? Before Papa courted Mama, did she yearn for beautiful words to come to her ears? I would not blame Mama if she once had pondered such ideas, nurturing them, entertaining them, cherishing them.

My day dreaming almost caused me to pass our own office, and opening the door that bore the gold words on the pane of glass "Whiting Insurance Company, Mr. Wm. B. Whiting, Agent.," I set my foot passed the threshold and immediately was keen to the absence of voices. Mr. Leslie Williams, the First Desk Clerk, barely raised his eyes to mine as he kept his face to his desk. Mr. Will Dashwood, the Second Desk Clerk, acknowledged me in the same manner. The two other females in the office, Miss Pauline Pordessa and Miss Julia Rochester are stenographers, timekeepers and assistants to the First and Second Clerks. As soon as I took in their solemn faces, I was confused as to the feeling in the air. It was not as if the tragedy of death had occurred, though the atmosphere was thrown out of gear. I put my lunch pail on the floor next to my desk, hung up my coat, and with a sigh, surveyed the chaos and disorder which had managed to pile up since last Monday. My effort to concentrate was futile, for the silence resembled that of a tomb. I glanced around me and the only sound that was audible was the faint rustling of paper. I noticed that the desk of Mr. Whiting's niece was vacant, and for the moment assumed that she was in her Uncle's office. The two young girls were busy with their pencils and note pads, and I did not understand why their typewriters were silent. I turned to Miss Pauline and Miss Julia and asked, "Are your typewriters defective?"

A finger shot up to Miss Pauline's lips and she pressed it into them. Her eyes scorned me, but not with the intent of meanness. Fear and trepidation was cast upon me, and I did not understand the reason for it. Miss Julia craned her neck toward Mr. Whiting's office, and listening for a moment or two, turned her head back to me. She then whispered in the softest tone possible. "Mr. Whiting does not want to be disturbed. He cares not to hear the banging of keys before ten 'o clock. It disagrees with his morning constitution."

"Miss Julia," says I, gentle in my scorning, "please do not speak about our dear employer in such a negative manner. I know he hasn't been well lately—"

"Miss Eleanor," Pauline whispered her interruption, "you speak of another Mr. Whiting, I sadly regret to say."

"What do you mean?" I questioned the two girls, but they did not have time to answer. A voice, one alien to my ears bellowed from within Mr. Whiting's office.

"Mr. Williams! Has he arrived yet!?"

Mr. Williams jumped out of his chair and stiffly stood outside the office before he reluctantly placed a hand on the door knob. Mr. Williams cautiously stepped inside.

"Well, is my accountant here?" asked the grumbling voice.

"Yes, Sir."

"Why are you still standing there? Are you deaf?"

"Not to my knowledge, Sir."

"Good, then I shall not fire you to-day. Tell him to step into my office at once!" the voice snapped.

Mr. Williams came out of the office and turning towards me, caught my struggle to understand what was taking place. "Miss Eleanor, Mr. Whiting wishes to see you promptly."

"Thank-you, Mr. Williams," I politely replied.

I did not know who this other 'Mr. Whiting' was, but as I stood and smoothed my skirt and straightened my belt, I did not appreciate his tone of voice and indignation towards my co-worker. Mr. Williams had forgotten to close the door so I softly tapped my knuckles on the frosted pane of glass.

"Yes, yes! Come in!" the voice sharply called out.

Upon entering, I thought the man who sat at my former employer's desk strongly resembled our Mayor, Hiram C. Gill. The man sitting in the chair had his partially bald head lowered as he was reading documents with silver wire spectacles balancing on his nose. He appeared to be in his early forties and may have been younger, but there was at least five to six inches of forehead, beginning from his eyebrows to the top of his crown where the sparse hair began. This fellow had the misfortune of being very round on top, and terribly narrow of chin. His head resembles an egg. My hands were folded quietly in front of me as I waited to be noticed by the new Mr. Whiting. He seemed quite absorbed in his reading, and producing a white handkerchief, dabbed his vast forehead. Finally he looked at me with hard, gray eyes instantly narrowing, and the two furrows between his eye brows deepened. Mr. Whiting's lips were not to be left out of the scornful stare. Thin and long and straight, they looked incapable of uttering one kind word.

"Where is my accountant?" he asked through pressed lips.

I let his words linger in the air while I looked directly at the nervous man with the displeasing personality.

"Well? Answer me girl!"

"I am the Accountant," I replied calmly and confidently.

The man gawked at me for a moment before he fell back in his chair, succumbing to the shock of being in the presence of a female accountant. A huff escaped from his mouth while his cold eyes were capable of laughing at me, and I could feel my face grow warmer and warmer over his ignorance and belittling attitude toward women.

He huffed again. "My Uncle never could pass up a pretty face. Of course pretty faces are good for business.....I've hired a few myself knowing that unskilled daisies lure clients in. As for my sister, she had neither skill nor beauty...the silly little imbecile! She did not belong here. Her place right now is suited in caring for our Uncle."

"Sir...."

"The name is Mr. Whiting!" he snapped. "Mr. Douglas Whiting."

"Mr. Whiting," I began again with a bit of sternness in my voice. "I will admit that your sister may lack some essential office skills, but to call your own sister an imbecile....why, aren't you being just a little harsh?"

"No!" Mr. Whiting folded his arms on the desk and leaned towards me. His eyes which are tenants to distrust and deceit bore into mine. "My sister, like so many other females are imbeciles. They are unteachable, ungifted, unwise, feebleminded, and have half-baked ideas of how the world works." Each word gave Mr. Whiting immense pleasure, for at the finish an unpleasant grin had been pulled across his face.

I stood there silently seething, my face very warm from anger. I wish I could have hidden my contempt from that man, but there is only so much a woman can do to disguise what she feels inside. My body was ridged; my hands were folded tight in white knuckles, and my teeth almost hurt from pressing them together, least insulting words only be kept in my mind!

"Now, according to my Uncle's payroll records, Mr. Leslie Williams and Mr. Will Dashwood are making $80.00 a month. The other two girls who make such dreadful racket on those machines make $55.00 a month."

I hoped that Mr. Whiting was not reading a look of surprise on my face, for I had no idea how much my co-workers were being paid. To reveal what we earn is a forbidden topic of conversation.

"But this is interesting. You, a female, make $100.00 a month. Now how is that possible?" Mr. Douglas Whiting raised his eyebrows. "And—" he adjusted his silly eyeglasses while bending his balding head down toward the payroll book, "—you are only here on Saturdays?" His voice let out a mocking squeak, and taking off his spectacles, he sat back in his chair and judged me with a nasty grin.

"I can see how my Uncle was easily misguided by your femininity, which you used to confuse the old man, no doubt."

"Mr. Whiting, it is clear that you think very little of me, even though you know nothing of me. As for your Uncle, I hold him in very high regards, morally and ethically. I am proud to have worked for him."

"I'm sure you did, especially since he was paying you $100.00 a month for a few hours here and there."

"Mr. Whiting, that is the wage for accountants in this city."

"Perhaps, for a male worker. A male working ten or more hours a day, six days a week. Not for girls." The word 'not' was strongly emphasized.

Although there was a chair against the wall to my left, it had not been offered to me. I wanted to sit down, but I continued standing.

Mr. Whiting opened a desk drawer and produced a black book which took up several minutes of his time in finding what he wanted from between the pages. As he held it close to his face, I read the gold words on the cover. NEW STANDARD AMERICAN BUSINESS GUIDE. My new employer ran his long thin fingers up and down and across the page, nodding his egg shaped head and verbally agreeing to himself. Suddenly the black book was closed and was tossed into the drawer. Mr. Whiting adjusted the silly little spectacles on his nose and informed me, without even looking directly at me for he was already engaged in other matters on his desk, that, until he found a full-time replacement for me, a male accountant, I will be making a 'generous' $2.00 a day on the days that I do show up. This shock was unanticipated. I stood aghast, bewildered. I quickly calculated that each hour on Saturday would earn me 25 cents an hour. Just 25 cents! For some reason I thought of the poor little paper boy who I had given 20 cents to not even an hour ago.

My thoughts of Roy were unseated from my mind as I was instructed to send Mr. Dashwood in. But I stood there starring at the insufferable human behind the desk, and I am not sorry to say that I may loathe him. One employer set the wage; another just withdrew it. I wonder how much less Miss Pauline and Miss Julia are making now. We are at our employer's mercy. The very act of bargaining for wages is intimidating to many women, especially those of us who are young and timid. I wonder if Mr. Williams or Mr. Dashwood negotiated their wages for their desk jobs. I do not think that any one of us was ever intimidated while the elder Mr. Whiting was present. But clearly it can be felt already, that Mr. Douglas Whiting is abusing his authority over his workers; the authority of male over female, age over youth. Miss Pauline and Miss Julia are close to me in age, but their frame of mind is harnessed in subjection; cowering to the stern, cold eye of the opposite sex; cowering almost instinctively. Young women such as they would rather change jobs, than face an employer in order to ask for a wage increase, or protest against low-pay. I have heard that some employers fire workers who were so brash as to request a raise.

My thoughts were interrupted by Mr. Whiting wondering what was the matter with me. I made my spine straight and lifted my chin. I hoped to appear courageous and speak without fear in my voice. "I do not think you are being fair, Mr. Whiting."

His gray eyes darted up at mine. "Oh, really?" If a pair of eye brows did not rise with his voice that alone would have given me fright.

"An individual cannot live on the wages that you propose. In this city, those wages are very, very low.....even less·than living wages."

I will never forget his snaring eyes which advertised his contempt for me as he pushed his chair back and slowly stood up. They dug into me, and clung onto my flesh. He stood close to me and asked me this. "Are you the primary family breadwinner? If not, your income is only a supplementary wage to your father and brother's income. Your small and uncertain wages will not cause massive economic suffering or political unrest. You females only need to make enough to cushion the family against adversity, and enjoy the flexibility to loosen the household budgets when a whim comes your way to purchase a new hat or something unimportant. Besides, why should I pay someone well, when I know that they will not be a lifelong worker? Any skilled male worker will argue that women are but temporary workers outside the home. Their true vocation is marriage and motherhood, and rigorous, expensive apprenticeship training would be wasted on even ambitious females. I do not know one person who wouldn't agree that women's first responsibility is to bear and raise children and maintain the home. Women are better suited to the domestic role than to paid employment." Mr. Douglas Whiting paused for a moment to catch his breath. He cocked his egg-like head and raised his eyebrows.

"You see, every male employer has come to realize that women move from school through employment and into marriage, much as their mothers and grandmothers had passed through a domestic apprenticeship on their way to husbands and child-bearing. Your brief years of work experience are but a small slice in a female's life before the long years of domestic life." He stepped closer and I could detect his body odor. I loathed the man before me.

"You should be grateful that I am paying you girls 25 cents an hour for 'social freedom.'"

On my tongue, spit was accumulating, waiting. What was I waiting for? Why did I wait so long? Unsaintly blood ran through my veins as he yelled in my face for Mr. Will Dashwood to come into his office immediately. I should have spat on his face then, just as Mr. Dashwood came in. I was excused and told to shut the door behind me as Mr. Douglas Whiting shook hands with Mr. Dashwood. Just before my hand lifted from the glass knob, I heard Mr. Dashwood being offered a chair and to make himself comfortable.

I can still remember how my heart beat rapidly, how it hurt. Under my high lace collar my throat was thick and throbbed, and the sudden sensation of strangulation seized my mind. My breathing became short and my chest rushed in and out. My hands flew to the back of my neck and unhooking the stock collar, it was quickly discarded. I looked at the beautiful wide band of lace, panting. I found myself frowning at it which suddenly looked out of place in the poorly lit room. My ears became aware of a voice softly calling my name.

"Miss Eleanor….." The soft voice of Miss Pauline was next to me. "Can Mr. Whiting do this to us?"

Movement of passerby's caught my attention and I turned to look at the men and women as they leered into our office for a moment. Such strange faces who poked their noses close to the pane of glass, as if they were on a sight-seeing stroll about the city, catching glances of female office workers here and there. Is this how a caged bird discerns its life when goggled upon?

"Miss Eleanor….?" a voice softly wailed. "Are you feeling ill?"

"No, Miss Pauline," I responded calmly, yet unemotionally, almost cold-heartedly.

Wagons carrying wares to market rattled by. Bells rang on trolley cars that followed predetermined paths about the city. Ladies swooshed by. The populace in sharp fashionable suits swarmed the sidewalks and darted between the powerful street cars as if they had authority over them.

I was aware of the sounds of the city. I was aware of the sound of my own voice. A soft little hand touched my sleeve, and Miss Julia said how sorry she was that Mr. Whiting was to find a replacement for me. She expressed her concern over her own future. It was then that I turned to her and Miss Julia and spoke the raw truth.

"The job will be yours for as long as you are willing to accept scanty wages on account of your gender."

I moved my eyes over to Mr. Williams, but he denied himself the courage to express his thoughts. How could he share in our sorrow? To express sympathy for our situation is an invitation which man has declined for decades.

"You will never have to worry about a man ever filling your position, ladies. It is not a virtuous thing for man to work for pauper's earnings." I paused. "Is it, Mr. Williams?"

The embarrassed young man kept his head down and moved his pencil across the lines of his large note pad.

I bent down and picked up my lunch pail and placed it on my desk. Now Mr. Williams turned his head and glanced at it, and then his eyes cautiously rose to mine. I removed my long coat from the stand and put it on. Miss Julia and Miss Pauline pressed a hand to their lace covered bosoms and gasped. Mr. Williams stopped moving his pencil.

I listened to my feet cross the wooden floor and my steady hand reached for the cool doorknob without pausing. The young woman who opened the door and stood proud interrupted two horribly surprised men. She did not care if the older man spat insulting words at her. It did not matter anymore. Her eyes bore into those of her former employer.

"Mr. Whiting," says I, addressing him triumphantly, "you will not have the pleasure of reducing me to poverty. I refuse to live as a destitute or be financially embarrassed. I presently resign from my position in this office. I happily permit myself to say that it is without regret that I sever my connection and association with narrow-minded employers such as you. Your character Mr. Whiting is a mark of personal failure, and happiness will always elude you. I pity you, Mr. Whiting, but I do not have to subject myself a moment more to men like you. Good-day!"

Whether or not he heard me did not entirely matter, for the door was slammed shut.

Removing myself from a place of employment which spanned over three years still seems like a blurry dream as I picked up my lunch pail from the desk and nodded to the girls.

"Miss Pauline, Miss Julia, it has been a pleasure working with you. I have valued our friendship as well. Perhaps someday we will meet again. Good-bye."

From the door of his smaller office, Mr. Douglas Whiting's voice filled the main office with hilarious threats that startled Miss Pauline and Miss Julia. I nodded my head to a stunned Mr. Dashwood, and walking passed the speechless Mr. Williams, I wished him a polite 'good-day.' I shut the door on my office endeavor and my hand touched the knob for the last time. My numb body floated passed window after window, ignorant of all the male occupants who were slaves to a desk and chair. A boy's voice rang in the air as I approached the corner.

"Miss, care for a paper to-day?"

I lowered my eyes from the view of passing trolley cars and looked into the dear, eager eyes of Roy. I forced a little smile on my face and told him honestly, "I'm sorry, I cannot afford one to-day."

The morning hour which was unknown to me was still chilly as I stepped off the corner and into the criss-cross traffic of Fourth Avenue and Pike Street. I have never been so bold as to intrude upon the rest of the world that lay beyond my little corner at such an hour. The feeling of trespassing in my own city foolishly and deceitfully hung in my thoughts. Mr. Whiting's ghost carried me under black cables which trolleys clung to, and over cold metal tracks which they faithfully follow. I went south, for it was familiar to me. Westlake Boulevard was at my back and Pike Street was under my feet. Somewhere ahead of me was Elliott Bay. I found myself making a left on Third Avenue, passed Union Street, passed Madison Street, passed the James Street Substation. I departed from Third Avenue and turned right onto James Street till I neared the corner of Yesler Way and First Avenue. I eased my pace as I neared a park in Pioneer Square.

Surrounded by elegant brick buildings and more trolley cars sat the beautiful pergola. From across the street where I stood, several pedestrians waited for the next car under the Victorian-style iron and glass structure which was erected last year. Sixty feet long and sixteen feet high, it is a popular cable car stop on rainy and sunny days. Although it would not provide much comfort from the damp morning air, I was drawn to it and settled myself down on one of many benches. My lunch pail sat next to me on the cold lonely seat. I shivered and my cold fingers turned my coat collar up. I had forgotten my leather gloves in my pocket and put them on.

My exhausted walk had taken me thus far; under lovely glass that arched toward gray skies. Where was the warm sun that I yearned for that would cast deserved elegance on the intricate cast iron? Had it deserted me, too? My body shivered again from the cold and the tears that ran down my face drew in the dampness and I wept more. My gloved hand fumbled in a pocket for a handkerchief and the horrible catastrophe which the morning unfolded on me, hit me square in the face and my constitution fell to pieces in the midst of curious but worried on lookers. My painful sobs filled the air and my embarrassment searched for refuge away from eyes that knew nothing of my troubles.

I made haste to the grand entrance that led to the underground restroom, and having found an empty stall, I wept for a long, long time. It was only after I had dried my eyes that I realized the restroom was dressed in marble and brass. I was in awe of what the world had to offer, even if it was flaunted in a ladies restroom underground. While men and women departed from the pergola somewhere above me, I wept again, for the truth of Mr. Whiting's words came to mind again. In a society which is dominated by men, intelligent women such as I deserve higher pay but will never secure it with men like Mr. Whiting. And yes, someday, I will be a wife and mother, and maintain the home while my husband works. But right now, as a working-class daughter, I should be paid fair while I hold an occupation outside my father's house. I thought that talent and ambition could overcome the disability of being a woman. I was wrong.

E...

April 9, 1910
Saturday

I have dreaded this morning and the task that had to be carried out. I have told Papa and the others the bad news. Papa could not finish his breakfast and has spent a good portion of the morning in the basement. Papa and Mama cannot hide their worries.

I explained that I was replaced by a man, which was not an entire falsehood—I just hastened my impending fate. John, Marie, and Alice act as if the financial pinch has already upset their tender carefree lives. A glance here, a look there. What do they know of the real world? Surely it is not taught in the classroom. In three years when John finishes school, he will make decent wages that he will be able to live on—all because he is a man.

It would be nice if Alice could get a position as a Page at the library on Saturdays. Perhaps John could assist a store merchant moving boxes or running errands. Perhaps, even Marie could do something at home.

I do not care for the heavy responsibility that is weighing my weary shoulders down. My dear Richard will be accumulating medical bills soon. How are we to pay for his hospitalization? How? I do not wish to write. I want to cry.

E—

April 12, 1910
Tuesday

One would have thought that I've sucked a whole lemon dry today because of my sour disposition. It is not a mystery to me what the main reason for my mental fit is stemming from. I expect the 'curse' to strike at any hour. The other reason for my dol-drums is the cold, damp weather we've been having all spring. Yes, the tulips and daffodils are in bloom, but last night they stood chilled while the air dipped to 31 degrees. I cannot keep my poor feet warm, nor my hands, nor my shoulders. Oh, when will the warmth of early summer come? A few robins are here, but not enough, and I suspect that they are waiting for spring to kiss the air so they may return to their favorite yards.

To-night at the supper table, Mr. Miller Sr. grumbled again about soup. Stuart Jr. and Todd also mentioned how tiresome soup night is. Only Nate continued to eat heartily as he always does and said that soup and bread makes for a delicious meal. I thanked him and very politely remarked to Nate, but not for his ears alone, "Do you wish to know why you have soup several times a week, Mr. Miller?"

Nate stopped eating and wiped his mouth with a napkin. He cleared his throat politely and glanced at his father and brothers who picked at my tasty meal.

"I can only imagine, Miss Eleanor, that the burdensome duties of washing and ironing alone fill up your whole day and do not leave any time or energy for an extravagant meal."

I stood there satisfied with Nate's reply, and searched the faces of the other Miller men as they chewed on sliced bread and glanced up at me. "With all due respect, Sir," I said while I had the opportunity to catch Mr. Miller Sr.'s glance, "men folk have no idea just how long

177

the cleaning and ironing process requires when I am forced to use out-of-date equipment that even my own mother does not use."

Nate looked at me. "Are you still using that old wash board, Miss Eleanor?"

"That I am. Have you seen anything new in this house during the past eight months that would assist in my chores, Mr. Miller?" I replied bluntly.

"Can't say as I have," Nate answered my question but was looking at his father, as well as Stuart and Todd.

Stuart leaned into the table. "Father, perhaps just this once we could indulge in the housekeeper's request. If it will quicken her duties so she can fix us meals that we are accustom to, I don't see the harm."

Mr. Miller Sr. was void of words as he bit off a healthy piece of bread, and while he ate he stared at the base of the candelabra. He let out several throaty grunts while contemplating his role in the situation. The liquor was brought to his mustached mouth, and with one large gulp the liquid was gone and the glass was put down with a thud. The flesh of his checks moved in waves as his tongue fished around the interior of his mouth. Mr. Miller Sr. pushed his chair back and planted the palms of his hands flat on the table.

I had been standing behind Nate with my hands concealed behind my back with fingers crossed in secret. Was there a chance that the hard, cold, and unbending father would submit to my needs, finally? If his answer was no, he would have left the supper table by now or continued on eating, ignoring me altogether. But no, not this time. I had a slight and fleeting chance that disappointment would not visit me to-day. Again, I was wrong.

Mr. Miller Sr. stood up and addressed Stuart, but gave me not the courtesy of looking in my direction. "Order whatever the girl wants, but tell me the costs. It won't matter to me since I won't be the one working to pay it off."

Mr. Miller Sr. was amused at his own little joke and laughed. He vacated the dining room, strode across the hallway and into the parlor. I could still hear him laughing.

Stuart also pushed his chair away from the table, grinning at nothing in particular, and having reached for his liqueur, he let it chase itself around the glass. He found great pleasure in this while eyeing me with heckling eyes. Stuart threw the vulgar liquid down his throat and wiped his mouth with his arm. He looked at me mockingly without ceasing his cruel laughter, and I knew that any luck that possibly still existed in the world, did not waste its precious time knocking on the Miller's door. His laugh consumed the last glimmer of light from the eye of hope; what was left was imprinted upon my face, and suddenly I burst into tears and ran to the kitchen, falling into one of the chairs at the table.

I let the tears run down my cheeks and wet my arms. I was tired, so tired! A bit of time went by when the door to the kitchen opened and Nate took up a chair across from me. He took my hands in his and I did not pull away. They were strong and rough, though warm and caring. I brought my weeping down to a sniffle and wiped my eyes so I could at least look somewhat lady like. Or is that possible after a lady has cried?

Nate smiled at me.

"Do I detect, under all that wonderful femininity, that boldness lies somewhere within?" he teased.

Nate's eyes were kind and gentle, and realizing that my face was growing warm from his attention, I did not think it would be wise to return his gazing affection.

"I should begin cleaning up," I suggested.

"In a moment. There is a matter in which I hope you will be agreeable with."

"Which is?"

Nate cleared his throat. "I would like for you to choose a machine for washing clothes, and whatever else you need that is 'up-to-date,' to make your duties lighter, if possible, while you are in this house."

I sat there in silence, stunned that this man was offering to do something that his father was refusing to do.

"Miss Eleanor, please do not look so….."

"Like what? How do I look?"

"Stubborn and tired," he replied.

"Is it a wonder, that I should be so tired? Your father, Stuart, and Todd are not sympathetic to what a woman does all day, or what goes on in her mind while she suffers over the hot range, cooking and heating water for washing…."

"Let me help you!" Nate's voice was growing impatient and he began to squeeze my hands a little.

"No! You can't! I won't let you…" I snapped.

"What you mean to say is, 'I would give anything to have a washing device, but I am too proud to accept one if it doesn't come from Mr. Miller Sr. himself.' Right?"

I lifted my chin and sniffled.

"Do the good people in Seattle know how stubborn you are?"

"Now that I have lost my job at the Insurance Company, the good people of Seattle will not see me anymore. I will end up a spinster like Marie will be. We can be spinsters together!"

"Eleanor, I am truly sorry about your job, but you are too handsome of a woman to end up in the ranks of spinsterhood. That, will never be your ending fate."

"You seem very sure of your convictions, Mr. Miller!" I replied, expressing a moment of justified sarcasm.

"Eleanor?...." Nate pleaded softly as I removed my hands from his and laid mine on my lap.

"Please tell me what is really troubling you."

"You really want to know?"

"Yes. Yes, I do."

I told him directly and honestly. I gave him the truth.

"Mr. Nate Miller, do you have any idea what it feels like to be offered poverty wages until a male accountant can be found to replace you?"

Nate did not know what to say as he appeared silent and stunned.

"What part has taken you by surprise, Mr. Miller. The poverty part? The replacing part? Have you never considered that a female could hold down an accounting position?"

He was obviously stunned and was searching for his tongue.

"I suppose all three. I had no idea that you were one."

"I am. I was."

"I'm sorry."

"Me, too."

I stood up, and while retying my apron strings I reminded Nate that a handsome face cannot pay household bills, nor a brother's medical bills. I rolled up my sleeves and looked at Nate solemnly.

"If Richard's illness should get the better of him, a handsome face will be of no use since it cannot buy a decent casket to lay him in."

I left the kitchen and cleared the dining room table by myself, as well as washing and drying everything. I watched Nate quietly remove himself from the kitchen, and I did feel sorry that I was so unkind to him, but my heart did not feel like making amends with everything happening to me and our family. Somehow I do not feel as if I owe anyone an apology for my behavior lately.

Nate did drive me home which was traveled in strained silence, except for a polite, "Goodnight, Eleanor," after he delivered me to my front porch.

After a nice bath, I found the Sears and Roebuck catalog and spent the rest of the evening in bed, dreaming of what could have been.

Goodnight, Eleanor

April 13, 1910
Wednesday

My dearest, dearest Richard! I cannot stop the tears—Did you not want to stay and say good-bye, or could you? How could we have said good-bye face to face? How can a tree branch not move when the wind blows against it? Can the stars in the heavens stay suspended without some unseen force? We could no more have seen you depart with Mama this morning to board the trolley which took you to the Interurban train which took you north—took you away from me.

I regret stepping into this house to-night—regret looking at the faces of my family—regret listening to the very quiet house as I stood in the living room. I looked at each face before they cast their somber glance aside. I heard Alice's voice call my name as I fled up the stairs to Richard's room—throwing the door open—I couldn't breath—I couldn't breath—dear Alice was holding me as I felt life draining from my body and soul.

Richard's bed was stripped—only a mattress on an iron frame—it could have belonged to anyone. Not even so much as a pillow or sheet to prove that Richard laid there.

"Be strong, Eleanor. Be strong..." Alice begged.

I collapsed on the bare mattress and let my body shake as I cried without control.

"Eleanor, I'm sure Richard is resting comfortably to-night. I'm sure he is being cared for in that nice place. Please, Eleanor...do not make this so difficult on yourself. You knew this day would come...didn't you?"

I rose off the bed in a fury. "How... how can you possibly! What gives you the-the right to call a place where people go to die—a nice place! You imbecile! What would you know about resting comfortably while you are coughing up blood all the time?"

Sobs and tears escaped from Alice. "Eleanor—you are hurting my feelings! Don't you think I miss Richard, too?"

I breathed deeply, "No—not as much as I."

Alice looked at me with angry eyes. "You are a very, very selfish person, Eleanor. You are not the only person in this house who is sad that Richard is so sick."

"Sad? Is that all you can come up with— is sad? Your brother is dying—and the only word you come up with is 'sad'?!"

"Stop it, Eleanor!"

"Yes, for you…that may be quite adequate," I cruelly admitted.

A hand swiftly stung my face—I broke out in tears, and in the blurry pain I saw a figure go to the doorway.

"I loved him as a brother—" she hesitated, drawing a breath. Her voice shook with anger; our eyes locking cruelly. Alice warning, I daring for the other to exhale into the suffering silence, sacred words. In order for such words to command the stage, feelings were disinherited; sisterly love was set aside. Her unmerciful expression had not changed, and then her lips slowly parted…

"If you cared for him any differently…you only have yourself to blame."

My eyes fell away from Alice's. I turned my tear-stained, hand-stung face away for a brief moment.

"Richard does not belong to you, Eleanor," Alice carefully breathed.

Somewhere within me, deep, deep in my heart, I could feel him, smell him, see him, hear his voice….I raised my chin. "Yes, he does," I said sternly. "He has always belonged… to me."

E….

May 4, 1910
Wednesday

I have not seen Richard since April 13th. John has taken up his room again after Mama thoroughly disinfected the iron bed, scrubbed the floors, and everything else. John isn't saying much, but I know he misses his older brother.

I write a note for Richard daily, and have John, Alice, and Marie do the same. Mama says he looks forward to our letters for it is the only cheerful thing in such a stark, depressing place. Only Mama and Papa have visited Richard since he was admitted 22 days ago.

Although the rest of us would dearly love to see him, Mama thinks it would be wise to wait. She does not want to risk the chance of her children catching 'something' in that hospital.

Richard's birthday is nearing on the 29th. He will be 23. I cannot imagine what it is like in that place, and I try hard not to. There isn't a day that goes by that I don't imagine myself bringing Richard armfuls of lilacs— the heavenly perfume snuffing out the likes of disinfectants.

I almost forgot. Back on the 30th of April, Miss Pauline's brother, Ambrose Pordessa, suffered head injuries during a fatal Interurban streetcar accident in Rainier Valley. Around ten at night, a runaway coal car struck a Seattle, Renton & Southern Railway car. The last coal car on a freight train broke free and rolled down a grade, striking the front of the car at an estimated speed of 40 m.p.h. Sadly, a judge visiting from Harrodsburg, Kentucky and a 13-year-old girl were killed. Incidentally, the girl's name was Julia Lee Rochester. Despite the age difference between Julia Lee Rochester, and the Julia Rochester which I know from the Insurance Company, I rang my former co-worker's house number just for my piece of mind. Apparently I was not the first one to inquire of her 'well being.' Julia is quiet shaken up after having read the article, too. Julia Lee suffered a skull fracture, injured internally, and both legs were broken. Fifteen others suffered injuries ranging from crushed hips, fractures, shock, cuts, and bruises.

This Sunday, the 8th, is Mother's Day. It will pass through this house quietly this year. Two years ago in '08, Anna Jarvis of Grafton, West Virginia began a campaign for a nationwide observance of Mother's Day, honoring the memory of her own mother, Mrs. Anna Reeves Jarvis. Anna Jarvis wears a white carnation, indicating that a person's mother is dead. A colored carnation means that a person's mother is living. Governor Hays requests a general observance throughout the state. The proper observance of the day contemplates that everyone shall wear a white flower, and if possible attend some church, where appropriate services will be held. (Someone failed to tell Governor Hays the significance of a 'white' carnation.)

This little poem was in the newspaper—

A mother's love—how sweet the name!
What is a mother's love?
A noble, pure and tender flame,

Mary Margaret Bayer

Enkindled from above
To bless a heart of earthly mould;
The warmest love that can't grow cold—
That is a mother's love.

Eleanor

May 16, 1910
Monday

The Snare — by James Stephens

I hear a sudden cry of pain!
There is a rabbit in a snare;
Now I hear the cry again,
But I cannot tell from where.

But I cannot tell from where
He is calling out for aid;
Crying on the frightened air,
Making everything afraid.

Making everything afraid,
Wrinkling up his little face,
As he cries again for aid;
And I cannot find the place!

And I cannot find the place
Where his paw is in the snare;
Little one! Oh, little one!
I am searching everywhere.

Oh, Richard dear, how I think of thee each hour! Do you know that with your departure, part of me went with you? In all our youthful years we have never been apart. To measure the depth of sorrow and pain that my heart is capable of inflicting is beyond my human ability. Please wrap your arms around me one more time, dear brother. Never let me forget the feel of your loving, warm embrace. I am afraid that I shall forget, someday, if you are taken from me.

Renouncement — by Alice Meynell

I must not think of thee; and, tired yet strong,
I shun the love that lurks in all delight—
The love of thee—and in the blue heaven's height,
And in the dearest passage of a song.
Oh, just beyond the fairest thoughts that throng
This breast, the thought of thee waits hidden yet bright;
But it must never, never come in sight;
I must stop short of thee the whole day long.
But when sleep comes to close each difficult day,
When night gives pause to the long watch I keep,
And all my bonds I needs must loose apart,
Must doff my will as raiment laid away,—
With the dirst dream that comes with the first sleep
I run, I run, I am gathered to thy heart.

Dear brother, I saw your sorrow late yesterday afternoon. The dark heavens opened and the torrent of your tears hailed down upon the earth. The branches of the lilac tree bent toward the ground under the weight of your unceasing sadness. Please do not cry dear brother least the branches snap and the beautiful flowers die. Though, you have every right to cry—I should not tell you what to do.

Olive Custance — by Lady Alfred Douglas

O! do you hear the rain
Beat on the glass in vain?
So my tears beat against fate's feet
In vain…in vain…in vain.

O! do you see the skies
As gray as your grave eyes?
O! do you hear the wind, my dear,
That sighs and sighs and sigh?…

…Tired as this twilight seems
My soul droops sad with dreams…
You cannot know where we two go
In dreams…in dreams…in dreams.

You only watch the light,
Sinking away from night...
In silver mail all shadowy pale,
The moon shines white, so white...

...O! if we two were wise
Your eyes would leave the skies
And look into my eyes!
And I who wistful stand,...
One foot in fairy land,
Would catch Love by the hand.

Goodnight, dear brother,
try to sleep....
love, Eleanor

May 23, 1910
Monday

The weather in Seattle is almost too fickle for me. Quiet suddenly, almost changing overnight, yesterday's temperature must have been in the middle 80's, with more than a touch of humidity hung in the air. John's honey bees have been rushing in and out of their box hives, scurrying here and there as time needs to be made up for the wet, chilly spring.

The lilacs are beginning to brown— I hate to see them go. When I visit the yard, I scoop up the lavender masses in my hands and breathed in the rich intoxicating perfume until my senses cannot endure further delight. Mama's bearded irises have been blooming, and the roses have just begun opening their petals.

A few neighbors have pink dogwood trees and are sharing them with Mama. There is a vase filled with them on the kitchen table and another in the living room. I keep forgetting to ask if her friends visit Mama, or does Mama visit them. Now that dear Richard is being cared for outside the home, I do hope that poor Mama will begin to go to her ladies tea parties, luncheons, card games, crochet gatherings, and devote her precious time to the church and to the needy of society. But if I am correct, I do not think Mama will. In order to indulge in the company of gay women while sipping tea and eating delicate cookies while your eldest son is coughing up blood—to pretend that all is cheerful—that is something which neither Mama nor I could manage.

Dear Richard, I do not know what to write you to-day, so I found another poem…..

by Laurence Hope
Ashore

> *But I came from the dancing place,*
> *The night-wind met me face to face—*
>
> *A wind off the harbor, cold and keen,*
> *"I know," it whistled, "where thou hast been."*
>
> *A faint voice fell from the stars above—*
> *"Thou? whom we lighted to shrines of Love!"*
>
> *I found when I reached my lonely room*
> *A faint sweet scent in the unlit gloom.*
>
> *And this was the worst of all to bear,*
> *For some one had left white lilac there.*
> *The flower you loved, in times that were.*

In church yesterday, a lady sitting in the pew ahead of us was unaware of a perplexing situation that she was putting our family through. You see, Richard, somehow on her way to church, she must have brushed against a bush or walked under a tree, for

on her back was a fuzzy caterpillar. I think John wanted to show it to her, which as you can imagine would have made the woman shriek. Marie did not want anyone to even touch the 'thing.' Alice thought it was 'interesting' while marveling at its ability to crawl in caterpillar fashion. Poor Papa and Mama tried to pay attention to the Mass but were caught up in the distraction. I wonder if our family was the only one to have noticed it.

What would you have done, dear brother? I know you and I would have had a good laugh, and no doubt would have received a light scolding on the way home. You cannot imagine how lonely church is without you. I try so very hard to picture you next to me…..please believe me dear Richard, that part of me has fallen ill because you are not with me in body. I wish with all my might that your strong spirit which is engraved on my heart could make up for your absence. I would make a marvelous doubting Thomas, for I need to feel the soft hair on your arms, and see your warm eyes, and touch your face to know that you are truly beside me. It is indeed, that very nature which is within me that is ill. To have been cut off from your brother is cruel and my heavy heart grieves constantly. Am I making sense, dear brother? Or, are these words hollow sounding, merely ink on paper? I feel inadequate at the moment—words, words, words. If only they had the ability to feel, touch, think, speak, cry—wipe salty tears from the lashes of a dear one.

Your birthday is near. You will be 23 on Sunday. I wish more than anything to be near you on that day. As they probably have told you, Mama and Papa feel it is best if the rest of us not come in contact with the impurities contained within the walls of the hospital. For days on end I have exhausted my mental parts, wondering what gift I can give you that doctors and nurses would approve of. While the purple lilacs were in full bloom I wanted to drench your room in the heavy fragrance, but unfortunately they will be a depressing brown by Sunday. Perhaps a bouquet of roses. Are flowers allowed? I would be crushed if you were denied a vase of Mama's roses—the first bunch this season—all on account of a friendly lady bug or spider escaping from the petals. The notion of disobeying Mama's non-visitation wishes distresses me, but for the first time in my life I must listen to my heart and not to her rules. (Please forgive me Mama.) Somehow I will try to find my way to your bedside on your birthday.

> Your loving sister,
> Eleanor

May 29, 1910
Sunday

Dearest Richard. Because life has forsaken you, my memory of you will be forever changed after to-day. Dear, dear brother! What has life done to you? Has our prayers which number in the thousands gone unheard? Why hasn't God taken pity on an innocent man? Why is He letting you suffer while the likes of the Miller family go about their corrupt lives, healthy? I do not understand this God of ours.

Our visit was very brief, wasn't it? I am very grateful to Mr. Nate

Miller for driving me. The roses which I cut from Mama's garden were supposedly for a friend who lived a few miles away. I did not feel right about making up a story to tell Mama and Papa, but I did not have any other choice. Nate was waiting for me a few blocks from the house—we rode in his father's motor car in silence.

Upon entering the grounds of the Tuberculosis Sanitarium, tall fir trees on the outskirts of the property did not dwarf the block long, three-story Tudor style building. At a distance it was impressive—if you could blot out the fact that the ill and dying were prisoners within those impressive walls. Nate stopped the motor car in front of the door way—another impressive sight in an effort to help visitors forget momentarily what is inside. I do not know how long Nate waited as he held the motor car door open for me. All I could do was raise my eyes to the intrusive building before us.

Yes, I know I was there—yet, I can calmly deny—for to really, really be there—means—that my mind must acknowledge that its two parts were there as a whole. Therefore, since neither will agree, I feel no obligation in the upkeep of my memory. For sometime now, a new Eleanor has been introducing herself to me…She is protecting me from what sorrow refuses to accept. She knows best what I can and cannot endure.

I must have floated over the herringbone laid bricks, up two small brick steps which were flanked by a lovely archway. More ornate trimming surrounded the out-of-doors foyer. Nate opened the door for me as I held the roses in my arms. He whispered that he would wait outside. Unfortunately, the other Eleanor cannot erase the strong smell of cleansers and medicines—the unsmiling faces of stiff older nurses in their pure white long dresses—my flowers for you were not allowed—Foolishly I assumed you would have had your own room, but against both walls beds were lined up one after another after another. Endless they seemed—all painted white over stark iron frames. To my right were low windows which began at about pillow height, and rose above the top of a nurse's head. At the top of the ceiling were ventilation windows which are kept open year round, I later learned. Dropping down from the ceiling were a few long rods with three short arms with glass fixtures attached.

I followed a cheerless nurse to your bed, but you did not recognize me at first because I was given a mask to wear over my nose and mouth. I was given a chair and was instructed not to touch anything— or you.

I am not sorry for having seen you—I shall not regret that I disobeyed our parents this once. I shall not forget the image of a dying young man, unsmiling, somber, your eyes lacking any hope for recovery. I can see your brown eyes, Richard. I remember exactly what a dying soul looks like through them. You know that you are going to die, don't you, dear brother? How many cloths did you use in the few minutes while I sat with you? How much blood did you cough up? Too much, I fear. There was so much I wanted to say to you. Oh, so much! But how does one make conversation while being surrounded by innocent ears that are starving to hear of news from beyond their stark walls.

I am trying to remember what I did say to you. Did I say anything? Or, did we just stare at each other—for what could be said? When I shut my eyes I force myself to picture you as a healthy man. It is difficult after to-day, but I shall try. I know that you would want me to remember you as you were a few years ago. Maybe not completely healthy, but you were happy, teasing, smiling, and so full of life....

I am sorry that I was sick after I left you...I knew in my heart that I would never see you again.

But then, I do not recall taking leave of your bedside—what I said to you—if we did speak at all—Did I really leave you, or am I still beside you keeping you company?

I can feel myself there, so yes, that is how it must be. Did I really walk by row after row of beds, away from you, away from you...down hallways, back to the door way.

Forgive me for not being as strong as everyone imagines me to be.

I cannot endure such penetrating grief which pierces one's heart.

E...

June—

In this month's issue of The Housewife, in the Editorial Outlook page, there is an article which I think I would like to share as I have pasted it onto this page. I mustn't ever speak of such things around Marie for she may be one of life's "unplucked blossoms."

An Every Day Tragedy

Some people imagine that to have a tragedy there must be murder or suicide but some of the deepest and greatest tragedies of human life are the living ones. And in a way we all have a hand in them whether we like to own it or not. Saying we do not believe a thing does not make it untrue, but sometimes we cherish this foolish belief.

A young girl surrounded by brothers and sisters, or else the only daughter, by some means or other never has had a proposal she cared to accept, and she gets up toward the thirties unattached. In spite of the fact that she is serene and happy, perhaps the mainstay of her parents, thoughtless people begin making remarks about "unplucked blossoms" and quizzing her as to why she never married. At first she regards the teasing lightly, but in the time the laughter and careless words hurt, and she determines to show everybody that she can get married is she wants to. The first man who proposes she accepts, regardless of everything, and the first act in the tragedy is presented.

Yes, it is a common happening, but none the less a tragedy. Many a woman well cared for and hedged in by every comfort, has deliberately thrust herself into untold misery by marrying a drunkard or a man in no way worthy of her, simply and solely because she wanted to show her friends she could be married. And she does not only ruin her own life, by doing so, but the lives of the children who should be a comfort and blessing to her. Be careful how you talk about "withering on the parent stem" and such foolishness. You may have a hand in some life tragedy before you know. It is easy to say girls should have more sense than to pay attention to things they hear, but how about yourself—you who are older and should be more sensible—are you never influenced by idle gossip? The best way to steer clear of having a hand in such troubles is to keep unkind and personal remarks to yourself, for personalities no matter how clever nearly always have a sting.

E—

June 5, 1910
Sunday

We have returned from church—a pointless endeavor on my part on having gone in the first place. If there were a drop of remorseful feeling within me, I may be astonished at my attitude toward God. But I feel nothing. My insides are numb, and what is around me does not matter anymore.

I am sitting at the little desk, gazing out the window that looks down on the street, and through the thin walls of our dear little house, I am listening to Mama crying in her room. She will be visiting Richard this afternoon. I cannot phantom the heartache that is ripping her soul apart. Papa will not be going—he cannot bear to see his son so close to death. Mama's first born. Her flesh and blood—I don't understand—I don't understand. Have I bolted my mental doors, refusing to let agony in— least it scrape away at my mental flesh? Oh, poor Mama! Her weeping has driven Papa outside—there he is—he pauses at the edge of the sidewalk and bends his head down. Hold on to your hat Papa…hold on to your hat. His hands slide into his trouser pockets and Papa has let his shoulders slump forward. I wonder if the neighbors see his shoulders shake as he sobs—as he turns left down the street, away from our dear little house.

Marie has entered our room and her tear swollen eyes do not see me. She softly shuts the door and strange low sobs from her body are shaking her bed. Her small, fragile back faces me. I cannot see her memories nor her tears. My own eyes are dead which is evident to the fact that I am numb— the flowers, the blue sky, the green foliage that I see means nothing. There is not a speck of recognition informing my head that these are things of joy. Joy has been amputated from my life.

The fate of Richard is robbing the life of those who remain— who must remain and watch death wrap its evil arms around my beloved brother. The disease chose its prey long ago. The victim's struggle is almost over. Suffering is pleading to drink the drug of Silence. Sleep dear brother, sleep in peace.

I will not look back on summer joys, or forward to summers of bright blue dye. Without you by my side, the evening earth will not smell so sweet, nor will the dew on flowers seem as clear.

Remember—Christina Rossetti (1830-1894)

Remember me when I am gone away,
Gone far away into the silent land,
When you can no more hold me by the hand,
Nor I half turn to go, yet turning stay.

Remember me when no more day by day
You tell me of our future that you plann'd:
Only remember me; you understand
It will be late to counsel then or pray.
Yet if you should forget me for a while
And afterwards remember, do not grieve:
For if the darkness and corruption leave
A vestige of the thoughts that once I had,
Better by far you should forget and smile
Than that you should remember and be sad.

From "The City of Dreadful Night"
by James Thomson (1834-1882)

The chambers of the mansions of my heart,
In every one whereof thine image dwells,
Are black with grief eternal for thy sake.
The inmost oratory of my soul,
Wherein thou ever dwellest quick or dead,
Is black with grief eternal for thy sake.
I kneel beside thee and I clasp the cross,
With eyes forever fixed upon that face,
So beautiful and dreadful in its calm.
I kneel here patient as thou liest there;
As patient as a statue carved in stone,
Of adoration and eternal grief.
While thou dost not awake I cannot move;
And something tells me thou wilt never wake,
And I alive feel turning into stone.

E...

June 8, 1910
Wednesday

How long have I sat facing this window... hour after hour—in my night gown—rain streaming down the glass in puddles—smudging my view of the gray world outside? The rain cries for me—it pounds and beats at the window—at the roof—I cannot see my dear Richard through the dark, shivering, wet skies...

I must read James Thomson again...

The chambers of the mansions of my heart,
In every one whereof thine image dwells,
Are black with grief eternal for thy sake,
The inmost oratory of my soul,
Wherein thou ever dwellest quick or dead,
Is black with grief eternal for thy sake.
I kneel beside thee and I clasp the cross,
With eyes forever fixed upon that face,
So beautiful and dreadful in its calm.
I kneel here patient as thou liest there;
As patient as a statue carved in stone,
Of adoration and eternal grief.
While thou dost not awake I cannot move;
And something tells me thou wilt never wake,
And I alive feel turning into stone.....

Oh, Richard dear! What shall I write? You are not with us anymore.....Your long, long vigil is over. You waited, we waited.... you knew it was only a matter of time, we knew it too, but the end is never supposed to come...even though the light grew dimmer and dimmer in your eyes. Perhaps you are not really gone...perhaps the household was not awaken in the dark, early this morning...and perhaps John did not answer the telephone—only to hand the receiver to Papa, but Papa could not speak, so Mama gently took it out of his hand. "Yes?" she said in a low, hesitating voice.

Our house, our dear little house was pitch black. I could not see faces— blackness poured into our little home and made it hard to breathe—rushing in, pressing upon us. Your being which is gone, suddenly left a massive void—I felt it in the blackness...it crept through the room, touching our skin with invisible fingers, paralyzing our limbs. It was not you which was felt, but of a ghost, running madly—swirling around each of us, sucking the particles of life from the air.

"I see...."

We heard Mama's voice...she was having difficulty breathing. The ghost of death had placed his lips against Mama's and was stealing the air from her lungs.

How we sat—frozen, pinned to where we were at that moment—I turned to stone on the steps of the stairway—fourth step up from the bottom—left hand side—leaning against the wall, hugging my cold body.

"I see…" My Mama sniffled and her voice was breaking.

Papa, John, Alice, Marie, and I…were we breathing? I could not hear air flowing from our nostrils, nor did death let us see each other. Had we all turned to stone?

Mama's words had separated—shock—she was polite to the doctor—her heart bled, crumbled, withered, her chest opened and it fell to the floor—thud—is that what I heard? The sound of Agony was groaning and crying at her feet. Did I hear it murmur Richard's name?

"Please…yes…you may begin the arrangements as we discussed…yes,… yes, thank you for calling…yes,… thank you… good-bye."

Mama and Papa became statues—years passed so it seemed before they returned upstairs; their painful journey back to their room. I will always remember how their feet sounded on the bare wood—slow, unhurried, step by step they forced themselves forward. The gripping of hands on the railing; gripping, grabbing, gripping, grabbing—moving upward. They had to move upward.

Oh, my beloved brother!! It would have been better if I had gone with you! Do you realize that my life cannot go on without you?! You have forgotten me!!!! I will not know how to live without you….I cannot, I cannot—I am coming dear brother….

Your adoring, loving sister,
Eleanor

Dr. Henry

In the hallway just outside John's room, Dr. Henry rests his hands in his pockets. His tired figure looks into the room where the deceased once lived. Richard's bed is neatly made he notes, and still, it does not seem possible that the young man whom he had cared for since birth is dead. It has been three days since Richard's last breath, one day since the funeral, three days since his sister has sat practically unmoved in the chair just inside her brother's room. John told him this much...

"She stares at Richard's bed as if he is lying there. She will not let anyone touch anything. If someone sits down on his bed she lashes out at them and orders them out of the room. She stares at the bed while backing up, puts her hands out to feel for the chair, often tripping."

Every day since Richard's passing he has looked in on her. He is worried. Very worried. Miss Eleanor has always been the strongest of the three girls—but now she is frightening him as her behavior is obviously stemming from shock. According to the family she did not go to the funeral but has been in the chair just after dawn on Wednesday. She has not ate nor slept, and she looks like hell. Dr. Henry let his head fall forward and rubbing his eyes he hears soft foot steps coming toward him.

"Dr. Henry?" whispered Alice.

He removed his hands from his tired eyes and let them focus on her.

"Mama has a cup of coffee waiting for you in the kitchen," Alice spoke as quietly as possible.

He let out a heavy sigh. "Thanks child, I'll be down in a moment."

The sound of her feet echoed in the stairwell, and he faintly heard her say something to her mother. Then he heard another voice...

"I am here Richard….I am here….I will not leave you…."

Eleanor whispered those words again, as she had done many, many times during the past three days. Her lips, which barely moved, were the only signs of life within the young lady.

"I am here Richard….I am here….I will not leave you…."

Dr. Henry remembered the cup of coffee and took out his pocket watch. Three o'clock. Papa would be at the kitchen table too, drinking his 3 o'clock coffee which is customary in Vienna, he was told. He made his way down the steps and paused at the landing. Mama, Alice, Marie, and John all looked at the doctor. Papa placed his coffee cup on the saucer and put his German newspaper down on the table and glanced over his glasses. Dr. Henry was tired—tired of telling the poor family, "No change…," so he brought himself over to the table and sat down without a word, sitting there with his hands covering his tired eyes as the aroma of coffee rose and filled his nostrils.

$\mathcal{N}ate$

In the hallway he waited for something to happen. Dr. Henry left hours ago and told the family to call him no matter what the hour, if, and when Miss Eleanor should snap. It killed Nate to see her hurting herself like this. It was strange seeing the woman he loved in her nightgown, her beautiful dark hair cascading down her shoulders, down her back....but the rest of her did not look like the young woman whom he met on Saturday, October 16th last fall. Nate's memory quickly brought back the lovely but limp figure of the fainted Miss Eleanor at the Alaska-Yukon-Pacific Exposition. Eight months ago…Eight months ago he knew he was in love the moment he saw her…And since that wonderful evening, there has not been a day allowed to pass without that incident playing over and over in his head. But this….over the past months she had been losing weight, growing pale, her beautiful singing had ceased long ago, her soft little smile gone. Gone….it all went away with her dying brother.

The gas light was turned down low in Richard's room; just enough light so Nate could see Eleanor, just enough light for her to see Richard's bed. As for the rest of the house, it lay in darkness, for light is not obligated to stay for sorrows sake.

A thought inched its way into Nate's mind. A disturbing thought, but not unreasonable, considering the circumstances; considering how close Eleanor was to her brother. Could it be possible, he wondered, that Eleanor was 'willing' death to come to her so she may be with her brother? He rested his head against the wall and let out a long sigh. Her unceasing murmuring of her brother's name lulled his eyes closed, and although Nate promised himself that he would rest for just a moment, the curtain of slumber was drawn and he joined the others in sleep.

But it did not last long, for a blood curdling scream was thrown into dark rooms. The family and the young man had been waiting for something to happen…for their daughter, their sister, his love—They all had waited for something to happen…for her to come to, for her to snap, but they weren't prepared to see the young woman's eyes glazed over in the terror of hallucination, grabbing one of the pillows off Richard's bare mattress—for poor Eleanor was watching little red men trying to climb up her brother's bed—she began hitting them repeatedly. She yelled at her family to get the little red men off Richard as they crawled like busy ants....

"Why are you standing there?!" she shrieked, running around the bed. "Don't you see them!? Can't you see them you fools?" her voice frightened those who heard it, for it was not her own. "Why don't you care?—" she sobbed.

She finally noticed Nate beside her and glared at him with wild eyes.

Eleanor pleaded with petrifying alarm, "Hurry Nate!" confronting him with appalling dismay. "Do something!!" Fear was thinning her voice, extracting breath from her lungs.

Nate grabbed Eleanor by the arms and tried to pull her to him. "Eleanor honey, there isn't anything after Richard....he's—"

She jerked her head towards the bed.

"Richard? Where?—"

A possessed cry left her lips. "Richard!— Richard!!— Where are you!?— Where are you!?"

She filled her lungs with her dead brother's name and hurled it against thin walls. Eleanor's face went colorless and her body would have hit the floor if a pair of arms hadn't been waiting for the fall. Nate scooped her body up and ordered John to immediately fetch Dr. Henry; ordered Alice to open their bedroom door and hastily asked, "Which one?" as he carried Eleanor's limp body carefully through the bedroom door. Alice pointed to the bed against the wall and under the sloping ceiling adorned in wallpaper. He gently laid her down and brushed the hair from her white face.

Marie, who hung onto the doorway as though she were nailed to it, was told to fetch a washcloth and a pitcher of water. Her parent's stood out of the way for the young man was taking matters into his own hands. They stood rigid with an arm wrapped around their stomachs while a hand stifled worries from tight lips.

"Tell Marie to hurry up!" Nate barked, his own voice now yielding to desperation from hours of worry and his inability to give aid to a suppressed mind. His control and influence were being undermined by a memory.

Alice went to the doorway to check on Marie but was almost run over by her, causing some water to splash on the floor. In the brief moment of jilted distraction, Alice removed the picture and wash-cloth from Marie's grasp and had it placed on the night stand while poor Marie was still in a quandary over the wet floor. And taking the washcloth Nate dipped it into the cold water, wrung it out, and tenderly pressed it against Eleanor's face.

"Eleanor honey," Nate whispered, his insisting words quivered, stirred by agony, "you must be strong...too many people depend upon you." Then taking a deep breath he lowered and softened his voice. "I need you—you have to know that by now." Nate's lips moved though only he heard this oath, "I am not going to let you go with him..."

As he spoke to her, Nate noticed that her breathing was growing shallow, and her already pale skin turning paler.

"Eleanor?—"

"Nate...Nate? What's wrong?" Mama wailed as she flew to his side.

"I don't know—" the words flew from his lips. Nate was not listening to his own voice as it communicated to all a reason to dispense unexercised panic. "Where's Dr. Henry!"

Papa couldn't stand it anymore. "Ach mein durftig kind! (Oh, my poor child!) Ach mein durftig kind! Teuer Got, gefallig tun nicht lassen todesfall anspruch ihr zu!" (Dear God, please do not let death claim her, too!) Leaving the room he covered his face with folded hands and shook his head in grief.

"Eleanor..." Nate lifted her upper body and pressed it against him. "Be strong my love! You cannot leave me! Don't leave me! Don't leave me..." Nate was crying as Eleanor's head fell back as he clung to her.

While Mama got down on her knees on the wood floor, pressing her eyes shut, she heard the young man weep as she prayed out loud. Alice and Marie quickly joined her as fervid pleading voices filled the room.

Sunday
June 19, 1910

Dearest Eleanor,

I pray that this letter finds you in better spirits and that you are regaining your strength so that you may come home and be with us girls. It is terribly lonesome in our room at night without you. I miss our hushed little chats while Marie is asleep. Do get well soon.

I am sorry to confess and I hope that you do not scold me, but Mama and Marie put on a lovely little graduation party for me yesterday—though it was not the same without my eldest sister to add to the conversations at hand.

Because our family is in mourning, I was very hesitant to even bring up the subject of my graduation—for I feared that in the midst of all that has taken place this month that, my commencement may have slipped dear Mama's memory. As it so happened, I was pouring over The Housewife magazine on the porch one day when Mama came to join me. She asked what article I was engrossed in and I replied in a little above a whisper, "A Rose Party for The Graduate." I could not speak bravely—for on one hand I knew that such expectations on my part were cruel, though on the other, I secretly pined for what so many other girls will have; those girls being society girls, of course.

I can only believe that Mary Sumner Wilkins, the author of such article, had envisioned luncheons and evening parties for frolicsome lassies and possibly lads somewhere in New York where the magazine is from. Such young people will be playing croquet on lush green lawns near the sea-side and playing other gay little games. I shant suppose 'those' graduates won't be wearing anything less than the best. Can you just picture it Eleanor— all the girls in crisp, pure white dresses, or lovely five-gored skirts joined at waist. Oh, Eleanor! Somehow, if I could be in the company of such fine dresses, even for a day—Oh, the China silks, the white linen and lace and trimmings!

Now, for shame! Look what I've done! You are laughing at me, aren't you Eleanor dear. You are probably saying, "That silly little Alice, she is forever thinking about designs and costumes." Yes, yes—and perhaps—Oh, Eleanor—I just thought of something simply divine! What if I went into the skirt and waist pattern business? I wonder how difficult it would be. Oh, now I'll never be able to sleep to-night with such entertaining notions buzzing around in my brain.

I must get on with telling you about yesterday's party.

Well, Mama must have known how badly I wished for even a small party in our yard, for she patted my hand and said that I should not be cheated out of sweet and pleasant things as I am stepping across the threshold of womanhood.

I nearly sprang out of my chair and hugged Mama in delight.

I sent thirteen written invitations and pasted a pink crepe paper single-rose to the upper-left hand corner of each.

Those invited were: Misses Evelyn Gibson, Mary Ballard, Hetty Hubbard, Grace Wooding, Lilly Inglis, Dora Walker, Elizabeth Hemphill, Rose Hart, Fanny Lyle, Mamie Barber, Myrtle Powers, Gertrude Peterson, and of course, Frances Harper.

Although the party's theme was "roses" Mama did not want to empty the few bushes we have, so in their place, I cut handfuls of fragrant sweet-peas and put them in canning jars for centerpieces. All the girls commented on the lovely smelling flowers and were delighted to learn that before their departures, each guest would be given a portion of the large wavy flowers on long stems.

By each plate I put a dainty homemade paper rose and inserted in the center a rolled up piece of paper with a "prophecy." I wrote each girl's name on the largest leaf so I could write laughter provoking with appropriate gentle sarcasm on pet fads and ambitions.

Mama thought that a delicate and not expensive menu would be:

Tomato Cream
Salmon patties
Stuffed Lettuce
Bread-and-Butter Diamonds
(sandwiches cut in diamond shape)
Strawberries and Ice Cream
Fortune Cake
Strawberry Punch

Mama and Marie baked a fortune cake iced pink with tiny sugar roses for decoration. The cake held the usual ring, dime, thimble, compass, pen point, and other little things. I cut the first piece, then by each girl in turn.

So far as amusements were concerned, we had fun doing puzzle patchwork where guests were distributed to small tables with a cut-up puzzle at each, and then hat pin prizes were given to the table that first completed a picture. (Mama bought a few pretty new hat pins made of real rosebuds metallized from your friend Miss Ernestine McAfee.)

I wish you could have been here for the festivities— your name was mentioned once or twice in passing—mainly from Miss Harper I believe. She does so enjoy being in your company.

On the whole, the occasion was one of success—my classmates and I laughing of our escape from the school room in the cool shade of our house. Our little group of emancipated females, knowing there had been many graduates before us, truly felt that we were the most important thus far.

The scope of topics enlightened on popular and not so popular teachers whom we bade farewell, exams we were free from, and which girls were packing suitcases in anticipation of a journey to a far away University.

One of us will be wearing a veil of black, for Mamie Barber will be joining the Sisters of Holy Names of Jesus and Mary, teaching at Holy Names Academy here in Seattle. This news did not come as a shock to us, for as long as we have known Mamie, that is all she has ever wanted to do; to teach and join a religious order.

As conversations go, we young females exercised great restraint in saving the most important topic for last. Matrimony. The question was raised. Had anyone heard of a bride-to-be among us? Very casually, and skillfully too, her timing drawn out superbly to the end, a tiny suppressed giggle escaped from Miss Grace Wooding. All heads turned in surprise for we had not an inkling that Miss Grace had so much of a beau to speak of. After some coaxing, she gave tid-bits on the groom to be, and after some pondering and guessing, both Lilly and Frances asked if the lucky young man was none other than one of our own classmates. Miss Grace blushed and said it was so.

For shame, for shame we scolded her lovingly for keeping such a secret from us. And for shame on me, secretly wishing that it was I instead wearing the long white lace veil, and I, receiving lovely wrapped gifts that would fill a whole room. Oh, the lovely dreams that each of us verbally envisioned caused happiness and envy to dwell in the same heart of hearts.

Matrimony, which is on every young girl's mind brought up the subject of one young man in particular, John, and where he was keeping himself. Gertie and Elizabeth thought it was naughty of me to not have invited John as they had seen him in a recent school performance and was quite smitten of him. The age difference of "only" two years, one of the girls noted, should not discourage or narrow our scope of determining a "good catch" if one is in view. This I noted, caused Miss Hetty's fair complexion to turn in shades of my party's theme color—pink.

Miss Frances Harper, who, knowing John's where-abouts on a Saturday, informed all curious ears that she thought she saw him down the block with a friend. While dear Gertie stood up pretending to imitate John, and upon reciting a few lines from "In Blossom Time" which was comical because it came from Gertie and not

John, I noticed one of us—a quiet little thing was entranced as she listened to Gertie. I turned slightly, studying her indirectly and with a reserved hidden smile, for it was not dear Gertie this young Miss glowed in admiration of; for if I remember correctly, at the Spring Recital, sitting with her family a few rows behind ours was Miss Hetty Hubbard. All attention, except mine was fixed on Miss Gertie, for I saw one shy little flower mouthing silently every word 'before' Gertie spoke it.

In Blossom Time
by: Ina Coolbrith

It's O my heart, my heart,
To be out in the sun and sing—
To sing and shout in the fields about,
In the balm and the blossoming!

Sing loud, O bird in the tree;
O bird sing loud in the sky,
And honey-bees, blacken the clover beds—
There is none of you glad as I.

The leaves laugh low in the wind,
Laugh low, with the wind at play;
And the odorous call of the flowers all
Entices my soul away!

For O but the world is fair, is fair—
And O but the world is sweet!
I will out in the gold of the blossoming mould,
And sit at the Master's feet.

And the love of my heart would speak,
I would fold in the lily's rim,
That th' lips of the blossom, more pure and meek,
May offer it up to Him.

After all good and lively conversation was used up, we hugged each other, wishing bright futures to all; hoping all paths be filled with nothing but joy and happiness.

Purely, and for the sole purpose of relating back to their own mother's as to what our home interior is like, the girls slipped through the house clutching their share of sweet-peas to thank Mama for the wonderful afternoon. With that task completed, they politely bade Mama good-bye and departed down the front stairs, which on all account was far more respectable than walking around the yard.

All were gone, with the exception of one. I hadn't noticed her at first because I was on the porch waving and throwing kisses to my classmates, but there she was, hesitating until she saw the girl before her leave. Mama, who noticed the shy and quiet girl who hung back until the time was right, gave Hetty all her motherly attention.

The interesting thing about Hetty, is, that although she is shy and doesn't talk a great deal, what she chooses to say and how she say's it, is far more worthy than Frances Harper's ability to prattle on and on. Thus, after the pleasantries of a "I have had a most delightful time," Miss Hetty congratulated Mama on raising such a fine young man as John—his memorization an attribute to note-worthy tutoring at home by his parents.

Mama replied and confessed that she could not take credit for such skills, for memorizing and reciting poems is what John does best, without her assistance.

And, by-the-by, with her shyness giving way in the comfortable company of Mama, a genuine sweetness drifted through the air like that of a bouquet of fragrant sweet-peas as she smiled a sweet little smile. In the space of a few minutes or so, and perhaps— without an agenda on her, Hetty and Mama talked and walked their way to the street, just as easily as a needle and thread makes a seam. I held back on the porch, for something in a woman's mind knows when to interfere, and, when not to.

Hetty Hubbard turned and smiled at me, thanking me for inviting her.

I in turn wished her the best, and if fate allowed, perhaps we would see each other's names in the paper under "Wedding Announcements"— someday.

While we waved and blew little kisses to each other, Mama was making her way up to the porch, waving to Hetty, too.

But, as fate would soon have it, Mama will be sipping tea and nibbling delicate cookies this week while in the fine company of one—Mrs. Hubbard.

Well, dearest sister, I hope this letter has kept you company as I am trying to keep you up-to-date on events during your absence. All is being maintained as such at the Miller's—I cannot say any more than that, for Mama made me promise not to upset you with little

matters that Marie and I should have known better about —so, I best close, least I tell all—

Thinking of
you, your sister, Alice

July 5, 1910
Tuesday

My room—our room—it feels like a stranger to me.

It is difficult to express myself… Where do I begin?

I spent twenty-three days in the hospital—resting, regaining my strength, gaining a little weight. I am ashamed for what I have put everyone through. I have been so inconsiderate—not considering Mama and Papa's feelings…

As much of burden as I was, I could not have helped myself for my constitution was broken.

Nate came to visit me every day, and with each visit he brought flowers. The nurses said I was the luckiest girl alive. Mama, Alice and Marie came once a week as to not interfere with my rest. Before I was discharged from the hospital, Mama and I went to the counter to pay my bill, but to our surprise (and relief), we were informed that it had already been paid in full. The young lady would not tell us who the generous person was. She didn't need to.

It is a little past seven in the evening. Yes, it does feel good to be home. I'm not sure who is the happiest to have me back home…Alice or Marie. In my absence, they have been working for the Miller's, and according to Nate, they had a pretty rough time of it. Soup and biscuits is all they dared to make, which raised Mr. Miller Sr.'s temper each night and caused plenty of crying in the kitchen. In my sister's letters, (which they took turns writing, when they weren't fiercely exhausted at night,) there were many unspoken 'thank-you's which I read over and over in the gloomy hospital. They had no idea what I did each day prior to their 'unappreciated, loathsome time working for such an unpleasant (Marie's description) and repulsive (Alice's description) family.' Mr. Miller Sr. frightened and intimidated both girls with his temper and gruffness, and Stuart Jr. could not be trusted with a turned back. According to Alice, he took liberties of freely gazing his eyes up and down her in the most vulgar way. And

206

of course, with each gulp of liquor his behavior worsened. And, if Nate had not been present to keep his drunken brother at a distance from Alice and Marie....both girls would have stayed home after the first day. But now they know. Now they know. Do they understand now what it must have felt like on the 29th of August last year, when Stuart Jr. brazenly pulled up in front of our little house and practically pointed his finger at me? Do they finally appreciate all that I have gone through since the 11th of September of last year?

One letter in particular I will not forget. Marie forgot to put the ice card in the front window one day and for the next three days the family ate canned food due to a warm ice box. Marie said the Miller's yelled and yelled at her, and she cried and cried. When the ice wagon came on the next delivery day, Marie had that card hanging on the window. Then it was Alice's turn to cry. One rainy day she forgot to put down a path of newspapers from the back kitchen door to the ice box, and across her clean floor was a terrible muddy mess. Although she must have felt like scolding the ice delivery man, it was her duty, not his, to protect the kitchen floor. Neither Alice nor Marie forgot those two duties again. It is twenty after eight. They should have been home by now.

And John....his only duties are caring for his bee hive and cleaning the chicken coop.

I can see an automobile coming down the road. It is slowing. It has stopped in front of our house. I can hear the front screen door creaking open, and creaking again as it closes. Papa watches Alice and Marie climb the steps to house. Creak—creak goes the door. Nate looks very somber as his eyes are down cast. Papa has put a hand on Nate's shoulder and is squeezing it. Through our open window the automobile sounds louder as it is thrown into drive and the wheels move forward. I am watching Papa as he watches Nate disappear down the street, but now Papa is pausing at the sidewalk, facing the house, looking up at our window. Something tells me that I should go to him.

Papa and I have returned from our little walk around the block. I have learned that the Miller's have filled a missing persons report for Todd and a roommate who has not been seen since Sunday. How terrible! Todd's disappearance is suspicious since his clothes and belongings remain at the dormitory. Mr. Miller Sr. suspects his son has been shanghaied from one of the saloons south of Yesler Way. The Seattle Star has been reporting for years that shanghaiing has been occurring at an alarming extent in this city. I'm trying to picture

Mary Margaret Bayer

Todd, waking after being rendered unconscious, on a foreign bound vessel, most likely to China. Poor Todd! Kidnapped for the soul purpose of compulsory shipboard service. Crews for ocean-bound ships are sometimes difficult to obtain says Papa, so sailors and non-sailors have been known to disappear without a trace.

I don't know how close Nate was to Todd, since Todd seemed to have spent most of his time at the University. But no matter, a loss is a loss. I can't imagine how Mr. Stuart Sr. is handling this. I'm sure it will be in the paper tomorrow morning.

It is late and Alice and Marie are in the bathroom getting ready for bed. They look exhausted! Alice said she was so glad to get home to-night. Neither Mr. Miller Sr. nor Stuart Jr. ate their supper, but each of them carried a bottle of liquor up to their rooms. Nate invited the girls to join him at the table, which they did.

I think I will return to the Miller's house tomorrow, but will have Alice and Marie help me until the end of the week.

Goodnight,
Eleanor

July 10, 1910
Sunday

I suppose I ought to put something down on this piece of paper, or else close the top of the fountain pen jar.

Another warm day. Yesterday was 86. To-day 82. Our bedroom is warm and stuffy—I dearly wish a breeze would sweep across this desk. The air is not moving outside—not a leaf stirring—too hot for my feathered friends to sing to-day.

We have been home from church an hour or so. I wish our friends and neighbors, who mean well, would put an end to their inquiries of how I am, and all their well intended sympathies for Papa and Mama. Such wearisome individuals inquire if we know so and so who is ill—only they know—only they care. Some people seem to keep a mental tally of the ill and those who do not recover. Is there a contest, which I do not know of, to see how many funerals one can attend in a week? Then come Sunday it is necessary to brag—what fools! I asked Mama on the way home why we must be polite to people who exhibit rudeness and think nothing of it. After a few moments of silence, all she could say was, "It's our Christian duty."

Thanks to John, my raspberries did not go to waste during my

208

absence. He picked them every other day and a nearby store bought them for a decent price. John gave me an envelope full of green-backs, and having given John a portion of the profits, I gave the rest to Papa. Any remaining berries will be used for jam, but there will not be enough to last through the end of autumn. Last years supply is already gone. Perhaps we should wait till winter when the delicious flavor of summer will be appreciated.

At dinner this afternoon, Mama told Alice and Marie that they will be helping me at the Miller's until September. I am sorry to say that my two sisters are being somewhat cool towards me. I'm positive that Alice and Marie assumed, as I did, that their days at the Miller's house were over last Friday. Alice had planned to speak to Papa and Mama about securing a summer job at the new library. She had seen an advertisement in the paper in need of a "Page" which pays $30.00 a month. From the look on Alice's face, it seems as if the subject had not been brought up yet. Poor Alice. I know how much she wants to work around all those books, and how she detests working at the Miller's which is 'killing her youth, her beauty, her vitality.' As much as I would like to have Alice help me and keep me company, I shall have to speak with Mama and plead on Alice's behalf.

Supper consisted of cold roast-beef sandwiches, potato salad and lemonade. Everyone was glad that the range did not have to be going on a hot day like to-day. We ate a late meal on the front porch as dusk was closing in. A breeze finally did stir around us as well as a few mosquitoes.

Alice is speaking to me again. Mama told her that if the job is already taken at the library, she will be helping at the Miller's. All for to-night. Hopefully we can sleep in this warm, stuffy bedroom.

Goodnight, Eleanor

July 11, 1910
Monday

Marie and I are home. What a beastly hot day it has been! Although it was only 80 degrees outdoors, it must have been in the high 90's in the kitchen. I spent most of the time in the kitchen instead of Marie for she cannot handle the suffocating heat while baking bread and preparing supper. Instead, she made herself useful with stripping beds and making them; cleaning the water-closets; dusting and other light duties. I wish Mr. Miller Sr. would be content with cold meat sandwiches, potato salad, and lemonade like our family had last night. But no! He and Stuart Jr. must have a meal! I don't think Nate cares one way or the other on these hot days.

I would assume that most men do not have an inkling how insufferable women's work is in the summer time. They do not care if the range must be fed wood and coal to heat gallons of water for wash day; for baking and cooking. I shall be glad when autumn and winter falls upon us once more. I even tried imagining that snow was falling in the kitchen, but it melted before it had a chance to land on me. I did have the back door and the two kitchen windows open, but it made little difference since not a breath of air stirred passed the window sills. I wonder if hell is made up of millions of ranges. Is there any difference between here and there?

When I could, I stood outside on the partially shaded stoop and watched the birds gather around the end of the drain pipe which is connected to the ice box. (I wish our ice box had a drain pipe instead of a tray which must be carried outside daily.) The cool melting water must be a treat for my little feathered friends. I was envious of them as they frolicked and splashed about. They did remind me to splash water on my own hot sweaty face.

Nate has been working very long days as he goes to work early to take advantage of the cool morning hours. He has developed a handsome tan which makes him all the more attractive and charming. While making lemon pudding to-day, I dreamt that Nate poked his bronze head into the kitchen to tell me that he was home, and looking at me with sympathetic eyes, he immediately found a wash cloth, wet it with cold water, and gently wiped my face and neck. He did this without saying a word, and his tender eyes kept me from whispering tender words of thanks. Nate smiled at me, and then kissed me on the forehead before he went upstairs and took his bath.

Yes, Nate did come home, and for a quick moment looked at me from behind the kitchen door. But ever since the kitchen has been unbearably hot in June and this month, he has quietly excused himself from helping out with the cleaning duties. Yes, Nate did look hot and dirty and tired as he stood there for a moment to say that he was heading upstairs to take a cool bath. A cool bath... Did he not see the sweat on my red, flushed face and wisps of hair clinging to my wet neck? Did he not see the huge circles of perspiration under my arms? Did he not recognize a woman on the verge of faint from heat exhaustion? Apparently not. What man would?

Marie and I did not speak on the way home—for that would require us to put forth one's strength which we could not spare on such a laborious task. As Nate helped us out of his motor car, he asked me if there was anything wrong. I did not trouble myself to answer his foolish question. I let out a heavy sigh, and without looking at him, I followed Marie into our house.

My bath is over and I feel like going to bed early. I am feeling a bit nauseated at the moment. I do hope tomorrow is cooler.

Goodnight,
Eleanor

July 13, 1910
Wednesday

Yesterday was a strange day weather wise. The morning was very cool so Marie and I wore light sweaters on our walk to the Miller's. Just after noon it rained for about fifteen minutes, and then gradually warmed up to 80. A very strange day indeed.

Alice began her new job yesterday at the four year old library. I envy her now… to be able to dress in nice clothes and feel like a lady… to mingle with other people… how lucky can a young woman be. Every day she can take the trolley to Spring and Madison, and dismounting from her click-ety, click-ety carriage, stand on the cemented (not dirt) sidewalk, and before she makes her way up the grand stairway to the front door, she'll lean her pretty head back and admire the height of the elegant yet stately building.

I wonder if I'll ever have time to borrow a book like thousands of others do. I cannot imagine having hours and hours of idle time just devoted to reading. How wonderful that would be. Alice informed the family to-night that a library borrower can deposit their books at local fire stations, instead of carrying them all way back to Spring and Madison Street.

At supper to-night, John asked Papa and Mama if he could look into securing a job with a new company called American Messenger Company located downtown.

Founders of the three year old company, James Casey and Claude Ryan, are in the position to increase the number of bicycle messengers. Mama isn't so sure she wants John darting between horses, motor-cars, street-cars, and pedestrians on those shaky two-wheeled contraptions called bicycles. John did point out that he is

211

almost in 10th grade and wants to be a wage contributor during the summer months like Alice. Papa said that he will talk it over with Mama. There is no doubt in my mind that John will be on a streetcar tomorrow morning applying for the job.

Oh, dear, I suppose that means I'll have to give Marie back to Mama. She needs Marie to help with the cleaning and washing. Oh, dear...

Goodnight,
Eleanor

July 16, 1910
Saturday

This morning I received a letter and photograph from my dear friend Mrs. Howard Wallingford. Minnie's picture of her holding an adorable baby is propped against a vase full of Mama's roses. The new mother is smiling tenderly, her head turned, glancing down at the child who looks blankly at me. The baby boy, Theodore Raleigh Wallingford is adorned in yards of lace cascading over his mother's lap. The new mother looks happy as any new mother should be—for she has brought life into the world. But sadly, my dear friend has a deplorable tale to tell...

Shortly after the baby was born, while the mother was recovering from the pain and exhaustion of having given birth, her husband and mother-in-law stood in the room talking.

"Well done my son," Minnie's mother-in-law announced, "you have finally given me a grandchild. Now you are entitled to your inheritance."

"Thank you, Mother," said Howard as an envelope was handed to him.

I am trying to picture it all....poor Minnie.... the confusion, the heartache, the deception...

"Don't you want to hold your son?" Minnie's question was cast at her husband as he headed for the door.

Minnie confessed, Howard turned and looked at me blankly before he coldly replied, "Why? I have what I need."

"The inheritance papers were tucked inside his jacket, and then my husband left the room without holding his son. I was still in a state of painful confusion as the truth was being made known to me.

I asked Howard's mother to please explain herself. She had this to offer…"

"Well, my dear, did you really expect my only child to marry without knowing if the prospect-bride was fertile or barren? I instructed Howard to lay with you, and when your menstrual discharge was arrested at the second month, I knew your mother would want a quiet wedding as her daughter was already with child."

Mother Wallingford smiled at the little bundle I held next to me. "You see Minnie, my son has illegitimate children—somewhere." Mother waved her hands about in the air as if they were butterflies. "Naturally, as far as I'm concerned, they do not exist. I told Howard that if he wanted any inheritance, he would have to marry and produce a grandchild. Naturally, not in that order."

Poor, poor, Minnie! I truly feel sorry for my dear friend. I wish I could visit my friend, but I would not want to be in the same house with Mr. Wallingford.

I am holding the photograph and am looking at a baby that was born almost eight weeks ago. What kind of childhood will little Theodore have as a Wallingford? The poor, poor child.

Eleanor

July 19, 1910
Tuesday

I thought summer had forgotten us earlier this week. The weather has been very cool—very much like autumn. I felt the premature stirring of autumn which made us women don our sweaters during the second week of July. We were very tempted several times to start a blaze in the fireplace, but Papa told us just to dress a little warmer.

John has been reminding us of his up-coming birthday on the 30th. I shall have to start thinking of a gift for him. He will be fifteen years old and going into the 10th grade in a few months. He is turning into a handsome young man, and during this past year his voice has deepened. I will say this about my brother…he has many wonderful qualities, two which I can name immediately; John is a hard worker and "I can't" is not in his vocabulary. Someday he will make a fine catch for some lucky young lady.

I was so glad to be able to hang the laundry outside to-day in the nice warm sunshine. I detest hanging things up in the dark and dingy basement when cool days forces me to do so. While I was outside, I glanced at the domestic help that was hanging wash also. They probably wonder among themselves why this household does not hire a china-man to do the cooking, and another for the domestic servant, and another for doing only laundry. These small-frame men from the orient wear tight looking little black caps on their heads with a long thin braid down their back. Few of the men have cut their hair; perhaps in an effort to fit into our culture. The china-men wear straight, loose tunics covering pants, and sticking out from under the pants are little black shoes. Now and then, when I am sweeping the front steps and porch, a Chinese domestic will be standing on a front porch opposite the Miller's watering two large pots filled with tall, white Calla-lilies. The china-man is courteous and polite as he bows to me. He goes about his tasks quickly and has a very serious face.

After having seen so many china-men on the hill, I asked Papa about these different people with silted eyes who speak an unrecognizable language. According to Papa, Washington Territory and Seattle would not have developed as fast if Chinese had not helped build the Western railroads, and now, as then, provide very low-paying help in lumber mills, canneries, hop farms, coal mines, and road construction projects. They flocked here when gold was discovered in the rivers of Oregon, Washington, and British Columbia. Right now their kind must live in the Chinatown quarter in Pioneer Square near 2nd Avenue and Washington Street because there are restrictive covenants by real estate agents and home owners that prevent the Chinese from living elsewhere. Also, they can not own land, and special taxes are put upon them. I do think that is very unjust. Any man who works hard and does not make trouble for his neighbor should be allowed to own land. Papa thought he read that the Chinese families are planning to move to the International District where they can establish food and import-export businesses, restaurants, laundries, hotels, churches, language schools, and gambling halls.

Although they look so different from us, I do not like the thought of a nationality being taken advantage of, just because they have come from a place, far, far away.

E—

July 27, 1910
Wednesday

Mama and I witnessed the first flock of geese taking to the south-bound skies Monday evening. We were resting on the front porch, making quiet conversation, enjoying the lovely hour; enjoying each other's company. Suddenly we heard "honk, honk, squawk, honk, squawk, honk," from above. I jumped out of my chair and ran down the steps to see the large brown birds with their long necks grace-fully flapping over our house. I stood on the walk and exclaimed to Mama, "Already? Doesn't it seem a bit early this year?"

"Oh, I don't know," Mama replied after a moment of reflection. "It is almost August...."

"Well, I don't think they ought to leave 'til September."

On Monday, Tuesday, and this morning, we have awoke to cool, gray skies. But gradually the gray thins and the sun quickly warms to 80 degrees by eleven o' clock or noon. And then, by evening, a nice breeze stirs and the air cools enough that a sweater is needed for outdoors.

Earlier this week (I forgot exactly what day), the robins, chick-a-dee's, starlings, sparrows, and finches appeared all of a sudden. It was as though their nesting duties were over and their babies had grown and left the nest. Now the parents are free to do as they wish. It pleases me to see them again.

Eleanor

August 2, 1910
Tuesday

To-day is Papa and Mama's 25th wedding anniversary. According to their wishes, it has passed quietly. Simple to extravagant cards from well-wishing relatives and friends grace the top of the piano. I cut a few hydrangea branches and phlox stems and placed them in the living room. Since the blue hydrangea bush and pink phlox are of the few flowering plants in the yard, I asked Papa and Mama to over-look the flower's meaning. Mama said that she has never understood why such a beautiful blue flower would say to its recipient, "You are a boaster and are heartless." On the contrary, the phlox means, "Showing no disagreement." I'm glad Mama liked my gift. I wish I could have bought her and Papa something fancy—something nice. They deserve something better than a handful of flowers.

By the way, John had a nice little birthday last Saturday. I made him a cherry pie instead of cake. He had to work on his birthday which he didn't mind. John loves his new job, but finds bicycling in downtown Seattle very physically challenging with all its steep grades. Mama has quite a time waking him each morning since he exerts so much energy during the day.

Forgive me, but I do not feel like writing much to-night. I should write a letter to dear Minnie soon. She sounds terribly home sick.

Goodnight,
Eleanor

August 4, 1910
Thursday

I cannot remember another August that was this fickle...Two nights ago, on Papa and Mama's wedding anniversary day, the moon lurked behind patches of dark clouds, its light resting on the edges of darkness here and there—its effect was quite eerie.

On Wednesday night, the wind howled a lonesome whistle through our bedroom window. I laid in my bed in the darkness, and wondered if Mr. Wind is just an invisible face with his cheeks puffed out, his lips circular, blowing swirling cool air against our window, and through the opening his breath becomes a song.

During the day the weather can range from warm, pleasant, cool, cloudy, or light rain. Although I detest hot days which are so common in August, women in this region who cannot escape laboring over the miserable range are having a period of welcomed reprieve. I am counting my blessings.

After supper to-night, John received an unexpected telephone call from Nate Miller, inviting him to go fishing Sunday afternoon. I think John was just as surprised as I was, and after receiving a nod of approval from Papa, John accepted the invitation.

"What's the matter?" Papa asked John as seeing that John had a puzzled look on his face.

"I wonder why Nate wants to take me fishing."

"Well..." Papa stretched out the word as he was thinking and reading the evening paper at the same time. "Mr. Nate Miller isn't a stranger to the family... after all, he has been driving your sister home for almost a year now. And, he does know how much you enjoy the sport. I can't imagine his father or brother wanting to join him."

I just had to let out a giggle at the thought of Mr. Miller Sr. and Stuart fly-fishing in a stream, or standing on the bank of a lake or a pier somewhere. John and Papa could not help themselves either and broke out in laughter too.

"It has been a while since I've taken my pole out of the closet...." John paused for a moment and stared at the maroon oriental rug. "I remember how much Richard used to love fishing.....used to love the outdoors.....it didn't matter if he and I came home empty handed. He just loved being outside...."

The living room was very silent and very still. We had not expected John to mention Richard's name so soon as our house is still in mourning. I held my breath and nervously stole a glance at Papa—his face was wrinkled in a painful way. He slowly rose, and dropping the newspaper on the couch, Papa faced the dark and empty fireplace. He placed one hand on the mantle and covered his face with the other. Pity and pain seized my heart, and standing beside my Papa, I put my hands on his shoulders.

"Ich im ganz recht, teuer tochter. Ich im ganz recht."

Papa nodded his head, trying to convince me that he was all right. But the truth is— none of us are.

I turned to look at poor John. His head was bowed and upon his face was a mix of sadness and frustration. I know that Papa isn't the only one who mourns....Papa's depth of misery is deep for one who is not with us. I wish he would talk to John or at least pat him on the shoulder, and tell him that it is OK to acknowledge one's mental anguish for a deceased son or brother. But Papa will not, for that is not his nature, nor the nature of his generation. John on the other hand needs to talk, needs the companionship of another man. I want to, but am afraid to talk to John about him missing his brother. Are certain things meant to be left unspoken by a sister? Or by the grace of God, is there an instinct in man which comes to the aid of another man when there has been a death in the family?

John left the room and ran upstairs. He did not shut his door quietly. I wish Papa would have gone to him. Poor John! I can't begin to imagine how lonesome he must be. Who can John really talk to? Oh, dear God! I am truly sorry for my selfishness in the past. At least

I have Mama and Alice to confine in. But who can John turn to? No one...except Nate.

> Thank you,
> and goodnight-
> Eleanor

John and Nate

To the right of the two men who sat on the grassy banks of Lake Washington, the early evening sky laid down a light pink blanket of clouds behind tall fir trees on the large spit of land next to theirs. Behind them, firs doted the shoreline, and passed the firs was a spit of dirt where a Touring automobile was parked. During the course of the afternoon, the atmosphere was frequently interrupted by the jingling of harnesses and the clip-clop of horse's hooves. Sunday afternoon lovers who snuggled against each other came in road wagons, road carts, and spring runabouts. Some buggies sported stylish automobile seats and snappy genuine leather tops bent front wing dash—a special automotive design—padded with leather of course. Couples of four and small families arrived in surreys with either leather tops or tops with fringes. These were more automobile like than buggy in appearance.

The handsomest family carriage by far was a Cabriolet. The two fishermen whistled low so the occupants could not hear. With father, mother and younger brother in tow, a young Miss eyed the two handsome men and smiled a pretty little smile. Her parents quickly noticed her unladylike behavior and urged the pair of horses to continue on, almost making a circle in the dirt along Washington Park Boulevard.

Nate gently elbowed his companion that sat on his left and grinned.

John had already begun to blush and felt embarrassed for doing so.

"What?" Although the young man of fifteen had turned his blushing face away, he was having difficulty suppressing the laughter which embarrassment brews.

"I think that pretty little blond with the blue eyes took an instant liking to you, John."

Now it was John's turn to poke an elbow in Nate's ribs.

"Don't jest! She was making sheep eyes at you, and you know it!"

"I don't think so John….I saw how that young daisy was trying to get your attention…"

"Oh, so you were looking at her too!" John accused Nate with a hearty laugh.

Nate raised his right index finger in the air to justify his glancing which any healthy man cannot avoid.

The older of the two cleared his throat and spoke in a mocking though serious tone of voice. "Only for a brief moment, my friend. You see, I was admiring the tufted seat cushions of upholstered leather; the poplar panels; the graceful patent leather double fenders; the handsome oil burning lamps; the black enameled leather top; the hickory spokes made of second year growth—no doubt. And, did you see the shiny black finish on the body and gear? Did you take notice of the rich Brewster green seat panels as they harmonized with the black body? The pillars and moulding on the body and seats were painted blood carmine. The gear, wheels and shafts on that attractive Cabriolet were painted Brewster green….but in the matter of seeing a blond haired, blue eyed female? Only for a moment—her head was interfering in the view of the auto curtain fasteners!"

John and Nate glanced at each other and then broke out in hysterical laughter.

"Does my sister know how wicked you are?"

"No. Not yet!"

"Are you going to marry her, someday?" John asked bluntly.

Nate replied, "Yes!"

"You sound awfully sure of yourself, Mr. Miller."

"I am. And please, no Mr. Miller. Just call me Nate."

"All right, Nate. What makes you so sure that you'll snag my sister?"

"Simple. I never take 'no' for an answer, and I always get what I want."

The young man turned to Nate and chuckled.

"Good luck!" warned John.

"How do you mean?"

"Well, for starters, you aren't going to win her over if she has to continue using that wash board that she's always grumbling about."

"Oh, no!" Nate gasped, smacking his forehead with the palm of a hand. "I quite completely forgot all about that! Oh!!" A long groan came from the man's lips as he shook his head. "Now I understand why your sister has been cool and withdrawn towards me since April! Nate, Nate, Nate! You fool!"

"That bad, aye?"

Nate shook his head. "Now I remember! One evening during supper, Eleanor had asked my father for an up-to-date washing devise, but he turned her simple request down. I remember how she cried... Then I told her to give me a list of whatever she needed to make her duties more manageable."

"Did my sister ever show you a list?" John asked.

"No. No, she didn't." Nate quietly confessed. "But I should not have waited for a list though. I should have taken matters in my own hands."

"Well, knowing my sister, she's probably waiting for your father to purchase some sort of contraption and park it in the middle of your kitchen floor!"

"I'm sorry to say, but it would have to snow on the hottest day of the year before my—father will buy one."

John let out a disappointed, "Oh..."

"Oh!" Nate exclaimed.

John turned and looked at Nate who was grinning a mischievous grin.

"Say, did you ever catch any hints as to what model of washing machine your sister might like?"

John thought for a moment. "I think it was from Sears and Roebuck, their newest ball bearing kind...was a little pricey for our family....over six dollars I think. But I suppose the contraption is worth every penny if we men don't have to hear Mama and the girls grumble and complain!"

"Yes, Sir! Won't she be surprised...right in the middle of the kitchen floor! Should arrive by train sometime in the middle of this coming week."

"Think you've got it all figured out, do ya?" John questioned his smiling companion who was reeling his line in.

"Know so!" Nate spoke with confidence and nodded his head to prove it. "Maybe this will make her happy and she'll start singing like she used to. Oh, what a voice your sister has! Sweeter than honey."

John let out a mocking laugh. "Are you serious? Do you really think a girl would get giddy over a washing machine, be gratefully in debt to you, sing like a canary to you, and then someday marry you?"

Nate paused a moment, flicked his line and grasshopper bait above the water, and when the lure went 'plunk,' into the water, he answered with a "Yep!"

"I don't get it."

"Don't get what?"

"Well..." John stopped short as he picked through his mind for the correct and respectable way to put his inquiring question.

He could see by Nate's side-ways glance, raised eyebrows, slightly wrinkled forehead and crooked grin that his friend wasn't quiet sure what his younger companion might throw in his direction. John finally decided to just come out with it.

"Are girls that easy to please?"

"Girls? I dunno…I wouldn't know what sparks their fancy at that age, but there can't be that much difference between pleasing a girl or a woman."

"Why's that?"

"'Cause they all have one thing in common."

Nate looked out on the water to check on the location of his floater.

John gave a slight sigh hinting of exasperation. "Well, do I have to guess, or are you going to draw this out while the sun goes down?"

"My dear boy! You live in a house full of females. Haven't you ever noticed what your mother and sisters wish for?"

"Well, I never hear Mama want for anything. If she does, you'd never hear about it. And for the girls…well…it's always something. A new pretty waist, and," John reached for the flimsy rim of his blue broadcloth cap and took it off for a moment, "…a new hat, more magazines, more lacy things, little purses made from walrus' and more hat pins. And, if all that isn't enough, the girls want to put even more things on their big hats! Ostrich feathers and pigeon wings. Roses, grapes and cherries!"

"That's quite a wish list all right. Say, just how happy was Eleanor when I gave her those two hats and the set of hair combs?"

"Oh, those! My sisters spent hours in front of their mirror admiring themselves, turning this way and that."

"So, am I to understand that they were 'pleased' with the 'things' that I gave Eleanor?"

John was quiet for a moment, and turning his head he saw that Nate's eyebrows were slightly raised. "Well, I suppose so…but those are just… silly things."

"For us men—perhaps. But, if any of those 'silly things' brings happiness and pleasure to a woman, and, if that happiness will lead to other accomplishments…"

"Like snagging my sister…." John interrupted.

"Like snagging your sister…then, it is up to us men to make sure that the women we care for receives 'things' now and then."

All of a sudden there was a jerk on Nate's line and he spun the handle forward. "It's like this," explained Nate as he unhooked the plastic grasshopper from the fish's mouth, "things to a woman are like—worms and grasshoppers to a fish. Here."

Nate had put the trout in the willow basket with the other two good size ones and handed the basket to John.

"Aren't you going to take any?"

"Nah. You take them."

"Gee…thanks."

"Well, I think we should be going," Nate suggested, glancing at the approaching buggies filled with young lovers, wanting to park along the water's edge to catch the enchanting sunset that was falling behind the tall firs across the water.

The two fishermen gathered the tackle box and poles and reluctantly put their gear on the back floor where a large lunch basket sat. In the passenger seat sat a very happy and content young man who watched Nate crank the starter handle and got the touring car chugging. Nate quickly got in next to John and adjusted the spark by a lever on the left side of the steering column. He explained that sometimes it takes a driver a year to know precisely where to set the spark and throttle levers before starting and how to adjust the choke just so. On the way home, Nate promised that he would teach John to drive, if John promised to go fishing with Nate again.

By the time Nate deposited John at his doorstep, both men, if not especially John, felt as if they had known each other for years.

And for John, he had found what his aching heart desperately needed…a brother figure.

August 23, 1910
Tuesday

"All right girls, let's get this article read so we can honestly tell Mama that we have done so," Alice let out a deep sigh as she retrieved the magazine from the dresser, and making herself comfortable on her bed she began.

Why I Married A Woman Who Could Cook
by William H. Hamby

"My dear, I wish that you could play bridge like my mother used to."

Did you ever hear it that way, you wives who read this page? Ah, no! Of course you didn't. And I fancy you will never read it so in the annals of man's yearnings. The old, old wish is usually unjust, for most wives of to-day cook far better than their husbands' mothers ever did; but the fact that even their mistaken yearnings are still for cooking shows which way men's hearts blow.

I married a woman who could cook, not primarily for the cooking, although that is of tremendous importance, but for the qualities such as ability and taste stand for. By a woman who can cook is not meant one who can, if she has to, endure the torture three times a day of getting "something that will do;" nor one who splashes and dumps together a meal we can "make out on this time;" nor yet one who goes to the kitchen semi-monthly and lectures the "bought cook" on how not to do it. I mean a woman who not only knows how, but loves to cook; a woman to whom a daintily set table is fine art, a carefully balanced meal higher mathematics, delicately flavored food poetry, and a good cup of coffee a true benediction.

Man's sentiment has been rather unmercifully mangled by the odd saws about his heart and stomach being twin brothers; "feeding the beast," and the like. We are ready to admit frankly that what a man gets to eat at home plays a big part in his happiness and accomplishments—yes, and his affections. A man must have a very strong faith in a reward after death to enable him to plod through forty years of married life without either a square meal or a divorce. Yet fond as man is of good cooking, it is not the food which she serves that wins and holds him, but the qualities in the wife which make her a good cook.

We can think only in material terms; and the mind always selects some physical manifestation to stand for spiritual conditions or truths. When your mind runs back to some very, very happy day, you find no picture there of your happiness, no conception of the wide, glorious spiritual uplift. But instead memory finds the rock on which you sat, the leaves that waved above you, the white sail in the distance, a voice, a look, a touch. All are physical things but they stand for a day of beautiful, indefinable spiritual ecstasy.

It is the same with those we love. Beauty, nobles, devotion alone are barren terms. We do not think of them. Instead we recall some feature, some act, some item of daily work and care, and these physical things stand to us for the deeper meanings.

And so, when the man on the street or on the lonely country road rides in the gloomy chill of a Winter's rain toward his home, it is no catalogue of abstract home virtues that stirs within his heart glad, eager anticipation. His mind seizes upon the light of the burning fire, the dainty white table and smoking, savory food; and a warmth and happiness steal through him soul and body. But really it is not the food nor the fire, but that there lies in the wife that which makes these comforts and this care. Only that is spiritual and not definable to his mind.

And thus it is when I married a woman who can cook and loves to, I did it not primarily for the cooking, but for the qualities this implies in a woman.

And what are those qualities?

First and above all, a love for home. A woman who loves to cook and can do it excellently is a born home keeper. Who ever saw one of that kind who did not want to keep house? And heaven have mercy on the souls and bodies of men whose wives have no home instinct! There are many people whose circumstances, location, or occupation make it impossible for them to have a home of their own; but if the wife has the home instinct she will make even a temporary abiding place habitable. Better the instinct without the home, than the home without the instinct.

Such a woman is orderly. No sloven was ever a good cook. It requires deftness and precision of movements and that requires mental grasp, alertness and concentration. These qualities not only make a woman orderly in her home but efficient and successful in her social and other activities outside the home."

E—

August 24, 1910
Wednesday

"Goodness!" Alice exclaimed as she stood behind Eleanor while she brushed her hair in front of the dresser table. "How much rain does God think we need?"

"Apparently, too much!" Eleanor replied. "I don't understand how we were suffering in 91 degree heat two weeks ago, and now this. We must have received a few inches just this afternoon alone...Ouch!!"

"Sorry..." Alice apologized as the brush hit a snag in Eleanor's long dark hair.

"Well," sighed Marie, "I suppose I'll make it my turn to read the next column

since Eleanor is getting pampered. Marie pushed her bed covers back and planted her bare feet on the wood floor, and going over to the tall dresser she picked up The Housewife magazine. "Now listen you two," Marie advised. "Mama just might ask us questions just to make sure that we have read this."

"Did Mama tell you that she would?" asked Eleanor.

"All she said was that I had to make sure that each of us read it, for in Mama's opinion, this article is probably one of the most important concerning a young woman's future happiness. Now, let's see…were did you leave off last night, Alice?"

"Start at the top of the second column."

"Right." Marie cleared her voice.

"The woman who loves to cook is usually of a wholesome temperament. A moody, brooding, disconsolate sort of woman is seldom a good cook. The woman of a cheerful outlook, the one to whom the worst can somehow be mended and all the good enjoyed, makes the finest cook. She has taste. She loves pretty things for herself because she enjoys them, and not because she wants to attract attention. She loves pretty things for her home because it makes it more delightful for those who live in it.

Again this woman who loves to cook possesses a fine mental and spiritual quality akin to that of the poet, the painter, the sculptor and the preacher. It is the spirit that loves beauty and fineness and pleasure; the spirit that gives to others the bread of life; the spirit of the student and yet the creative and inventive quality of the discoverer. The player who must see the next note before he knows what to strike is not a born musician. So the cook who must go by set rule is not a born cook. The genius cook knows how to pull and push this stop and that, to deftly touch here, and intuitively add there, putting in and withholding ingredients, and all with such ease and sureness that the result is a symphony in brown.

And, too, she who loves to cook is nearly always good company. Keen mentally, original, wholesome, clear-sighted, she sees things as they are, yet know they are pretty good.

Judged as cooks women are divided into four classes. And this classification is the most valuable document that can be placed in the hands of a young man who hopes after awhile— Valuable because it not only indicates what he is going to get, but largely what he is going to be."

"I wonder if Mama is going to make John read this too," Alice interrupted.

"Of course. She said that she will make sure he does. Like Mama said, a man needs to consider whether a pretty young thing can cook or not. A handsome face and figure does not fill a husband's stomach nor makes home life pleasant. May I continue?" asked Marie.

"If you must," said Alice.

"First: Those who can't and won't. This class includes both those who are too mentally dull or physically lazy to learn, and those who have no home instinct. With right instruction and sufficient inducement many of the ignorant ones might have been—and may be yet—taught to cook fairly well. Many of them have never learned and knowing their failures hate to do it, just as we all dislike to do what we can not do well. The husbands of these have that seedy, boarding-house look which haunt men who never get over the notion that anyone, fool enough to marry as they did, has little chance of success. The other sort—those without the home instinct—are often brilliant and accomplished; but they were never designed to marry. They were created to fill that part of the statistics which reads: "Number of women more than men—seven per cent." If they do marry—and alas! they do—their husbands usually get a divorce or a contract to travel for something.

Second: Those who can not and will. This division embraces that very distressing class of women who make cooking a drudgery—and eating a punishment. Some of them cook from a sense of duty, feeling they must do their part but hate it—and do it abominably. Some of them cook because they have to—it is that or worse, and worse would be awfully bad. Few of them make any effort to learn. Their only object is to get "something" done enough not to produce immediate cramp colic, and get it on the table in some sort of shape within an hour or two of meal time. They "get" three meals a day for forty or fifty years without even learning to mash potatoes or boil eggs."

Marie put the magazine down on her bed and yawned. "I can't imagine anyone married for that long without learning to mash potatoes or boil eggs! Alice…it's your turn to read a column."

Alice put Eleanor's hair brush on the dresser and settled down on her bed with the magazine. Meanwhile, Eleanor picked up Marie's brush from the dresser and standing behind her, began to brush her hair.

"Ready?" asked Alice.

"Ready," echoed Eleanor and Marie.

"They serve sloppy victuals, over-seasoned and under-seasoned food stuff, burned on the crust and dough inside: four varieties of food of the same kind one meal and nothing of any variety the next.

Their table looks like a nightmare that has been trying to catch a train while half dressed, and their housekeeping matches the table. Some of these women are real good, pious, devout, emotional; some are club women; some are semi-business women. But a great many are simply ignorant, untrained women who have never known any better and never been inspired to learn. They know nothing of the pleasure of learning and the joy of doing one's work well. Some of the symptoms of the husband of this kind of a cook are: drunkenness, dyspepsia, insomnia, billousness, dirty linen, bent back, bad temper, grouch and woe. Few of these husbands are ever known in the gates—but many of them are known behind them.

Third: Those who can and will not. This style of woman has allowed her natural instinct to become perverted. Either her affections have gone awry or else she is consumed by some outside ambition. She is often brilliantly attractive, and often disastrous. Single, she sometimes accomplished a career; married, she usually ends two. Her husband has a flower in his buttonhole, a taint on his breath, and a pistol in his hip pocket.

Fourth: Are the women who can and will. God bless them! And there are lots of them to bless. Really this civilized America is pretty full of good cooks, of women who love their homes and take pride in their work. There are already millions of them, and more are learning. This is the woman who is not a drudge, nor a slave to her household work. She reads, she plays and sings, perhaps; she has her clubs, her charities, her church work. But still home is the place of all places that she loves. And her deft fingers and dainty taste make the kitchen a place of sweet incense, the dining room a place of delight, and the living room a haven of rest. She bears her common lot of burden without too much complaint, she does her work cheerfully, she asks for her natural rights, and gets them."

"I wonder," Alice interjected," if Mr. Hamby has included 'voting' as a natural right?"

"Probably, as long as it involves something to do with cooking and eating!" Eleanor huffed.

"She makes the best of the bad, and better of the good. She is a woman of sentiment and sense, of spirit and flesh, of vision and practical work.

Now, of course, I do not mean that every woman ought to cook three, or one meal a day, or even one a month. That will depend on circumstances. But I do mean that it would be fortunate, indeed, if every woman were a good cook and took pride in it. Whether a woman cooks the meal herself or directs it done, she should know the food values, know the best ways of preparing and serving food, and take pride in doing it or having it done excellently. It should be as much a matter of pride to mix and bake a perfect cake or batch of bread as to write a poem which is accepted for publication, or to paint a picture which secures exhibition. Indeed, I am not sure that the cake or bread triumph is not the greater for so many can share in the results of the glory.

Any woman of ordinary intelligence can learn to do this. Not all can be poet cooks or genius cooks—as is mine—but all can be good cooks, and in learning to be that most women will learn to enjoy the work of preparing a meal.

With the many inventions in the culinary line cookery is no longer the drudgery…"

"How would he know?" Alice huffed.

"…that it was when the wood-burning stove needed to be crammed with heavy logs every hour or so; when coal ranges were of uncertain temper and the oven a matter of chance, as much so as the church fair grab bag, for no cook was exactly sure what would come out, no matter how carefully it had been put in."

"Mr. Hamby must be from the east coast, and his lucky, perfect wife must be fortunate to cook and bake on a gas range," Eleanor spoke to Marie's reflection in the mirror.

"Sugar loaf does not require being broken from its cone shape by chisel and hammer, nor does roasting call for the tedious turning of the spit. Really great intellect, even genius has been put to work to improve and lighten this domestic science, and as much of the brains so exercised belong to the men it shows pretty conclusively the sex regards that matter as well worth serious attention."

"What doesn't belong to men?" exclaimed Eleanor with a sigh. "They own the business world, run the political stage, and only pass laws if it benefits them. They own the home while the wife is only married to it. I think I should like to write to 'Mrs. Hamby' and find out what her true point of view is on this 'domestic science' called cooking."

"You should," replied Marie.

"Now let me finish…just a few more li—" Alice yawned suddenly, "a few more lines, then we can go to bed."

"Sorry," said Eleanor.

"The well-fed family is the contented, happy family. I defy a man to do his work properly, to think out important matters if he has a lump of lead falsely called biscuit clogging his digestive apparatus; if he has been sent from the breakfast table with his appetite dulled but not appeased by half-raw, half-charred chops or steak, hard potatoes, pasty cereal and muddy coffee. I defy any teacher to get rational school work from a boy or girl who is fed in such fashion. I defy any one to blame either man or children if they seek other quarters for comfort as soon as the chance offers."

"Done!"

Alice handed the magazine to Eleanor, who in turn placed it on the tall dresser.

"Let's go to bed," Eleanor yawned, putting Marie's brush on the dresser table.Marie scrambled into bed first, leaving the task of blowing out the light up to Eleanor.

In the dark room, Alice mumbled one more thought before drifting off to sleep.

"I can't wait until tomorrow night, Eleanor, when you get to read the final 'words to the wise' by a man who has to tell the world, 'Why I married A Woman Who Can Cook.'"

"Good-night, Alice!"

"Good-night, Eleanor."

August 25, 1910
Thursday

"All right, girls," announced Eleanor. "Settle down. Let's get this column done with so we can start looking at the new fall fashions in other magazines. Oh bother! Where did you leave off Alice...?"

"Um...somewhere at the top of the left hand column I believe..." Alice answered with a bit of uncertainty in her voice.

"Found it—ready?" Eleanor inquired with weak enthusiasm concerning the article that would enrich their understanding of another point of view from a man.

Alice and Marie laid on top their beds in their nightgowns and echoed a gloomy sounding, "Ready..."

"The woman," Eleanor began, "who from such ignorance—willful ignorance—or from laziness fails to feed her household properly is interfering with business and with education, is literally driving her husband and children away from home. The man into the saloon, maybe, the children into the first place that promises to feed them well. If she does not understand and fails to take means to inform herself as to the selection of the best materials and ingredients she is playing traitor to her husband and children, and acting as supporter to the tradesman. If she does not make proper use of good materials when they are furnished she is a waster of her husband's money and a destroyer of her family's health.

Is it worth while?

Is it worth while for the woman herself, her husband and children, to enjoy three meals a day instead of suffering three bargain counter feeds? Is it worth while for them to have strength and health, clear eyes and springy steps? Is it worth while for the home to be bright and orderly and the meals on time? Is it worth while for the members of a family to look forward with eagerness and pleasure to the home coming? To anticipate gleefully the deliciously cooked even if simple viands which will be set before them in cleanly attractive guise, presided over by a good-humored, neat womanly woman?

Is it worth while for the tired man, after a day's battle with the complicated problems of business, and another battle with the elements, it may be, before he sees the lights of home, to be suddenly invigorated and encouraged as that gleam falls across his pathway, knowing full well what it betokens, what plans for his comfort and cheer?...."

Eleanor's eyes fell to the picture of a young man returning home. Rain and wind pushes upon his back and his umbrella; his galoshes stepping in unavoidable puddles as he rounds a brick wall, his head turning towards a house, his house! The lights are glowing and warm, and behind the door, happiness and contentment—everything a man desires and hopes for. Eleanor pictured Nate walking home in the rain after a long day at work, and wondered if he would have a smile on his face and a glad heart, knowing that she was preparing a wonderful, tasty meal for him? It occurred to her that Nate and his fellow co-workers may ask each other how well their wives fare in the kitchen. She would hope that Nate would say to the other men that his 'domestic help' is a wonderful cook, and the men in return would be jealous.

"Say, daydreamer...." Alice snapped her fingers in the air.

"Huh?" Eleanor looked up. "Oh...I was just..."

"Daydreaming?" teased Alice.

"And I bet Mr. Nate Miller was in it too!" Marie chimed in.

"Oh, you two hush!" Eleanor wished that her rosy cheeks were not warm, for she knew that they were betraying her most intimate thoughts.

"Isn't it worth while for his heart to beat warm as he thinks of the woman whose influence and management has made his home a haven of peace and happiness to be longed for during the day and joyfully returned to at night? Aye indeed it is worth while. Not only for the comfort and health it imparts but for the affections it holds and the spirit it develops…"

Eleanor stole a glance at her sisters and saw that she was not the only one who could not hide the effects of a stirred heart, for what young woman could deny not wanting her husband to think of her during the day, and hurries home into her waiting arms at night?

She smiled and continued on.

"Go to your Bible if you want a vital illustration of these facts. Look up the story of the wayward boy who turned his back upon his home and wandered off into evil ways. Note carefully that very human experience and don't make any mistake in understanding.

It was not the memory of the father's admonitions that brought repentance to the heart of the Prodigal Son and turned him homeward but the remembrance of his mother's cooking.

And when the years slip away and the children are grown up and leave the nest; as their memory turns fondly to the old home, instinctively it lights on one of two scenes: Either the twilight hour when they gathered about the mother's knee before the fire, listening to the loved stories read or told; or it will be the golden glory of the table laden with its delicious, steaming foods which sent out such teasing calls to the hungry child, presided over by this wholesome, cheerful mother, the one who brought all these things to pass.

And in the light of after years, when the child has come to understand the spiritual meaning of material things, he will look in memory at the delicious food, the well-kept home and see in them the skill, the wisdom, and the abiding love of Mother—and will instinctively turn to packing his grip that he may catch the holiday train for the old home."

The room was quiet, except for the magazine that Eleanor folded and slowly placed on her lap. The three sisters were quiet indeed, for their heads were slightly bowed while they sat up in their beds contemplating the words of truth from a man who must know from experience what made him and fellow men decide to marry a particular girl.

"Oh…now I understand," Alice quietly murmured.

"Me too," agreed Marie as she slipped into bed.

Eleanor rose from her bed and put the magazine on the tall dresser and then blew out the light. Making her way back to her bed,

Eleanor realized why her wise Mama wanted them to read such an article.

As everyone settled under the covers making bedsprings creak, the room remained voiceless, for many tender thoughts flitted through sleepy heads. And for one young lady, she was picturing herself setting a pretty, dainty table; a delightful fire warmed the adjoining living room, and, until sleep overtook such dreaming, Eleanor stood next to the range dressed in a breathtaking evening dress of Arabian lace and China silk that brought a smile to a certain young man's tired face.

August 31, 1910
Wednesday

This past Sunday I saw my first Nuthatch. It was a thrill seeing a new bird for the first time. But more enjoyable that day was taking the streetcar to Woodland Park with the family. The outing was a first this summer....In the past, every pleasant Sunday was spent strolling through a park, resting along a riverbank, or wading ankle deep in the cold tingling saltwater along some beach heavily adorned in seashells and sand dollars. Once in a while starfishes can be found stranded on the shore during low tide.

I wish we owned an automobile so our journey would be quicker, but I suppose I should be thankful that streetcars deposit persons just about anywhere in this city. Of course, if we could afford an automobile we would not be coming to Woodland Park. I will explain momentarily.

Papa boarded first, then John carrying the lunch basket. Mama was looking out the window the whole time, taking in sights that she has not seen for a while. She did not say very much on the way, and realizing this, the rest of us did not bother her.

I couldn't say how many miles are involved from our house to Woodland Park, but at the bottom of our hill, the streetcar turned onto Beach Drive (which faces the shore of Elliott Bay), continued on the long stretch of Fifteenth St. West., where a bridge took us over a narrow point of Lake Union, then zigzagged along-side the narrow stretch of Lake Union until reaching Woodland Park Avenue which heads north past the Fremont Substation. The streetcar finally came to a stop, letting families off to find their favorite spot under a tree.

We settled in the shade of maples and cedars and ate cold chicken, potato salad, pickles, peaches, cake, and lemonade. The weather was perfect—sunny with a slight breeze. Oh, how dear Richard would have loved it there—lying down on the picnic blanket, resting his head against my lap, arms folded on his chest, eyes closed, pretending to nap. Sometimes I think he did drift off for a short time. I can still see his brown hair gently lift and fall as a breath of wind swirled around our lazy bodies…Richard loved the out-of-doors, loved life, loved to have my fingers run through his hair as he drifted off to sleep. You seemed to need a lot of rest, didn't you dear brother? You were always weary. Do you know how precious your breathing was? Yes, I adored even that! How could I not? There was nothing in your nature that displeased me.

The park could not have felt lonely for there were many families visiting her last Sunday. Families such as ours, the "middle-class," the "working-class," the "employed-class," are sorted out and segregated to Woodland Park, Madison Park and Volunteer Park. These places are for families of all classes, colors, and nationalities, and can only be reached by streetcars—hence their names— 'streetcar parks.' I spoke to a black woman at this park some time ago, and she told me that it took her two hours to get here from Rainier Valley, and that this park is one of the few where a black woman was free to visit.

You see, when the newly rich and wealthy of Seattle were building their elegant homes and begun to concern themselves with boulevards and parks, they sought places where a black woman or china-man would not go and no streetcar came near. The fine homes of the well-to-do are on the south and west slopes of Queen Anne Hill, on the west slope of Capitol Hill and around Volunteer Park, and along the ridges above Lake Washington. It would not take a newcomer long to notice that the further away from the streetcar the more expensive the house, and for the wealthy, their aim is seclusion. For these houses are not meant to be seen or enjoyed from the street or from a distance, but are lived in by people who themselves never want to see the street. Years ago, the wealthy lived downtown while they put up new attractive office buildings, but they separated themselves after their fortunes were made, and those remaining downtown were the less affluent.

I am thinking of Madison Park….we have not been there this year. It is not one of the new parks but a public carnival easily reached by streetcar. H. A. Chadwick, writer for the Argus had this to say about the grand park.

"We have a Coney Island now, a playground for the Industrials, a breathing spot for the Employed….The whole show is one inharmonious medley of sounds, and therein lied the charm of the resort for the people who go there. It is all cosmopolitan to a degree, mixed, unexclusive—it is of the people, for the people, by the people, a democratic arrangement to always appeal to certain kinds of Americans. But you don't see family parties there to spend a quiet day out of doors, nor mothers with nervous children, nor society girls with their fiancés."

What you won't see at Woodland Park are Gibson Girls, or young men with their eye on Alice Roosevelt look-a-likes. Ah…. but these families can arrive in automobiles and have family parties here if "they" wish. We would see a display of snobbery, and of nervous mothers with nervous children. "They" can play in our parks, though we do not have access to theirs. The Olmsted brothers have done well in convincing the city to put into public policy that the whole hillside above Lake Washington in Rainier Heights be acquired for the wealthy. To let cheap houses mingle in one of the best residential districts would retard the rise in property value, and give such people undeserved views or seclusion. These individuals have segregated themselves great distances from the cheap houses, and it seems as though our city has no other interest than that of its wealthy citizens. It has made parks and boulevards exclusively for carriages, and no one strolling or driving on Lake Washington Boulevard could fake the genteel style of near royalty. Needless to say, I was surprised to find out that Nate took John fishing along the Boulevard. Even Nate and his fancy touring car were ignored by the parents of the blond haired, blue eyed Miss. They were probably surprised to come across two men who looked like they belonged to a class that is excluded there, and one they wished to avoid.

I best turn in for it is late.

Goodnight,
Eleanor

September 4, 1910
Sunday

It has been a year—has it not, since I was at this very desk saying that there were too many hornets about? A year has passed. What good can I say on its behalf? There are so many days that go by in envy of my little feathered friends…how I wish to be one of them—carefree, oh, how carefree! The chickadee's have found their way to the Miller's yard where the drainpipe from the refrigerator drips continuously, giving them a cool drink or a little bath if they wish.

And speaking of the Miller family, since Todd's disappearance, it seems as if the walls are gradually falling in around them. The tension between Stuart and his father is terrible; sometimes unbearable. According to Nate, Stuart's drinking is out of control. In a way, I think Nate feels sorry for him. Although they do not treat or care for each other as brothers should, I think Nate understands why Stuart is turning on his father. Stuart has always been expected to be just like his father and has not had much say in the matter. The son who has been under the thumb of the father is lashing out with his claws, though in the process, also hurting himself.

I have been cooking less and less these days. I never know if Mr. Miller Sr. or Stuart is going to join Nate for supper. If Stuart does come home before I leave, he stumbles into the dining room and grabs a roll or a slice of bread. The smell of liquor precedes him, and his loud boisterous nature can be heard throughout the house. I do not care for the way he looks at me, though I am very thankful that Nate is there to protect me. I hope Nate is never late in coming home.

From behind the kitchen door as I am cleaning up, I clearly hear Stuart inform any listening ear of his daily visits to the gambling parlors, saloons, and brothels. It gives him great pleasure to report his gambling losses to his father, and for Nate, he speaks about this woman or that woman in the 500 room brothel on Beacon Hill.

On Friday night while driving me home, Nate stopped the automobile and apologized for Stuart's ill-behavior. Nate was quiet for a moment or two before he shyly turned to me and asked if I might enjoy a stroll in one of the parks next Sunday. I replied calmly (my poor heart was all a flutter) that I would have to ask Mama and Papa for their consent first. Nate understood.

At this moment John and Nate are fishing somewhere. It would be wonderful if they brought home a fish or two for supper.

I best go downstairs and see if Mama needs any help getting dinner ready for it is almost half-past eleven.

Eleanor

September 6, 1910
Tuesday

Our warm nights are gone—oh, how I do miss them. The pleasant, sweet air that filled our room after a warm day has slipped into the memory of a season gone by. Autumn, oh, autumn. Your nippy air and winds from the north; leaves from branches pile under trees; branches sway to and fro. Autumn, oh, autumn! You are here again, again so soon.

It was very chilly last night on the way home, and nearing our house, I could see smoke waving from the chimney. Once inside, I found everyone gathered in the living room around the fireplace.

I'm afraid I have some disturbing new to tell. I had scarcely changed out of my work clothes when Papa asked me to join him in the living room where he was reading the newspaper. Papa informed me that there was some sad news about my former employer at the Insurance Company. Immediately I thought that Mr. Whiting Sr. had passed on, but as Papa handed me the paper, my eyes found the horrible story.

On Monday morning, Mr. Dashwood, Mr. Williams, Miss Pauline, and Miss Julia found Mr. Douglas Whiting slumped over his desk with a gun in his hand. Mr. Whiting's partially bald head and silver wire spectacles laid in a pool of blood after he inflicted a fatal shot to his head. Mr. Williams was quoted in saying that his employer was found with his nervous little eyes still open. Miss Pauline fainted at the terrible sight, while Miss Julia, having a slight bit more constitution about her, only lost her breakfast. But as Mr. Will Dashwood informed the reporter, the suicide of Mr. Whiting shocked him, but knowing the personality of his former employer, the incident did not entirely surprise him. Mr. Douglas Whiting, he said, was a high-strung fellow—acting as if he were about to jump out of his skin at any given moment. He was never happy, and dealing with him on a daily basis was insufferable. "I believe he lead a very lonely life, absent of a loving wife and adoring children." Having done his research, the reporter concluded that Mr. Douglas Whiting chose to terminate 41 years of personal and business failures. I will telephone Miss Pauline and Miss Julia tomorrow to see how they are handling Mr. Whiting's death.

Yesterday, John started his sophomore year in high-school, Marie is a junior, and lucky Alice is working full time at the library. She has been indulging in clothing purchases on her lunch hour, for Alice feels the need to look sharp for the citizens of Seattle.

I must close and take a hot bath, wash my hair and dry it by the fireplace so I do not go to bed with a damp head. Speaking of washing—I almost forgot. Yesterday, upon arriving at the Miller's, a wonderful surprise was waiting for me in the kitchen. There sat the newest and most expensive ball bearing washing machine that a certain persistent Miller could buy. And yes, I cried happy tears, and yes, the new washing device did make my day a little easier. And for once, my silly pride did not get in the way.

Goodnight, Eleanor

16 Highland Drive., September 5, 1910

Dear Miss Eleanor:—

Presuming somewhat upon our former acquaintance, I hope to be pardoned for this little note, which is to ask permission to correspond with you, and also to have the pleasure of calling on you at your home.

Anxiously awaiting a favorable reply,

I am very truly your friend,
Mr. Nate Miller

Miss Eleanor,
6th Avenue West

6th Avenue West., September 8, 1910

Dear Sir:—

Our former acquaintance, though not extensive, has been pleasant, and I do not find it in my heart to object to your kind request.

With pleasure I subscribe myself,

Your sincere friend,
Miss Eleanor

September 11, 1910
Sunday

My guest has departed after a pleasant visit with the family.

Mr. Nate Miller had planned to take me to Luna Park—Seattle's Coney Island of the West, but the sky which I had been keeping an eye on all morning turned darker and darker. Nate arrived with rain drops on his suit. Behind Nate's smile and mine, we felt imprisoned by the rain, for we were horribly anxious to be alone with each other. I'm sure Mama and Papa understood our plight, but they could no more control the weather than we could.

I am grateful to everyone for making Nate's visit comfortable. Papa enjoyed listening to Nate explain how things are going with the construction of the Oregon and Washington Station. Although Nate is not on the Smith Tower construction team, acquaintances from the A. Y. P. Exposition are, and they keep Nate informed on how it is coming along. They expect the 42- story building to be completed sometime in 1914, which will be one of the tallest buildings in the world. The owner is Lyman Cornelius Smith who owns a large typewriter-manufacturing firm.

John and Nate chatted on about fishing which bored us girls, but made John happy. Mama sat in her chair working on an embroidery piece. She asked a few questions about Nate's involvement with the Alaska-Yukon-Pacific Exposition. We were all surprised to learn that the buildings which were not meant as permanent fixtures for the University, were constructed of materials which would demolish easily, and the huge columns which thousands passed by upon entering were cedar trees painted white.

About one o'clock, Mama, Alice, Marie, and I excused ourselves from the men's company to put dinner on the table. The meal was simple, yet delicious, and Nate gladly accepted a second serving of everything. During the meal it was extremely difficult keeping my eyes from lingering on Nate, and not wanting to embarrass my guest, a good portion of my time was spent playing with my meal and looking at everyone else.

The rain continued while coffee and pear cake was served close to the warm and cheery fireplace.

Oh, how I wished to tell Nate how handsome he looked in a suit. Papa and John did not change their suits after returning from church either. Alice wanted me to wear one of her new purchases, and has reminded me several times since Nate's departure, that she caught him stealing glances my way.

As the evening came to a close, we were permitted some privacy on the porch. The rain had ceased, but the air was cold and damp. Mama had given me a warm sweater, but the chilly air still managed to sneak under it. Unfortunately a shiver ran up my back and Nate apologized for keeping me out in such unfavorable weather. He thanked me for an enjoyable afternoon and hoped that I wasn't too disappointed in not going to Luna Park. If the weather cooperates next Sunday, we will go. Time to bath and wash my hair.

All for now, Eleanor

September 18, 1910
Sunday

For the first time in almost a year, I hobnobbed in the assortment of social and economically diversified families at Luna Park. Although we were by no means alone on the trolley car, or barely out of earshot of others on the boardwalk, to-night was a first for us.

Nate looked so handsome in his single breasted, three button medium gray suit which covered his tall physique. From his stiff black beaver hat, to his crisp white shirt and silk tie, down to his polished kangaroo skin shoes, Mr. Nate Miller was catching the fancy of many females who tried to solicit the eye of my beau.

As we ushered ourselves across the vast pier of boards, we were in awe, knowing that under our feet, pilings had been driven deep into the tide flats allowing the park to be built out over the water of Elliott Bay.

Strolling leisurely, Nate draped his arms behind his back, and I held mine in front, keeping my little handbag close to me. (I brought the velvetta one that's trimmed with small colored beads with the chain handle.)

Pausing near the balloon and the band shell, Nate asked if I cared to go on any rides. I thought the Figure Eight Roller Coaster might be too much, least I lose my hat to the wind. So Nate suggested the Chute-the-Chutes, the Cave of Mystery, the Canal of Venice, the Original Human Ostrich, the Joy Wheel, Merry-go-round, and the Giant Whirl that spun six boat-like fixtures over the Salt Water Natatorium and the boardwalk. Nate did not seem disappointed that

I chose the Merry-go-round. At least I did not have to worry about losing my hat.

As dusk set in we roamed aimlessly around each ride, watching people enjoy themselves, listening to the clatter of the roller-coaster and the happy screams that came from its riders.

Oh! What a wonderful delightful time I had. The drudgery of tomorrow will be eased by my memory of to-night. Oh! The wonderful sounds and smells and the music floating from the band shell—I wanted to sample everything! I wanted to indulge in the excitement that Nate was treating me to. While sitting in the Cafe that stood on the pier's edge, we watched a small ferry deposit more young people at the Park. After finishing our sandwiches, we strolled by the Dance Palace which is a popular place for a young fellow to bring his gal and dance the night away. Nate did not ask me if I cared to go in, nor did he show interest to go in, so we stayed on the outskirts watching couples dance and listened to the music for a while. It occurred to me that perhaps Nate does not know how to dance. I suppose not every man does.

Having seen all the rides and sampling a few amusements on the crowded pier, we had a soda at what is known as the "best-stocked bar" on Elliott Bay. Although the rides and amusement stands are popular, and the Dance Palace draws crowds, and on hot summer days the Salt and Fresh Water Natatoriums are filled with swimmers, it is the longest bar on the bay that is the main enticement. Unfortunately, West Seattle residents are angry that "boozers from Seattle," are overrunning their community.

Oh! The magic of Luna Park at night! Nate escorted me to the edge of the boardwalk where the glittering lights danced and played across the water on the lapping waves before us. It was then that Nate gently cleared his voice and spoke.

"Miss Eleanor, although I am fond of your hat, it is preventing me from wrapping my arms around you."

"Mr. Miller!" I gasped in surprise. I kept my eyes straight ahead of me, plunging them into the darkness beyond the dancing waves. Yes, he had taken me by surprise for my thoughts were not as his were! I drew my hand up to my laced neck and felt my heart beat at my throat.

"I beg of you, my dear Eleanor, if I am your beau, please tell me what liberties that permits me? Please relieve my curiosity for I am about to go mad! My affections and desires for you increase daily. When I am with you my heart is full of passion as you stir the inmost recesses of my manhood." Nate paused and looked down at me. "I know Miss Eleanor, that you do not have an unruffled part in you this very moment."

"Mr. Miller! Please!" I half begged, for I was taken-back by his unapologetic passion that was being revealed to me. I turned my back to him and felt my checks burn and my body quiver, and as my mind staggered, I wished there had been a railing to place a hand on.

"Eleanor, turn around and look at me," Nate pleaded as he endured my silence. He spoke my name again, only this time it was lower and deeper in his throat.

I am keenly aware that Nate has a vein of affection for me, though up till now, I did not know how deep. I did not know how agitated he was with our cordial relationship, for under our circumstances, what is permissible? I want to expand our liberties too, for Nate and I have both suffered at the hands of social sensibilities. Are the liberties between Nate and I, pending on what other couples do? Should the development of our relationship be held to the bondage of Victorian times? To say that I have never wondered what life would be like—if men and women were socially emancipated...I would be telling a falsehood.

Nate placed his strong hands on my shoulders, and turning me around to face him, he whispered eagerly, "What can we not be obedient to?"

I dropped my chin for I was not sure if I wanted to see his blue eyes, and placing a gentle finger under my chin he lifted it, and I did see Nate's piercing eyes, and yes, they were telling me that as a man, he wanted and needed more.

In the moments that followed, I was speechless while starring lovingly into Nate's eyes— my mind was in a state of confused intoxication. How was I, a modest young woman of Christian delicacy, able to answer such a question from my new beau? "What can we not be obedient to?" Such indelicate inquiries would be thrown away if sent to "The Question Box" in The People's Home Journal magazine. (The column is for readers', offering help, counsel and encouragement.)

I'm afraid my eyes deceived me, for what I was about to suggest was a simple gesture on Nate's part—to offer an arm to me to loop my arm through. But as I stood so close to Nate, being with him in a different atmosphere and remembering his physique on a few occasions—my shamefulness was revealed to him. Then it happened quickly, very quickly. Nate had his arms around me and his warm lips found mine. His urgent kisses wetted my face, and then found my lips again. I felt his right arm tightening around my waist, pulling me closer to him as his left hand supported the back of my head. I must have been holding onto his neck…I must have.

Then suddenly, there was slipping and tugging, and then my head felt light. A strong hand held my head again, and I realized that Nate had torn my hat off. I should have, at that moment, cared how my hair must have looked; cared what others were thinking of our indecent behavior, but I did not. I did not even care about my hat. I was claimed by love's savagery. Our thirst for this silent, splendid human yearning was strong—and it went unpunished. No one apprehended and escorted us to the exit of Luna Park. I could feel my hair escape from the combs that Nate gave me, and down my back my hair fell, and a sigh escaped from his lips.

"Oh, your beautiful hair…someday, someday…" Nate breathed into the night air.

He held me close and whispered in my ear. "Someday, soon I pray, I will behold you with loving, adoring eyes as you let your beautiful hair tumble down over your soft, fair skin. Oh, Eleanor," he lamented, "do you care for me as I care for you?"

I nodded my head. "Yes."

Nate smiled. "I should not have even asked, but a man needs to indulge his curiosity in such matters."

My combs were retrieved from the boardwalk, and as I tried to re-do my hair, I asked Nate, "And now, Mr. Miller, I too am curious about another matter."

"What about, my dear?"

"Now that you have thrown my hat into Elliott Bay, what shall I tell Papa and Mama when they ask about my bare head?"

"Well…." Nate began, rubbing his chin, "I suppose you'll have to tell them the truth. Your lover tossed it into the water…and he'll buy a dozen more to make up for it."

"Or…I lost it on the Roller-coaster."

"I'm corrupting your morals, aren't I?"

"Yes, Mr. Miller, you are."

The night air was growing nippy so we decided it was time to return home via the trolley. On our way across the boardwalk, we heard laughing and giggling coming from dark corners. Unfortunately there were girls hardly fourteen years old, mere children in appearance, mingling with older men, drinking beer, smoking cigarettes and singing. I stepped closer to Nate and he offered me an arm which I gladly accepted.

Goodnight, Eleanor

October 1, 1910
Saturday

Our bedroom is a bit on the chilly side this afternoon. As I sit at our desk and pause to observe the quiet, fog covered day outside, I am listening for noise within our little house. Only gentle stirrings of the basement door opening and closing, and the iron rounds clinking back into place as Mama checks on the fire in the range stove.

John is delivering messages somewhere up and down the streets of Seattle. I hope he is keeping a sharp eye in this fog that is trying to thin itself as the hours pass. Alice is at the Public Library. She has been after me to come and visit her there for weeks. Maybe next Saturday. I'm not quite sure what Marie is doing downstairs. Probably reading or working on an embroidery piece—or something.

In light of the on-going and recent articles in the paper concerning female workers in the Triangle Shirt Shop in New York City, I happened to come across a poem by Thomas Hood, entitled "The Song of the Shirt." In front of the warmth of the fireplace, I was reading the book that Richard had given me on my 21st birthday last December. It is a long poem to copy using a fountain pen, but I think it deserves to be copied again. Here it is

Thomas Hood
(1799-1845)
The Song of the Shirt

With fingers weary and worn,
With eyelids heavy and red,
Plying her needle and thread,—
Stitch-stitch-stitch!
In poverty, hunger, and dirt;
And still with a voice of dolorous pitch
She sang the "Song of the Shirt!"

"Work—work—work
While the cock is crowing aloof!

And work-work-work
Till the stars shine through the roof!
It's oh! to be a slave
Along with the barbarous Turk,
Where woman has never a soul to save,
If this is Christian work!

"Work-work-work
till the brain begins to swim!
Work-work-work
Till the eyes are heavy and dim!
Seam, and gusset, and band,
Band, and gusset, and seam,-
Till over the buttons I fall asleep,
And sew them on in a dream!

"O men with sisters dear!
O men with mothers and wives!
It is not linen you're wearing out,
But human creatures' lives!
Stitch-stitch-stitch,
In poverty, hunger and dirt,-
Sewing at once, with a double thread,
A shroud as well as a shirt!

"But why do I talk of death,-
That phantom of grisly bone
I hardly fear his terrible shape,
It seems so like my own,-
It seems so like my own
Because of the fasts I keep;
O God! that bread should be so dear,
And flesh and blood so cheap!

"Work-work-work!
My labour never flags;
And what are its wages? A bed of straw,
A crust of bread-and rags.
That shattered roof-and this naked floor-
A table-a broken chair-
And a wall so blank my shadow I thank

For sometimes falling there!

"Work-work-work
From weary chime to chime!
Work-work-work
As prisoners work for crime!
Band, and gusset, and seam,

Seam, and gusset, and band,-
Till the heart is sick and the brain benumbed,
As well as the weary hand.

"Work-work-work
In the dull December light!
And work-work-work
When the weather is warm and bright!
While underneath the eaves·
The brooding swallows cling,
As if to show me their sunny backs,
And twit me with the Spring.

"Oh but to breathe the breath
Of the cowslip and primrose sweet,-
With the sky above my head,
And the grass beneath my feet!
For only one short hour
To feel as I used to feel,
Before I knew the woes of want
And the walk that cost a meal!

"Oh but for one short hour,-
A respite, however brief!
No blessed leisure for love or hope,
But only time for grief!
A little weeping would ease my heart;
But in their briny bed
My tears must stop, for every drop
Hinders needle and thread!"

With fingers weary and worn,
With eyelids heavy and red,

A woman sat, in unwomanly rags,
Plying her needle and thread,-
Stitch-stitch-stitch!
In poverty, hunger, and dirt;
And still with a voice of dolorous pitch-
Would that its tone could reach the rich!-
She sang this "Song of the Shirt!"

October 4, 1910

I found a nice little poem in a Good Literature magazine from October 1900.
It was written by: Lucy Larcom

When The Woods Turn Brown

How will it be when the roses fade
Out of the garden and out of the glade?
When the fresh pink bloom of the sweetbrier wild,
That leans from the dell like the cheek of a child,
Is changed for dry lips on a thorny bush?
Then scarlet and carmine the groves will flush.

How will it be when the autumn flowers
Wither away from their leafless bowers;
When sunflower and starflower and golden-rod
Glimmer no more from the frosted sod,
And the hillside nooks are empty and cold?
Then the forest tops will be gay with gold.

How will it be when the woods turn brown
Their gold and their crimson all dropped down
And crumbled to dust? Oh, then, as we lay
Our ear to earth's lips, we shall hear her say,
"In the dark I am seeking new gems for my crown"—
We will dream of green leaves when the woods turn brown.

October 10, 1910
Monday

Oh, what a day! What a day! Where do I begin?

I suppose I'll start from the beginning. It had been raining almost steadily all day. It was a quiet autumn day as the pitter-patter sound soothed my nerves. But my nice day was about to turn upside down.

Nate and his father suffered through another silent meal without Stuart. It is seldom when they do speak to each other. After supper we went our separate ways. I cleared the table and cleaned up the kitchen. Mr. Miller Sr. retired to his room upstairs, and Nate read the evening paper in the parlor next to the fireplace.

I was drying the dishes when I heard a loud commotion from the other room. Nate yelled my name and hurrying out of the kitchen and through the dining room, I saw the body of Stuart lying on the threshold of the front door! I screamed—for blood was coming out of his nose and onto the floor. His face had been badly beaten, his eyes swollen and cut, as well as his mouth. I couldn't help notice the red that was splattered on his white shirt that I had spent so much time cleaning and ironing.

Nate yelled for his father to come down, and when he appeared, Mr. Miller Sr. stood at the top of the stairwell holding a drink in his hand.

"What's the matter with him?" Stuart's father barked.

"He's hurt!" Nate yelled up to his father. "Please call Dr. Henry!"

I cannot express my feelings enough when that cold hearted man laughed.

"I guess the 'Green Goods' swindle caught up with him! If that dumb boy can't avoid being caught, then he deserves what he got." Mr. Miller Sr. put the drink to his lips and appeared to have finished it. He then turned around and disappeared.

We would have starred longer in disbelief at the spot where Mr. Miller Sr. had just stood, if Stuart's painful moaning hadn't attracted our attention.

"Wait here!" Nate ordered.

Quickly stepping over his brother's body, Nate ran down the porch steps and to the street, looking all around him.

"No one's out there…" he breathed bounding up the porch stairs. Nate got down next to Stuart and cradled his head in his lap, talking to his brother, asking him if he could hear his voice. All poor Stuart could do was moan in pain as Nate pulled him inside the house.

"I'll call Dr. Henry," I said as I turned toward the dining room and for the kitchen.

"Hurry!"

While we waited for Dr. Henry to arrive, Nate carefully carried his brother up the stairs and laid him on the bed. It was very strange to see Nate do that, because I believe that Stuart still has not accepted and even resents his brother's presence in the big house. At that moment I felt sorry for Stuart. He did not look or act like the man I used to know. He was like a hurt animal, and yes, I felt sorry for him, and for any other man who grew up with a father like Mr. Miller Sr.

Dr. Henry arrived and I led him up to Stuart's bedroom. On the way, he asked where Stuart's father was.

"In his room," I replied. And then I added, "drinking."

When Dr. Henry entered Stuart's room, his eyes fell on Nate and he smiled.

"Good evening, Nathaniel."

"Good evening, Sir. Thank you for coming. Looks like my brother got himself into a bit of a scrape."

"I'd say so," Dr. Henry agreed as I helped him take off his long coat. I briefly left the room to call Papa and Mama to tell them that Stuart wasn't feeling well, and that I would be detained for a while. When I approached the upstairs landing I could hear Stuart raising his voice and using profane words. I hesitated at the doorway, and Nate came out in the hallway and closed the door. Nate thought it would be best if I waited downstairs until he could drive me home. An hour later, Dr. Henry came down and reported that Stuart was cleaned up, the cuts over his eyes stitched up and wide strips of cloth were wrapped around bruised ribs. Dr. Henry handed Nate a bottle of pain pills and gave him directions for usage. Then Dr. Henry put his hands into his trouser pockets and rested his eyes on the fire that I had made hours before.

"It's hard seeing him like that, especially since I brought him into this world."

There was a strange moment of silence. Nate slowly turned his head toward Dr. Henry and asked, "You did?"

"Yes, all three of you, and hundreds of other babies…" Dr. Henry's thoughts were lost in the fire that his eyes adhered to. His face was downcast and weary, and he looked like a man in low spirits. Perhaps he was thinking of all the babies that were taken up into heaven shortly after birth, or the children who succumbed to a disease for which there was no cure for.

I cleared my voice and asked both men if they cared for a cup of coffee. My offer was declined which I was glad of. Nate escorted Dr. Henry to the door and thanked him for coming, and then Nate came back to the parlor and spoke with me. It was difficult for Nate to hide his concern in the matter of his brother staying in the house while I was there. Dr. Henry, I am told, will stop by every day to check on Stuart, but I believe it is me who Nate wants Dr. Henry to look after. When I told Nate that everything would be all right, I tried to put on a brave face and smile, but inside I was a little frightened. I have cause to worry for I know what Stuart is like when he drinks.

Nate was standing by the fire looking at me, and suddenly he opened his arms and I did not hesitate to have them wrapped around me. It felt so wonderful to have strong, caring arms embrace and comfort me. I laid my head against his chest and savored every moment of intimacy before I was brought back home.

> Goodnight, my dear Nate
> Eleanor

October 19, 1910
Wednesday

Stuart has been home for nine days; seven of those I have spent with him. I am thankful that he spends many hours sleeping while I work. When I bring a meal to him, the previous tray is usually untouched, though a bottle of liquor seems to find its way next to his bed.

He has been reduced to a pitiful sight. His face is unshaven and dark; his hair uncombed and dirty; and the stench of liquor has over-taken the air in his room.

I do not have any doubt that the stronghold which liquor has on a man, will be the downfall and ruin of the Miller men— except for my Nate. The Stuart Miller who came into our yard last September no longer exists. I pity Stuart and am sympathetic to his situation, since I now have a better understanding of what life must have been like for him. Having grown up without a mother, and having Mr. Miller Sr. as a father….. I am very grateful for the parents I have. If Stuart had been brought up in a loving home, perhaps he wouldn't have had to resort to swindling people out of their hard earned money, throw his money away at gambling, drinking himself sick, or falling into sin on Beacon Hill.

Every day as promised, Dr. Henry pays Stuart a visit. If Stuart is awake, Dr. Henry tells him that he shouldn't be mixing pain medicine with liquor. The room is then filled with profanities and yelling, and Stuart orders Dr. Henry out of the room. To-day, just before he left, Dr. Henry glanced back up the stairs and said that Stuart is probably going to drink himself to death at the rate he's going.

I am looking forward to Nate's visit to our house on Sunday. Since our lovely visit to Luna Park, the weather has been too damp and cold to enjoy a stroll in a park. I believe Mama and Papa have really taken a liking to Nate, and they look forward to his visits. John, Alice, and Marie do, too. But I do wish it was spring or summer so we could picnic under the shade of a tree, or take a leisurely boat ride for hours on Lake Washington —just the two of us without prying eyes watching a girl and her beau sharing an intimate moment. We could catch a motion picture at one of the numerous theater houses downtown or in Pioneer Square. Handfuls of movie houses or nickel-odeons are springing up everywhere. On 2nd Avenue, Thomas Edison opened his own a few years back, rightfully named, Edison's Unique Theater. One of these Saturday's Miss Ernestine and I will have to catch a streetcar and spend an afternoon seeing silent movies. It has been a long time since we have spent a day together.

All for now,
Eleanor

October 22, 1910
Saturday

Alice is home from the library and she's brought Miss Frances Harper with her. I can hear them talking with Papa and Mama down-stairs.... now I can hear their feet coming up the stairs.

Miss Harper has just left after an hour and a half visit. What a talker that young lady is! I can see how easily it would be for her to speak in front of an audience. She can go on and on and on! We (Alice, Marie, and I) were filled in with the latest news concerning the upcoming November 8th election that will give Washington State male voters a chance to ratify Amendment 6 to the state constitution granting women the right to vote. If it so happens, the 14-year grid-lock in the National Woman's Suffrage Crusade will be broken, and

Washington will become the fifth state in the nation to enfranchise women.

I must tell what Miss Harper has done! I can't believe it! She made us promise not to tell our Mama or else she may not be welcome in this house again. After we crossed our hearts a few times, Frances told us that she has not worn a corset for the past few months. She sat proudly, her chin raised, and with determination set solidly on her freckled face, she boasted a wide grin. We stared at Miss Harper with our mouths open, our eyes riveted to the independent, daring feminist who sat on Alice's squeaky bed. It gave Frances great satisfaction to inform us that her steel corset lay hidden at the bottom of a drawer beneath layers of underskirts, corset covers, lace drawers, and gowns. She asked us why we looked so shocked. Our reply was that we had never known a female who did not wear her corset. Marie almost went as far as calling it unladylike and wicked. Miss Harper then stood up and challenged Marie.

"Is that so, after decades and decades of trying to make man understand that women are not to be held in bondage or kept captive by the restrictions and duress set by men? We have not been put on this earth as their slaves, and we certainly deserve the same rights as men! We are just fourteen days away from possibly the greatest event of our lives! Our lives will be changed, and hopefully the lives of others will be made safer and better in the factories, if and when we can begin passing laws.

Is giving the right for women to vote unladylike and wicked? Is being able to breathe and move freely unladylike and wicked? Why must a woman have her figure altered forever on account of what man wants? I can breath, Marie! I can bend over!"

Miss Frances Harper bent herself forward and touched her fingers to the floor.

"Look! Can any of you do this?" she exclaimed.

"No…" was our collective sigh.

I was looking at Miss Frances and she looked at me.

"Eleanor, you need to do it. Just leave it off! You will still have a lovely figure with your small waist and curving hips."

My cheeks were glowing a little for it is not the custom for females to pay compliment to another on her figure.

"Of course, your…" Miss Frances placed her hands near her breasts and gestured as to push them up, "won't have the lift and support they do now. But to be able to breathe!"

What will Miss Harper do next for the sake of woman's rights?

Eleanor

November 5, 1910
Saturday

The skies are very dark to-day, making the afternoon hour of one o' clock seem like early evening. I think at any moment it could begin to rain. I myself do not mind the rain—if I can look at it from indoors. I find it comforting. But for those like Nate whose employment places them outdoors— I worry about the health and safety of him and other men.

Papa has just put some coals on the fire and in the range as he has passed through the kitchen again. Mama has taken to her favorite chair to work on some piece work. I have been helping her with the monotonous job on the week-end. To-day she is wrapping silk flowers on pieces of wire, which will be put on ladies hats. Our woman's work is done, for the time being, until a quarter-till-three when a kettle of water must be heated for Papa's coffee. Then he will settle down and read The Seattle Daily Times.

Now the rain has begun, and is tapping with little 'pings' on the kitchen window. I think I will join Mama and will take a look at the paper to see if another article has been written about the Equal Suffrage Amendment vote. With male voters going to the polls this Tuesday, there has been a disappointing number of articles as to why Article VI. of the Constitution should be changed. In its place, there are near full size advertisements from The Bon Marche and Frederick and Nelson's Department stores for the latest 'Hobble' skirt which is fashionable on the east coast. With such a small circumference around the ankles, I do not understand how a woman could walk in a natural way since she would have to take short strides. I think I will join Mama now by the cozy fire.

I have cut and pasted an article in my journal that The Seattle Times printed to-day. I read it to Mama when I found it, and both of us wonder if society women in Scattle are like those of Chicago and New York. Here it is.

The Law of the Picket

The Society Woman in a riot is proving a difficult problem for the police of Chicago to solve, just as it was a difficult nut for the New York police department to crack when they encountered a similar situation a few months ago. It is something new, and a "new something" which seems likely to give us all "something" to think about.

To be frank at the beginning, there is no convincing proof that any of these society women are risking their physical comfort in the midst of a mob of working girls because they "love the cause," or because they have any deep-rooted conviction in it. They are out in the crowd because it has come to be a fashionable thing to do—because they have nothing else to occupy their minds and because there is some excitement about it.

Certainly such an interest and such an active part taken by such a class of woman is bound to have a beneficial effect upon the working women who are vitally interested. It is a good thing for the working class if these women of wealth and culture can take an interest in their more unfortunate sisters. But it is a strange thing that these women cannot take any interest in the working girl until after she has become involved in some difficulty, with this interest terminating at the end of the excitement.

Girls who work—particularly those who work in the manufacture of clothing—seem to be notoriously underpaid. It is not necessary to go into the evils of that system at the present time, but it might be a good thing if these women who are so anxious to get into the streets and join these girls in fighting the police when they are on strike could devote a little of their spare time at other periods in doing something to help them—to make life seem a little brighter—and to aid them in meeting the world without yielding to the almost overwhelming power of temptation.

These society women, however, have done at least one thing, and that is to determine the law which they ask the girl strikers to accept as their platform. Among them they have husbands, fathers and brothers who know the law—who, while they may not be able to keep their women folk from mingling with the crowd, have at least been able to advise them of their rights.

They have prepared a list of "Don'ts" which it might be well for any striking labor organization to follow—The "Law of the Pickets." If that law should be followed there would be little or no trouble with the police, or with anyone else, but the fact that the women who have prepared this law under expert legal advice are having trouble with the police would seem to show that they cannot even follow it themselves. To summarize this list of "Don'ts," the law is something like this: Don't walk in groups of more than two or three; keep moving; walk alongside of anyone with whom you wish to argue; don't get excited and talk loud; don't touch the person to whom you are appealing and don't use abusive or threatening language.

This sums up the rights of the picket very well. The picket has the rights of any citizen—the right to walk the streets in an orderly manner, to speak to anyone and in general to argue any point she wishes to argue so long as the argument does not become offensive or disorderly.

And yet with that advice to guide them these women in Chicago have succeeded for several days in having the police reserves called out and some of them have been arrested. It is apparently very difficult for a woman to be calm when she is much interested. (The End)

I suppose by now, my dear Minnie in Portland, Oregon is a woman of 'society.' She writes regularly and her letters are interesting, and though I appreciate hearing from my good friend, Miss Minnie has taken the position of Mrs. Howard Wallingford very well. During our last correspondence, she informed me how many people her husband employs to keep them in leisurely comfort.

One Chef
One Nurse
One Housekeeper
Two maids
One Head coachman
One Second coachman
One Butler
A Head gardener and a helper

Minnie is still begging me to come for a visit so she can show me Portland.

During a recent Sunday drive when they were having favorable weather, the Wallingford's and friends drove around the city so they could be seen in their handsome coach pulled by two dapple-gray and two matching chestnut horses. The horses had to be paired with the opposite color and diagonally, so two front horses were gray and chestnut; the one's behind where chestnut and gray. When two coaches pass, Minnie says that etiquette on such encounters is very strict. On first meeting, one bows; on the second, one smiles; on the third, one looks away.

Minnie has no shame in admitting that she has put Seattle behind her, as she was quick to accommodate herself to living in a mansion with the upper-crust families of her city. Her husband's wealth, and that of his parents, gave them admission into the inner circles of glittering people who have more money than they have time to use. The rich and the very rich spend it competitively to impress and to outdo one another. (I wonder what Minnie would think if she saw Mama and I doing piece work so our food budget isn't so worrisome) And to think of all the parties and balls the rich people put on. The elite come by the hundreds to such spectacular functions, wearing costumes that cost thousands.

"Millionaires," Minnie reports, "put on masked balls which costs shocking sums in the thousands. As rich as we are, we can only hope for that someday."

It has been reported that the very rich on the east coast, while spending their summers at Newport, have no difficulty throwing $100,000 parties and wearing $5,000 costumes. One can only wonder how long such wealth will last if spent at that rate. I can see how such 'society women' would enjoy joining the poor working girl in a riot. They do not have to work. Their father's surely will give them anything their little hearts desire. They do not 'love the cause.' They are bored and have nothing else to do. They join for the wrong reason because there is some excitement about it. But what about the poor working girl in the factory, and those who work in the manufacture of clothing? The girls in the Triangle Shirt Shop? Why are there no articles in the paper that educate the public of the 'evils of that system?'

I wonder if Miss Frances Harper will be handing out pamphlets at a polling place on Tuesday. I think I will pay her a visit and see if I can join her.

Eleanor

November 7, 1910
Monday

Yesterday, in the coal mining town of Black Diamond, sixteen men were killed in an explosion. In the Pacific Coast Co. Lawson Mine, five bodies were could not be recovered due to the slope that caved in on the miners. Sixteen men, some brothers, half had wives and children. Ten were Italian; three were Belgian, one Polish, one Austrian, and one Finn. Dave Lunden, the oldest and a Fire Boss was 34. Matt Galope, the youngest, was 19. The poor victims of this tragedy all made $3.15 a day, with the exception of one, who made $3.80.

Men who wore mine rescue gear that was shown to the public at the Alaska-Yukon-Pacific Exposition, were allowed entry into the hazardous atmosphere.

I am very thankful that my dear Nate does not have to work in such dangerous conditions as those poor men did. I pity the poor wives with children. What will they do? I pray each day that God watches and protects my dear Nate.

Goodnight,
Eleanor

November 8, 1910
Tuesday

It is good to be home. Miss Frances Harper and I spent the good part of the morning handing out literature in the cold rain. I did not go to the Miller's to-day. Nate understands how important this is to me and granted me a day off. My poor shoes are close to the fireplace drying and I've taken a hot bath to warm my bones. While Mama heated a bowl of beef barley soup for me, she expressed interest in wanting to have joined us girls, but standing in the rain for so long would not have been wise for a woman her age. Mama says that she is proud that one of her daughter's helped in the suffrage cause.

During the late afternoon, Miss Harper came by with the paper and was very excited because there was an article that could have been written about us. She stood in front of the warm fire and read it to Mama and me.

Suffragettes on Job.

The damp and bedraggled
suffragette, her political ardor
uncooled by the disagreeable drizzle

25

lent a novel touch of color to the polling places to-day. At every voting place two or more determined women, in most instances with a "Vote-for-the-First-Amendment" automobile at their command, stood in the downpour, dealing out moist literature to nonplused males.

Though awe-stricken at this sacrilegious invasion of the places once sacred to masculine machinations, the average voter couldn't help but wonder who told him that suffragettes were thin and iron-jawed, for most of the self-appointed electioneers were neither. Some there are who think that the all-wise generals of the suffragette forces, knowing man's weakness, deliberately appointed the most beautiful of their number to act as poll workers.

Rain proved the most terrible blow to the "Taxation Without Representation is Tyranny" forces. Every woman knows that it is hard to be self-possessed and convincing when one's hair is wet and all straggly and persists in getting into one's eyes.

Rain is the true test of power in politics, however, and more than one earnest worker succumbed to the attacks of J. Pluvius.

Try Psychic Influence

When smiles and literature failed the women tried "psychic influence." "Psychic influence," explained a Ballard suffragette to a mere masculine molecule unable to fathom the intricacies of female politics, "is

used as follows in helping our grand
and noble cause, which, by the way,
you must be sure and vote for. Have
one of these circulars."

"When we see a man enter the polls
who has refused to read our highly
instructive pamphlets we try to
influence him by thinking intensely
to place an X after the 'Yes' for the
first amendment."

"For instance, do you see that big
fat man with a red face? He has
just entered the booth. Now I will
say over and over again to myself,
placing my thoughts on him: 'Vote
for the first amendment, vote for the
first amendment,' and so on until he
leaves the booth. We thus expect
to obtain additional votes by taking
advantage of the inferior quality of
masculine gray matter."

The courteous treatment which
the women were accorded at all the
voting places from Georgetown to
Ballard was the subject of no little
favorable comment to-day."

Mama cleared her voice and was the first to speak.

"Isn't it interesting how the weather started out as 'disagreeable drizzle,' and then quickly was called 'rain?'"

"Well, I don't care for that reporter's lame idea that some how we 'appointed the most beautiful suffragettes to act as poll workers,'" huffed Miss Frances.

"Frances," I asked, "did you happen to read that article a few days ago about society women on the east coast wanting to join the cause because they think it is fun and exciting?"

"Yes, I did! Can you imagine the nerve of them? Well, yes, I suppose I can. Oh! And do you know what made me most upset about that article?"

Miss Frances hardly paused long enough for us to ask when she put her nose in the air and spoke as if she were an aristocrat.

"'There is no convincing proof that any of these society women are risking their physical comfort in the midst of a mob of working girls because they "love the cause," or because they have any deep-rooted conviction in it. They are out in the crowd because it has come to be the fashionable thing to do—because there is some excitement about it.'

I would love to see one of them stand with us in the cold rain for hours. The poor dears!"

We had a good laugh over Miss Harper's comical gestures and her prissy voice. Mama fixed some tea and served cookies for us all by the cozy hearth. What would we do without a fire to gather around? I think Mama really enjoys listening to Miss Harper because she is so well informed on women's rights and has taken such an active interest in the cause.

I'm sure thousands of Washington women wait in eager anticipation for tomorrow's news.

All for now, Eleanor

Nation Will Be Called United
Equal Suffrage States of
America—Suggested as
New Name for Nation,

STATE
CONGRATULATED
ON PROGRESSIVENESS

Resolution Wants Local Legis-
lature to Ask New York
Solons to Put Question Up to
Empire State,

NEW YORK, Friday, Nov. 11.—"The
United Equal Suffrage States of Amer-
ica" will be the name of this country if
the suggestion put forward by Mrs. Mary
Ware Dennett, corresponding
Secretary of the National Suffrage As-
sociation, finds favor.
Mrs. Dennett spoke at a meeting held

last night at Cooper Union to celebrate
the victory of votes for women in
Washington. She made the motion in
seconding a resolution proposed by
Mrs. Ida Husted-Harper, congratulating
the men of Washington on the courage
of their convictions, and the whole
state on its progressiveness. The resolution was adopted unanimously. Mrs.
Carrie Chapman Catt presided.

"We come here to-night," she said,
"to celebrate our first victory. We now
have five suffragist states and only
forty-three more to get. That's pretty
good and will be better a few months
from now, when we meet again. That
will be after the Legislature of New
York has passed a bill for us."

Mrs. Harriet Stanton Blatch introduced a resolution calling on the
Legislature of Washington to invite the
Legislature of this state "to place before the voters of New York the full
right of free born citizenship," (for
women).

"Some years ago," she continued,
"Mr. Roosevelt was asked if great
meetings and speeches would help
votes for women. He said:

"No, the best thing to do is to gain
another state in the West."

"Well, we have done that but unfortunately the universal adviser is now
silent. He is as close as the oyster
from Oyster Bay, so now we must
pick our way in the dark."

The resolution of the Legislature of
Washington was seconded and adopted.

November 13, 1910
Sunday

Oh, what a wonderful day! Our dull, gray, wet skies could not dampen my spirits to-day! It is a little past six o'clock and Nate should be home by now.

The light of day has left so I must write in the kitchen instead of the bedroom.

As promised, Nate rode with us in the trolley to St. James Cathedral this morning. I was amused by his roaming eyes that took in everything. The ornate dome, the choir which blessed us with their beautiful singing, and the rows and rows of people gathered—all speaking in Latin. Nate was confused by the Latin but tried to follow along. John enjoyed sitting next to Nate. I'm glad they are good friends. On the way home, Nate asked Mama and Papa if he could join us next Sunday. They said yes, of course.

Next month is my birthday. Is it possible that a year has gone by? Time is a strange thing, is it not? It was then, that my dear Richard gave me the book of poems. Oh, my dearest Richard. I know you are gone, but there is a part of you which is not. I can see you by the range, buttoning your shirt, smiling at me, waiting for a kiss on your cheek. It has been suggested, that time heals sorrows— lessens the agony of a broken heart. Let time pass, but I do not want it to take away the agony of a departed loved one—least the memory of my beloved brother becomes faded in the depths of mind. If thoughts and visions of Richard cannot be separated from tears and grieving, I am happy to have both. Oh, how did Lord Tennyson Alfred word it?

Let Love clasp Grief lest both be drown'd
Let darkness keep her raven gloss.
Ah, sweeter to be drunk with loss,
To dance with Death, to beat the ground.

Another poem from Lord Tennyson Alfred comes to mind...

"O That 'Twere Possible"
O That 'twere possible
After long grief and pain
To find the arms of my true love
Round me once again!

When I was wont to meet her
In the silent woody places
Of the land that gave me birth,
we stood tranced in long embraces
Mixed with kisses sweeter, sweeter
Than anything on earth.
A shadow flits before me,
Not thou, but like to thee.
Ah, Christ, that it were possible
For one short hour to see
The souls we loved, that they might tell us
What and where they be!

The clock in the living room rang out seven o'clock just now. I should finish soon. For some reason, Stuart Miller's face just came into my head. He was angry and crying at the same time. His eyes were red and his face which has not seen a razor in over a month was horribly scruffy. As I stand in the hallway tomorrow, waiting to knock on Stuart's door, I will wish that I did not have to go in. The same man who insisted on having his sheets impeccably ironed has not allowed me to change them in over a month. The horrible stench of body odor, liquor, opium and vomit is almost too much for any human to bear. I will have to throw open his windows while he is passed out on his bed or on the floor. Dr. Henry has stopped coming. What can a doctor do if a man is bent on destroying himself? Nate tries to speak to his brother when he is not asleep, but Stuart wants to be left alone.

I suppose this could be a half-blessing, but Mr. Miller Sr. has fallen into a deep depression himself, and consequentially, Nate informs me, very few nights are spent at home. On his Saturday routes, John has seen Mr. Miller yelling and swearing as he is physically removed from saloons.

Before Nate drove me home on Friday, he spoke to me in the parlor, saying how concerned he is with his father and brother's well being, and how his father is bringing financial ruin on the family. Through his own greediness, wickedness, and sinful nature, Mr. Miller is on the verge of loosing the house due to gambling. I wonder if Mr. Miller Sr. just does not care anymore.

Next Sunday after church, if it is not raining, Nate would like to take me for a drive to look at neighborhoods.

> Goodnight, Richard
> Goodnight, Nate
> All for now,
> Love, Eleanor

November 14, 1910
Monday

I sit before the cozy fire at the Miller's. Outside it still rains. It has continued without ceasing since last night, beginning around bedtime. It began as a pitter-patter upon our roof but gradually the rain drops fattened and the pitter-patter turned into a pounding sound. I was content with both for I do love the sound of rain—as long as I stay dry, which was not the case at all this morning. My goulashes kept my feet dry, but as for the hem of my skirt—it will have to be washed.

The laundry is soaking, the bread is rising; the hands on the clock seem content in provoking my impatience in getting the day over with. It would be difficult to explain the feeling this house has had on me lately. There are no demands put upon me. It feels as if Nate is the only one living under this roof. I am not to speak of his family's financial troubles, for Nate has confidentially communicated many things to me which are not to leave my lips. The Miller's reputation for crooked business dealings has been a well known fact for decades. Has their activities eventually caught up with them? Are people's prayers finally being answered? The high and mighty tower of the Miller family is crumbling fast, and as their witness, I should dismiss myself soon least I be injured by the tumbling ruins.

I have returned from a brief visit on the front porch. There is not an automobile or delivery truck in sight, nor anything pulled by ox or horse on this once dirt road. These grand, yet lonely looking homes on the slope of Queen Anne Hill sit beside a long stretch of mud as far as the eye can see. The young trees next to the sidewalk have lost nearly all their yellow leaves. I did not see one domestic on a single front porch. I would think that Nate should be home to-day. My lips have been praying intermittently throughout the day for his safety. How I wish he were here with me now. I miss the warmth of his lips and the comfort of his embrace. Take care, my dear Nate. Please take care....

A rumble of thunder has filled the skies. I wonder if it woke Stuart at all. I should go see how he is.

> My dearest Nate,
> you are always in my
> thoughts.
> Affectionately, Eleanor

November 27, 1910
Sunday

Nate could not join us this morning due to having a bad cold. I was very disappointed after he called to let us know about his health, though Mama appreciated his thoughtfulness of not wanting to spread unwanted germs.

Dinner consisted of Mama's beef barley soup, bread, raspberry jelly, and cake for desert. I believe we are having chicken pot-pie and left-over cake for supper.

Since dinner, I have written Minnie and my two uncle's back east. Unfortunately they could not make it out here this Thanksgiving. Possibly next year. As soon as Minnie heard that women in Washington State will now be able vote, she wrote right away, congratulating our men that they did the right and noble thing. Oregon men have yet to decide if they want women to vote or not.

It has been quiet in the house to-day— a drowsy, sleepy, lazy day. I miss Nate very much. Wish he was here. I think I will join the others in the living room and read for a while before us girls have to prepare the next meal.

> Good-day
> Eleanor

December 2, 1910
Friday

Do you know what happens tomorrow? Last year on the 3rd it was very cold, very cold indeed as the temperature dipped to 30 degrees. Mama baked an Irish apple pie; Papa built a little keepsake box for my hair and hat items; Mama crocheted a pair of delightful butterfly doilies; Marie made me a lovely card; Alice baked mouth watering cookies and other delectable; John entertained me with his harmonica; and dear Richard....oh, my dear, beloved Richard. Thank you so kindly for the book of poems that you gave me last year for my 21st birthday. I am most sorry for the tear stains that dot the pages...I thought my tears would dry and disappear, but the stains from my grieving and deepest sorrows after your passing are still evident. It does not seem possible that a year has gone by. Oh, my dearest brother, if only I could see you again!

Sometimes, when I come down the stairs in the morning, I can see you standing at the range, buttoning your shirt, warming yourself, smiling at me. I have not, and dare not mention this to anyone in the family least they will think I've gone mad, but I can honestly say that your presence is very much with me. Although your body is not with us, the rest of you are quite intact. It is not as if I can literally hear your voice in the air, rather, I hear it in my head and in my heart. It is, and please note dear brother, that I do not say 'as if' this may be all a figment of my imagination. You 'are here' with me, only I cannot 'see' you.

From my earliest memory, you and I were blessed with a special gift that other siblings could have turned their backs to. I know in my heart, that in the course of history, few sisters were as fond of a brother as I was with you. We were devoted to each other, adored each other. We held a natural affection for each other. You were my darling, my pet. You were charming, affectionate, tender, and sensitive. I spoiled you. You were a man after one's own heart. Mine. Was I the apple of your eye? Was I your pet, your favorite, your devoted, your dearly beloved? Were our souls not betrothed to each other? Were not our minds filled with enchantment of the other?

Not even my beau, Mr. Nate Miller, has come close to such qualities aforementioned. That should make you happy. Though, I truly hope that you are not displeased that Mr. Miller is my beau. I know that you and he did not have a chance to get very well acquainted, but please understand dear brother that I believe him to be of good moral character, honest, courteous, and hardworking. Papa and Mama like him very much, as well as the rest of the family.

Please do not worry about John. He and Nate are wonderful friends. And no, my jealous brother, Nate has not replaced you. Nate knows more about you from John than from me. John is a young man who needs to talk to someone. I hope you understand. You would be proud of your little brother.

Well, my dearest Richard, tomorrow I shall turn 22 years old. I am anxious to see what everyone will give me. Is it that late? The clock on the fireplace mantle has rang out nine gongs. I best leave the warm kitchen and make my way up to our chilly room and prepare for bed. Alice just came in the kitchen and asked if I wanted to have my hair combed by the fire.

> Goodnight,
> dearest Richard,
> Eleanor

December 3, 1910
Saturday

We all thought it would snow sometime during the night while we laid in peaceful slumber. The air was very chilly and even Papa went out on the front porch to feel and smell the air. The sky had been solid gray all yesterday afternoon— the kind of gray that can only promise snow when the air is cold enough. How lovely it would have been, I thought, if we had awoke to a bright morning, and rushing from our beds had discovered a white world outside. But it was not to be. Mother Nature did not give me a white sparkling gift on this my 22nd birthday.

I have lit the gas lights in the living room for the late afternoon hour is upon us and dusk has settled in.

I am in front of the cozy fireplace with Papa who is reading his German newspaper. His face is serious but not still. His eyebrows shift up and down; his mouth curls at the corners, thus making his already thin lips appear thinner. I doubt very much if he realizes that he sighs and shakes his head.

Mama and Marie are in the kitchen making my birthday supper. I have offered to help them with the cooking 'chore,' but was told by my dear Mama, that a woman should be free to do what she wants on her special day. She also whispered with a little smile and her voice breaking, that I may be a married woman by next year so I shant spoil her last chance to cook me a birthday supper. I feel guilty though, sitting here, relaxing my efforts while poor Mama and Marie are fussing in the kitchen.

The words which Mama spoke seem strange to me—those about possibly not being here on my next birthday. Is it possible that Mr. Nate Miller could propose marriage so soon, and that he and I would

truly be betrothed to each other? Does it all seem a far away dream
until those magical words "Will you marry me?" fall from a man's
lips? Then, and only then, will my dreams appear clearer. All those
nights, when Alice, Marie and I have spent wondering and wishing
what every young woman hopes for. From what type of house I
shall want to have, the furniture I shall desire, the china and place
settings that will grace our lovely table. We, as thousands of other
young women do, who pine and dream on setting up their own
house someday, have spent countless hours turning the pages of
Sears, Roebuck Catalogue. Everything from sad irons, stove furnishings, ball bearing washing machines, all wool carpet in a handsome
red, with green scroll and leaf effect (Sears sent me a sample).
Nottingham lace curtains, china silk piano and mantel drapes, my
very own Minnesota sewing machine that I'll place next to a bright
window so I can make baby and children's clothing. We have even
discussed little details such as tooth powder. With a dreamy smile
on her face, Alice has confessed that she is jealous after hearing all
of my lovely dreams. She wishes too, that she were getting married
soon so she might have an excuse to pour over catalogues. But as I
have continually reminded her, Mr. Miller has not even proposed to
me, nor has asked Papa for his daughter's hand in marriage. Such
wishful planning has also had an affect on Marie, for she has broken
down more than once and dampened her handkerchiefs.

It is 4:19 p.m. and it is dark outside. Supper smells wonderful.
We are waiting for John and Alice to come home from their jobs. We
will eat, sing "Happy Birthday!" and I will open presents. I suppose,
and think I shall, cry while opening my gifts to-night. Nothing will be
the same once I'm married, will it? I am holding back a tear or two,
and Papa has asked if I am catching the sniffles without glancing up
from his reading. Knowing he could not see me, I shook my head
nonetheless and replied, "No, Papa."

"Der ist gut...." he mumbled from behind his paper.

I shall stop writing now for it is too dark to see what I am doing.
Will finish later.

I have returned. It is late. I heard the clock chime ten-thirty while
I was in bed a short while ago. I sit before the fire and have added a
few more coals to the dying embers. I don't think Papa would object
if he knew I was using a little extra coal. There is no joy to be had
while sitting next to a cold and lifeless fireplace, is there? I should
think that perhaps this is the first time I have ever been downstairs,

with the dark at my back, in the still and silent night of our little house.

My family sleeps above me. I am drinking from the cup of enchantment that my mind is exploring. This room seems odd, almost feeling like a stranger to me. The light from the fireplace gradually merges with the darkness. Familiar furnishings about the room take on new forms and uneasy features. My imagination is not embracing such derangement and muddling which my mind is being subjected to. Does the living room become its own wilderness after we depart for the night? Have I intruded upon something which has been unknown to me all these years? If indeed I am in a new wilderness, I can honestly say that the hour of my intrusion has marked me an outsider; a foreigner. Does this room not understand that it is I, Eleanor? Does it not recognize me in my long night gown and robe? Oh, what a perplexing situation! How does one communicate with walls and furnishings? Yes, Eleanor, it is absurd! Simply tell them that you had difficulty sleeping and wish to keep the fireplace company.

Tell the darkness that lurks behind you, that to-night was a wonderful night. That after John and Alice arrived home, we all sat down to oven-baked chicken, green beans, scallop potatoes, baking powder biscuits, gravy and cranberry sauce.

After the dishes were washed and put away, I was brought into the living room and was ushered to a 'birthday' chair by John. We have never had a 'birthday' chair before, so this must be something he thought up himself. John cleared his voice in an attempt to cease the chatter, and failing, he went over to the piano and loudly hit a few notes which followed by everyone singing "Happy Birthday" to me. Then, as family tradition has it, Papa, being the head of the household went first. He got up and stood behind a blanket covered rectangle object that I had not noticed in all the excitement. Papa removed his pipe from his lips just long enough to speak.

"Eleanor, mein eldest daughter, ich wish zu jeder happiness from diese tag forward…" My dear Papa sniffled and reaching for a handkerchief in his trouser pocket, promptly rubbed it under his nose and returned it to his pocket. He cleared his voice."Dis gift vas made bei Richard and myself….he…he wanted zu geben ihr something that ihr could pass auf zu your kindlich."

I stood before my gift and hesitated to even touch the blanket. My throat was thick as the thought of my dear Richard filled me with sadness. I found it hard to swallow and the tears in my eyes did not help me to see clearly.

"Come on Eleanor," John half-complained, half-begged, "aren't you going to see what's under the blanket?"

"Leave her be," Mama's voice softly cooed.

From behind me I heard the soft rustling of skirts, and touching my arm Alice whispered, "It's OK if you cry. We understand. This is what girls are supposed to do," she informed everyone matter-of-factually. "Would you like me to unveil it?" she whispered.

I nodded my head and wiped my eyes.

Alice grasped the material in the middle and slowly rose her hand until the gift was revealed to all. There before me was a beautiful table chest that was about four feet long and maybe three feet high. It sat on handsome turned legs, the wood was stained dark, and a fancy scroll was adhered to the front of the chest.

"Now you can begin to put together your trousseau for your wedding night and honeymoon," Marie informed me.

"Ah! I don't want to hear that girl talk. All this wedding nonsense is for the birds!"

"Now John," interrupted Papa surprisingly, "this is a special time in a young woman's life. We mustn't rain on their happy planning. Recht mutter?"

Mama smiled lovingly at Papa and nodded her head. "You are correct. Preparing for your wedding day, and bearing children are two of the greatest joys in a woman's life."

I went over to Papa and had intended to kiss him on the cheek, but in my tear filled wistful moment that played with my emotions, I wrapped my arms around him and cried. That started Mama crying, which in turn made Alice and Marie cry, too.

"Oh, for Pete's sake!" wailed John. "You're all a bunch of silly gooses!"

"Mama, make him stop!" Marie cried. "We're not a bunch of silly gooses!"

Papa patted me on my back.

"Hier, hier!" Papa reassured me.

Finally, we settled down and dried our eyes.

"Mama is next," John announced. "Mama," my brother spoke as if he were introducing her to us.

"Thank you, John." Mama said. "My dear daughter, on this your 22nd birthday, I want to say how pleased I am with you. You have turned out to be a fine young lady, a true joy..." Mama's voice broke suddenly at the word 'joy,' and more tears filled her eyes. She dabbed her tired eyes with her handkerchief while holding a white tissue wrapped package that waited in her lap. "Happy Birthday, my dear," she said, sniffling as she handed me her gift. I rose from my chair and receiving it, I kissed her on the cheek.

"Thank you, Mama. Thank you so much for a wonderful birthday."

"You are very welcome, my dear," she replied.

Sitting back down, I untied the pink silk ribbon and carefully folded back the white tissue paper so it could be used again. Suddenly I let out a gasp when I saw yards of white lace. "Oh, Mama!" I squealed. "My first tablecloth!"

I unfolded the yards, revealing rows and rows of delicate scroll and leaf designs which are very much in vogue now-a-days. Suddenly I realized something drastically important. "Mama," I awkwardly began. "I don't feel right that I should accept this since it must have emptied your purse."

"Thank you for concern, but my hands have not been idle this past year as I've been selling embroidery items at Fredrick and Nelson's Department Store."

"Don't forget all your piece-meal work too, Mama," Marie reminded her.

Mama smiled and nodded at Marie.

I kissed Mama again on the cheek and told everyone that they will be my first dinner guests to use the lace tablecloth 'someday.'

"I'm next! I'm next!" piped Alice as she slightly bounced up and down on the seat of her chair. I noticed that Mama's eyebrows were frowning as she gave Alice a disapproving glance as my sweet energetic sister sometimes displays a lack of lady-like behavior. My sister crossed the room and gave me a heavy square package which was wrapped in thick layers of white tissue paper with a pink silk ribbon about it. As the layers of tissue fell away, my eyes took in a large handsome celluloid and plush photograph album.

"Don't you like it?" Alice asked with a sweet voice and a long face as I had fallen silent while my hand brushed the plush cover on the back.

"Of course I do. It's just that…"

"Now Eleanor, can't your sister give you a special gift from the labors of her first job?" Alice sat there smiling at me with her hands folded in her lap and her ankles crossed. She was the picture of a proud young lady, her back straight and tall. I should have pressed on with my objection, but knew it was a worthless effort on Alice. I feel terrible knowing that the album must have cost her about $1.65, when she makes a mere $30.00 a month at the library. For this reason, it is worthy of description: The central decoration is a beautiful bouquet of roses, with buds and leaves, all in their natural colors, while the background of the front is in delicate cream and lilac tints. The bouquet of roses is surrounded by a handsome gilt border, has a heavy new style, gilt extension clasp and gilt-edged leaves. Crimson plush covers the back. The entire interior is of deep cream color, with gilt lines, and is one of the finest and handsomest I've ever seen. I am most anxious to fill it.

Next, Marie scurried across the room with her gift and gave my shoulders a quick squeeze. She quickly took up her seat next to Mama and glanced at me shyly. More tissue paper and pink ribbon revealed a lovely framed embroidery piece with a very practical saying;

> "Eat it up
> Wear it out
> Make it do
> Or do without"

At each corner lilacs, pansy's, tulips and daffodils rests on flowing green ribbon.

I thanked my sister very kindly for Mama made it known that Marie had been working on my present since last December.

And finally, John stood up with much pomp and ceremony. He cleared his voice and placed a hand upon his chest.

"My dearest sister, what can I give thee, this I asked of myself. Thee, being a kindred spirit to poems, are thou not?"

"Yes, John, thou knowest I am," I laughed.

"How glad of heart I am to hear thee profess thine words!" admitted my brother.

"I'm surprised your roll of greenbacks hasn't sprung from being so tight!" Alice teased with laughter in her voice.

"Let's see who's laughing when I buy my own automobile someday!" John retorted.

"Now, now…All right John, please present Eleanor with your poem," Mama whispered.

"Yes, Mama. It's called, '*A Ride With Santa.*'"

"I met an old man on the road

One winter long ago,
One cold and wintry Christmas Eve,
When fields were white with snow.

"Hello, old chap! Pray, whither bound?"
Of course I could not tell
It was that good, that jolly saint,
Whom children love so well.

"Hello, old chap! I wish that you
Would take me on my way.
That is of course, if you have room
Within your tiny sleigh."

The old man laughed a jolly laugh.
"Climb in, my friend," said he,
"I have a team beyond compare,
As you right soon shall see."

He whistled once, he whistled twice,
We sped o'er hill and dale,
A thousand times a thousand miles,
And still we left no trail.

And when at length we did draw rein,
"Twas in a wondrous land,
With fairies, sprites and gnomes and fays
At work on every hand.

Ten thousand dolls were seated there,
And jumping jacks galore,
And horns and frums and tops and guns—
A million toys and more.

Of course you've guessed now who it was,
That funny little man.
And this I know, that Santa Claus
Will bring you all he can."

The cheery little room suddenly was filled with loud applause. John was the center of attention. He stood there so tall, casting a shadow behind him on the wall. His handsome features are teetering between youth and adolescence.

"Thank you, thank you! You are too kind."

John continued bowing before his audience.

"Well done!"

"Bravo!"

"Magnificent!"

The mantle clock has finished its long mid-night announcement. I have placed more coals on the fire. I am feeling a bit sleepy as the coziness of the fire is lulling me deeper and deeper into dreamland. I will finish here, steal an afghan from the couch, curl up in this chair, close my heavy eyes and think about all the wonderful gifts I received to-night.

As wonderful as all those are—there is no more precious a gift, as my dear, dear family.

> Good-night and good-
> morning,
> Eleanor

December 11, 1910
Sunday

In the warmth of the kitchen this morning, a few stomachs growled in protest of wanting breakfast before church. Our starvation which begged for cinnamon rolls, scrambled eggs and milk would have to wait. We made conversation of the bleak, cold, damp weather outside our walls that soon we would have to step out into. The street car would be cold. Our feet would be cold and would continue to be cold all through church. Not until our arrival back home could we do something to thaw our flesh from the damp Pacific Northwest winter climate.

The telephone startled us for it never rings before church. John got up and answered it.

"Good-morning, Mr. Miller," John greeted the caller.

A "Hello, John," was faintly heard from where we sat.

"Do you wish to speak to Eleanor?" John asked.

There was a pause.

"Hello? Are you still there?"

"Yes. I'm here. Please tell her that I will call later."

I could faintly hear Nate's voice—something was wrong.

"I will. Whom do you wish to speak to, Mr. Miller?"

"Your father, please."

John turned to us, and looking directly at Papa made a gesture with the receiver saying, "Nate Miller would like to speak with you, Papa."

The kitchen was very quiet, each of us glancing at someone else, puzzlement crossing our faces. We all wondered, "Why would Nate Miller want to speak to our Papa early Sunday morning?"

Papa slowly raised his small frame from the chair and took the receiver from John. He greeted Nate in his thick German accent. He stood very still next to the box on the wall. His face was still—almost like a stone. The words he used were kind and sympathetic, but they lacked any emotion.

"Is there anything we can do to help you, Mr. Miller?"

By now, we were dreadfully anxious and curious as to what the nature of Nate's call was about.

"Very well. Yes, thank you for calling. Yes, I will inform her. Thank you. Good-bye."

Papa put the receiver back on its hook and just stood there staring at the linoleum floor.

"Dear..." Mama gently began, "what news did Nate Miller share with you?"

Papa did not answer Mama right away, because, if I am not mistaken, I thought I saw Papa trying to hide a smile.

"Papa—" Mama had to speak to him again.

"I'm sorry," replied Papa, clearing his voice. "There is one less Miller this morning."

"Oh, dear..." Mama sighed.

"Gosh," exclaimed Alice, "first Todd, and now Mr. Miller Sr."

"It is not Mr. Miller Sr.," corrected Papa. We looked at him. "Stuart Jr., is dead."

John was as curious as the rest of us yet braver so he asked, "Papa, what happened to him?"

Papa cleared his throat. "I was not given any details, but Nate believes that upon discovering his brother that he had passed away sometime during the night."

"Children, Papa..." Mama already had her eyes closed and her hands folded in prayer. "Let us pray for the soul of Stuart Miller... despite who he was and what he did to his fellow man."

I do not think Nate told Papa anything other than what we were told concerning Stuart. Only Nate, Dr. Henry and I know the truth.

I have returned. It is a little past the hour of two in the afternoon. The house is quiet without Nate's presence. We are so pleased to have him accompany us to church on a typical Sunday. Nate happily suffers through endless card games, piano playing and sing-a-longs, a light meal, followed by coffee and men talk around the fireplace. And while the men converse (much to the delight of John), us women prepare a nice meal in the kitchen and lightly speculate what our ears cannot hear.

But not to-day. My heart is sad and heavy, partially because I have seen what the evils of vice and sin can do to a man. Yes, even I feel sorry for Stuart Miller who is no longer part of this world. My heart wants to reach out to Nate, the grieving brother—the brother who is now alone.

Despite their differences, despite their later childhood without a mother (I still do not know any more than that...perhaps Nate will share those memories someday), to-day he must go about the task of burying a brother. I wish I were with him. I want to be with him. Mama and Papa offered to assist in the details that a young man should not have to go through. Nate politely declined any help. I only wish that my poor dear Nate did not have to buy a coffin, find an undertaker, and watch his brother be lowered into the cold, dark, brown earth. They say it is six feet down...but I do believe it's deeper. Don't you think so? Mama says that there will not be a viewing in the Miller's parlor; the lights will not have to be on for three days...

No, I was not particularly fond of Stuart, but all the same I feel sorry that he did not know what happiness was. To die as he did seems such a dreadful waste; even for a Miller...

All for now,
Eleanor

December 12, 1910
Monday

The misery of it all...I cannot think of more fitting words to describe to-day.

Papa, Mama, and I rode the cold streetcar up the hill to Mount Pleasant Cemetery this morning, pausing briefly at the intersection of Queen Anne Avenue North and West Galer Street where the motorman hitched us to the counterbalance cables. I didn't mind the wait…it kept us away for just a while longer.

Papa and Mama and I spoke but a few words on the way. I know that the only reason they went to Stuart Miller's funeral was out of respect for Nate.

I remember how worried I was, wondering if Mr. Miller Sr. was going to be there for his son's funeral. As the streetcar went along Sixth Avenue West and turned left onto McGraw Street, my stomach was in knots. After depositing riders here and there, by the time we reached Seventh Avenue West, we were the only passengers headed for the cemetery. Having been informed that the next streetcar would not be by for half-an-hour, the streetcar rang its departure bell and went back down Seventh Avenue.

The miserable dampness had already found its way through my clothing—a depressing thing—considering how many layers were on me. Such included a gray ribbed fleece union suit, warm under-skirt, my long gray plaid coat, my fascinator on my head and gloves on my hands.

Papa and Mama turned their attention to four men. One, being Nate, another, a man of the cloth, and two undertakers who stood waiting with shovels in the hands.

I have not mentioned Mr. Miller Sr., have I? I wonder if Stuart would have cared at all if he knew his father was not present. What a grim and lonesome thing it would have been if we had not been there for Nate. I'm glad we decided to go.

As our cold feet stepped across the wet grass, my eyes were fixed on the two men holding shovels. Their heads were bowed—though not out of reverence for the dead. They were beyond miserable. Their shoulders slumped forward—I saw one shiver—I saw the knees of the other shake. Their cold, dark eyes lifted from under thick eyebrows. If they had necks, they disappeared into raised coat collars. I can only imagine the contempt they must have felt—burying the dead in the middle of winter. Although the gravediggers had been speech-less and almost statue like in appearance, I saw the lips of one move. This made the man wearing the church cloth turn an ear slightly but did not look behind him. A frown was quickly seen on his face.

I had been paying too much attention to the undertakers to not have noticed what was not there. It quickly hit me that the casket holding Stuart was already in the ground. I eyed the mountain of earth next to the dark hole in the ground.

Nate gently squeezed my hand. He shook hands with Papa and

nodded to Mama. Insignificant small talk almost seemed forbidden—what could be said?

I stood on Nate's left and Papa and Mama stood on his right.

I could not help notice Nate's red ears, red nose, cold cheeks. Oh, my poor, dear Nate!

The man who wore the church cloth was eager to be done with his task. The skin recoiling, chattering of teeth, shivering, goose flesh weather was to blame for his hasty words. His right hand made the sign of the cross in the air as he clutched his black bible against himself with the other. He turned to Nate and quickly put out his hand, but my poor Nate just stood there, confused that the whole service lasted all of a good three minutes or less. The man of the cloth wasted no time in picking up Nate's hand that hung at his side, shook it twice, and with a turn of his back his speed across the wet grass removed him from us.

Needless to say, his tactless departure momentarily left a sick feeling in my stomach. This feeling swept over each of us—or was it the nippy wind that decided to stir all of a sudden? And to make matters worse, the two men who had been holding shovels stepped forward, and feeling no obligation to acknowledge Nate a few moments of quiet reflection, planted their tools into the dirt. Nate began to lunge forward, out of instinct I suppose, but Papa caught his arm and turned him around. The remorseless sound of dirt hitting the wood coffin was too much for Nate to bear. We walked briskly into the wind that was painful against our cheeks. I can almost see it laughing at us as Papa and Nate held their hats in place; while Mama and I grabbed our hoods about our necks while the tassels blew behind our backs.

We went home in the Miller's automobile.

Oh, somber, somber day. Do leave us quickly! I wish to get on with my life with the man I care for. Dear Lord, please take care of my dear Nate.

Thank-you
Eleanor

December 20, 1910
Tuesday

Five days till Christmas. This should be a joyous season....
And yet, my thoughts are with Nate. I have not set foot in the

Miller's house since Stuart's death. It is difficult being away from Nate, not being able to take care of him as a woman should. I do not know how he is getting along and this worries me greatly. Mama says he needs time to sort things out and get his brother's affairs in order. I cannot forget to call Nate to-night and invite him to Christmas Eve dinner and to midnight Mass. Mama has gently warned me that Nate might decline our invitation—considering all that he has been through. If our invitation is not agreeable at this time, I shall be gracious and not take his absence to heart.

Papa and John found a nice tree in the vacant lot a few blocks away. It proudly stands in front of our living room window. I have been baking gingerbread men and star shaped sugar cookies for ornaments. Marie is making more German star ornaments. Fragile glass balls and bells dangle from scented branches, as well as the wish-bone from our Thanksgiving turkey. John was fortunate to bring home tin foil from his messenger job. It must have been used for packing purposes for it very hard to come by otherwise. He was quite happy to obtain it and having cut it in long thin strips, the tinsel now glitters from branches when the sun decides to appear.

In-between baking and washing, Mama and I settle down in our chairs before the fireplace with bowls of popcorn and cranberries. While needle and thread are busy, I ask Mama what Christmas was like when she was a little girl. I can't remember a more enjoyable nor pleasant time spent with Mama. It has been years since I've had her all to myself. As a child, she received dolls, caps and mittens, while her brothers would get trains, building blocks, and caps and mittens, too. Her mother would get pretty dishes.

I almost forgot. John is going to be in the Christmas Pageant at school to-night and will be reciting two poems. They are as follows:

Christmas Fires

When bright Christmas fires are glowing
And the fields are white with snow,
Down beside the fair Penobscot
There comes back the long ago.
From Bohemia's gilded castles
Do I longing flee again
To the bygone dreams of boyhood
'Mid the pine-clad hills of Maine.

How we children watched the chimney
Till our eyes closed fast in sleep;
How we waited, watched his coming!
But we never got a peep.
How we shouted in the morning,
"Merry Christmas!" —sweet refrain—
As we emptied all our stockings
Filled by Santa Claus of Maine.

Oh, the joys and toys of Christmas
In that home of olden time!
By the great log fires a-glowing
I can hear the voices chime,
Father's, mother's, sister's, brother's,
Reunited once again;
Oh, the turkey, pies and puddings
Served on Christmas up in Maine!

The second poem is:

At Christmastide

Now deck the walls with mistletoe
And shining wreaths of holly
And though the wild winds shrilly blow
Where wintry wastes are white with snow,
Wrapt in the Yule-log's ruddy glow
We'll laugh at melancholy.

For on the ebb-tide of the year
Has come the festive season
When care and woe should disappear
And every soul be filled with cheer,
When life and youth seem boubly dear
And folly links with reason.

And when the viol's mad refrain
Sets every foot to dancing,
Let every heart that long has lain
In sorrow's shade grow light again,
And every tongue take up the strain

Of melody entrancing.

Ay, deck the walls with mistletoe
And shining wreaths of holly,
And while the light hours lightly go,
Let every eye with luster glow,
Let mirth around the fireside flow
And one and all be jolly.

Composed by Hilton R.Greer

I think the Christmas program should prove to be entertaining and delightful. Perhaps it is what we need to lift our low spirits.

All for now,
Eleanor

December 21, 1910
Wednesday

What should have been a delightful time at John's Christmas program last night.... I best start at the beginning.

Sitting at the dressing table in our room, I had fussed over my hair till my arms were quiet tired and I was near tears. I wished to do something different with it besides putting it on top my head in a loose bun. Marie and Alice also stood behind me helping each other into their finest dresses. A knock sounded on our door and John's voice spoke though it as he was wondering if he might speak with Alice. They closed our door and removed themselves down the hallway, as all I could hear was muffled voices. Then John's footsteps echoed up the landing as Alice came back into the room with a twinkle in her eye. I asked what John wanted.

Standing behind me, she cleared her throat and lightly whispered into my ear, "Nothing…"

"Eleanor dear, I saw a lovely new hair style in one of your magazines recently. You seem to be having difficulty with your hair to-night…." at that Alice removed the pins from my horrible attempt of a bun and my long hair fell over my shoulders and to my seat. My efficient sister had the hair brush in her hand while asking Marie to find a certain magazine and go to a specific page.

"Is this the one?" Marie asked, bringing it to us and holding the magazine open so we could gaze at the breathtaking photo.

"Oh!" Alice exclaimed, thrusting a hand upon her bosom "isn't that just the loveliest hair style any woman could ever want?"

"I wish my hair was thick enough to manage Josephine curls," sighed Marie.

"Your hair is just fine," I reassured my sister with a kind smile in the mirror.

"Thank you for saying so, even though all three of us know that God inflicted me with the straightest hair imaginable. A terrible thing it is for a woman, any woman to have to suffer for the rest of her life! But that is something that neither of you shall ever have to worry about. You two were favored by God from the beginning. Time has only enhanced what He has given you."

Alice and I were somewhat speechless. What could we say in our sister's defense? She had judged herself and us correctly. To say that she was in the lot that was blessed with a handsome figure, a pretty face and thick hair would be a falsehood. I was grateful that Alice continued to brush my hair while I sat looking at myself in the mirror. Our poor Marie does have her short-comings, through no fault of her own.

"Now Marie! Who's to say that straight hair isn't a blessing? Why...you must take notice of how long it takes Eleanor and I to brush out our uncooperative pile of mess every morning."

"Well....yes," Marie agreed reluctantly.

"And truth be told, there are times that I wish I had straighter and finer hair so I wouldn't have to spend forever in front of the range drying my hair," added Alice.

"What about you, Eleanor?" Marie looked at my reflection in the glass.

I could see Marie in the round mirror—sitting on the edge of the bed facing us. Our eyes were studying each other. Oh, how I wish she had turned out differently. I could not help take in her long neck, her thin shoulders, and the figure under her dress that did not have many curves for a young woman. And if lacking female curves wasn't punishment enough, Marie also lacked the second most important feature a woman can possess—a healthy bosom. The first, of course, is her crown and glory—a beautiful head of hair. In due time, Marie could fill out, but in all probability and pure honesty, she will never achieve what Alice and I have. And so, I sat looking at my poor sister in the mirror, and suddenly I found myself rising off the chair. I do not know what part of me decided to do so, for I would rather have been the spoiled recipient of Alice's brush. But my tongue has never been as quick or cleaver as Alice's, and therefore, my moment of hesitation was lost in obtaining vanity.

"Marie....come take my seat and let Alice fuss over you."

A gasp of surprise left Marie as she clasped her hands together.

"Truly?" Marie asked, disbelieving such an offer.

Alice was taken back at this sudden turn and she carefully eyed me in question and of slight annoyance. I shall not say that Marie has never been groomed by Alice or I....only that we prefer to groom each other. That sounds cruel, perhaps, excluding a sibling from a relaxing time between two females.....

Was our intentional partiality wagging a finger at us now?

I read Alice's face and she read mine.

The small clock on the dresser ticked away the minutes— it seemed that it would be Marie's good fortune, not mine, to be the center of attention at the Christmas Pageant to-night. Time would permit the grooming of only one person. Our momentary glance understood this. I felt a pang of remorse for my slowness to respond to Marie's question. It should have been me on the bench, not Marie. It should have been my hair that Alice would have loved to have put into Josephine curls. I tried to smile at Marie while suppressing my rising envy. While Alice began to brush Marie's hair I picked up the magazine and ran my eyes over the picture of the lovely young lady who's bent head was youthful and elegant. Her eyes were dreamy, her nose perfect, her mouth desirable. And draping low over her creamy shoulders, yards of soft material drifted within the forbidden recesses of her soft bosom.

At that moment I did not care if my emotions were about to be displayed, for I tossed the poor magazine on the closest bed and strode into the little closet in huff. I crossed my arms and bit my lip for tears were on the verge of spilling out. I let out a sniffle and Marie asked if I was catching a cold. Dear Alice answered for me, lovingly shrugging off any suggestion of tears, instead, she wisely placed the blame on the dust in our closet.

I did find a suitable skirt and waist and belt, and then turned my attention back to my hair which ended up in its usual plain bun.

As our youngest sister was being transformed, I sat on my bed watching, giving an occasional smile or nod of approval here and there. In my heart, I knew how important and necessary it was for Marie to be lifted up from her lowly life—even if it was just for one short evening.

In the time that it took to dress myself, Alice's skillful hands turned Marie's hair into two figure eights which looked very lovely. Then Alice put one of her own dresses on Marie. Alice had quite outgrown it, though kept it without handing it down to Marie. With hair pins in place and lace collar affixed, Marie stood up, and Alice and I smiled.

Our sister looked at herself in the mirror. There was a different look in her eyes. A different glow in her cheeks. Our sister was feeling something for the first time. Was Marie sensing something about herself that the rest of the female race takes for granted every day?

"Eleanor," Marie asked, "am I as pretty as I feel?"

The question hung in the air....It was not intended for Alice. Just me.

"How pretty do you feel?" I asked gingerly yet slyly.

"Very pretty!" beamed Marie.

I smiled at Marie and at myself for my cleverness at having my sister answer her own question.

"It will be a wonderful evening. I know it will. I shouldn't be so excited and giddy over a little Christmas pageant, though I would feel more complete...." She paused for a moment to add a touch of soft pleading, "if only I had..." As Marie's voice trailed off her eyes slipped over to mine. Why was Marie making me out to be a stool pigeon, again? Her dark brown eyes were filled with a hint of possessing the upper hand—rare indeed in Marie's shadowed life. I understand this feminine accomplishment which is as natural as breathing to most females. We learned this as little girl's, as miss's, as young women. In this world of men, women do not have the same privileges, thus it is to our advantage to use what God has given us to obtain an upper hand. Women understand this and we would be fools not to utilize what is at our disposal. And men? They are perplexed as well as aroused. They comply to our whims and fancies, for we are creatures that they wish to cling to.

I thought I heard Alice's soft voice speak my name.

"What? I'm sorry..."

"Marie was wondering if she may wear one of your pendants."

"Oh...." my voice was already withholding her simple request.

"Please, oh, please," Marie petitioned again. "Please, please, please?"

She had placed a frail hand on her throat and attempted to form a pout. Ironically, in the hour that had passed, Alice and I were part of a performance; unplanned at first, but upon its birth, Marie quickly bit into her plan and was now relishing in its ascendancy.

"Oh, do give in, just this once Eleanor..." Alice cooed.

I let out a protesting sigh and nodding my head I said, "All right." I opened my drawer and produced the velvet lined box that Papa had made me last year. Settling myself back on my bed, I opened the lid and held up a heart shape locket, several nice pendants on chains, and a Genuine Amber bead necklace. Alice took the necklace and smiled, telling Marie how lovely she would look in it.

"No, its not quite what I had in mind. What about—that one?" My sister was pointing to the beautiful solid gold soldered links—the 18 inch rope chain—the pendant set with fine blue stone and pearls. My birthday present from Nate. I have not had the pleasure of wearing it in public as of yet.

"I'm sorry Marie, perhaps after I have worn it first. You do understand?"

Marie gave me an interesting little look after something had crossed her mind.

"I suppose I shall have to settle on something plain and ordinary....just like me," she sighed.

"Now Marie," Alice quickly came to my aid. "Do not be cross. It is only right that Eleanor should wear her birthday present first, and then if she wishes for you or I to wear it after such time, that is up to her."

"Why don't you wear it to-night?" asked Marie.

"I want to wear it the next time when I'm with Nate."

Just then Mama's voice called to us from the bottom landing, informing us that we needed to be downstairs in five minutes. Marie quickly chose one of the other pendants and left the room.

When I arrived downstairs, John looked at me from head to foot disapprovingly. He quickly turned to Marie with a shocked and surprised look on his face. John turned back to Alice who was shrugging her shoulders. It was too early in the evening to understand the whole of it. Finally we were all gathered in the living room, our coats on and ready to turn the gas lamps off when Marie said that she had forgotten something upstairs.

The night air proved to be chilly as we walked down the hill passed the vacant lot where Papa and John cut our tree from. We took our time and stepped carefully on the wood-plank sidewalk that protected our shoes and skirts from the dirt streets. John and Marie led the way in the dark, then Mama and Papa, then Alice and

I. We looped our arms together so the black night wouldn't seem so frightening. I wish the city would install street lights on our block so one doesn't feel as if they are walking blindfolded. When the clouds roll away at night we can see twinkling stars and the moon lights our way. But not to-night. All I could hear was our shoes clicking on the wood that was bringing us closer to the trolley car lines. We had to wait perhaps five or ten minutes before one arrived, and by that time our faces were quite chilled, and since trolleys do not have any means of heat, we stayed chilled. John sat in front of me and I could hear him whispering his lines. I wondered just how nervous he was.

Arriving at the two story brick school, John proudly led us down the halls which were lit by electricity, and to the auditorium which was also lit by electricity. Thankfully the building had central heating! John told me to sit almost to the end of the row but to save the isle seat for him—just in case he was allowed to sit with the audience after his recital. I was instructed not to let anyone sit there. Everyone except Marie removed their coats and put them on the backs of the chairs. Marie claimed she was still chilled as she often is since she does not have much meat on her bones.

Alice and I immensely enjoyed the quiet pageantry and display around us. And yes, I felt horribly unfashionable and wished I hadn't been so stubborn earlier. Even Alice looked more stylish than I. The fashionably gowned woman this winter is wearing frocks and dresses as the very slender silhouette is being sought after according to the women in this auditorium. A tunic drapery seems popular as supple material of soft satin and crepe de chine are used for dresses when a woman goes out for the afternoon, for visiting, matinees or teas. Oh, how we sighed! The cashmere, the fine French serge and wool-back satin, the silk and wool-poplin. Braiding, bands of hand-embroidery in oriental colors, lace yokes, collars and undersleeves….sigh! Striped gray and white silks, light grays and dark grays.

A lovely blond woman made her presence known as she took her sweet time choosing a seat two rows ahead of us. Alice caught my arm and whispered to me, "Look at her costume of blue French serge….black satin bands trimming the lace collar and yoke, and all that lovely lace undersleeves under her short sleeves that is trimmed with more black satin…."

"I wonder what kind of gowns and walking costumes Minnie wears?" I asked out loud.

"Oh, Eleanor, just so we do not die out of curiosity, you must ask her!"

"I will."

"Oh,…I think the program is going to begin," Alice whispered.

The house lights were dimmed, and the huge purple velvet curtains separated and were drawn aside. Lights lit up the stage where a piano stood waiting, a star hung from above, and an assortment of Christmas related props waited to fulfill their duty. As a woman settled herself at the piano bench and played a short introduction tune, a nicely dressed gentleman came on stage, introduced himself and then promptly opened the program. Just as he took his bow and was exiting the stage, I heard a man's voice ask,

"I beg your pardon, Miss. Is this seat taken?"

Before I had a chance to think, the figure of one Mr. Nate Miller sat down in the vacant seat reserved for John.

"Oh!"

"Sorry if I startled you," Nate apologized.

"This is quite a surprise," I confessed in a whispering voice.

"Didn't John tell you?"

I could only shake my head as I knew I must have looked so plain and ordinary in Nate's eyes. If I had known, I would have put on one of my Sunday dresses and worn the pendant from Nate. Due to my stubbornness I wore neither which was no one's fault except my own. I managed to forget about my lack of costume as Christmas songs were sung and short plays made us giggle and laugh. The house lights went up and there was a brief intermission. It was in the course of stretching our legs in the hallway when I noticed that Marie still wore her coat. While Mama and Papa greeted Nate and made pleasantries, I had a strange feeling that Marie was avoiding me. I thought it was very odd that she was covering up a lovely dress that she should have been flaunting. And then it happened. Alice approached the coat clad Marie and asked her why she wasn't showing everyone her pretty dress. Again, Marie said that she was cold.

"Nonsense!" Alice replied.

"Truly, I am…" Marie half stammered.

"Even so, there are too many handsome young men here to-night!" Alice hinted through a playful smile. "It must come off if you want to catch the eye of an admirer."

Before Marie had a chance to protest, Alice quickly removed the coat, and there hanging from Marie's neck was my pendant. All eyes fell on my sister as her cheeks turned red and a dreadful silence fell upon us. Nate, not understanding the enormity of Marie's exposure was the first to speak.

"Marie, may I pay compliment on how lovely you look to-night."

Our sister having been caught in self-perjury, managed to thank Mr. Miller for his kind words with a slight nod while her dishonest eyes looked down.

"I see that your hair is in a new style,…. and that Eleanor was kind enough to loan you her pendant."

I fixed my scolding eyes on my sister, and at that moment, I did not care if other people saw the sourness of my character. I do not know if Nate was looked in my direction or if he was admiring Marie while I wore an unpleasant face. I hope for my sake he was looking at Marie. Although I have been wise enough to have never placed myself in the awful position Marie was in, I'm sure at that moment my sister would have died rather than face the humiliation and punishment of her crime.

"Yes…Alice is quite good with a brush," Marie feebly answered.

"You are lucky to have two wonderful sister's who care for you," replied Nate with a kind smile.

Looking back, it really was an awful conglomeration of Papa and Mama not understanding what was going on. Nate was confused. Alice and I were betrayed.

Thankfully there was stirring in the hall, and with the announcement that the second half of the program was to begin, we took up our seats. As the lights were dimmed once more, our brother and the woman pianist came out together and took their places. Oh, how handsome and mature John looked on stage. How proud I was of him. I know dear Richard would have been beaming, just as Papa and Mama were to-night. John began by introducing himself, then announced that he would begin with a Christmas poem entitled "Christmas Fires." The audience for the most part was still and quiet enough for John to start, I thought.

"What is he waiting for?" Alice whispered as she bent her head toward mine.

Still, John waited.

Nate asked, "You don't suppose John has forgotten his lines?"

I smiled and suppressed a little giggle.

"I don't think so. What you are watching is John eating up every morsel of attention he can get to-night," I explained.

Our dear brother stood there graciously smiling until a dropped pin could have been heard. He then bowed to the pianist and her fingers softly flowed over the keys.

> *"When bright Christmas fires are glowing*
> *And the fields are white with snow,*
> *Down beside the fair Penobscot*
> *There comes back the long ago…*
> *How we children watched the chimney*
> *Till our eyes closed fast in sleep;*
> *How we waited, watched his coming!*
> *But we never got a peep…"*

The softness of her mingling notes with the poem's carefully spoken words brought tears to my eyes. The cheering and applause John received was quite spectacular as it went on and on. He began his second poem titled "At Christmastide."

> *"Now deck the walls with mistletoe*
> *And shining wreaths of holly*
> *And though the wild winds shrilly blow*
> *Where wintry wastes are white with snow*
> *Wrapt in the Yule-log's ruddy glow*
> *We'll laugh at melancholy.*
>
> *For on the ebb-tide of the year*
> *Has come the festive season*
> *When care and woe should disappear*
> *And every soul be filled with cheer,*
> *When life and youth seem boubly dear*
> *And folly links with reason.*
>
> *And when the viol's mad refrain*
> *Sets every foot to dancing,*
> *Let every heart that long has lain*
> *In sorrow's shade grow light again,*
> *And every tonque take up the strain*
> *Of melody entrancing.*
>
> *Ay, deck the walls with mistletoe*
> *And shining wreaths of holly,*
> *And while the light hours lightly go,*

Mary Margaret Bayer

Let every eye with luster glow,
Let mirth around the fireside flow
And one and all be jolly.

There was a brief hush in the auditorium before a stunning roar of clapping and cheering broke forth. You could feel pandemonium rise and swallow every softened heart that was captivated by my glowing brother! And yes, my tender heart swelled with pride as I cried. Suddenly, Nate stood up which gave everyone permission and the courage to follow suit. He clapped heartily and showered John with a string of "Bravo's!"

The young man on the stage was so sure of his speaking abilities, so confidant, so mature, so in love with his captivated audience. I saw Mama dab her eyes when I leaned forward to see how John had affected her with his performance. My hands were quite numb when the clamor died down.

And what happened next is partially due to my own fault and ill-preparedness, for I knew it was close to coming, but not so soon nor so suddenly. To my horror and dismay, I was so far from home and too close to Nate when I realized that a light 'occurrence' was starting. I could not stay seated for too much longer least I ruin my garments and dress; least everyone see the spot of the curse! I wanted to cry because I was a woman...I wanted to hide from my shame... "Oh, God," I prayed, "do not let anyone notice my curse or I will die!" I cried silent tears and then turned to Alice. How she knew I'll never know, but she whispered, "I'll follow you," and discreetly excusing ourselves we quickly found the ladies room.

Yes, I did cry, and Alice kept saying, "You poor, poor thing! You poor, poor thing!"

"What are we to do!?" I sobbed helplessly. "I wish I could die! Oh, just let me die!" I wailed.

"Now, now! Let me think. There must be a way to save your dignity...." Alice paced the black and white checkered tile floor. "Eleanor, please stop crying! I'm trying to come up with a solution!"

"I'm sorry!" I snapped, "but you would be crying too if your dress was ruined and a good portion of Seattle was on the verge of discovering it!"

"Not if I can help it!" Alice started for the door.

"Alice! Don't leave me!" I wailed.

"I'll be right back with our coats."

"What will you tell Mama and Papa!? Oh, no!" I gasped, my sobbing escalating into a shriek. "What about Nate! How will I ever!?"

Alice came back to me and held me by the arms, her voice very stern.

"Listen Eleanor…I'm sure you are not the first woman on this earth to have ever been taken by surprise by an evil day. Are you unfortunate? Certainly! Unlucky? Yes! Will you die of humiliation?"

"Yes!" I answered, stomping my foot like a child.

"Not if I can help it! I'll be right back….stay put!"

Alice had her hand on the doorknob and was partially out when I stopped her.

"What will you say to Papa and Mama and Nate?" I fretted as my heart beat increased and my skin began to moisten with nervousness.

"Don't know yet…but I'll think of something before I reach the auditorium," my dear sister almost laughed at her undecided plan, discarding the words with a wave of her hand before she shut the door and disappeared.

I will be forever in her debt for her unflinching character and clear thinking. At the moment I am lying in bed with a wonderful hot water bottle on my stomach and at my bed-side sits a warm cup of chamomile tea. My blessed dear sister is trying to wash the stain from my garments….what sister would do that for another? Bless her a hundred fold!! How can I ever repay a sister who retrieved our coats, told family and Nate ever so discreetly that a cloud had come over me….that we would take a trolley home, and yes, we would be very careful not to speak to men on the way home. Alice had exited so quickly that poor Nate and John was given an explanation of 'a feminine headache' after the program was over. Nate drove the family home in his nice automobile.

And my pendant? Marie apologized for disrespecting other people's property and placing it on the dresser, she pleaded that I must hear that 'still small voice within my heart' that wants to forgive her. I informed my sister in a cool tone of voice that I did not hear no such thing. I did not care to look at her nor forgive her when she came in this room. She will have to suffer….just as I have to-night.

Alice says that there isn't much hope for my dress…..

Goodnight,
Eleanor

December 22, 1910

Since Eleanor no longer occupied the house with her domestic duties, nor filled his evenings with her soft voice and feminine presence, he spent what was left of the night in front of the parlor fire eating roast beef sandwiches and reading the paper. Nate dreadfully missed Eleanor. He missed talking to her. Missed just knowing she was in the house with him. Of course, he missed her wonderful meals, but considered himself a lucky man to have partaken in them while he could.

Nate put the paper down in his lap and let out a deep sigh. Although he enjoyed reading practically every column in the paper, his concentration was very poor as many details were occupying his mind as of late.

Not long after Todd's kidnapping back in June did Mr. Miller Sr. fall into fits of depression. His returning home in the early morning hours had become more and more common, as was seeing his intoxicated large rumpled body sprawled across his bed. Upon wakening, he lumbers groggily down the grand staircase holding onto the banister for support, and still wearing wrinkled suits from two or three days prior, he yells in a loud slur the names of his two favorite sons throughout the near empty house. His father would stay only long enough to sleep the alcohol off, and according to the urgency to sustain his life long dependency, he was gone again, without a shave or bath.

Here and there, either by a meeting of chance on the trolley, or by a nightly phone call, Dr. Henry asks how things are, asks how Nate's father is dealing with the death of Stuart Jr. and the disappearance of Todd. He does not offer help for the drunkard, nor is condescending toward his vices. Rather, Dr. Henry and Nate are spectators—an audience of a drawn out play—the audience having its day of quiet reckoning....There is no need to mock or sneer at the dying actor. Both men clearly understand that one day Mr. Miller Sr.'s ill-health will turn upon him with deadly effect. Though he is barely at the living point with the disease, and further punishes himself by devoting considerable time to the relief afforded by alcohol, Dr. Henry has touched on the possibility that Mr. Miller may become an easy victim, like Todd, of a 'Shanghai' set-up in one of the many taverns of the city. Or, a more likely victim for robbers, depositing his body among the waste and filth in an alley; attracting curious mice and rats to scurry over the beaten, cold, lifeless body of a once pompous and pitiless man. The healthy population of scavengers and parasites would feel no need to express pity or sympathy for the victim; only gratitude toward the robbers. Somewhere in Seattle, such things are permitted to cease life; it wraps its dark cloak from various vices and waits to claim the flesh of drunks, bootleggers, low life, and occasionally the unsinkable from high society.

In the early morning hours when his father comes home from hours of gambling and drinking, he slams the front door and loudly makes his way up the staircase, through the blackness of the house and to his room. Nate hears the clumsiness of a drunk man from his own room. He hears his father thud against the hallway wall, and sometimes Nate goes to his door and opens it enough just to see his father's figure slide against the wallpaper and crumple in a worthless heap on the oriental flooring. He looks at the body but is not inclined to feel sorry for it. Nate remembers the night in the parlor when his father laughed at his appearance, laughed at his only possession—the steamer trunk, and tried to humiliate his son who was probably penniless.

At night, Nate turns on the bedside lamp and picks up the picture of his mother and him, letting his fingers run down the glass as if he could feel his dear mother. The sound of his mother's sweet voice comes back to him when fond memories picture them together. It all comes back in a fuzzy way which is still comforting to him after all these years. Nate remembers how kind and gentle she was, rarely raising her voice at her children. It was cruel, very cruel for a child to have lost his mother at such an early age. And still, at the age of 28, there was an aching void left in his life. He and his mother were very close. Nate was not like Todd and Stuart. He thoroughly enjoyed being with his mother, listening to her read to him, listening to her play the piano—one of the few joys she was allowed. The only time his father and brothers joined him and mother to church was on Christmas Eve. Although his mother did not have any say in the matter of who should go to church, she was very pleased that one of her sons faithfully joined her every Sunday. This arrangement did not bother Nate in the least since it meant that he had his mother's attention entirely to himself.

After his mother's death, Nate felt that his brothers lack of sympathy stemmed from not knowing her as well as he. Within a week, Stuart began to turn on Nate with unrelenting spite. He accused his younger brother of coveting their mother's attention, which of course was absurd. For some ridiculous reason or excuse, Stuart did not think that he was welcome in his mother's 'little circle' which consisted of her and Nate. And for that he would never forgive his brother. This vindictiveness of course was the sudden void caused by a mother not being there….and what was Stuart thinking all these years…to carry on like his father, and then one day pretend that his character meant nothing? If indeed, Stuart had suddenly come forth from the cloud of oblivion fostered by his father, he was rudely awakened by whatever grief he felt.

It was useless, trying to explain to Stuart that his mother did care for him. He asked Stuart one day if he really thought his ill mother was going to live forever. Was he waiting for a certain time, perhaps while she breathed her last to whisper, "Mother, I love you."

Stuart had thrown the first fist. Nate finished the fight.

Even at a young age, Nate was acutely aware that loyalties to their parents were divided: Stuart and little Todd sided with their father. Nate was drawn to his mother. This separation was obvious but never spoken between his mother and father. At least not in front of the children. To Stuart, being the oldest by almost two years and Todd, four years younger, it mattered little. They thought, through the influence of their father, that their mother did not care for them. They were sadly mistaken, for quite often she would tell Nate how it saddened her heart that two of her sons held her in "low estimation." Sadly, it was a way of life in the Miller household. Nate understood early on that his parents were in a loveless marriage that imprisoned a young woman's hopes forever for a happy home life.

Not too long before his mother's death, Nate was at her bedside reading to her when he put the book down and asked her a question that had been weighing on his mind for some years. He apologized if wanting to ask was inappropriate, for he knew it was a subject that a son should not be discussing with a mother. But years of suspicion had waited long enough and the days left for his mother were few. Whether it was courage or curiosity, he found himself inquiring, and to his surprise, his mother wanted him know the truth.

It pleased her greatly that one of her sons cared enough in wanting to know, and so, she did not hesitate to tell her Nathaniel that it was an "arranged marriage" for the benefit of her father who treated the engagement and marriage no differently than a business transaction. Her mother literally betrayed her own daughter by refusing to acknowledge the fact that Mr. Stuart Miller who was to be their son-in-law, earned his living off the misfortune of others, swindled the innocent and robbed the naive without blinking an eye. As long as their life style was guaranteed to rise from modest means to elegant prosperity, Mr. Miller could not be viewed with disfavor. Difficult and painful as it was, Caroline understood how her adoptive parents could be so agreeable with the temptation of wealth laid at their feet in exchange for their beautiful young daughter. It did not matter to them that their seventeen year old daughter wished to be further educated at a University with her friends. Nor did they bother, or care, to take into consideration that their only child was in love with another man. To allow the notion that she had a mind or feelings of her own would not be of any benefit to them. She begged and petitioned her mother to rebuff Mr. Miller's empowerment over them, but to no avail. At night she offered up prayers, beseeching of her Creator, to spare her from a life of misery, sorrow, heartache and bitterness from a man who was dispassionate and possessed no soul. A man who derived pleasure from gambling and drinking, and seared the downtrodden if they were foolhardy or valiant enough to claim they were wronged.

During the night she shed inconsolable tears, driving her physical being to illness. If she was to marry against her will, Caroline summoned what strength she had left to protest and took it upon herself to pack a carpet bag. To do nothing would be regretful. To take a decisive step at least gave her hope. She had managed to steal away from the house, and with determination made her way through the dark and dirt lined neighborhoods of Seattle until she found a carriage that would deliver her to her beau's house. But upon entering the carriage, she quickly learned just how possessed her husband-to-be was. The grim reality sank in as two hired men escorted poor Caroline back to her parent's house.

Sometime during the early hour when the sun promised another day, she yielded to her fate. Young Caroline did not turn her back on God when she stood at the alter that horrid morning. And for her parents, unearned wealth was theirs when their daughter became Mrs. Stuart Miller.

There was a small wedding breakfast and gifts to be brought back to a strange house. There was no post-wedding trip to be taken. In the matrimonial chamber that evening, her new husband, without mincing the matter, informed his young wife that she was for breeding purposes only. He needed a wife to produce legitimate children to carry on his name. Anything more that he desired, he would look elsewhere. And he did. It was no secret to her sons that their father had mistresses at his disposal; housemaids and governess' were no exception. If an illegitimate offspring was the result of her husband's sexual vice, the poor girl was simply bought off, dismissed and readily replaced.

During Nate's childhood, there was a stranger in the house who rarely spoke to his middle son, and when he did, it was carried out with disapproval and criticism. Nate never did understand why his father inflicted such verbal punishment upon him. He could not find just cause in his thinking why this person whom he called "father" treated him as if he was almost—unwanted. Somewhere within, his character was never hungry or half-starved for his father's affection or approval. This, in itself must of been a blessing. A child so young as Nate would have been a withering thing to society— a product of a "father's cast-off."

Since Todd's disappearance and Stuart's passing, his father has been rushing destruction upon himself. It did ·not matter to Nate what his father did to himself.

Nate rose from his chair. He put his hands in his trouser pockets and stood before the fire. A few forbidden words were muttered into the fire.

He let his eyes fixate on the hot flames for a while, but a knocking sound interrupted his thoughtless gaze. Nate lifted his head, and listening more intently, he made his way to the front door, where the knocks persisted until Nate opened it.

Two rosy-cheeked gentlemen stood on the porch and breathed into the frosty air. The older of the two who sported a reddish mustache looked in the neighborhood of thirty, while the other looked younger than Nate.

"May I help you?" Nate greeted the two men.

"Good-evening, Sir," the older man replied, and commencing to clearing his throat, he donned an aristocratic-business like air. "We apologize for the late hour, but there is a matter of great importance which we need to discuss with…"

"Why, gentlemen," Nate exclaimed, "will you look at that! You have snow on your coats and hats. How long ago did it begin to fall?"

The two men looked at each other, shrugged their shoulders and replied, "Perhaps an hour or so ago?" they ventured.

"Well, this is a surprise," Nate smiled.

"I beg your pardon, Sir, but considering your family's financial situation, I would think not," the mustached gentleman was quick to correct.

Nate looked passed the men and said, "The snow...Isn't it a wonderful sight? See how something so small and unassuming can cover the dirt and make everything so clean and bright."

Nate nodded to the men in a way that they felt obligated to twist their upper bodies slightly in order to have another look at the cold snow without moving their feet from the front porch.

"Maybe we'll have a white Christmas after all," Nate sighed in a wishful voice.

Someone cleared his throat. "Sir...we—"

Nate saw his words in the frosty air.

"Forgive me! Where are my manners? Please do come in and warm yourselves by the fire," Nate apologized, opening the door with its beautiful lace design etched on the oval glass. He welcomed the two strangers in, extending an outstretched arm.

Cautiously, the two entered the foyer, and while removing their hats they quickly eyed the interior of the Miller home with interest. They followed Nate into the parlor and he made a gesture towards the warm fire that the men did not hesitate to go to.

"I'm sorry that I cannot offer you refreshments or coffee. Our housekeeper is...no longer employed here," Nate spoke casually to the befuddled men who were not expecting such hospitality.

The younger man finally spoke. "Well, yes, thank-you, that is quite all right," he stammered.

"Are you Mr. Miller...," the other inquired a bit impatiently.

"Yes," replied Nate.

"Mr. Stuart Miller Sr.?

"No," answered Nate. "That would be my father, owner of this house, though...." Nate hesitated, "as to his where-abouts.... unknown at this moment."

As Nate sat in his favorite chair picking up the newspaper that had fallen on the floor, the men nodded, quietly issuing throaty apologies.

"Care to have a seat, gentlemen?" Nate offered, glancing at the crushed plush sofa. "Best Roman Divan my father's money could buy," he quipped.

The men took a moment to run their eyes over the piece of furniture that would easily cost an average male worker a week's wage. It was handsome with its carved oak back, claw feet and deeply tufted seat. There was no doubt in their minds that their wives back home would be envious of such luxuries.

"If you like, you may flip a coin for it. I'm sure my father will never miss it." Nate reached into his pocket and produced a penny. "Now, who will be head's and who will be tail's?"

The room was silent except for the crackling from the logs in the fireplace. Nate glanced up at the two perplexed gentlemen.

"It may prove a little difficult if I do not know who and where to send 'that' tomorrow," Nate nodded in the direction of the sofa.

"Are you serious, sir?" the younger one half-laughed.

Nate rose from the chair and put out his hand.

"I am Mr. Nathaniel Miller, pleased to make your acquaintance. And yes, I am quite serious."

"Well...my name is Mr. Fredrick, and this is Mr. Berg."

Both men shook Nate's strong hand and suddenly the penny was placed on the back of his hand. "Gentlemen?"

Mr. Fredrick and Mr. Berg glanced at each other with raised eyebrows. They did not know what to make of the situation, but since nothing was to come of this bit of amusement, they let Mr. Miller make light of the awkwardness they were placing upon him. After all, it should not have been the duty of the son to put on a good face for the father. Having made their choice, the coin was tossed.

"Mr. Berg? Do you have a wife?"

"Yes, sir. Quite new in fact."

Nate chuckled at the man.

"I'm sorry that your friend won the toss for the sofa, but would your wife object to...." Nate's voice trailed off as his eyes roamed over the room. He rubbed his chin and finally offered, "...an assortment of smaller furnishings?"

At that Mr. Fredrick turned to Nate with a twitch of annoyance, knowing that they were part of a cat and mouse game—they were the fools on the end of the string. Any patience, which Mr. Fredrick thought he could bear with composure was clearly disregarded.

"Mr. Miller," said Mr. Fredrick in an irritated deep voice, his chin now raised.

"Yes, Mr. Fredrick?"

"Although, you have shown us nothing but hospitality since we've stepped through your door, you have taken us off our course to carry out an unpleasant, though necessary duty."

Mr. Fredrick gathered every sense of professionalism about him, in preparation of dispensing words of doom. He spoke slowly and enunciated every word, for to be living in a mansion in the Highland's, Mr. Miller was ill-dressed for the society around him, and thus would be judged accordingly. In the privacy of his arrogant mind, Mr. Fredrick even went so far as to ridicule Mr. Miller's attire while boasting of his own fine suit that he was able to purchase due to a recent raise in pay.

"As his son," Mr. Fredrick stiffly began, "you must know or be aware of your father's failure to pay the mortgage on this house."

"Yes. It has come to my attention, recently," Nate replied calmly. "How many months would you say, precisely?"

Mr. Fredrick opened his long coat and produced an envelope from a pocket inside.

"Let's see," he mumbled as his fingers took out a document and turned the pages."Here…It will have been five months since the bank has not received payment from your father."

Nate shook his head.

"A shame at that."

"Mr. Miller, forgive me if I'm receiving the impression that you may not be feeling well?" Mr. Berg carefully assumed.

"No, I'm doing quite well, thank you."

"Forgive me, too," said Mr. Fredrick, "but considering what this document means to you and your family, are you not taking this news….er….rather lightly?"

The question from the bank representatives did not need to linger on Nate's conscience at all. To weigh their question a moment more may have given indication to them that he cared about his father's mansion which sat among rows of other mansions; cascading down the slopes of Queen Anne Hill, overlooking glorious Mount Rainier, the Cascades and Lake Union below.

Nate's simple reply was, "No."

"But, Mr. Miller," exclaimed Mr. Fredrick while looking around the elegant parlor, "what a loss this will be to your family." Mr. Fredrick took this opportunity to sweep his feasting and slightly envious eyes over the imported lace curtains which protected the palm trees from the western sunlight. The exquisite woodwork and trims on walls and ceiling were envied as well. Expensive oils hanging from dark wallpaper above the dark wood did not go unnoticed either. Nestled with the head in the left corner from the window was a magnificent, massive and strikingly handsome Empress couch. Mr. Fredrick admired the deep carving of a roaring lion under the curving biscuit tuffs where he could lie his weary head at night. And no doubt the four heavy claw feet would stand guard while he rested his equally weary body. Opposite the couch in the right corner was a splendid office desk and chair, and directly next to, against the wall leading out of the pallor stood a combination bookcase and writing desk with a swell bent glass door.

"What a loss indeed!" Mr. Fredrick sighed at last, very unaware that the pining in his heart was noticed by all.

Nate leaned against the fireplace and crossing his arms comfortably, smiled at Mr. Fredrick and Mr. Berg.

"Gentlemen, what you see is only a house. An empty house at that. If it had been a home, there would of been..." Nate stopped himself short, then let out a heavy sigh."This place means nothing to me. It is not my home, Mr. Fredrick, therefore, I feel no loss."

A sympathetic silence washed over the three men.

"Well, now," Nate piped up in a half cheerful way, "I believe there is a document that you wish to give to my father."

Mr. Fredrick looked at Nate with an approving nod and smile, and putting the papers back into the envelope it was given to him.

"I suppose neither of you gentlemen have a Christmas stocking hiding in your coats?"

"I'm afraid not," replied Mr. Fredrick. "The Mrs.' has them hanging from hooks on the fireplace."

"Don't you have a stocking, Mr. Miller?" asked Mr. Berg.

"Not this year. Perhaps next," Nate smiled at the possibilities of his future.

Mr. Fredrick, Mr. Berg and Nate left the parlor, but not before Nate implored their help in extinguishing the parlor lamps on their way out. The only light which poorly illuminated the fine parlor was from the dying fire. Then Nate opened the fine glass door with its breathtaking etching and joined the somber men on the porch who had put hats on their heads and drew coat collars snugger against their necks. Filling up his lungs with the cold air, Nate let his warm air fill the night and then folded his arm against his heavy flannel shirt.

"I think you may be right about the snow," said Mr. Berg, trying to keep his voice somewhat light.

"Yes, I do, too," agreed Mr. Fredrick, hoping his voice delivered the right amount of 'minimal gaiety.'

"Think we'll have a foot or more in the next three days?" Nate breathed into the frosty air.

"By the size of the flakes...I shouldn't wonder," said Mr. Berg smiling wryly.

"I have every confidence and assurance that Old Man Winter will not disappoint you, Mr. Miller," Mr. Fredrick nodded, without yielding to a bit of pessimism.

The three men had made their way in the soft snow to the cold black iron gate, which after passing would lead two of them down the snow covered sidewalk, and with candles glowing behind windows from towering houses, guide them to the nearest trolley and back to their cozy homes where families waited. And standing at the cold black iron gate would be a man who at least, Mr. Berg was in awe of. He had never come across the likes of such kindness, such character.... especially from such a strong bodied man.

As the delightful snow descended on Nate's head and clothing, Mr. Berg and Mr. Fredrick appeared to hesitate in front of the huge house that was ill lit from within. Their breaths took turns warming the flakes that fell into such momentary paths. Their eyes lifted to observe the grand height of the residence with its nicely slopping roof and saw the small wave of smoke linger across it; a testimony of dying embers back in the parlor's fireplace.

As every home in sight having chimneys poking through roofs, the heavy presence of smoke filled the air. Mr. Berg began to cough and then Mr. Fredrick coughed.

"You should be going home now to your wives and children..." Nate suggested.

The two men turned around on the sidewalk to face Nate as he was shutting the gate.

"Sir?" Mr. Berg politely inquired, but upon his slight hesitation, he noticed that Mr. Miller only looked at him in response. "Will you be staying here much longer?"

Nate did sigh, but not with a look of despair about him.

"No, I shall not," Nate answered.

"I see," Mr. Berg sniffled and rubbed his cold nose while glancing at his snow covered feet.

"You best be getting home to your new wife. I don't want to be blamed if you catch something right before Christmas because I kept you out in this weather," Nate smiled.

The younger man smiled back.

"Mr. Miller, please do us the honor of staying with my wife and I, that is, until you secure another residence," Mr. Berg nearly begged.

Nate sniffled himself, and looking down at his own snow covered feet he had to clear his voice.

"Well....that's just about the nicest offer I've ever had, and I do thank you. Your kindness Mr. Berg is worthy of praise. I believe, and I'm sure that even Mr. Fredrick would agree, that a newly married couple should spend their first Christmas alone. Perhaps I may pay you and your new bride a visit sometime?" Nate suggested instead.

"We would be delighted to have you come by."

The two men regarded each other with mutual warmheartedness, and offered each other a lingering handshake.

"Merry Christmas, Mr. Miller."

"Merry Christmas, Mr. Berg," and nodding to Mr. Fredrick, Nate wished him good tidings also.

"And to you too, Sir!"

Mr. Fredrick was the first to turn and advance in the direction of Col. Blethen's imposing column mansion which sat on the corner of West 6th and Highland. His feet crunched in the new snow until he realized that his partner was holding back.

"Mr. Berg," he called through the thick falling snow.

Mr. Berg glanced at the distant figure of Mr. Fredrick, but instead of acknowledging him, turned to Nate with a hopeful twinkle in his eye.

"Mr. Miller,....I.."

Nate raised his eyebrows.

"Was there something else, Mr. Berg?"

"Well, I was just wondering if you will be going to mid-night mass on the twenty-fourth."

"I suppose I will. And you?"

"I suppose I should. Might be a nice way to start off Christmas, or married life, or something..." Mr. Berg pondered thoughtfully. "Do you mind if I ask where you 'suppose' you'll be?"

"Probably at Sacred Heart Church."

"On...?"

"Second Avenue North."

Mr. Berg nodded his head slightly. "I suppose I should catch up to Mr. Fredrick. I'm sure his feet are quite numb by now and his shoes are spoiled," a huff of warm laughter filled the air.

"If they are, tell Mr. Fredrick that I know where he can receive dozens of fine shoes at no charge," Nate replied with a small grin.

"Well, good-bye, and if I should never have the fortunate chance of meeting you again, I wish you a blessed Christmas and a brighter New Year."

Nate smiled and nodded at the young man, and watching him jog in the beautiful white snow, he thought he saw something fall from under Mr. Berg's long coat. By the time Nate opened the gate and made his way to where he thought he saw the object drop, the two men had passed Col. Blethen's mansion, turned left and headed down the hill of Sixth Avenue. Nate looked down and around him but only saw white, until his foot stepped on something. He picked up the sign and brushed the snow off, and turning it over, white flakes stuck to the black printed words. He looked at the footprints of Mr. Fredrick and those of Mr. Berg, and looking up at the new electric lamp post he fixed a boyish gaze on the flakes that swirled before the bright light.

Eventually, Nate turned and made his way back to the cold black iron gate.

He slowly opened the beautiful front door with its delicate etched glass and went inside the lonely, empty house.

He took a few hesitating steps toward the grand staircase and stopped.

Between the dining room window and the imported lace curtains, Nate leaned the sign against the cold glass. He began to feel a pang of remorse as he made his feet back out of the room. Then something made him stop. He starred at the table and at each chair that once belonged to someone. His thoughts did not give way to mournful nor gloomy memories; rather, to an unfamiliar heaviness; a comfortless feeling pulling down his spirit.

"Good-bye," he faintly breathed.

He went down the foyer without glancing into the dark parlor because it held too many memories there. The grand staircase solemnly led Nate to his room where he picked up the picture of he and his mother. Oh, how his heart hurt for her. Oh, how he wished that she was there with him.

"Oh, Mother!" he half cried, "why did you have to leave me? Why? Why?"

As the world slept under a blanket of quiet white, little Nathaniel dozed off as he watched the snow from his soft warm bed. His mother sat with him, brushing his soft hair with her fingers, lulling him to sleep with tender songs. And then, while the world was warm and sleepy, he felt her sweet kiss on his forehead as she tenderly whispered, "I love you..."

December 23, 1910

Nate listened to the six splendid gongs from the grandfather clock below as he slowly awoke in his warm bed in the semi-darkened room. He knew that the hint of brightness that came through the window meant that the wonderful snow was still there. Thinking of the white covered world pleased him and made him smile. The seventh and final gong rang out. Someday, he promised himself, someday he would have a clock of his own, in his own home that would faithfully and cheerfully ring out the Westminster chime.

The thought of taking the grandfather clock for his own crossed his mind, but he did not know if it was originally his father's before he married his mother or not. His father's residence was almost fully furnished when he brought his unhappy new bride home. During their married life, if a piece of furniture fell out of favor with his father, for whatever reason, if in fact there was one, it was replaced with something grander and more expensive. Nate's mother was never consulted whether she wished for something to stay or go, or whether she was fond of a particular style or not. Her feelings and opinions in a male dominated household was entirely cast aside. Nate could not recall his mother mentioning where the grandfather clock came from, but chances were that it belonged to his father.

When the time drew closer for Nate and Eleanor to marry, Nate would make sure she was involved in certain decisions. For some time he had been trying to get a feeling of where she would like to move to, taking into consideration, of course, his earnings, his small bag of fortune, and what kind of neighborhood they feel comfortable raising a family in. Although it pleased him in knowing that he could buy a nice house, maybe quite not as grand as those in the Highlands, but a nice one, he wanted to put distance between them and himself. Nate did not feel at home in the lower Highlands where the rich were assured quiet and elegant living.

Though, to have truly "arrived," one removed oneself to the privacy of a Colonial, Tudor or Georgian style mansion which stood out in the open with enough trees and other foliage to give a country feel. No lot could be smaller than five acres. In The Highlands, houses were not meant to be seen or enjoyed from the street or from a distance, but to be lived in by wealthy aristocrats who cared not to see the street.

Nate did not go to work in expensive suits nor dine in fine restaurants at noon. He did not seek the society of other males in the exclusive Rainier Club where wealthy business men gathered in the great banqueting hall to drink and smoke. Nor did Nate care for the comfortable for-men-only atmosphere of barbershops, clubs and saloons. His neighbors never saw him retreat to barbershops where the reek of cigar fumes and whiskey filled the air. Nate was not interested in the company of men, who, while waiting for a 15 cent shave, browsed through spicy magazines and ogled at the ladies who hurried passed the door. Nate did not want his hair color altered with hair dyes as to preserve the youthful look that society men desired. Nate was not one of them.

There was something spellbinding about the chimes that caused Nate to stop thinking, stop moving, stop worrying. It held him captive, demanding his attention. Someday he would have one, too. But the sounds were gone, and his thoughts shifted to his father.

During the night he hadn't heard any loud voices or profanities throughout the house, nor any thuds which would have indicated that his drunk father had somehow and miraculously found his way home, once more. Perhaps he would stay away until Nate had returned from work; stay away while the contents of the parlor could be loaded onto two or three wagons, with the exception of the desk that was filled with long overdue bills. It wasn't as if the drunk cared for anything in that room. And besides, what was his father going to do 'if' he did notice the empty room? The uncertainty of his father's return bothered him more than he wanted to admit. His initial cheerfulness towards the morning had quickly dwindled to an attitude of gloom.

Nate laid in bed for a few minutes more wishing he did not have to go to work. He knew he would have to pack the picture of he and his mother back in the trunk and haul it to the trolley somehow, or, if things did work out in his favor, load the trunk on the wagons with the parlor items. Nate hoped that the snow covered hill wouldn't prove too difficult for the wagons pulled by four horse teams. Such worries were turning into unpleasant thoughts which swallowed up the gayness he felt upon rising.

He would not be spending another night in the room that he had occupied during the last fourteen months. He would have to find a room downtown after a long day at work. Though, before any of those things could take place, Nate needed to have breakfast at a cafe, then go through the cumbersome and time-consuming task of putting together a lunch at a delicatessen or grocer. He truly missed his ready made lunches that Eleanor prepared for him. And among other things, he missed having his clothes cleaned by her and her alone. Since her departure, a China-man in a single-horse drawn, small covered wagon picks up his soiled laundry on the front porch, and delivers it back to the front porch.

Besides, being very much in love and taken with Eleanor, Nate also wanted all the conveniences and comforts attached with marriage. These thoughts alone, besides love, encouraged contemplation in Nate's head as to when he should ask the question. Nate had admitted to himself, that living alone in a hotel while deliberating matrimonial ideas was not going to secure him a wife, and further waiting may lead Eleanor to look for a more earnest beau.

Flinging the bed covers off his warm body, he let out a huff of annoyance as the chilly air hit his body. He shaved and dressed for the cold day, and making his way down the steps to the cold black iron gate, he paused and turned to look at the dining room window. Nate wondered what his father's reaction would be upon noticing the foreclosure sign. Although the events from the previous evening were firmly in place, the new day brought forth a remorse that lives at the bottom of every unseen soul. This feeling was not aimed at the individual who solely would be affected by the irreversible decision of the bank, rather, only toward a house that held cherished memories there. For when a man, such as Mr. Miller Sr. has lived his whole life spiting the world with a relentless grudge, such circumstances are only inevitable; nearly predestined in the eyes of others.

It would be difficult to find a trace of compassion toward his father who was roaming somewhere in the bottom-most layers of society. But this feeling of remorse, as slight as it was, had managed to creep into his conscience and made him look at the grand homes across the yet utilized white street, and he wondered if any of the occupants had taken notice of the sentenced house of Mr. Miller Sr.

Nate opened the gate which led to the empty and abandoned street, and stepping on the crunchy snow, his presence was laid bare to the world. He felt a tingling of unwarranted desperation pushing against his back as his foot steps quickened along the street. At the corner his heartbeat was duly felt and Nate cursed for it had no reason to act so. He couldn't help but wonder if Colonel Blethen's daughter, Florence, was observing him from the view of an upstairs room. And across the street at the Duffy home, did Gilbert happen to see the last Miller boy hesitate on the corner, while waving to his fiancée in the mansion with white columns and Roman scrolls? Nate cursed under his cold breath, because, although he didn't give a damn, he did.

He quickly turned away from Highland Street and down the slope of Sixth Avenue West where he boarded the trolley. They pick up more riders at the corner of West Galer Street, and before turning right onto Queen Anne Avenue, the trolley stopped again before it headed into the heart of downtown Seattle.

In the course of an hour, he was fed a hearty breakfast, noticed that the pedestrians had begun swarming to department stores while he had a girl behind a delicatessen counter make him lunch. There was almost a buzzing sound in the air as he stepped out to the street where he would wait for the next trolley.

The ridership on the trolley was far above its normal capacity with standing room only. The usual frigid temperature of the unheated car did not deter the hordes of holiday shoppers from boarding. He was, on the most part, indifferent to the people around him. Day after day he rode to work and came home from work taking minimal interest in the activities around him. If a gentleman sitting next to him cared to initiate polite conversation, he would graciously lend an ear least be accused of having a tarnished character.

But this morning was different. He had no desire for conversation nor for listening to business discussion or gossip around him. Perhaps if he kept a nonchalant stare at the horses, carriages and delivery wagons outside his window, he may avoid notice of the cheerful merry-makers, soliciting the attention of any poor soul for their sheer amusement. They with parcels of shiny boxes and colorful ribbons, spoke in loud merriment and ignored a passengers wish to be deep in thought.

Unfortunately, Nate's seating companion was an unfavorably suited man with worn out button holes and frayed sleeve cuffs. Nate could sense that he was being looked over as a prospect and esti-mated from his own work ensemble that he would be an easy target to a sales adventure or scheme. The suited man introduced himself but was ignored by the quiet man next to the window. Although Nate heard the prattle of his slippery and polished voice, he shut the fellow out, but this did not disquiet the salesman. Matter-of-fact, to Nate's dismay, his shunning only spurred the boasting man on, assuring Nate of 'brighter opportunities' if he would accompany him to a cafe where they could take up matters privately. Thankfully the trolley neared Jackson Street and came to a stop. Standing up, Nate looked down at the despicable man and said, "If you were a parasite instead of an obnoxious human being, I would have squashed you under my foot long ago!"

Nate and fellow workers were thankful to disembark the crowded trolley, but as they stood close to the work site, it was very quiet. A sign had been put up, giving all workers notice that construction would not continue until weather conditions improved. This gave the other men cause to grumble and swear while Nate hid a secret smile.

On his way north, back up to Third Avenue, Nate saw the Hotel Plaza from the corner of Third Avenue, and turning east on Pike Street, the building was sandwiched between Westlake Boulevard and Fourth Avenue, with the American Hotel directly across the street to the east. The crowded trolley came to rest in front of the American Hotel, and stepping onto the sidewalk, he looked up at both hotels which were five stories high and decided on the Plaza because of its unique sad-iron shape.

After renting a nice yet modest room on the third floor on a monthly basis, Nate walked back to the corner of Fourth and Pike, peering into the windows of the Seaboard Building as he rounded the sidewalk and continued east on Pike Street. His next task of hiring wagons was relatively easy since he was on one of the busiest market streets in town. His only difficulty was convincing the drivers to venture up treacherous Queen Anne Hill and back down again with loaded wagons. After a few declines, Nate realized that he had to bribe drivers with the promise of a new delivery wagon, and, if they made it to Mr. Berg and Mr. Fredrick's home successfully, he would buy each a new team of horses. With verbal formalities and handshakes out of the way, Nate sat next to one of the drivers as the two wagons and eight horses headed for the long climb up Queen Anne Avenue.

On the way, Nate prayed that his father would not be there and would not show up while the men were loading the furniture to take away. That would prove to be an interesting situation—one that Nate wished to avoid. If his father was home, he would likely be in his bedroom passed out on the bed and wouldn't be aware of the commotion below.

The two drivers took their time and were cautious. Nate's seating companion mumbled once or twice that he was glad the snow wasn't any deeper or else he doubted very much that the horses would make it up the hill. Close to an hour later, tired horses and cold men pulled up in front of the Miller's house. Nate told the men to wait while he went inside to check on something. Upon inspecting his father's room which was absent of a body sprawled on the bed, Nate and the men quickly carried the sofas, chairs, the round table; paintings, pillows, palm trees and parlor lamps; the mirror over the fireplace, the expensive lace curtains, and the Oxford Cylinder Talking Machine with dozens of unused cylinder records to the wagons. Then going to his room he picked up his trunk, and with a sigh, left the room for the last time.

Nate stood just outside the naked parlor. The only items remaining were the desk and the rose-green-beige carpet. The room was impoverished and naked; as if a woman's most private garments had been taken from her. It was very unfamiliar to him, appearing reclusive, barren of any happiness.

His attention turned to the drivers who waited outside in the cold; thoughts of his father witnessing a robbery by his own son; looked again at the naked room that had been filled with joyful memories of him and Eleanor. But those memories had taken leave, or at least were attached to the items loaded in the wagons. Nate realized that his heart was pounding and the feeling of remorse had found him again. He turned around to look at the grand staircase and at the dining room, and at the foreclosure sign still leaning against the window. The trunk was picked up and put on the porch, and slowly closing the front door, he hesitated. And then, for the last time he let go of the glass knob.

His trunk finally in the wagon, the drivers turned their teams around in the wide road. He was glad that the driver spoke to the horses instead of him. He was glad to be leaving Highland Street. Only, he couldn't help turning his head back to look at the mansion that was lonely and grieving like a child. The house he was abandoning was speaking to him. This he was sure of. It was crying out to him. Nate turned and drooped his head forward so he didn't have to see it, and as the wagons turned down the hill, its cry grew faint till it could be heard no more.

The home of Mr. and Mrs. Fredrick was at the bottom of the hill, almost at the intersection of West Mercer Street and First Avenue. Nate, posing as one of the drivers, simply informed Mrs. Fredrick that her husband won the Roman Divan sofa from a client and left it at that. The woman's personality resembled that of her husband. As she ushered the men and the sofa into the noisy and cluttered room, her hands were either folded at her chest or balanced on hips with pointed elbows.

"Well," Mrs. Fredrick said with smug sarcasm as she set her face in false surprise, "how do you like that!"

The three men watched four young children shout excitedly, bouncing on the expensive sofa and shoving each other off. The haggard mother did not glance or fret over her undisciplined children, nor was she alarmed when one came crashing to the floor.

"Won't Mr. Fredrick be flabbergasted...." she said with the same amount of sarcasm.

"Why is that Ma'am?" Nate asked the weary looking woman.

"Oh....well," her hand waved in the air as if she was driving off a fly, "my husband thought for sure that Miller fellow was playing him for a fool. You know, knowing that he was going to get those papers. Oh, well, it doesn't matter... I'm just glad to see a snob from Millionaire Row roll down the hillside once in a while," she huffed, putting a lazy hand on her left hip.

Nate slightly tipped his hat to the rude woman and made for the door, but he could not go just yet. He politely asked the drivers to wait in their wagons.

"Ma'am, you've never seen this Miller fellow, have you?"

"Well, of course not!" she replied smartly.

"Did you know that your husband was given that sofa as a Christmas gift, and although this Mr. Miller really didn't know your husband at all, he did not judge him or his family. That wouldn't be right, would it? Is Mr. Miller a stranger or a snob because he lives in a different neighborhood than you?"

Nate stared at the rude woman with raised eyebrows.

Mrs. Fredrick eyed Nate with a cool stare, and with her arms placed under her bosom, her lips opened.

"I'd say a little of both," she smirked.

Nate gladly departed without wishing her a Merry Christmas.

The Berg's home was on the outskirts of the business district, just far enough away from the Denny Regrade project that was sluicing tons of earth from First Avenue to Pike, around Bell Street and Cedar Street.

Beginning in 1903, it was decided that the land would be lowered several hundred feet so horses and wagons could manage the future gradual slope, and for perhaps a better reason; sewage control, which on the part of daily high tides and the steepness of the hill did not help. To the south, another hill was once laden with virgin timber, until 1852, when Henry Yesler built Puget Sound's first steam-powered sawmill on a wharf, but was destroyed by the Great Fire of 1889.

Nate and the men could see the work taking place as forced water from Elliott Bay was turning the hillside into a haunting and spooky sight. The eerie landscape was due to several stubborn homeowners who refused to have their homes either torn down or moved, creating an effect of a forsaken house perched on a narrow slice of earth several hundred feet high in the air.

The two wagons traveled down Broad Street and turning left on Western Avenue, the presence of salt water grew stronger as they neared the water. Relieved upon their arrival, Nate glanced around at the small weathered dwellings which were occupied by unskilled workers who lived near sawmills, shingle companies, packing plants, and railroad lines, oddly mixed with boarding houses for sailors and fishermen, drifters and the unemployed. Looking down on the bay and closer to the heart of the city; cooks, waiters, domestics, hotel managers, and janitors lived in apartments adjacent to and above offices and showrooms.

A noisy flock of adult white gulls soared closely above, sporting their dark gray backs and yellow beaks, while younger gulls wore pale tan coats for their first and second winters. Looking for an easy meal, their loud whining 'whee-ee' and 'cow-auk' sound could briefly be drowned out from a steamship's departure blast, or from the shrill of a Mosquito Fleet steamer ferry horn from the Coleman Dock south of them. Or still, from the coal bunkers perpetual clanking racket along Railroad Avenue.

Directly below the Berg's shanty was Pier 69, one of seventeen in the necklace of terminals which made up the Port of Seattle. The Pier was built by the Rosalyn Coal and Coke Company to export riches from Black Diamond, Renton, and Newcastle elsewhere. At the foot of Battery Street, conveyors were dumping earth from the Denny Regrade onto barges which would be taken out on the bay and dumped. Consequently, large mountains threatened navigation and dredging was necessary. The foulness from the canneries, fishing piers and oil depots drifted off shore and lingered on the hill. The surroundings would make his dear Eleanor grateful to be in her present neighborhood.

As Nate thought of Eleanor, a young woman peeked out from a square pane of glass dulled from the salty air. A moment later she came down the steps with wetted bangs and a glowing face.

She was a small framed girl, above average in appearance, though not as handsome as his Eleanor. Her hair was in a simple bun and she wore a practical solid dark gray skirt without any detail to it, while her white waist had a touch of embroidery on the front. Nate quickly compared her apparel to Eleanor's and felt pity on her, for she was wearing the costume of scanty wages. She seemed out of place in her dismal surroundings, yearning not for wealth or riches, but simply to live on a well-thought-of street where pleasant shade trees grew and quiet evenings were spent on porches. On a street where she wouldn't have to mask her shame with a smile. But Mrs. Berg did not let the influence of the bay dishearten her spirits. She immediately filled the chilly air with cheerfulness which turned the men's attention from the commotion below. She held her hands up to her flushed cheeks and was near a state of speechlessness.

She then turned to Nate and held his hands in hers exclaiming, "Oh, Mr. Miller, what a pleasure it is to finally meet you!"

Nate casually looked at her and feebly said, "I'm sorry Ma'am, but I'm only one of the drivers. You must have me mistaken for someone else."

"Oh, no!" her warm and youthful voice giggled. "My dear husband sat me down the other night and told me everything about you. I recognized you right away just from his verbal description."

"Guess I can't say anything more…can I?"

"Now, before anyone does anything or goes anywhere, I want you all to come inside….it might be a little cozy space wise, but that don't matter. I happen to have a pot of warm stew on, fresh bread and butter. And I'll put on a pot of coffee too, while you're washing up. Now, all you men aren't going to argue with Mrs. Berg because I know how cold you are just by looking at you."

Nate looked at the two drivers and said with a grin, "You heard the little lady."

"That's right, so just tell those horses to stay put and make sure you stomp your feet before coming in. This little place may not be grand but at least I can keep it clean."

Before Mrs. Berg picked her skirts up, she turned to the wagons and stole a glance at the contents. "Oh, my! Oh, my!…" she giggled in delight.

Mrs. Berg made them wash their hands and said a little prayer before the meal, and to the men's amusement, she talked almost non-stop. And out in the harbor an incoming boat blew its horn and she told the men which steamship it was by name, where it was arriving from, and what cargo it held. When no one was so bold as to ask how she knew such things, she let them in on her little secret, which, God forbid, Mr. Berg could never know about. To relieve her mental state-of-being from going mad inside her little dwelling, she ventures down the hill and visits families along the way. Then, as far as her courage allows her, she keeps a safe yet respectable distance from the wharves. When the weather is agreeable, she brings a lunch, reads a book, or just takes in the activity on the sparkling water as steamships and freighters from the Orient dock as the open trade continues on the Port.

The men found her company pleasurable as she kept the atmosphere bubbly. She informed her guests that she and her husband thought it was prudent to start saving immediately after they were married five months ago. She also hinted of wanting to start a family soon, but knew it would be best to find a home with more than one room as their bed was nestled in a corner opposite from where the table was located.

Finally, with content and warm bellies, the men unloaded everything except Nate's trunk and put the furniture into the now tightly packed tiny house. Mrs. Berg was just as excited as a child, clapping her hands and squealing in delight. Everyone had a good laugh, though Mrs. Berg was laughing the hardest of all. She gave everyone a little kiss on the cheek and sent them on their way with a thick slice of bread and butter wrapped in wax paper. She waved to the men, wishing everyone a "Merry Christmas!"

Heading back up the hill and back to the Hotel Plaza, Nate said how very glad he was that Mr. Berg should have such a wife as Mrs. Berg. The driver agreed and admitted, he wished for his wife to be more like Mrs. Berg.

After a very long day, the horses came to a stop alongside the American Hotel. Nate paid the two drivers sufficiently so they could purchase new wagons and younger horses. Holiday greetings were exchanged. Then with care, Nate crossed the bustling street with his trunk, weaving between trolley cars, delivery wagons, carriages, and a few honking automobiles.

Entering the Hotel Plaza, Nate went up to his room and placed his wet and dirty shoes on the floor at the end of the bed. And finally, he laid his weary body on the delightful bed, falling sound asleep with a happy smile on his face.

Christmas Eve Day

At ten o'clock Christmas Eve morning, John boarded the crowded trolley and headed downtown to meet Nate in the lobby of the Hotel Plaza. After briefly showing his room to John who was curious as to what a hotel room looked liked, the two went back to the lobby and discussed where they should go. John handed Nate a list of what the girls were hinting for, and told Nate that he had informed Mama to expect a turkey to be delivered Christmas Eve day. He said Mama was so pleased that she didn't have to cook a darn goose for Christmas dinner. Papa loves eating goose, John admitted, but it is Mama who must deal with the great amount of grease the bird produces while it cooks.

The city's sidewalks were filled with shoppers entering and exiting department stores, jewelry and watch stores, millinery parlors and toy stores. It was hard to tell which of the two were more excited about their shopping excursion that was planned a few weeks in advance so John could have the day off. Nate felt like a little boy, filled with awe and tingling wonder, while John felt very mature and independent while in the presence of an older man.

The bell over the door of "McAfee's Millinery Shop" rang and the young lady behind the counter glanced up to see her best friend's beau and younger brother step through the door. Miss Ernestine was fussing over a female customer but politely excused herself while the woman made up her mind between three hats.

"Mr. Miller....this is a pleasant surprise!"

"Merry Christmas, Miss McAfee," Nate casually nodded to her, smiling.

"Merry Christmas to you, too! It's been a little while since your last visit." She paused and lifted her mouth to form a shy little smile. "It's good to see you, again."

Miss Ernestine's words hung in the warm air of the millinery shop, dangling tenderly from her lips. She did not realize until after they were spoken, just how wrapped in sincerity and longing they were.

Nate noted something in Miss McAfee's feminine voice that he hadn't heard before. He was sure that Miss Ernestine was not, and by no means was insinuating such once-concealed "interest" in her best friend's beau. However, according to Miss McAfee's blushing

314

face, Nate could not have been too wrong. Something had come to light, and this caught him quite off guard. His male instinct caused him to be ill at ease; his eyes obeyed and became passive, falling away to his shoes, though, all the while, that same male instinct caused natural curiosity to bloom.

Finally, Nate offered in reply,"Thank You."

The young lady with the pretty auburn hair, brown eyes and lovely complexion lowered her eyelashes and wished her cheeks did not feel so warm. Although the handsome man was her best friend's beau, it was beyond her womanly strength not to feel weak and shy around Mr. Nate Miller.

Many, many times, Miss Ernestine thought that life was unfair since she did not have a beau, while her friend was able to claim one of the most handsomest men she ever set her eyes upon. Yes, she was happy for Eleanor. And yes, she wanted a man just like Nate Miller. And, if for some reason Eleanor decided not to marry Mr. Miller, she would be more than happy to be his wife. Many, many times she dreamt of summer picnics with him. Dreamt of lovely walks in parks with him. Dreamt of his enchanting voice speaking to her, dreamt of touching his handsome face....

"Miss McAfee, you have met John, Eleanor's brother, haven't you?" asked Nate.

Miss Ernestine cleared her throat for she was visibly embarrassed for harboring such intimate thoughts in Mr. Miller's presence. Her pretty complexion had turned a deeper color of red and she wished that he wasn't so handsome for he affected her senses in every part of her womanly being. Why, she wondered, did God have to send him into her store? It was unfair of God to place such temptation in front of her. How was she to ward off certain thoughts if God kept bringing Mr. Miller into her store? It was not fair. And yes, at that moment she envied her best friend. And for a moment, a quick and fleeting moment, she even felt the sting of hate. Maybe not toward Eleanor herself, but for Eleanor's fortunate circumstances which brought the two together. It would be wrong to hate her best friend. Eleanor was sweet and well deserving of a good man. Eleanor deserved happiness in her life. But what about poor Ernestine. Didn't she deserve a wonderful man, too? Was she asking too much out of life for a little happiness? To be loved. But if love should never find her, she would settle for a man who found pleasure in caring for a woman. To be cared for by someone—anyone—would be better than living the reminder of her life above the millinery shop, in the apartment she and her father occupied.

If Ernestine could not have Nate Miller for a beau, he had no business making her heart flutter and her mind race. Ernestine almost felt dizzy in his presence. No other man affected her the way he did, and it showed. She tried composing herself as best as she could.

"Hello, John. It's been sometime since I've seen you. My, you have grown! You must be—sixteen?" Ernestine guessed, glancing at Eleanor's brother with lowered eyelashes and a little smile.

"Fifteen," corrected John who held his cap in front of him and nodded to Miss Ernestine. There was a twinkle in his eyes and a shy smile surfaced as he glanced down at his cap.

Ernestine smiled and half-winked at Nate while willing her body to relax.

"Now, what sort of mischief are you two up to to-day?" she asked, knowing fully well that Nate Miller was going to make another nice purchase for Eleanor, and perhaps, being Christmas, an additional three more hats for Eleanor's mother and two sisters. Ernestine smiled. She had to keep smiling. She had to pretend that it did not matter that she never received gifts from a man, not counting her father, of course. Ernestine was feeling the sting of hate creep into her heart again as she smiled her sweetest smile. At that moment she wished Nate and John would leave. Trying to mask her emotions was killing her. Thankfully a voice spoke.

"Miss…I think I'll take this one," the forgotten customer at the counter interrupted her thoughts, which was a blessing.

"I'll be right with you," she informed the woman. "Why don't you two look around and see what you like," Ernestine said as she made her way behind the counter.

As she boxed the woman's hat and rung up her purchase, she looked at John and burst out in laughter. Nate had placed a hat on John, but before he could remove it, a few passerby's glanced in the shop and saw John. The woman holding the hat box had missed it all and did not understand what all the laughter was about. Ernestine thanked her for coming to their shop and wished her a very 'Merry Christmas.' And as she left McAfee's Millinery Shop, three pretty young ladies came in and immediately fixed their interests on John and Nate.

Ernestine knew the twinkle in the young miss's eyes, knew their cute little laughter, and saw the lowering and fluttering of eyelashes.

From behind the counter she watched their young bodies turn while admiring hats and shoes, lace and ribbons, jewelry, tea pots and dolls. John and Nate had moved on to hair pieces, books and games, and although trying to be a gentleman, John could not help stealing a glance at the girls, who just a few years back, would not have caught his attention at all.

Although amusing, Ernestine wanted to rid the shop of the young girls, who, she was sure of, had doubtful intentions of opening their little purses.

"May I help you?" Ernestine politely inquired with a business-like tone of voice, as she stepped out from behind the counter with her hands behind her back.

The girls apparently must not have seen Ernestine and were somewhat startled by the young woman approaching them. Ernestine could not have been more than three to five years older than they. The girls took this opportunity to face Ernestine which allowed them full view of the two men. The less bashful of the three spoke in a most sickening sweet voice which should have caused her words to drip onto the carpet.

"We are just looking...." she sang, tossing her little nose in the air.

"I see...." echoed Ernestine. "Might you girls be interested in perhaps... new hats?" she inquired next.

The girls shook their pretty heads while avoiding the storekeeper's discerning watchful eye.

"Perhaps a book, a game, new ribbons...." Ernestine suggested.

"We would like to look around, if you don't mind," said another, turning her little nose up, practicing an air quite new to her.

The third decided to join in the fun, and not wanting to be left out, the unskillful young actress clumsily slipped up her aristocratic voice. Miss Ernestine wanted to laugh at the little fool, and she thought she almost heard a short laugh escape from Nate. The girl immediately began to blush and her eyes dove to the ground. The first girl quickly came to her friend's aide and half-snorted in the air, "There isn't any harm in 'looking' is there? After all, we don't know if you have anything to our liking," she breathed.

Ernestine smiled at the young women, and taking a step toward them she slowly whispered, "No, there isn't any harm in looking, but I do know that we do not have anything to your liking to-day."

"And how would you know?" snorted one of the girls.

"Because, those two men whom you have your little sight-seeing eyes on, happen to be my brother….and my husband."

A gasp of air left the three girls as their faces froze and their aristocratic shells crumbled.

"I beg your pardon, Ma'am," one of the girls quickly whispered as they slid to the door hoping their skirts would not rustle as they made a hasty exit. The bell above the door was still tinkling as the girls disappeared down the sidewalk.

Miss Ernestine dusted her hands against each other as she was glad to be rid of such nuisances. She turned to Nate and John and saw a little twinkle of curiosity in Nate's eyes.

"I'm terribly sorry about that….." Ernestine attempted to apologize with a chuckle in her voice.

"And what made those girls leave so urgently, may I ask?" Nate half whispered.

"I…." Ernestine paused, wondering if she should tell a lie. But then, if she did, who really would care? Things were not going to change if her tongue did lie.

"I….I told them that you were my husband."

There. She had said it. Husband. My husband. It sounded so nice just to say that word. Husband. But Nate Miller was looking at her with a peculiar expression on his face.

"Oh,….yes,….that certainly would do the trick!" he laughed.

Nate smiled and said that he would have to remember to tell Eleanor about the joke Ernestine had pulled on the three girls. John on the other hand seemed a bit disappointed without the attention of the girls.

Finally, the two men, with Miss Ernestine's help, decided on four hats.

Christmas greetings were exchanged once more and the little bell above the door rang as Nate and John left the shop. Ernestine watched them from behind the painted words on the window. The two men did not look back as they quickly disappeared among the other shoppers. Why would they look back? What reason would either of them have to turn back and wave? Surely the millenary's daughter would be tending to other matters directly after their departure and would not give the two men a second thought thereafter. But they would be wrong. Very wrong. Ernestine looked at all the happy shoppers passing her window. Men, women and children. Men, men, men. More women. A few children. People glanced at her but she did not care. She did not care if her throat was tightening and sobs were building in her chest, nor did she care if passerby's saw a young lady weep with her hands covering her face on Christmas Eve Day.

****

With hat boxes in tow, Nate and John entered a butcher and meat shop and ordered a turkey. Nate was told that the delivery truck would be making a delivery to Eleanor's street sometime that afternoon.

With that task out of the way, the two men headed toward First and Cherry Street and almost walked passed the jewelry store of Albert Hansen. Advertisements in the Seattle Daily Times read 'Precious Stones, Rich Jewelry and Silverware of the better grades at reliable prices.' Next door was an Optical Department, also owned by Mr. Hansen, specializing in nose glasses and spectacles. John and Nate faced the window display in silence. Once or twice they turned their head to eye the other, raised an eyebrow or scratched a chin. Their eyes nervously ran over items which were nestled around strategically folded blue velvet. Such items, little as they were, marked the end of bachelorhood for a carefree man, for size held no comparison to their meaning once placed upon the finger of a love smitten female.

Nate turned to John and winked.

John caught his breath in surprise when he understood what Nate's wink meant. "You're gunna snag my sister, aren't you?" John exclaimed in a raised voice.

"I told you I would, didn't I?" Nate replied confidently. "Come on, let's see what Mr. Hansen has inside."

Upon entering, Mr. Hansen was assisting a few customers but nodded to Nate and John, acknowledging their presence. With hands behind their backs, the two men looked over silverware and serving pieces, nodded in approval at the watches in the long glass display cases, as well as pendants and broaches. But what Nate needed to see was where Mr. Hansen was, and when seeing the two young men standing idle with their hands behind their backs, Mr. Hansen stood up and excused himself from his customers.

"May I help you gentlemen?" Mr. Hansen asked.

Nate cleared his voice. "I would like to look at some rings."

"Certainly, please follow me."

Mr. Hansen went back behind the glass display case while John and Nate crept up beside the seated customers.

"What sort of ring do you have in mind, Sir? A delicate little one to place on a pinkie finger? Or, is this a Christmas gift for a sweet-heart?"

Nate stood motionless, biting his lip while Mr. Hansen waited for a response. He realized that his heart was thumping terribly, and no longer did he possess the confidence he had but a few minutes ago. John and Mr. Hansen was looking at him now. Nate opened his mouth and thankfully the words spilled out.

"En-gage-ment....I'm looking for an engagement ring. Please."

Nate let his chest fall as he breathed a sigh of relief.

Mr. Hansen smiled, for he knew how to handle such customers who soon would be standing at an alter and saying 'I do.'

Nodding, Mr. Hansen smiled and replied, "Of course."

He showed Nate an array of gold rings, silver rings, simple rings, and rings adorned with diamonds.

After several minutes Nate turned to John and asked, "What do you think?"

John turned to Nate and laughed, "You're asking me?"

"Well....yes. You are her brother."

"That may be so, but when it comes to this stuff, you're on your own!"

Mr. Hansen smiled at the two men and said that perhaps that they would like to take more time to decide. He excused himself and went back to fussing over his previous customers.

Finally, after too much pondering and sighing, John offered, "Well, I don't know....How would a guy know what a women wants, them being so fickle and all."

The woman sitting down at the counter turned and scowled at John. "I beg your pardon!" she huffed.

"Oh, not you Ma'am. I'm referring to my sisters," John quickly apologized to the middle aged woman who lifted her nose while turning away from him.

"Maybe you should bring Eleanor down here so she can pick something out herself," John suggested.

"Good idea John. Good idea." Nate said in a breath of relief. He looked up at Mr. Hansen and nodded at the man who pretended to have not heard.

"Will you be making a selection to-day, gentlemen?" Mr. Hansen asked.

"I'm afraid I will have to bring my....fiancée next time and have her select a ring, if that's all right?"

"Certainly. Was there something else you saw that she might like for Christmas?"

Nate looked at the shiny pendants and pointed to an attractive one that he was picturing around Eleanor's soft neck and resting on her healthy bosom. Mr. Hansen carefully handed the pendant to Nate and studying it a moment he nodded in approval. The gift was placed in a nice box and wrapped, and having paid for his purchase, Nate thanked Mr. Hansen and wished him a Merry Christmas.

"I will look forward to seeing you again. Merry Christmas, gentlemen."

John and Nate were so relieved to be heading out the door that Mr. Hansen had to remind them of their four hat boxes on the floor. After closing the door behind them, they breathed in a huge gulp of air and slowly let it out.

"I'm hungry," Nate declared. "How 'bout you?"

"Starving!"

Making their way back to the Hotel Plaza they decided to put the boxes back in Nate's room and then have lunch before they finished their shopping. They covered the distance of a few blocks before Nate opened the door to Frey's New Cafe. The warm delicious air hit them, and remembering their manners, Nate and John removed their hat and cap. Nate made eye contact with one of the four waitresses as he and John stood next to a display case filled with cigars and trinkets. On top the glass case sat a potted fern which was four arm lengths directly across from a palm tree and a mission style rocking chair. And across the black and white checkered floor was a shiny banister next to the palm tree. The flight of stairs led customers to private dining rooms above the cafe.

Against the left wall were six tables covered with white linen, four chairs to a table. In the back left corner a mission style dresser housed silverware and linen. Each table had long stemmed flowers in matching vases, and above the tables were mirrors with a hook for a hat and a hook for a jacket or coat. Half way up the two long and one short walls, just above the mirror and hooks was light colored wall paper, while a dark maroon filled the upper half with gold designs dripping from the edge of the ceiling. The right side of the cafe was identical except for a door at the back which presumably lead to the busy kitchen which was catering to a full crowd.

One of the waitresses hurried over to Nate and John and said that it may be a while before a table would be available. Nate nodded and said that they would wait, and not more than ten minutes had passed when a front table emptied. The dishes were cleared and the two men were escorted to the table. Upon receiving the menus, John was told to order 'anything' he wanted. But when the young man opened the menu and noticed the prices his eyes grew wide, but Nate whispered to him and said, "John...I mean it. Anything. My treat."

John looked at the menu again. Roast Pork and Apple Sauce 20 cents. Boston Baked Beans 10 cents. Mashed Potatoes 5 cents. Lemon Layer Cake 5 cents....His mouth was watering already and to make matters worse, a waitress appeared at a table across from them with a large serving tray. She carefully unfolded a little table and placed the tray on it. John and Nate eyed the wonderful looking food as the waitress put the dinners in front of her waiting customers. After depositing the folding table and tray to the back of the room, she came to their table and took their order.

John decided on chicken, mashed potatoes, salad, bread, and apple pie. Nate ordered roast beef, buttered beets, cold slaw, mashed potatoes, coffee and rhubarb pie for desert.

In-between bites, John asked Nate a lot of questions about where he and Eleanor were planning on moving to, when could he come for a visit, and would he and Nate still go fishing once Nate was officially a married man.

Nate's answers were 'not sure yet,' 'as soon as they buy a house and furnish it,' 'and by all means, yes!'

"And speaking of fishing, I would like to give you a new rod and reel for Christmas. Do you mind if it's not a surprise?" asked Nate.

"Do I mind?!" John mumbled through his apple pie. "Gosh no. That would be just swell!"

"Good. Almost done?" Nate asked, wiping any rhubarb pie crumbs from his mouth.

Shoving the last fork full of apple pie in his mouth, John nodded his head then mumbled, "Yep."

Nate just had to laugh and shook his head. "I didn't think you could put all that away."

John patted his content stomach and sighed. "I hope you and Eleanor find a place close to us so I can come over and have dinner with you often."

"I think we better go before you order another slice of pie," Nate chuckled as he carefully pushed his chair back and stood up.

***

Back outside, the streets are alive with shoppers hurrying to and fro. Bells on the front of trolley cars ring out in the nippy air while delivery wagon drivers holler and whip their teams as they rush in front of the clanking things. A patrol officer here, a patrol officer there twirl their sticks, ignoring the motionless panhandler on the corner. Nate and John nears the weathered and wrinkled man who is crouching against the stone building with his head down and arms wrapped around his old, soiled coat. He has a box next to him against the wall so it does not interfere with the foot traffic going by. His eyes are red and watering from the cold as they stare at the snow trodden pavement in front of him.

A coin here, a coin there is dropped into the box. The old man would like to say thank you or nod his head, but he is too cold to move, too tired to try. He supposes that it is Christmas....whatever that is supposed to mean for a homeless old man. The edge of women's skirts swish close to his numb feet...the seams on his leather shoes broke long ago; a string which he found in a dumpster is tied around his shoes to keep them from flapping.

Two pairs of feet slows and pauses in front of him. A hand puts a few dollars in the box. The old man should say something, but his face is too cold to move. He thanks whoever it is with a tiny nod as his eyes are still downcast. The footsteps move away from him. Then they come back. Two young men crouch down to look at him and he puts a dry red hand on the money box. Then the older of the two speaks softly and tells him that they would like to find him a nice warm room and feed him a hot decent meal.

"No one," said the young man, "should have to live on the streets. It is not humane."

The old man listened to those endearing words. A warm room. Food. A bed. He blinked his eyes and knew this was a ploy to get him near an alley so that the two young men could beat him, take his money and leave him for dead. The old man thought about this. If that was their intent, if might be a good thing to go with them, for God was taking his time in calling him home. He did not want to suffer anymore. The old man looked up at the two men and was surprised how kind they looked. He hoped that they were just nice looking young men with bad intentions, and nodding to them, he was slowly and painfully lifted up. The boy handed him his money box, and walking some blocks they stopped outside a boarding house. They entered a dimly lit hallway and was met by a woman who pinched her nose and complained of the urine stench. She ordered the three out of her place, but the young man reached inside his pocket and handed something to her.

"Will that be sufficient for a week's stay for my friend?" he asked the stunned woman.

When she managed to find her tongue, she cleared her voice and replied, "I suppose so…."

The old man could not believe what was happening to him. Perhaps there really was a God that had sent these two men to him. He heard the soft voiced one instruct the woman to give him a bath, wash his clothes, feed him, and make him comfortable. The woman began to argue, but the soft voiced man said that this old man was someone's son, someone's brother, someone's forgotten father. He would return in a few days to check on the old man, and if he should find him neglected, her establishment would be closed down.

The old man turned to the young men and tried to smile. "God bless you!" he stammered, his crooked yellow teeth showing as he spoke. "God bless you!" he blinked and sniffled as his red swollen eyes were filling up with tears.

"I'm Nate and this is John. I'll be back in a few days to check on you. Merry Christmas."

The old man nodded to Nate and John and then followed the woman down the hall to a room. That night, as he slept comfortably for the first time in many years, he closed his eyes and thanked God for this little bit of good luck. And then, sometime during the night, God answered his prayers and brought him home.

***

For the rest of the afternoon, Nate and John were not as talkative as before. They were thinking about the old panhandler and wished they could have done more for him. John even told Nate that he really didn't need a new fishing reel and rod. Somehow, they just didn't seem all that important. But Nate disagreed and bought him one anyway. Both men were exhausted when they came back to the Hotel Plaza, and boarding a trolley for home, John carried two hat boxes and his fishing gear with him.

After a sound rest, Nate put on his good suit and boarded a trolley car for Eleanor's house. The car was chilly and he was anxious to be with Eleanor and her family. Such thoughts warmed him as the trolley car made its journey away from downtown. Nate wished for tomorrow to hurry, and God willing, he would not be alone, anymore.

He was deposited at the corner a little after six in the evening, and making his way a few blocks in the snow, he arrived at the cozy little house. He could hear someone playing the piano as he knocked on the door. Papa opened the door for Nate, and taking his coat and hat he wished him a "Merry Christmas." Two more wrapped hat boxes were placed under the tree with the other gifts. Eleanor removed herself from the piano stool and greeted Nate, letting him take her hands in his.

"Oh, you poor thing!" Eleanor exclaimed. "Your hands are freezing! Come over by the fire and warm them up."

Eleanor led Nate to the fire, and leaning closer he whispered in her ear, "I prefer warming my hands this way…" His soft voice had more than a hint of desire in it which caused Eleanor to blush. They glanced up to see Mama coming out of the kitchen with a big smile on her face. Nate quickly let go of Eleanor's hands and hid his hands behind his back.

"Thank you so much for the wonderful turkey. He's so big, I think I shall have to adjust the oven racks tomorrow." Mama held Nate's hand and let him kiss her on the cheek.

"Oh, my!" Mama giggled as she put a hand on her cheek.

"Merry Christmas!" said Nate. "Thank you for inviting me."

"It's our pleasure!" Mama said with a twinkle in her eyes.

"Can I help you in the kitchen?" asked Eleanor.

"No, no. Everything is just about ready. Why don't you entertain Nate with some more Christmas songs."

"Yes, Mama." Eleanor was more than happy to play as to avoid kitchen duties.

At last, everyone gathered around the kitchen table and enjoyed a wonderful meal, and afterwards, Nate surprised the women in the house by rolling up his sleeves and employed a not so cheerful John to kitchen duties. Mama was ushered to her favorite chair by the fire. While Eleanor, Alice and Marie put the leftovers in the ice box, Nate washed and John dried the dishes.

Finally, Nate and John left the kitchen, and rolling down their shirt sleeves they joined the others in the living room by the fire. The hours before midnight mass were spent listening to Eleanor, Alice and Marie take turns at the piano, looking at Christmas cards the family had received, and bringing up more coal for the fire.

Between a full stomach and the pleasant music, Papa put his

head back on the sofa and was asleep in no time, and shortly there-after, Mama was softly snoring in her favorite chair, too. Nate and John played cards and yawned and tried to stay awake while the girls fussed over themselves.

At last, the clock rang out eleven times, and Papa and Mama awoke from their long naps. Standing up to stretch, Papa glanced out the window and announced that it was snowing.

The crowded trolley car emptied its passengers, depositing the family and Nate in front of Sacred Heart Church. Music and voices were heard as sleepy people were drawn up the stairs and through the doors where pews were filling up rapidly. The scent of cedar boughs filled the air and swags with red ribbons hung from the end of every third pew. Red poinsettia's graced the area around the altar.

Nate looked down at Eleanor and smiled. He never imagined that his life would have turned out like it had. Surly God had a hand in his good fortune of meeting Eleanor that night on the Fair grounds. Nate breathed deeply and sighed with a smile on his content face. Yes, he was a very, very happy man.

Suddenly there was a finger tapping his shoulder.

"Mr. Miller?" the voice inquired.

Turning around, Nate and Eleanor took in a young man and his young wife.

"Mr. Berg! Mrs. Berg!" exclaimed Nate.

"Surprise!" said Mr. Berg with a big smile on his cold face. "I bet you thought you would never see us again."

Nate turned to Eleanor and said, "Eleanor, I would like you to meet two of the nicest people in the world. Please forgive me, but I do not think I know your first names," apologized Nate.

"How do you do!" Mrs. Berg put her hands around Eleanor's and gave them a warm squeeze. "My name is Georgina, and this is my darling, wonderful husband, Cary."

"I'm very pleased to make your acquaintance," Eleanor nodded at Mr. and Mrs. Cary Berg. "Would you care to sit with us?"

There was a twinkle in Mrs. Berg's eyes and a quick little smile on her youthful face. "Oh, please!" she whispered in delight as they made their way up the isle to an available pew.

As it turned out, Nate and Eleanor, and Mr. and Mrs. Berg sat behind the pew that Eleanor's family took up. This bit of separation gave Nate great pleasure as he thought he was able to hold Eleanor's hand without her parents knowledge. His touch though lasted a few moments as Eleanor carefully slipped her hand away and folded them in her lap. Again, Nate covered her hands with his strong right hand, and this time his fingers would not let go. Georgina sat to the right of Eleanor, and detecting her uneasiness she leaned close to Eleanor and whispered, "My dear, it's quite all right. See, Mr. Berg is holding my hand, too."

Eleanor turned her head slightly and saw that Mr. Berg had his hand over his wife's hand. Eleanor could not believe it! Such behavior was never seen in church because it simply was not done. Period. The Berg's were married, and therefore such physical contact was allowed— outside the walls of God's house. But to have Nate hold her hand in church! Eleanor's face was warm and her heart was racing. What if Mama or Papa happened to turn around and catch her and Nate?

The young girl leaned towards Eleanor again. "Enjoy what God gave you and what He has given you," whispered Georgina wisely. She began to move her head away but stopped. Georgina's voice was almost too soft to hear, but Eleanor understood the young bride. "You are a very lucky girl. If you want to please and keep your husband-to-be, it's best to let him have his way."

Georgina and Eleanor's eyes met as they stood up for song, their hands falling discreetly at their sides. The young bride innocently smiled at Eleanor and began to sing, "Silent Night."

Death comes: even to Rats

At the corner of West 6th and Highland Street, he stops his exhausted large body to take gulps of whiskey between panting breaths. Curses and profanities fall from his lips after climbing the steep hill that trolley lines have not been laid to yet.

The breath of Mr. Miller Sr. fills the cold air and tiny snow flakes begin to fall around him. He takes a few steps forward but his intoxicated clumsy body almost stumbles in the snow and he has to reach for the cold, black iron fence with his bare hand. As he clings to the cold iron, he makes his way to the gate of Col. Blethen's mansion. Mr. Miller turns his head to stare at the grand house with its towering white columns yearning to reach the sky. Every large pane of glass was announcing the joy of the season by spilling warm yellow light onto the snow. Sounds of music emanating from a piano escaped from the walls of the Blethen home.

Mr. Miller crinkled his weary hateful face and spit on the other side of the fence, onto the Blethen's snow covered lawn. He hated the Blethen's. Hated the Duffy's. Hated everyone on his street. Mr. Miller's heart was feeling tight and a strange feeling was going through his arm. The hand that the bottle was holding pressed against his chest and his face whinst in pain. When the pain subsided, the drink was brought to his lips again and the empty bottle thrown into the Blethen's yard.

Following the black crutch east, he finally reached his own gate and his own front steps, and hesitating on the porch steps, he saw something in the window. At first, his blurry eyes were not sure of themselves and were brought closer. A violent yell which rendered the air from deep in his gut shattered the peace and tranquility of the blessed evening.

"Damn you all! Damn the whole world!"

He rubbed a fist against his mouth and mustache and wiped the spit away that came out with the words. And from the window the foreclosure sign was seized, and standing on his front porch Mr. Miller fought the thick paper but could not tear it until it was brought to his teeth.

"Who do you people think you are!?" he seethed. "Don't you know who I am!? You don't deserve to be my neighbors! You bunch of filthy scum!!"

The front door was slammed shut, and making his way into the dark house the hall light was turned on and going through the dark parlor he found more drink in the billiard room. As he made his way back through the parlor, what was left of his senses told him that he stood in an empty room. The light from the hall made obvious the fact that a robbery had taken place. The only pieces remaining were the carpet and desk. His body turned and jerked about in disbelief, his mouth open until the drink was brought to his mustached lips again. Mr. Miller turned to the fireplace and saw a white envelope leaning against the mirror, and placing the drink in the crook of his left arm against his thick body, he opened the contents.

From the depths of hell a roar filled the house and the glass that was filled with strong smelling liquor ran down the front of Mr. Miller's rumpled clothes. Profanities and the glass were smashed against the lonely, dark fireplace.

"I'll find you and then I'll kill you…that's what I'll do!!" his voiced boiled in anger. "I'll stuff this right down your throat!"

A wall suffered a blow from Mr. Miller's fist as the man spat out loathsome words from his cold spirit. The house whimpered in pain.

"Merry Christmas to you, too!" Another hole was put in the wall.

Mr. Miller Sr. strode over to the desk, picked up the chair and threw it across the empty parlor. An evil smile grew on his face as the sound of the chair hitting the floor pleased him. He went over to it again and threw it against a wall. He threw it again and again, and finally, when quite out of breath, he managed to pick it up and hold it over his head. All silence of what should have been ceased, when the sound of shattering glass disturbed the blessed night.

A drawer is opened from the desk and a pistol is removed.

"I'll find ya. I'll find ya all right!"

A bottle of liquor is found. The foreclosure note is stuffed in one pocket and the pistol put in an inside pocket. His coat unbuttoned, his bare head and his damaged hands are without protection as he makes his way down the walk. And behind him, a house stands— weeping, grieving—her heart pierced from loneliness and desertion. The chill of winter sweeps through the broken window and rushes passed a door that the last Miller refused to close.

He gets on a trolley but his repulsive smell and behavior gets him removed after a few blocks. His sense of warmth from the effect of the alcohol is deceiving him as he walks through the cold night air. He slips and falls and he loses the foreclosure notice as it is blown into the middle of trolley tracks. His futile attempt to retrieve it leaves him frustrated and exhausted. He sees a church steeple in the distance but his eyes are beginning to blur.

Mr. Miller slips and falls in the snow once more. He swears that he will make it to the church. Swears he will kill Nate. He is very near the church where he sees the soft warm glow spilling out from stained-glass windows onto the snow covered steps. He hears the strain of Christmas songs escaping into the night. He has stopped to catch his breath, drinks more liquor because he is thirsty; stops because he is too tired. He falls down on the steps and his eye sight is blurred. He sees a figure walk passed him. "Good for nothing drunk…" As the figure disappears into the church, a rush of voices and organ music hit him, and then it softens as the doors close.

He turns on his back; an effort which takes all his strength, and stares unemotionally at the snow flakes that land on his face. He feels warm and comfortable on the bed of snow…he sees a little boy playing in the snow with his brothers and sisters.

He sees his controlling, unaffectionate mother in the distance; a nanny leads him away from her and to the nursery. Cold tears wet his face and then a stranger appeared to him also, but he could only see his back. He looked very much like himself in stature, and when the man spoke, he sounded like himself, too. The man was speaking to a child, but the figure of the child was too blurry, but this did not stop the man from inflicting verbal punishment on the child. A butchery of words were sent forth, slayed with criticism and disapproval. Mr. Miller could feel the child wither and cry, which whipped and spurred the man's temper. A glass filled with liquor was thrown at the poor whimpering child, narrowly missing his head, shattering glass on the wall behind him. Shrills and cries, as if from an animal, hurtled objects about the room, screaming as if he was maddened by demons. Several uncles came and took his father away, placing him in an insane asylum. Their father was never to be seen again.

The poor drunk turned onto his side, tucking arms and legs closer to his body as he sobbed in fits, his tears spilling through the snow. And then, his sobbing ceased, leaving him breathing with great difficulty. Suddenly the music from within the church rose to a feverish pitch and a hand slid inside his long coat. The organ hit a series of high glorious notes, and as he stared blankly at the snow flakes he mouthed, "Write about this Mr. Blethen…"

And across town, in another church, the bells rang to announce the hour of midnight, to declare that Christmas morning was nigh.

Christmas Morning

Nathaniel Miller swore as the razor cut the underside of his chin. He could not see himself in the mirror and wiped a white towel over it.

"No, not now…" He grumbled to himself for not letting the steady hand of a barber do a better job while Nate could have been relaxing under a warm towel and soothing facial lotions. He looked down at his shaking hands. Nate was thankful that his room had its own private bathtub and privy. He did not care to share a privy with other people if he didn't have to.

The cut finally under control, Nate was able to dress and put on his Sunday shoes that were shined the afternoon before. His hair was wetted and combed back, with the usual part on the side. A fine turn down linen collar was attached to his neck which was restrictive and uncomfortable. Nate looked at himself in the mirror. As much as he hated wearing collars, they did make him look proper. Next he attached a silk shield teck-tie to the stiff collar. Finally, with his jacket on and his long heavy coat waiting at the foot of the bed, Nate went over to the dresser and picked up the picture of he and his mother.

"Merry Christmas, Mother…" Nate whispered tenderly.

In his heart, Nate wished more than anything that his mother could see him now; wish that she could give him words of loving encouragement. Nate began to feel old wounds again and tried to will them away. In difficult times, he let memories comfort and guide him as he wondered what his dear mother would do. But to-day, he needed her horribly.

"Well, Mother, wish me all the luck in the world. To-day I am going to ask for her hand in marriage," Nate whispered out loud. "I'm a little scared." He tried to lighten his voice with a small laugh, but sighed. "I think you would approve of Eleanor and her family. I just wish you were here to meet them." He paused again and sighed. "I will tell Eleanor everything about you….every little detail I can remember…." Nate bit his lip and pressed the picture frame against his chest. He drew in a painful breath. "Oh, Mother! Let her say yes…let her say yes!"

The picture was carefully put back on the dresser and a small package tied in string sat next to it. Nate had been waiting a long,

long time to open the package. On her death bed, Nate's mother gave it to him. She also gave Nate explicit instructions that it was not to be opened until he was of marrying age, when he truly, truly had found a young girl who could make him happy for the rest of his life. His mother made him promise that he would not open it till then. There had been many, many times when his pain and curiosity almost revealed the contents, but he would not go against his dear mother's wishes. He would wait.

***

Eleanor greeted Nate at the front door. She was very lovely indeed; her shiny dark hair looking freshly washed, rosy-glowing cheeks and heart-stirring brown eyes. Someday soon, he prayed, she would be his and she would greet him every night at the door. Then, and only then, would she be able to wrap her loving arms around his neck and kiss him with tender lips. It pained him that he could only wish her a "Merry Christmas."

The little house was filled with all the delights and smells of Christmas. Music from the piano and John's harmonica brought smiles and laughter to the morning. Breakfast was done. The dishes were washed and dried and put away before any presents were opened. Finally, everyone gathered in the front room around the wonderful fire that popped and crackled now and then. Nate stood with his back to the fire and near to where Eleanor sat opening her gift from McAfee's Millinery Shop.

Mama could only thank Nate with misty eyes and a kind smile, for social nonchalance was falling away to wistful-sentiments as she ran a hand over her new hat.Alice and Marie squealed in delight over their new hats, and John showed everyone his brand new fishing pole that had been waiting behind the tree.

Nate received boxes of baked goods from each of the girls.

John gave Nate 50 yards of Italian silk trout line. The spool had cost him all of 72 cents, but since it was for his future brother-in-law, it was 72 cents that he did not mind parting with.

Nate had been watching Papa and was wondering if he felt left out since Nate had not given him a gift. It did not seem so, for Papa leaned back against the sofa, smoking his pipe, enjoying the morning festivities.

Alice stood up and said that she wanted to try on everyone's hats, and wished for Marie and Eleanor to follow her. But Nate cleared his throat in a gentlemanly way which immediately caught the attention of everyone.

"But first, if everyone could have a seat, please."

Nate waited for all to be seated and for all eyes to rest on him.

"John, could you and your mother trade places, please?" Nate asked.

John's eyes were bright and a wide smile grew on his face for he was sure that the moment had finally come when Nate was going to spring the question. And having traded places with his Mama who now sat next to Papa, Nate began.

"I want to thank you all for inviting me to share Christmas day with you. You have no idea how much this means to me," Nate smiled.

"You are welcome," replied Mama.

"I wanted to give the whole family something as a token of my heartfelt appreciation for the kindness that you have bestowed on me…"

Nate looked at Papa and took a few steps forward. He put a hand inside his suit, and taking out an envelope he handed it to Papa.

"Sir, this 'was' your mortgage on this house. Merry Christmas!"

The room was cast in silence and all movement halted, that is, until Mama started crying and Papa, whose eyes were moist, stood up and hugged and patted Nate on the back saying, "Daken ihr!" Marie, Alice and John shook hands and hugged Nate, too. Then Papa went over to the fireplace, and with all eyes on the mortgage papers, they were tossed into the flames and consumed. Papa started to sniffle so Eleanor went over to him and comforted him. This started Eleanor crying which set the rest of the females crying. And within a few moments there was joyful sobbing, smiling faces and handkerchiefs here and there.

John came and stood by Nate and said in a good natured way, "Now look what you've done!"

Nate leaned closer to John and whispered, "What do you think they'll do when I propose to your sister?"

John turned and looked at Nate. "Oh, golly…all heck will break loose!"

Excusing himself from John's company, Nate strode over to Eleanor and asked if she might want some fresh air. Donning their coats, gloves and rubbers for their feet, they made their way onto the porch and down the steps. Eleanor put on her fascinator and tied it under her chin. The sun was beginning to come out which caused a hint of glare on the snow while it twinkled like one enormous shiny gem. They walked hand in hand up the hill. It was so nice being alone with Eleanor, holding her hand, listening to their footsteps in the crunchy snow. When they thought they were a safe distance from the house, Eleanor stopped and suddenly kissed Nate as she held his face in her hands. Nate pulled her closer and wished there weren't so many layers of clothing between them. He was aware that Eleanor was revealing natural inclinations as she pressed her body to his and let out soft little moans of frustration that escaped from her lips. Nate also realized that they had put themselves on public display and regretfully had to separate himself from her loving embrace.

"Nate...what is it?" asked Eleanor.

He looked down at her and whispered, "Your neighbors are watching..."

Suddenly her face turned color and quickly faced her back to the curious houses, but pressing against windows across the street were little faces as well. Eleanor let out a gasp and put her hands over her face. Nate took her by the arm and said, "Let's keep walking."

When they reached the corner and were laughing at the embarrassment of it all, Nate gathered Eleanor's hands in his and looked steadily and lovingly at her.

"Eleanor, I cannot live another day without you near me. You must know that I am deeply in love with you. Perhaps you have doubts and fears, that love is a luxury, and passion is for only a few. If you say 'yes' for the sake of companionship, I will try to understand. But I am a natural man, filled with unsown seeds..."

Eleanor's eyes were sparkling for the words of love were filling her heart.

"Since the moment I held you in my arms at the Exposition, you have become such a part of me. If you say no, I will go completely mad, for I will not know who I am."

Then, removing his hat, Nate knelt down in the snow.

"Eleanor, will you please be my wife?"

Oh, the love that radiated from her face would never be forgotten.

"As the new snow clings to the world, I therefore will cling to my beloved. My heart also aches for you constantly. It weeps when you are not near. And yes, I do want your companionship, but promise me that your love be year-round, not only in the spring when the air is laden with perfumes, violets, roses and apple blossoms. I want you to kiss me until your seeds run dry."

The two lovers continued walking until they fell into each other's tight embrace again. Each kiss grew more and more passionate and desireful as Nate unbuttoned Eleanor's coat and slid his hand around her small waist. It was quickly decided that they should marry as soon as possible, for the urgency of certain God given needs were proving to become unbridled. Nate and Eleanor wisely admitted that a long engagement would be sheer torture, both emotionally and physically. They spoke of a summer wedding, and then wondered if they could truly be submissive to social and sacred obedience. Nate told her that he heard that long engagements were one of the surest ways of breaking down even the strongest nerves. Nate loved Eleanor too great to cause her disgrace.

Eleanor shared an intimate thought when she remembered when Alice had read an article to her one night. It seemed silly and old fashioned at the time, but now Eleanor understood what Alice Preston was speaking of.

"Our love rouses the emotions and passions which is harmful to have roused and played upon; that it wakens and stimulates feelings and instincts and desires that should not be wakened."

Nate grabbed Eleanor and kissed her roughly.

"Too late! You awoke mine when I first laid eyes on you…." Nate breathed heavily in her ear.

"Not I!" Eleanor teased. "My emotions and passions will be yoked and held in-check till our wedding day," she smiled proudly.

"Is that so?" inquired Nate.

"Yes."

"Well, I hate to tell you my love, but your eyes are anxious with eagerness," Nate tenderly but honestly informed her.

"Oh, Nate! Truly? What I am to do? How can I ever go home now? Oh, this is terrible! Nate darling, say something!"

"Eleanor, my love! It's quite all right. This is not sudden."

"How do you mean?" Eleanor softly wailed.

Nate smiled at his love. "You have looked this way for many, many months. I've just never told you so."

"You beast!" Eleanor pretended to pout and be angry.

"My dear, dear darling…it's called 'being in love'."

Eleanor turned to him and gave him a kiss.

"How about May?" Nate offered as a suggested month for their wedding.

"April…"

"April? April it is."

"March…"

"March? March it is."

"February…"

Nate laughed. "February? Are you sure? We will have to find a house in two months. Can we do all that?"

Eleanor snuggled up to Nate and replied, "If not, I will surely die shortly thereafter. I must be delivered from being socially muzzled and religiously shackled. If you do not unchain me, my death will be on your head."

"As soon as the snow melts we will start looking in earnest," Nate promised.

"And I will make my dress and veil."

"Eleanor…"

"Yes?"

"I think we may have overlooked one thing…"

"What is that?"

"I haven't asked your father if I may take you from him!"

As the two lovers slowly walked back to the house, Eleanor smiled and said, "How can Papa say no after you gave him the house as a Christmas gift?"

Upon their arrival, Nate and Eleanor's faces announced the wonderful news, for the front room window was filled with three anxious faces.

And of course, Nate was quite relieved when Papa shook his hands which threw the household into another blissful fit of more hugging and crying.

The atmosphere in the house suddenly lost its tranquility as it prepared itself for a voyage. Time had taken a huge step forward. Certain things felt settled while the anticipation of the unknown lie only a few months away. Love set life in motion.

Before the noon-day meal, the girls retired upstairs to plan for the soon-to-be wedding. Mama came in too, crying and dabbing her eyes. She agreed that a short engagement was best, though it would be hard seeing her first daughter go so soon.

Downstairs the men quietly reclined before the fire, discussing possible neighborhoods and such business that a future father-in-law should take up with his future son-in-law.

And amongst the happy and tender tears in the crowded upstairs room in the little cozy house, a new name fell from someone's lips.

Mrs. Nathaniel Miller.

"Dearest Nathaniel..."

Many thoughts occupied Nate Miller's mind as he returned to the Hotel Plaza sometime after two in the afternoon. The trolley was near empty and the city streets were almost barren of life. Nate almost floated off the trolley and into the lobby where the clerk was engaged behind the Sunday paper. He was reading about a drunk who killed himself in front of St. James Cathedral the evening before. A person in the congregation recognized the deceased as Mr. Stuart Miller Sr. The clerk glanced up and then looked back at the paper. When it hit him as to who was hurrying across the lobby he cried out, "Say, Mr. Miller!"

"Sorry...in a hurry!" Nate replied without looking at the clerk.

Nate had suddenly remembered what was waiting for him after all these years as he crossed the marble floor.

The clerk snapped his fingers and mumbled, "Darn...wanted to ask if they were related by any chance."

The elevator was ignored as Nate's powerful legs cleared three steps at a time, and reaching his door out of breath, he quickly found the key and closed the door behind him. Nate leaned against the door, breathing, breathing, staring at the box, staring at the picture of him and his mother. His panting was not quiet in the otherwise hushed room.

"Mother...." Nate looked intensely at a long ago image of his dear mother, taken while in her early twenties. "She said, 'Yes."

He changed out of his suit, and carefully hanging it up, put on something more comfortable. He washed his face and splashed cold water on it. Nate let out a deep sigh in the privy room, for he was horribly anxious as the tightness in his chest could not deny. Nate needed to face whatever waited for him on the dresser, and sitting down on the bed, he was trying to picture his mother wrapping the box with her own fingers while she was very sick. The string was undone and the paper carefully folded back. Nate's heart was beating faster as he took the top off the box. Inside was another box, and slowly opening the dark blue box of crushed velvet, there was a lovely intricate silver and diamond ring. Nate did not recall his mother ever having worn such a ring.

His eyes were brought to the folded envelope that bore his name on the outside. Nate read his mother's cursive handwriting. "To my dearest, Nathaniel." For a long time he was only able to stare at her lovely handwriting, for he could not bring himself to open the envelope just yet. But terrible curiosity overcame him, and unfolding the two page letter he began to read it very slowly.

"Dearest Nathaniel,

I shall not be with you much longer…this much I know. A mother should never have to write her son a letter as this, but I feel that if I do not do it now, I shall be too tired later on to tell you the truth. My dear son, please do not hate me for what I am about to tell you."

Nate took his eyes away and sucked in the air about him. He didn't know if he could go on. He wasn't sure if he wanted to, but he looked back down at the paper and continued.

"Years ago, a wonderful young man wished to marry me. We were deeply in love and wanted to be man and wife, but my father did not approve of him. Not on account of him lacking good morals and such, but because I was bought by another. I was given over and forced to marry a man whom my father knew. It was money which brought happiness to my father. I was made powerless from the beginning to the end.

As for the ring…it was the only reminder of the true love I had and lost. It was given to me, and should have been worn as a sign of a man's love for me. But instead, I wore the ring of another which was a constant reminder of his merciless, mental and physical empowerment over me.

My son, a woman's heart needs to be filled with love. Both my heart and my body were dying for love….and the bearer of the ring never strayed too far from my view.

As you matured, I think your 'other' father had suspicions. You were so different in your manner, your being. You were nothing like Stuart or Todd.

He helped your brother Stuart and your brother Todd come into this world. But the greatest day for me, was when he laid 'our son' upon my breast.

My dearest boy, you are my son, and the son of Dr. George Nathaniel Henry.

If you should ever meet someday, please, my dear, be kind to him. He loves you just as much as I do.

I am tired my dear.

339

Until we meet in heaven someday, do not forget how much I loved you."

Love,
Mother

If You Should Ever Meet Someday...

Nate stood at the window and stared at the quiet street below. His mind was numb and emotionally drained. He had cried quiet sobs several times since reading and re-reading the letter. So many things made sense now. So many things...His father was not his real father. Stuart and Todd were only half-brothers; half-brothers who did not exist anymore, unless, if Todd could ever make it back home after his youthfulness had been spent.

As Nate watched a few wagons make their way passed his window, traveling along Westlake Avenue, certain little thoughts came to mind. Little things that only now made sense, like when he injured his back and Dr. Henry came to check on him. He had never forgotten the look in Dr. Henry's eyes. Never forgot the tone in his voice when Dr. Henry called him 'Nathaniel' instead of 'Nate.'

All these years his real father was right here.

Slowly, very slow, the reality of it all began to sink in. And when it did, the words were softly spoken from Nate's lips. "Dr. Henry 'is' my father..."

Such words, Nate discovered, birthed an invisible force inside him—suddenly gripping at his heart. And upon its conception, Nate felt a sense of warmth and a strong yearning that only grew stronger by the minute.

As he walked down the stairs to the lobby, Nate knew that he would not be interrupting Dr. Henry's family on Christmas Day. Eleanor had said that Dr. Henry did not have any family as far as she knew. Nate wondered if he never married because he was so very much in love with his mother.

His fingers were shaking as he held the receiver in his hands, and his voice was not steady either when he asked the girl on the other end to place his call to Dr. Henry's residence. And when Dr. Henry's voice did come on the line he could hardly speak. Nate asked if he could pay him a visit concerning an important matter that could not wait.

The desk clerk did not pretend to not have heard the conversation as the telephone box was in the lobby.

"Everything all right, Mr. Miller?"

Nate slowly hung the receiver on the box and began to go back up the stairs.

"Mr. Miller!"

The desk clerk called to Nate a second time, but to no avail. He was either being dismissed, though more likely, according to the clerk's notice which was an occupation in itself, Mr. Miller was quite absorbed in his own thoughts. The desk clerk snapped his idle fingers once more, for this Miller fellow who had fallen under his prying observance, did not relieve him of his immediate boredom.

In his room, Nate put on his warm coat and hat and placed the letter and ring box inside his coat. Presently, as his body moved independently from his intelligence, any worries which should have been present, were not. Nate looked at the picture of his dear mother but did not say anything.

He left the Hotel Plaza, boarded a cold trolley and headed to Dr. Henry's neighborhood. Nate was taken to a comfortable little area where mansions were not to be seen; only single-story bungalows filled with working-class families. Where the hours of summer were probably spent in the street throwing and catching baseballs or kicking a ball. Where families knew each other.

When the driver announced the street's name, Nate removed himself and walked a block or less to a corner where children were throwing snowballs at each other from behind snowmen. A few children flopped backwards in the snow, swishing arms and legs to create snow-angels. They ceased their fun for a moment and asked, "Hey, Mister— you lost?"

Nate shook his head but asked which house belonged to Dr. Henry. The rosy cheeked children pointed to the fourth house down. Nate tipped his hat and slowly proceeded to walk in that direction. But at the second house he began to loose his nerve, and it occurred to him that this whole thing could blow up in his face.

And what about Dr. Henry? The poor man might be horribly embarrassed or ashamed that his real son now knows the truth. And what would others say about Dr. Henry's indiscretion from decades earlier? Surely, this would damage a good man's career. Nate had not thought about that, and mentally chastising himself for his impulsive action, turned and started in the opposite direction. But then he stopped for a man's voice was calling to him…

The figure of the sweater clad Dr. Henry stood on a small stoop and he seemed to be waving to the two snowmen erected in his front yard, created by the children next-door, no doubt.

Dr. Henry greeted Nate and wished him a "Merry Christmas" as the young man navigated his way up the walk to the house. Nate returned the greeting and paid compliments to the snow figures that guarded the house.

In the course of hospitalities and hidden anxieties, Dr. Henry took Nate's outerwear and hat and hung them on the coat stand near the door. Nate's arrival was considered timely, for the water heating on the range was almost hot enough for a late afternoon cup of tea.

While Dr. Henry excused himself to the kitchen where little sounds of china and silverware could be heard, Nate stood near the fireplace where he took in Dr. Henry's residence. The room was smaller than average— room enough though for a single man. Comfortable yet practical pieces were arranged as such so the cozy room would not look cluttered. On a nearby table, a simple little tree of no more than two foot in height supported an assortment of homemade dangling ornaments from its fragile branches. Nate smiled. No doubt more contributions from the neighborhood children. And behind him on the fireplace mantle were dozens of delightful cards all signed in precious scribble.

On the whole, after the atmosphere had seeped into him sufficiently, Nate concluded that Dr. Henry's residence was one of tidiness, cleanliness, and livable comfort for a middle-aged bachelor.

"All right...here we are," announced Dr. Henry as he came into the room carrying a tray laden with two cups and saucers, a tea pot, napkins, and a plate of cookies.

"Aren't those sweet," Dr. Henry nodded in the direction of the Christmas cards. "I think— the thing I like most about children, is that they never forget who brought them into this world." He stopped and sighed with a smile on his face. "And their mother's keep me well fed too, especially during the holidays. You'd think by all the tins of goodies they've sent me, that I should be about the size of that Santa Claus fellow. They're all sweet dears, until a foul baseball comes sailing through a window."

Nate laughed a soft laugh which made Dr. Henry realize that he was still holding the tray while prattling on like an absent minded fool, and apologized for doing so.

"No apology necessary, Sir. I'm glad that the neighborhood children care for you so much."

The tray was put down, and in the manner of having made tea for himself for quite some years, Dr. Henry was not about to hurry the ritual. Nate was handed the first cup and was told to choose the cookies of his liking—and not to be bashful about it.

The two men retired beside the warm fire, casually sipping on the tea, nibbling on a tasty cookie, withholding conversation for the moment. The fire crackled and popped which brought a smile to Dr. Henry's face. And the "wrrr" sound of the mantle clock prepared itself before three splendid Westminster gongs filled the room. Dr. Henry sighed a happy sigh.

Dr. Henry's gentle and easy-going nature was appreciated, for the mood he created so far was proving to be grounds for quiet reflection. In-so-far as Nate could tell, he had not aroused Dr. Henry's curiosity as to why he wanted to visit the doctor all of a sudden. But Nate knew better than to tease fate, for that small, unrealistic bit of hope that laid at the bottom of his stomach was gone as soon as the doctor cleared his throat.

"Now," Dr. Henry began, carefully setting the china cup back on its saucer, his eyes lifting to Nate, "what brings you to this neighborhood on Christmas day?"

A dreadful panic that Nate had never felt before ran through his veins and it showed.

How, oh, how, was he to share such news he had just learned an hour or so earlier? Would his visit prove disastrous, causing Dr. Henry to turn on him, for the man that his mother knew long ago may have been a different man then. Was it worth the gamble? He did not know anymore because he felt close to ill; he wanted to run, but if he did, he would never hear the truth from Dr. Henry himself.

Dr. Henry was looking at him pensively, waiting for a reply.

Nate paused, and then sighed in frustration.

"I'm sorry, Dr. Henry, I… just quite don't know how to say this."

Dr. Henry smiled and raised a curious eyebrow. "Well, I suppose the best way to say something is to just—say it."

The doctor smiled a kind smile that should have put Nate at ease. And then quite suddenly, out of no-where, a thought took hold.

"Well, sir," Nate paused, "this morning I proposed to Miss Eleanor, and she accepted."

Dr. Henry's face was still for only a moment before it burst into happiness. The older man put his tea down and stood to shake hands with Nate. "Oh, my dear boy! How happy I am for the both of you! She is a wonderful girl."

"Yes, yes she is."

Dr. Henry made his way over to the fireplace, standing at the hearth rubbing his hands together before the warmth. "And when's the big day to be?" he cheerfully asked.

"Apparently, a few months from now," Nate half-chuckled.

"My, you young folks sure don't let any grass grow under your feet, do you?"

"To be honest, just between you and I, I would have let a bit more grass grow...I think Miss Eleanor is anxious to have a home of her own," Nate admitted.

Dr. Henry nodded his head.

"Yes, yes..."

The tea that Nate was holding suffered all loss of interest and was placed on a nearby table. He cleared his throat and mindlessly tapped his fingers on the ends of the sofa chair.

Dr. Henry glanced at the young man, who, in his estimation was looking overly distressed and glum for the suitor who had captured the heart and hand of Miss Eleanor.

"Something else is on your mind, isn't it?" Dr. Henry asked in a kindly matter-of-fact, stirring tone that made Nate immediately abandon all finger movement.

"Yes, sir—"

"And, you didn't come all this way for tea and cookies, did you?" Dr. Henry softly asked.

"No, sir—" Nate replied respectfully.

"Well then, best come right out with it. You're not looking too well keeping whatever it is all bottled up," Dr. Henry smiled.

Nate looked at Dr. Henry and then let the words come out very carefully.

"Before my mother died, she gave me a box and made me promise that I would not open it until the day I proposed marriage to a young lady."

"Oh..." Dr. Henry's face had turned ashen quite suddenly. "Oh, I see..." he whispered.

Dr. Henry slowly sat down and starred into the fire.

Nate wanted to say something, wanted to take back the previous moment for the awkwardness laid heavily upon both men. Nate was so dreadfully sorry that Dr. Henry was suffering on account of him.

"Well..." Dr. Henry said at last, finally ending the terrible silence with a shaking voice, "may as well go on," he suggested.

"Are you sure?"

"No..." Dr. Henry breathed, "but if you don't, it would be like taking a step forward with your foot suspended in the air, then not allowing it to touch back down. Seems to me, like that foot would have to come down sooner or later." Dr. Henry paused. "Right?"

"Yes, sir," Nate agreed.

And with Dr. Henry's permission, Nate continued, choosing his words carefully.

"Well, as I just told you, Miss Eleanor and I will be married this spring....and when I returned to my hotel room this afternoon...."

Nate looked into his father's eyes. The man who was his father, his real father after all these years. Dr. Henry was waiting and his eyes spoke for him.

Nate went over to the coat stand and brought forth the letter and the box.

"I was allowed to open this..."

Nate put the small dark blue box made of crushed velvet into Dr. Henry's hands.

"The ring..." he gasped. "The ring!"

Nate was not sure if Dr. Henry was going to collapse, or fall apart in a fit of uncontrollable sobs, or both. His shaking fingers opened the box and a hand flew to his mouth and a few sobbing breaths escaped from behind his hand.

"I have with me...a letter," Nate whispered, handing it to Dr. Henry. "You may read it if you care to."

The ring box was held tight in one hand while Dr. Henry took the letter from Nate in the other. Nate removed himself to the fireplace hearth and tried to abstain from glancing at Dr. Henry who was carefully taking the letter out of the envelope. A painful sigh was heard as the letter was opened and held quiet in Dr. Henry's hands.

"Dearest Nathaniel,

I shall not be with you much longer...this much I know. A mother should never have to write her son a letter as this, but I feel that if I do not do it now, I shall be too tired later on to tell you the truth. My dear son, please do not hate me for what I am about to tell you.

Years ago, a wonderful young man wished to marry me. We were deeply in love and wanted to be man and wife, but my father did not approve of him. Not on account of him lacking good morals and such, but because I was bought by another. I was given over and forced to marry a man whom my father knew. It was money which brought happiness to my father. I was made powerless from the beginning to the end.

As for the ring...it was the only reminder of the true love I had and lost. It was given to me, and should have been worn as a sign of a man's love for me. But instead, I wore the ring of another which was a constant reminder of his merciless, mental and physical empowerment over me.

My son, a woman's heart needs to be filled with love. Both my heart and my body were dying for love....and the bearer of the ring never strayed too far from my view.

As you matured, I think your 'other' father had suspicions. You were so different in your manner, your being. You were nothing like Stuart or Todd.

He helped your brother Stuart and your brother Todd come into this world. But the greatest day for me, was when he laid 'our son' upon my breast.

My dearest boy, you are my son, and the son of Dr. George Nathaniel Henry.

If you should ever meet someday, please, my dear, be kind to him. He loves you just as much as I do.

I am tired my dear.

Until we meet in heaven someday, do not forget how much I loved you."

Love,
Mother

"Until we meet in heaven someday, do not forget how much I loved you..."

Dr. Henry's voice crumbled and he broke down sobbing, covering his eyes.

Kneeling beside the sofa chair, Nate murmured, "You loved her very, very much. Dr. Henry—I am so very glad that you loved my mother the way you did."

"Oh, Nathaniel!" cried Dr. Henry, "I've been waiting twenty-eight years! Twenty-eight long years for this day! Oh, the thousands and thousands of times I wanted to say something, but couldn't. I'm sorry...your mother made me promise. It killed me to watch you grow up with...him, and then you left my sight for those fourteen years. Then, you came back! You—came back!" Dr. Henry took in a much needed breath. "Nathaniel, my son, please give me the best Christmas present in the whole world."

"I, Nathaniel, am proud to call you 'my' father, and equally proud to know that I am 'your' son..."

Dr. Henry rose from his chair still clutching the letter and the ring box, sobbing joyfully, embracing his own flesh and blood.

The decades; those spent and gone; years that wishful pinning cannot return; memories—memories. If life was to move forward, the past had to stay just that—the past.

Though, as far as the disappearing sun was concerned as it reluctantly dipped below the wintry pink horizon, bidding good-night to all the cold and tired, though happy children that were brought indoors by loving mothers, the memories it had created were magically formed into twinkling tiny diamonds, high above the cold, clear, dark, Seattle sky.

The End

Bibliography

Books

Cohn, William. *A Pictorial History of American Labor*

American Dreams—One Hundred years of Business Ideas and Innovation from The Wall Street Journal

Ford: 1903 to 1984

Tannenbaum, Edward R. *1900 The Generation Before the Great War*

Sale, Roger. *Seattle, Past to Present*

Woodcock Tentler, Leslie. *Wage Earning Women: Industrial Work and Family Life in the United States, 1900-1930*

Fisher, Chris C. *Birds of Seattle and Puget Sound* Lone Pine Publishing, 1996

Wood, Geo. M.D. and Ruddock, E.H., M.D. *Vitalogy (Encyclopedia of Health and Home) 1912, Chicago*

Zieman, Hugo (Steward of the White House) and Gillette, Mrs. F. L. *The White House Cook Book*, The Saalfield Publishing Company, 1907

LeGallienne, Richard. *The Modern Book of English Verse*, collection of famous poems, The Sun Dial Press, 1939

Roe, E. T. *New Standard American Business Guide, Gordon G. Sapp Publisher, 1912*

Time-Life, *This Fabulous Century 1900 – 1910*

The Good Old Days—They were Terrible!

1908 Sears, Roebuck Catalogue, A Treasured Replica from the Archives of History

Swallow Reiter, Joan. *The Women-The Old West*, Time-Life Books, 1979

Reeves, Pamela. *Ellis Island- Gateway to the American Dream*, Barnes & Noble, Inc., 1998

The Triangle Shirt Shop Tragedy, New York City

Sheet Music

Sheet music owned by Anna M. Nist, author's Great grandmother
"I Love You In Spite Of All" Copyright, 1893, by Chas. K. Harris

Sheet music *"Dreaming"*, *Woman's World magazine, November 1910*

Poems

A Woman's Work Good Literature magazine, June 1900
When The Woods Turn Brown Good Literature magazine, October 1900
Christmas Fires
At Christmastide Good Literature magazine, December 1900
A Ride With Santa
In Blossom Time Good Literature magazine, June 1900
An Autumn Prayer by S. W. Gillilan, The People's Home Journal, November 1909

The Modern Book of English Verse
  A Denial by Elizabeth Barrett Browning
  To-night by Louise Chandler Moulton
  When I wander away with Death by Louise Chandler Moulton
  The Snare by James Stephens
  Renouncement by Alice Meynell
  Olive Custance by Lady Alfred Douglas
  Ashore by Laurence Hope
  The City of Dreadful Night by James Thomson
  Remember by Christina Rossetti
  The Song of the Shirt by Thomas Hood

All other articles and pieces of interest from magazines;

The Housewife, March 1909; June 1910;
The People's Home Journal, September 1906; September
1907; November 1909;
Good Literature, January 1900; November 1900; December
1900; April 1900; May 1900; June 1900; July 1900; August
1900; October 1900;
The Housekeeper, December 1902; April 1903;
The Ladies World, May 1891
Harper's Weekly, January 25, 1902
Home Life, September 1910;
Life, January 10, 1889; December 19, 1889
Woman's World, October 1909; May 1910; September 1910;
November 1910
Modern Women, July 1905

Newspaper articles on microfiche from The Seattle Times,
The Seattle Star and the Auburn Argus.

Rocky Reach Dam, Wenatchee, Washington
Museum of History and Industry, Seattle, Washington
Seattle Public Library
The City of Auburn Library
History Link.org

Acknowledgements

Special thanks to:
Thom and Gail of "Icebox Memories" who graciously answered my questions.
Seth Dalby, MAS fieldwork student, Seattle Municipal Archives
The Auburn Library staff who assisted in many ways at the beginning.

To my Great Aunt Geraldine Reisinger Evenson, who, without sharing fond memories of her family, this book would not have been the same.

And last but not least, to the three men in my life, my husband John, and sons Morgan and Andrew who supported me through the ups and downs, brought me lots of coffee and snacks galore for the past few years, I will be forever grateful!

About the Author

Mary Margaret (a.k.a. Margie) McDermand arrived in this world along with a twin sister in Seattle, Washington on April 10, 196? -- must I? After 9 years of childhood in Seattle, the family which consisted of six girls and one boy needed more room and moved to a 20 acre farm in Maple Valley. Margie graduated from Tahoma High School and later from Highline Community College. In between those two establishments of education, life experiences included; working at a thoroughbred race track, waitressing, running a housekeeping business, volunteer fire fighting, and eventually, working at the Boeing Company where she met her husband, John Bayer. Married going on 15 years, and the mom of two boys, ages 10 and 12, Margie and her family currently live in Auburn, Washington.

The author enjoys bird watching, gardening, cooking, baking, and growing raspberries for jelly to give to family and unsuspecting friends such as the mail carrier. Up until recently, Ms. Bayer was a Cub Scout Leader and sang in her church's Folk Group.

For as long as the author can remember, she has always been the sentimental sort. As a youngster, the McDermand family descended upon Victoria, B.C., and there in one of the museums the author could hardly be removed from a certain exhibit. To the rest of the world it was perhaps just a bunch of "old stuff from a century ago," but to one young girl it was the beginning of a hard to explain association with a time period only known to great-grandparents. Again, as a teen-ager, while taking in the "Underground Tour of Seattle," (a preserved portion of Seattle after the Great Fire of 1889) while surrounded by old brick walls and dirt floors, the author was vividly aware of what was once there.

With a love for storytelling, a fascination with people, places and events, and needing a place to keep "family history in one place," and for reasons so stated above, Ms. Bayer's 2nd novel was inevitable. If someone were to ask what the author's definition of a job well done is, her answer would be this: when the emotions of the reader are roused to the point where characters are spoken as live breathing persons...forgetting that it was, after all, only a story. Or was it?

ISBN 1-41204726-9

9 781412 047265